Worldwide Praise for the Erotica
of STARbooks Press!

"If you're an avid reader of all-male erotica and haven't yet discovered these torrid anthologies, you're in for a treat. ...These books will provide hours of cost-effective entertainment."
- Lance Sterling, Beau magazine

"...This writing is what being brave is all about.
It brings up the kinds of things that are usually kept so private that you think you're the only one who experiences them."
- Gay Times, London

"A huge collection of highly erotic, short and steamy one-handed tales. Perfect bedtime reading, though you probably
won't get much sleep! Prepare to be shocked!
Highly recommended!"
- Vulcan magazine

"...Some readers may find some of the scenes too explicit; others will enjoy the sudden, graphic sensations each page brings. ...A strange, often poetic vision of sexual obsession. I recommend it to you."
- Nouveau Midwest

"'Dreamboys' is so hot I had to put extra baby oil on my fingers, just to turn the pages! ...Those blue eyes on the cover are gonna reach out and touch you..."
- Bookazine's Hot Flashes

"I just got 'Intimate Strangers' and by the end of the week I had read it all. Great stories! Love it!"
- L.C., Oregon

"Yes, it's another of those bumper collections of steamy tales from STARbooks. These stories are well-crafted, but not over-written, and have a profound effect in the pants department."
- Vulcan magazine, London

"...Touching and gallant in its concern for the sexually addicted, 'Angel' becomes a wonderfully seductive investigation of the mysterious disparity between lust and passion, obsession and desire."
- Lambda Book Report

Book of the Month Selections in Europe and the U.K.
Available at Fine Booksellers Worldwide

LOVERS WHO STAY WITH YOU

A New Collection
of Erotic Tales
Edited By
David MacMillan

STARbooks Press
Sarasota, FL

Other Books by STARbooks Press

Non-Fiction A Charmed Life:
Vince Cobretti
Lowe Down: Tim Lowe
The Best of the Superstars 1990
The Best of the Superstars 1991
The Best of the Superstars 1992
The Best of the Superstars 1993
The Best of the Superstars 1994
The Best of the Superstars 1995
The Best of the Superstars 1996
The Best of the Superstars 1997
The Best of the Superstars 1998
The Best of the Superstars 1999
The Best of the Superstars 2001
The Best of the Superstars 2002
What Went Wrong?
When Boys Are Bad
& Sex Goes Wrong
Legends: The World's Sexiest
Men, Vols. 1 & 2
Legends (Third Edition)
Tarnished Angels (Ed.)

Fiction
Billy & David: A Deadly Minuet
The Bigger They Are...
The Younger They Are...
The Harder They Are...
Angel: The Complete Trilogy
Angel: The Complete Quintet
A Natural Beauty
The Kid
HUGE
Strip: He Danced Alone

Fiction (Continued)
The Boys of Spring
Seduced
Heartthrobs
Dangerous Boys/Rent Boys
Barely Legal
Mad About the Boys
Lover Boys
In the BOY ZONE
Boys of the Night
Secret Passions
Beautiful Boys
Juniors
Come Again
Smooth 'N' Sassy
Intimate Strangers
Naughty By Nature
Dreamboys
Raw Recruits
Sweet Temptations
Pleasures of the Flesh
Juniors 2
Fresh 'N' Frisky
Heatwave
Taboo!
Fever!
HUGE 2
Virgins No More
Any Boy Can
Seduced 2
Wild and Willing
Fantasies Made Flesh
Saints and Sinners
Latin Boys
Living Vicariously
A View to a Thrill

ISBN: 0-7394-6454-X
Printed in The USA.

TABLE OF CONTENTS

Editor's Note

The editor and each of the authors represented herein advocate the practice of safe sex at all times. And, because these stories trespass the boundaries of fiction and non-fiction, we've changed all names and other identifying details in order to respect the privacy of those involved.

The Consumate Lover
David MacMillan

When the previous draft of this introduction began to look like a paper for the American Psychiatric Association on the significance of vampires as a source of secondary sexual fulfillment, I knew it was time to tear it up and start over. I mean -- right! -- the stories *are* meant to get you thinking about bed. But definitely not about sleeping any time soon.

The question could be asked why I wanted to anchor this collection of gay erotic romance in the vampire legend in the first place. After all, it would only take a naked Bela Lagosi drifting towards this gay man's bed to make me lose all interest (probably for ever and ever).

Cecilia Tan in her 1994 introduction of *BLOOD KISS* gives three reasons why she believed the vampire was the perfect subject for erotic fantasy. The vampire has always been viewed as sensual. The vampire has always been outside the bounds of propriety, representing "otherness". And the vampire has always embodied both life and death. Her belief is still valid nine years later and her reasons resonate with emotional truth.

Though seen as a hunter in legend, the vampire persuades his victim to put aside qualms and accept him. He's sensual. He touches. He caresses. He plays to his victim's sensual cravings. He makes himself the consummate lover and calls for the victim to come play.

He is "other", unbound by propriety or morality. We would call him amoral. Marriage, gender, relationship mean nothing to him. He has the power to help his victim put aside all the baggage society has put on him as well. Thus, while being able to take whomever he wants without a twinge of conscience, he does so by leading the object of his desire to want him.

He straddles the great divide between life and death, a foot on each side. He is a threat to his victim because of that and all the sweeter for it.

Twentieth century writers have carried the vampire legend a long way past the old Count with his fangs bared and blood lust in his eye. The book cover for *DRACULA* and film posters from the 1930s to the 1960s of fair damsels swooning before his hypnotic powers helped propel the transformation along.

By the end of the 1980s, Chelsea Quinn Yarboro had created vampire protagonists any reader could identify with. Romance publishers were opening up to "paranormal romance" and millions of bored housewives swooned over sexy, sensual *hunky* vampires after their husbands went to work. Anne Rice's vampires gripped the gay reader when they appeared -- for the first time, the pan-sexualism of the vampire was firmly put forward. LeStat and Louis certainly had a thing going in Louisiana, as did LeStat and Armand in Paris. And they were so damned sensual.

By the end of the 1980s gay liberation had progressed to the point that gay publishers could produce gay novels and even erotic anthologies without starting a book burning.

Firebrand Books gave us Jewelle Gomez's *THE GILDA STORIES*, Dodson and Roche edited gay male erotic anthologies, followed by Cecila Tan's pan-sexual *BLOOD KISS*. Rhinoceros Books introduced us to Gary Bowen's *DIARY OF A VAMPIRE* and the incestuous Rafael. Alyson gave us Jeffery McMahan's funny, erotic *VAMPIRES ANONYMOUS*. The 1990s threatened to become the decade of the gay vampire. The vampire had become a sex object to gay *as well as* heterosexual readers.

While heterosexual fantasy and romance may presently be overstocked with vampires, the gay reader has suffered a dearth of them since 1996. Yet, gays as consumers gobbled up *DIARY OF A VAMPIRE*, *VAMPIRES ANONYMOUS*, and *DESMOND* as well as the anthologies released by Circlet, Alyson, and Cleis.

I was just as famished as other gay readers. I *wanted* to imagine consummate gay lovers who were immortal (imagine if you will a Johan Paulik-look-alike lover in bed with you tonight -- and a hundred years from now, appearing not a day older). Yeah! I could contemplate that sort of forever. Fortunately, STARbooks gave me the chance to imagine just that.

I proposed this anthology as a combination of non-formula romance and erotica married to the vampire legend, and the folks at STARbooks were generous in their support. I also wanted real stories -- no interchangeable, cardboard "tabs A" and "slots B" with shagging being the sole action -- and a truly fine international group of writers came through for me.

Before I read Barry Alexander's *Night Wings*, I had occasionally wondered if it was possible to maintain an erection whilst chuckling, sniggering, and outright laughing. Read this darling story and find out for yourself. London haunts the reader in Richard Bellingham's *Street Angel*, his word pictures are so well drawn. I suspect that the English countryside's motorways will never be viewed quite the same after you've read Bill Crimmin's *Eternity*.

After Anne Rice and Poppy Brite made southern Louisiana the virtual home of the American vampire, this anthology wouldn't be complete without a story evoking the sweet, warm other-ness of that state. Grant Foster, from the American Northwest, captures it as completely in *The Willows* as a native son would have. And Jordan Baker, who is a native son, evokes the strangeness that is New Orleans in *The Hunting Trip*. Simon Sheppard gives the reader a stark picture of gay Amsterdam in his story. Daniel Ritter gives us another stark picture of the vampire's soul in *The Right Of It*.

Canadian Shane Yorston's *Love, Sex, and A Vampire* addresses the question of which is more important in a mortal man's life -- love or sex. Murray Brown's *The Right One* takes us to Charleston, South Carolina,

where he seeks to find out if a victim of spousal abuse can be made whole again. James Lincoln's *In Every Vein* gives the word "fixation" a whole new meaning.

The eleven stories mentioned above are only the beginning, however. I've selected only the best stories from two continents for you. I hope you'll enjoy them as much as I did -- and let the folks at STARbooks know that you enjoyed them.

David MacMillan
Atlanta GA 2003

Down For The Count
David MacMillan

My breathing had almost returned to normal. I opened my eyes and pushed back on my knees, smiling down at the lad whose arse still held most of my thick, still hard, nine inches. His legs wrapped around my waist, his heels rested at the beginning of my bum crevice, and his buttocks raised a foot or two off the blanket.

He grinned and reached up to touch my chest with his spread fingers. "That was very good, Engländer," he told me in thickly accented German. "You make me want always more -- since the first time…"

He wiggled his bum on my dick inside him and his face became thoughtful as his dark eyes clouded. "Again please, Jonathan?"

I wondered for a moment if I should use a new condom but realized that I could lose the moment if I did. I grinned down at him as I began to withdraw several inches of my mast from his hole.

We shagged under the trees beside the dual carriageway the communist government had built into the foothills of southeastern Hungary after the world war and the Germans had repaved for the young democratic government that had taken over nearly fifty years later. He moaned continuously as I plowed him thoroughly. He wanked himself to another orgasm; I remained still as the muscles of his arse spasmed and clutched at my prick inside him.

When his orgasm had subsided, I began to fuck him again. He bucked up to meet my every thrust. His erection rode his cum-slickened belly like a pendulum, his foreskin bunched behind the bell-end. He grabbed handsful of blanket and stayed right with me as I gave him everything I had.

I was finally close to my destination, ten days after leaving London. Another day and I would be in the Carpathian Alps and at the border between Hungary and Romania. The day after, I'd set up camp and finally be able to start earning the grant that had brought me into the very bowels of Europe. Where the red-throated bat was supposed to live.

I had cashed the check last month from the newly formed National Trust For The Preservation Of the Red-Throated Chiroptera -- five thousand pounds for a summer in the mountains, studying the blighters.

The Trust reckoned there weren't many of the things left after more than 45 years of communist mis-rule and wanted to make a start on counting them before bringing their plight to international attention. I was supposed to tag as many as I could and learn something of their behavior.

I still wondered a bit that the lads at the Trust would use an undergraduate in biology at the University of London to study their pet, but not enough that I ever considered giving the money back. Fortunately, dear old dad was a successful solicitor in London and I'd talked him into the use

of his Land Rover and was on my way to Folkestone and the Tunnel as soon as the check had cleared.

Orgasm grew over me, pulling me from my random thoughts. I looked down at the dark-haired, dark-eyed beauty beneath me. His eyes were closed, perspiration beaded on his forehead and matted his hair. His breathing was ragged as he moaned in Hungarian. His bollocks rode his shaft. My strokes became shorter and harder as I pounded his arse. I closed my eyes and surrendered to the pressure growing in me and threatening to make me explode.

A glob of cum erupted from his dick and arched over his chest to splat across his face. He was on his fourth or fifth orgasm of the day now. His muscles spasmed and grabbed every one of my nine inches buried in him. A second volley belched from his prick and landed on his chest as I exploded deep inside him.

I watched him while we dressed. It seemed that the deeper into the continent that I'd driven, the heavier the sex-drive of the locals became.

I'd been shagging French arse before I was even out of England. He'd been naked and we were on the back seat of the Land Rover before the train left Folkestone, his feet on the ceiling as I entered him. More French boys followed, then Germans, and finally Austrians. Even a Yank I'd given a ride to in Bavaria. And, now, Hungarians. University students, like me. The Euro lads making their way home for the summer.

Before I was fully past Budapest, I'd seen this beauty with his thumb out. In less than an hour after I'd picked him up, he had my flies open and was deepthroating my pride and joy as we drove along the Danube. That had been yesterday. He still hadn't had enough of my cock; and I was happy enough for the attention. I had him for the rest of the day, as his village was on the border and I was going his way.

His fingers traced my cock through my shorts as he drew closer. "Tonight, you will sleep with me in my bed and keep your sausage in me the whole night, yes?"

I shrugged.

"Tomorrow, I see my fiancee and must begin to give her what she wants; but, tonight, I want what I want."

"I'll try," said I and climbed into the Land Rover.

Back on the carriageway, I felt him studying me from across the cabin. "What's wrong?" I finally asked.

"You truly go into Romania?" he asked. "Into the mountains there?"

"That's where this bloody bat lives and I was paid a lot of dosh to tag and study his sort," I explained.

"There are stories, Jonathan…" He turned to look out his window. "Legends really -- from before the communists. From even before the war…"

"What kind of legends?"

He blushed before chuckling. "You must remember that my people --
and the Romanians as well -- were very ignorant then. Very superstitious,
like the gypsies…"

"And…?"

"They tell of dead men who rise from their coffins to drink blood. Of
young men who travel too deep into the Romanian Alps and sometimes do
not return home."

"Count Dracula!" I cried, trying to swallow the laugh that had made its
way to my throat. "He's been the subject of dozens of horror films in the
west -- maybe hundreds."

I succumbed to the fit of laughter that welled up in me. "He's always
the ugliest bloke, and I don't do ugly…"

I managed to glance over at him as I wiped my eyes. "You don't
believe that stuff do you?"

"Be careful with any young man you may meet while you are there,
Jonathan." He grinned suddenly and his hand was in my lap. "I would like
to think I will have this again sometime."

I was on the mountain that the National Trust had selected as having the
best likelihood of finding a cave of red-throated chiroptera. I had set up
camp at the edge of a meadow beside a stream where I could wash. I had
also started a stash of dead limbs for a fire.

I was at a higher elevation than I liked but, then, my research had
taught me that the red-throated bat was a cave dweller. A mountain cave
dweller to be exact, preferring the tree line or higher. So, I was breathing
faster and taking deeper breaths -- and my lungs ached from the
unaccustomed exercise.

It was nearly twilight when I'd cooked my meal of tinned ham and
potatoes and began to eat. The chill of the coming night forced me to wrap a
blanket around my shoulders.

I'd felt lonely almost immediately after I left the Hungarian lad. And
horny. I'd had a boy beside me for the past eleven days, each of them
offering up his arse for our mutual pleasure. Now, neither my prick nor I
had anyone.

With the Land Rover well stocked with English food in tins, I reckoned
I wouldn't hear a human voice until I left camp at the end of August, much
less have a lad doing anything to help make us both feel good. I was already
slipping into shock at the onset of my sudden celibacy.

Bats squeaked in a sky that was becoming indigo with but a few streaks
of pink and orange left. I shivered in the blanket I'd pulled close around me,
moved closer to the fire, and tried to follow their sounds -- trying to gauge
the direction of their flight. Tomorrow, I had to hunt for their caves and
hope I found at least one red-throated bat I could report back to London.

I lost all sense of time as I sat there following the sounds of bats across
the night sky. Stars twinkled coldly in the chilled, thin air. A wolf howled at

the other end of my meadow and was answered by its mate in the forest behind me. They were both far away and I felt no fear of them. I watched flames taste each stick of wood I placed among them and, slowly, begin to feed on it.

A bat glided near me in the dark -- a large one -- I could feel its passage in the crystal air around me. I knew it had come close, but that didn't pull my attention to it. It dived down for another inspection, and this time I got the impression of something the size of a cat or even a small dog.

I smiled at a sudden thought. At least I was still of some interest to something.

I pushed myself to my feet. I glanced in the direction of the stream and shivered again. One thing I was definitely going to have to do was rearrange my hygiene habits. There was no bloody way I was going to freeze my bollocks off washing myself at night. Better to do that in late afternoon before the sun started to go down. Definitely. I might shrivel in the daylight, but I could lose my nearest and dearest part of me to frostbite as cold as it became with the onslaught of dark.

I climbed into my sleeping bag within the tent and thanked dear old dad for insisting that I get the down, heat-keeping one at Harrods as I began to warm up. I wondered if the dark-eyed Hungarian was thinking of me as he gave his girl his nice cock. I wondered what all of the lads over the past few years really were thinking about when they took me into their arses.

I slept to strange dreams of flying over darkened landscapes and being forever free. And of one screaming giant bat after another pummeling my arsehole in mid-flight. I wasn't sure if my screams were of pain or of pleasure.

I suspected pain because I'd never allowed anyone to get close to my back entrance before.

The next morning I made real coffee. And drank it before I could convince myself that I was ready to face the world. I was an addict. A good French roasted bean beat any instant, and it wasn't even a contest. Fortified and in shorts and vest, I headed up the slope for the tree line and the caves I hoped to find in the rocks there.

I'd found two caves before I stumbled across the first bat. The blighters in the third were barely longer than my middle finger. Little mice with wings. I understood then why the Germans called them Fledermaus -- they certainly did look like flying mice. With sharp teeth.

I was glad National Health had insisted I be inoculated against rabies as well as other nasty viruses. Of course, the little buggers I'd found didn't have a slash of red on them, much less near their necks.

It was late afternoon before I returned to my camp. I was perspiring profusely even in the growing chill. My bollocks itched as the hairs of my ball sack caught in my briefs and pulled. I stank. It was definitely time I had a wash.

I stripped off slowly, enjoying the show I put on -- even if it was only for me. Naked, all nine inches of my thick, erect cock jutted out ahead of me from its bed of dark ginger. My left hand formed a fist around my dick and slowly began to stroke. My right hand caressed my smooth chest until I moaned. Its forefinger and thumb closed on a nipple then and pulled. I groaned and my hand picked up speed on my stiff member as my eyes closed.

Phantom hands caressed my shoulders and moved down my back until they were kneading my bottom. My prick grew harder as those hands established possession over me. Phantom lips nuzzled my neck and then my shoulders as a phantom dick plowed the crevice between my arsecheeks. My bollocks tightened in the cooling air.

I was more sexually aroused than I had been during the eleven days I shagged my way across Europe. And, strangely, I wanted to be possessed. I wanted to be possessed as I imagined myself being at this moment. I longed for it. I leant forward, offering my back entrance to the phantom dick behind me. I gasped as I imagined it entering me. I shuddered.

I cummed. Hard. Jizz shot out of me to land on grass five feet or more from me. My knees went weak and I sank to the ground.

As I got up, I couldn't understand this side of me. I'd never given more than a passing thought to the idea of letting a lad use me as I'd used those who surrendered to me. Now, since I'd entered this mountain retreat, my every sexual thought seemed to be of me with my legs spread.

I sat by the fire wrapped in my blanket and nibbled on a ham and cheese sandwich as darkness descended over my meadow in the Romanian Alps. My mind flitted from subject to subject like the butterflies I'd seen all morning.

I was at peace. I was glad that I had come on this mission.

Bats squeaked, taking their soundings, as the cold stars came out one by one. The wolves from last night howled to each other as they hunted. I took a deep breath and told myself I needed to get to bed. There were more bat caves to explore with the morning sun.

"It's Saturday night in Transylvania," I told myself, speaking out loud just to hear a voice. I lit my fire and began to strip off. Of course, it wasn't night yet. That was another two or three hours away. But it was later than I normally washed and I suspected my balls were going to be blue from the cold of the mountain stream. I wanted a warm fire waiting for me.

I had trekked around my mountain the last three days, exploring any cave I could reach easily and some I couldn't. I had found little bats and large ones, but not a single blighter had a red swab at its throat.

Back from the stream, I dried off quickly in front of the fire -- my teeth chattering and my body shuddering madly. The sun was just threatening to go down behind the trees to the west and the evening chill had a noticeably

nasty bite to it. The goose pimples that covered my body refused to believe that there was a balmy June evening beginning to cover London.

I scurried to the tent to find warm clothes and reminded myself I really needed to wash my things. Soon. Perhaps I'd take my first Sunday in the Carpathians off and do mundane things like wash clothes, I told myself as I pulled on briefs, corduroy trousers, and a flannel shirt.

I wrapped a blanket around my shoulders and, leaving the tent, started for the fire and another meal from a tin.

[*Who are you?*] a voice asked.

I stopped in my tracks and looked around hurriedly. It was strange I couldn't put a direction to the voice. My gaze finally traveled the meadow from my fire to the trees. A man stood there in the deep shadows.

"I'm Jonathan Harker," I called out. "Who are you?"

[*May I join you then, Jonathan Harker?*]

I realized the man had no accent at all and thought that passingly strange. "Sure, come on over and sit. I was just about to make dinner, would you join me?"

How was there another Englishman out here on the side of a Romanian mountain?

Damned good that he was! In three days, I'd become a bit daft with only myself to talk to. I didn't want to think about what my state of mind would be like in three months.

[*I shan't eat,*] he said as he stepped closer to the fire.

Or closer to me -- he seemed to be avoiding the fire.

[*But I would introduce myself -- and meet you, as you appear to be camped on my land.*]

I was getting the impossible feeling that what he was saying was appearing directly in my head, none of that muck about bones and nerves knocking together in the ear to let the brain hear sounds.

The thought of it was more than a bit scary. No school test I'd ever taken had suggested I had ESP, which would leave him with an elevated level of telepathy, like perhaps a space creature would have. I calculated; I was 50 kilometers from my Hungarian lad's village and the people there -- and they'd been the last people I'd seen.

I hadn't realized that I had tensed up until the geezer stepped out of the shadow and I saw his lips moving as he spoke. I relaxed with relief when I saw that he was young and was the best looking lad I could remember seeing. I smiled in real welcome as he drew near.

My cock tingled and started growing slowly across my crotch as I took him in. He wasn't much older than me but had a boyish face that actually made him appear younger than me. Brown hair fell in a fringe over his forehead. Light brown, almost blond -- but not quite. Liquid, brown eyes watched me: intelligent eyes. A scar across his chin. He knew I was checking him out. A smile that belonged on an imp crossed his face. He had secrets and laughs that he would share -- but only if he chose to do so.

He wore hiking boots and corduroy trousers -- though of a strangely different cut than mine. They had an old fashioned sense about them, like I'd seen in photographs of German boys from before the war. He also wore a peasant's blouse, thin cotton opened to just above the waist, exposing much of his smooth, tight chest. As he drew closer, I noticed that there was a birth mark just below his adam's apple. It only made him more desirable. I wanted him. My dick stretched all the way out to my hip and tried to push past its cloth barriers.

"Are you from here then?" I managed to ask, sounding half intelligent. "You speak English so well…" I opened a tin of boiled potatoes and poured them into a pot before placing it beside the fire. I pulled the blanket closer around me and wondered at his thin shirt.

His eyes twinkled and there was an eternity behind them if I ever fell into them.

[*I am from here,*] he told me. [*You like my English then, Jonathan*?]

I like you! I want you! Christ! This lad could get a dead geezer to erect.

"What's your name?" I asked and pulled the lid off the remainder of the ham from three nights ago.

[*I am called Dracul. Vlad Dracul,*] he told me and I had the distinct impression his lips were forming different words than the ones I was hearing.

This time, however, the sense of wrongness didn't trigger suspicion. My brain simply noted it. As it had the bat guano I'd stepped on in cave after cave the past three days.

[*Why are you here on my mountain*?]

I told him in as few words as possible. About the National Trust and what a wonderful opportunity their program was for me. How I'd not, however, found even one red-throated bat the past three days.

All the while, his eyes twinkled and my prick throbbed. I was trying to pretend it wasn't there, but there was all this sexual tension between us. An itch flared deep in my bum. Christ! I hoped he wanted me. I'd even allow this Vlad to take my cherry arse, I was so horny.

He grinned. His whole face got into it, even his eyes.

[*You are that Jonathan Harker then!*]

"I'm the only one I've ever met," I told him. "Why?"

He chuckled, a nice sound coming from him. [*I am the National Trust for the Preservation of the Red-Throated Chiroptera, Jonathan -- it is my money you have traveled on to reach my land. Was the voyage a pleasant one?*]

I stared at the lovely lad standing before me. I was mesmerized by his beauty. By my desire to touch that beauty. All else was forgotten. Or nearly so.

I realized that he was dominating me, his beauty was, and that, if I weren't careful, I would soon be a well-buggered lad. Instead of frightening me, the thought excited me.

He stepped closer and took my hand as he squatted beside me. His impish smile told me we were going to have fun.

[*There is but one red-throated bat left in the world, Jonathan,*] he told me. [*Me. And I would prefer not to be studied too closely.*] He looked into my eyes and searched for my soul. [*But I have wanted you since first I saw your photograph.*]

"I..." I was leaning towards him and his face swam towards mine. I felt his lips touch mine, chilled by the night quickly descending upon us. His free hand came up to spread across the crown of my head and pulled me hard against him. His tongue slipped between my lips and past my teeth. We were kissing and I was harder than I had ever been.

He sat back on his heels and laughed.

[*I had hoped -- but there is no good way to ask such things as sexual preferences on application forms, is there?*]

I shook my head slowly, still lost in his eyes studying me.

[*Eat your dinner then, Jonathan Harker. We have all night to come to know each other, yes?*]

The itch deep in my arse flared in anticipation as I shoveled the ham in my mouth along with the potatoes -- untasted.

"You've wanted me?" I managed, trying to organize into questions the half-formed thoughts sloshing through my brain.

Vlad smiled and his fingers caressed my nearest arsecheek.

My resistance to him and what he wanted wilted even more. I had had an active sex life as a top with a number of lads since I entered puberty: thinking about it now, it seemed a bit illogical not to try what they so obviously had enjoyed. I more than suspected that this lad of the mountain would be the perfect candidate to try it with.

[*I have wanted you since I first saw your photograph. The one that came with your application.*] He smiled. [*But, then, I was looking for someone like you. That is why I set up the National Trust in the first place. To find someone who would make my entry into England a smooth one -- my new life there a pleasant one.*]

"You're coming to England then?" I asked around another mouthful of ham and potatoes.

His fingers moved upward, slipping under the blanket and exploring the lines of my back through my shirt. My prick strained against its cloth prison. He nodded.

"You're going to give up this?"

[*Once when the world was young, isolation was the safest way to live. Violence was everywhere, no further away than the reach of your arm...*]

"It's still a pretty violent world," I mumbled.

[*True, Jonathan. But there is law now to stem the violence and sometimes reasonably intelligent men to administer it.*]

"Give me a moment while I wash up," I told him and pushed myself to my feet, finished with my dinner. I hurried to the stream and rinsed out my pot and plate.

I could only think of Vlad Dracul, imagining his naked body against mine. Kissing him. Learning to know his cock and learning what it could do for me. For both of us.

I had never lusted for another man as I lusted for him. I had wanted men before, but for the relief they could provide me. As a cute face plastered against my crotch as the tip of my nine inches worked past his tonsils. A sweating, shivering body reaching for orgasm as I shagged his arse. Those had been my lusts before this night.

As I returned to the fire and Vlad, I thought it deucedly strange that I had so suddenly and completely reversed myself. I did not resist the new knowledge but simply accepted it.

I didn't see him as I returned.

"Vlad?" I said, barely giving breath to his name. I reached the fire and still saw nothing of him. "Vlad?" I called, louder.

[*I await you in your bed, Jonathan,*] he called. [*Our bed to be. Come to me now.*]

His voice was low and sultry, closer than my ear. I realized that too; yet, my brain refused to question yet another piece of strangeness about the man who had come into my life only to possess me completely.

I couldn't get into the tent fast enough. He lay nude on top of the bedding, his skin palely translucent in the faint light from the fire. His cock was a flag pole jutting straight out from a dark bed of pubis. I threw the blanket off my shoulders and my fingers attacked the buttons of my flannel shirt. A small smile covered his face as he watched me strip off.

I did not feel the night chill as I squatted to take off my boots. I did not feel it when I stood back up and pushed my trousers and underwear over my hips and down my legs to step out of them. I stood naked before him. For his inspection. And my body was aglow with heat.

[*Do you want me, Jonathan?*]

Want him? I craved him like a smoker needing a nicotine fix. Like an addict needing heroin.

I nodded numbly.

[*Even now that you know who I am?*]

Who he was? Did I know that? Who then?

My brain began to work -- feverishly. But logically. There was no fear, no rejection, as I touched one fact after another. One happening that, I could see, tied to another. It took only moments.

Yes, I knew him. He was the Hungarian lad's legends come true. He was the fear of the unknown come true. He was Count Dracula, alive and well on the cusp of the new millennium.

"You've not spoken to me once, have you, sir?" I asked, subdued before my new knowledge and recognition of his title. "I mean, with your tongue and lips and breath?"

He chuckled. [*How can I? I speak no English.*]

"Mind to mind," I mumbled. "No need for language…" I stared down at him, fixing his image in my mind's eye. "How old are you, my Lord?"

[*Close enough to six hundred years that it doesn't matter.*]

Count Dracula, all right. Also Vlad the Impaler. Vlad Dracul, overlord of the far eastern borders of the Holy Roman Empire when the Turks invaded Europe.

"Did you really impale all those poor Turks, sir?" I asked.

[*Poor Turks…?*]

I felt the disbelief behind his thought.

[*They would have beheaded my men if I didn't kill them first. I had had enough. There was nothing to stop them between where I stood and the Emperor -- except me and my soldiers. We had enough prisoners. I had their heads cut off and put on stakes. It smelled but it also sent their comrades running…*]

I felt his thoughts touch mine and then, almost reluctantly, pull back.

[*Jonathan, I will not control you.*] He sighed. [*Sex with me and the future course of your life must be yours to decide with no influence from me. To this, I have committed myself. I would have you with me. I want you. But you must decide.*]

"My future?" I asked hesitantly.

[*If you will join me in immortality or grow old and die.*]

Hmmmm ... That didn't seem to be much of a choice -- even without thinking about it. There were only dear old dad and the housekeeper.

I didn't think they would mind. Give the old girl a nice stipend and dad a juicy case -- no, they wouldn't mind. Then, there was Vlad's six hundred years -- I wondered what London would be like in AD 2600. What the world would be like.

"I'm yours," I told him and lay beside him. I turned to face him. "Just be gentle with me, sir. It's my first time."

He pulled me to him then. As our lips touched, his fingers found my arse crevice.

[*This is mine first,*] he told me as our tongues dueled. I pressed against him, my fingers finding his cockskin and pushing it past his helmet onto his shaft.

He rolled me onto my back with him lying on top of me. My legs parted and he slipped between them, his dick oozing precum onto my bollocks.

My tongue found his fangs and I jerked beneath him.

[*It will not hurt, Jonathan. You will barely notice the transition.*]

I pulled away from his lips and his tongue. "I want to notice it!" I growled. "It's going to be the only time I change from being human to

being a…" I gazed into his eyes and smiled as I fell into them and continued to sink.

[*You will. I only meant that it will be painless. And it will not be tonight at any rate.*]

I stared up at him and made to protest. I had never been one to put off getting what I had decided I wanted.

He chuckled. [*You must get us both to London -- with your vehicle -- before you can completely join me.*]

My legs felt weightless and rose slowly up along his sides as his gaze held mine. The tip of his prick slipped under my bollocks as my ankles crossed behind his neck and my arse rose off the sleeping bag to meet his cock.

In the woods beyond the tent, a wolf howled as the count's cock found my puckered entrance and he leant into me to kiss me. Far across the meadow, the wolf's mate answered as Dracula began to ease into me.

I was expecting pain. The virgins I'd shagged through the years had certainly shown enough of it when we'd got down to the nasty. Instead, his cockhead met no resistance as it pushed through my sphincter.

[*I have taught your body to relax, that is all,*] he told me as his prick slid into me and took possession of me.

I ground my arse experimentally on him buried deep in my bowel. I felt the fullness he gave me and the massage of my prostate that my grinding provided. My eyes bulged as pleasure began to radiate out of my arse.

He broke from our kiss as he began to plow me. I groaned as I rode this new pleasure, and his lips began to nibble at my ear. His strokes were slow and long, waves of pleasure rose in my arse and crashed through my body, and I rode them. My hard cock rode between our bodies and my bollocks tightened quickly.

I gasped when I felt the rasp of the count's tongue on my neck and rode another wave of endless pleasure and forgot his mouth and what was in it. I groaned my ecstasy as his fangs bit through my skin and bucked up to meet his slow thrust into me. I exploded between us as he began to lap at the trickle of blood on my neck and continued to fuck my arse.

My dick stayed hard and Dracula continued to shag my arse. He continued to lap at the blood welling in the wound in my neck as I writhed under him, caught up in pleasures as high as mountains crashing down on me. Pleasures I had never imagined. Pleasures I knew that I would know through eternity.

Again, my bollocks rode the shaft of my prick. I rose into a technicolored sky as I climbed swiftly towards another orgasm.

"Cum with me!" I growled and grabbed his arsecheeks to direct his thrusts. "Give it to me."

He sped up his rhythm, his thrusts came short and fast. Pushing me. Forcing me. I went over the edge and sailed the technicolored sky. Riding the wind. Forever.

His crotch crashed against my inner thighs and pressed hard to them. I wheezed as I pulled great gasps of air into my lungs. Only slowly did I become aware of him on his knees still between my legs watching me, that impish grin making his eyes twinkle.

[*Will you be mine, Jonathan?*] he asked, his fingertips brushing my smooth chest.

"Will I?" I growled. "Just try stopping me, Count Dracula!"

He grinned. [*Good. I shall meet you back here tomorrow late in the afternoon -- you will be packed by then?*]

"Where are you going now?" I demanded and grabbed his arm.

He laughed. [*There is one thread of truth about us in the old legends -- we do poorly in the sunlight. I also have treasure secreted on this mountain since before the Empire ended.*] He traced my lips with his finger and smiled. [*I shall need money once I am in your country -- unless you intend to support me.*]

I hugged him to me and he was gone. I slept well that night for I knew I would have tomorrow and forever.

Sex, Love, And A Vampire
S. D. Yorston

"I want to…"

His tongue slid from my earlobe to stroke my neck, making my blood rush and the veins in my neck throb almost as hard as my prick. The nip of his teeth against my skin made my cock jump and my balls buzz.

"No…"

The word came out as a sigh, heavy with longing and the rush of fear. It was too much, too far. Too soon. I wasn't ready.

His hands moved up my thoughts to cup my crotch, his fingers teasing the outline of my stiffened cock through the stretched denim of my jeans.

I wasn't wearing underwear -- that was the way he liked me to be -- and the thin fabric clung to me like a second skin itching to be shed.

"Please…"

The word was whispered softly into the hollow of my shoulder. His breath against my bare skin moved upwards, a moist heat that left in its wake skin yearning for more flame. His tongue darted out at my earlobe once more and the nip of his incisors soon followed.

He wasn't cold at all, nothing like Stoker or other writers try to make his kind out to be. He was real. He wanted me, all of me, and I wanted to give him all that I am; yet I knew I couldn't. The scent of his cologne and, beneath that, of his own musk with its own need and urgency were a flavor at the back of my throat.

"Yes!"

There were tears. The desire to have him was that strong, that intense. Damn me, I no longer cared…

The sharp twin stabs of his teeth cut through me. I creamed right there, his hands on my fly and then on my dick as it spat out its own life essence for him. His lips milked my throat; the twin holes new openings into me he could probe with teeth and tongue. The orgasm seemed to go on for hours. His lapping and sucking making the night melt itself into this moment.

When it ended, I was lying limp in his strong arms, his tongue licking closed the new openings his teeth had cut into me.

"Am I going to die?" I asked.

He smiled in the dark, the moonlight from the bedroom window touching on features that belonged on Michelangelo's David.

"Not this night. Not ever." He bent forward to kiss me on the mouth and I tasted the copper tang of my own blood. "One more thing you can do for me, Thomas."

I went cold, knowing what he wanted, what he had asked from me before. This wasn't the first time that he'd tasted of my blood, but it was the deepest we had ever gone, so deep that I thought he might have gone too far

and this time would be my last.

I realized this is what I got off on when I'm with him: death lying so close to hand, the adrenaline of knowing this time could be my last. In a way, it was the death in him that attracted me as much as the beauty of his face and body.

Moonlight show on his fingernails like liquid pearl flowing uphill as his hand moved to poise over the throbbing vein in his own throat.

"No." This time there was true strength behind my voice. "I don't want that, Andrew."

His smile faded and darkness grew in his eyes. He had explained this to me. For his kind there was no orgasm of the body that could match the sharing of one's blood with another. I felt guilty as I always did, for taking what he'd given me and not returning it.

"You have to, Thomas. You've lost too much this time."

His voice carried fear now.

But the lethargy had returned to me like the soft enveloping of down comforters. I wanted to sleep and a part of my mind realized that this was his plan all along, to take me so close that I'd have no choice but to accede and give him what he'd hungered for all these months.

"Transfusion…"

The word took a universe of concentration to get past my lips.

He scowled and for a moment I thought that he might force it on me, a rape that would surpass even the first night we spent together in that alley outside the club. He got up from the bed, however, and went into the kitchen.

I heard the fridge open and close and, moments later, his steps as he moved to the bathroom. He returned with the IV bag and needle.

The prick of the sterilized steel was cold sharpness in the wake of the heat we'd just shared and the blood was cold as it entered my veins. He climbed back in bed with me, the heat of his body wrapping around me as I drifted off to sleep.

Morning was a savage attack on my senses. I felt like I'd just come off a weekend bender and was sore to my bones. My head pulsed, and the light coming through the bedroom window was an agony. Andrew wasn't in bed with me, but a large glass of orange juice sat on the night table beside the bed. I knew a full breakfast was in the oven, kept warm since dawn.

I drank my orange juice and wondered at the situation I'd gotten myself into. I'd been living with Andrew for the past six months in his expensive apartment above Charlottestown's bustle.

I still had my own place across town, a link to my old life before I'd met him. Before he'd found me in that alley, half- stoned and wanting only a good fuck before morning.

I picked up the phone beside the glass of orange juice and dialed into work.

My secretary answered on the other end. She sounded properly chipper and I hated her for it.

"It's Tommy," I said, astounded at the rasp in my voice.

"Tommy, you sound terrible," she told me. "You okay?"

"Not really. Well, I think it's just a cold or something. You know how I feel when one starts on me," I babbled. "Sounds worse than it actually is…"

I caught myself and got down to business. "I don't think I'll be in today. Could you see if Frank or Sharon can take my interviews for today?"

"Sure thing. If they can't, I'll reschedule them for next week, okay?"

"Thanks," I told her, nodding approvingly to myself at having found such a gem. "If I feel any better this afternoon, I'll stop in."

"Get yourself some rest and drink plenty of orange juice," she said before hanging up.

I smiled and looked at the glass in my hand. "Sure thing."

The shower after breakfast got me feeling almost human again and I sat in the living room, wrapped in a robe and staring off into nothingness.

I needed to make a decision.

I'd checked the refrigerator after breakfast. Two units left. Another night like last night and Andrew might not be able to get me back. I didn't know if I'd prefer him to fail or succeed. He offered me so much, yet to take that step was to leave so much behind.

I dressed and left the apartment at about one in the afternoon, catching a cab downtown just to walk in the crowds and reaffirm my own sense of me. I was still weak, but, as I stopped at a crossing, a bike courier in tight shorts and tee caught my eye with a wink and I found myself wondering what sex felt like.

I mean real sex. Not the bloodletting that Andrew called sex.

I could barely remember…

I wanted to remember what it felt like to have a cock in my mouth, a man's sweat on my tongue, and his hands on my hips as he rocked his prick into my ass. The real thing.

I wanted to remember what it was like to be human.

The office was busy when I walked in. My secretary was unflappable as she greeted me from her desk.

"You look like shit, Tommy," she said.

Her dark hair was up and her angular face was bright and cheerful, as usual.

"Yeah," I agreed, "but I thought I should get some work done on the Anderson account. How did Frank and Sharon make out?"

"Fine," she answered, "Though Frank was a little put out. I rescheduled a couple of things, they're on your desk."

I spent what remained of the day trying to lose myself in work, going over account charges, checking programmer's hours and installation and

maintenance fees. But the numbers didn't want to chill the fire of indecision in my soul. I stopped and stared out the window with its view of the city skyline and the St. Lawrence River beyond. A decision started forming and I wondered if Andrew would kill me for what I had in mind.

The club was as noisy as I remembered it being on a Friday night, the thumping of bass a second heartbeat rumbling from the soles of my feet to my chest. There were plenty of men there, most attractive, all looking for the same thing. I hadn't been there in over six months, a lifetime in the place, and was surprised that I actually managed to dress decently.

Wandering through the crowd, the old ways of the place came back to me: I liked club-hopping on the weekends, liked the anonymous sex, the physical release and the lack of any real commitment. Standing in a corner I wondered at why I'd come. If Andrew knew where I was he wouldn't be pleased, possessive as he was of me.

I wondered if I was at the club to flout my need and test the boundaries of our relationship? If so, then did Andrew really mean that much to me?

I shook my head, unable to get a grip on an answer.

I needed the feel of human flesh; I needed the taste of a real man, not the unreal, though wondrous, feel of my immortal lover. I knew what he wanted from me, a commitment that I wasn't sure I was ready to give him yet.

Or was I? I needed to know; I needed to be sure that what I was feeling was real.

He was nameless, the man I found. Just someone at the club. Attractive, even pretty -- in a mortal way.

His skin was tanned, not Andrew's pale alabaster. His eyes were blue and clear, ponds of light compared to the depthless oceans that lived in Andrew's gaze. His physique was toned, definitely a club regular. But he was full of imperfections that I suddenly craved.

He stood loose and lanky, not with an unearthly grace. He moved with the fumbling steps of a mortal, his pace matched to the thumping beat of the music. He was dressed in jeans, a size too small to show off his rounded butt and the mound of his crotch. The thin cotton of his muscle tee showed off a nice chest and accentuated the lines falling from his chest to his waist. He held a drink in one hand and watched the crowds with a lazy hunger.

I walked over to the bar and ordered a drink. Standing next to him I could feel the heat of his body, smell the cologne and sweat of the night. The DJ changed songs and the tempo in the club kept pace.

I didn't care who he was, what he was called, where he worked, or what he liked in bed. I only wanted him to notice me so that we could leave and I could make myself human again. His eyes slid over me and his full lips smiled.

I returned the smile and offered him another round. He accepted and in fifteen minutes we were out of the club and in a cab, headed for my

apartment.

The door closed and I pounced on him, desperate. My hunger almost as great as the hunger I saw in Andrew after we went for a few days without what he called sex. I kissed those full lips and tasted the night on his tongue. A human taste that was completely unlike Andrew. Earthy and animal and pleasant.

His hands moved over my ass, kneading my cheeks through my jeans. I ran my hands over his muscular back, the fabric of his shirt moist with his sweat from the club. His mouth moved to my neck and I stopped him.

"Not there. I want your mouth other places."

He smiled and his hands left my ass for my chest as we moved to fall on the couch. Me sitting on the cushions and him kneeling on the floor, hands roving over my chest and stomach.

He leaned forward and kissed me through the cloth of my shirt, his lips teasing my swollen nipples as his fingers cupped my crotch and kneaded my balls. His lips wandered lower until his teeth undid my zipper and found my rock hard and naked cock. His tongue rasped over the head of my prick, swirling around the knob. I closed my eyes and watch fireworks dance. His tongue probed the piss slit, dipping into me while his hands squeezed my balls and a thumb began to explore my pucker.

I was about to cum, a good healthy normal orgasm, when I stopped him. I wanted to cum inside him. I wanted to feel mortal heat wrapped around my prick when I creamed. I needed to feel that heat, needed to live that moment.

But first I wanted to taste mortal flesh again.

I got him up from his knees. He looked dreamy, his lips swollen and his eyes pleasantly dazed. For a moment I just gazed at him, wanted to stop time and study the expression on his face. Then I switched our positions, had him sit on the couch while I licked his chest through his shirt. I pulled the damp cotton from his body, my cock jumping as he lifted his arms and pulled off his shirt. I watched the play of muscles in his chest and arms, the slither of strength beneath his skin.

I devoured his chest, lapping at his nipples and feeling them gorge with blood beneath my lips, little buds of sensation that made his breath come faster. I licked the underside of his pecs, the smell and taste of his skin became my universe as I slid my way lower to his navel and laved it like a thirsting man drinking from a pool of water.

The thin forest of hair leading to the waist of his jeans rubbed against my chin, silky and soft. I undid his pants and mouthed his hard cock and swollen nuts through his briefs. He ground his crotch in my face, his hands coming down to press on the back of my head, his fingers stroking the back of my neck.

I pulled on the waistband of his briefs and he obliged me by lifting his hips free of the couch as I slid jeans and briefs from him. His dick was as

pretty and human as the rest of him, full and proud rising up from a nest of silky warm hair that smelled of musk.

I buried my face in his pubis, inhaling the clean scent of a mortal man. I licked the insides of his thighs, teasing a drop of precum from his swollen dick. Then I flicked my tongue across the knob before swallowing his cock, my lips sliding down the length of it until my nose was once more buried in his thatch.

I cupped his warm and swollen balls in my hand, cradling them to my throat as his breath came in great gusts. His cock began to twitch and I pulled off him, watching it throb angrily as the head dipped and waved.

"Fuck man," he moaned. "Finish me off!"

I smiled up at him, wondering if he was getting off on seeing me positioned so, his cock looming over my smiling face. I raised my head and sucked one of his balls into my mouth, his groans filling my living room as his hands once more came down to stroke my hair.

"Fuck, yessss…!"

I raised his legs over my shoulders, angling his hips up to expose the globes of his ass and began to stroke his pucker with my thumbs as I licked his perineum, my lips outlining the taut flesh there before I flicked my tongue over his tight bud.

He gasped and for a moment I though he might cum, but I waited until his breathing slowed and then began tonguing the smooth flesh of his ass, going deep into him, making the silken skin there a part of me. His groans grew louder before I finally decided he had had enough.

I slipped out from under him and stood up, shedding the rest of my own clothes as he nibbled on my dick and licked my balls.

I pulled a condom and a small tube of lube from my jeans before I tossed them. He grinned at me when he saw them and lay back on the couch, lifting his legs to prop his feet against my chest.

I slid the rubber on my dick and kissed his ankles. He closed his eyes and sighed deeply as I spread lube over his hole, letting a couple of fingers slide in.

I placed the sheathed head of my prick against his tight opening and leaned forward to kiss his pouty lips. The warmth and tightness of his ass clinched around my prick as I slipped into him, the tight heat almost making me cum.

"Fuck me, man!"

I pulled out of him slowly, the pull of his ass almost too much to bear. I entered him again, and the whole world was awash with sweat and sighs.

He raised up and his mouth was on mine again -- then on my chest, his teeth teasing my swollen nipples. His mouth moved suddenly to my armpit, licking the hair there and I almost shot in him, the sensation was so unexpected. His mouth was on mine again, and the taste of my own sweat on his tongue was nirvana.

We switched positions so that he rode me, his ass pummeling my hips,

grinding life into me through my prick. I leaned into the back he presented me and kissed the line of his spine, my hands cupping his asscheeks as he moved up and down my pole.

He stopped and grinned at me over his shoulder. He rotated to face me, my dick still inside him and his ass driving me insane as he moved. His grin widened as he positioned his knees to either side of my chest. Then he was bouncing again, bobbing on my meat while I tugged on his balls and he jerked himself.

I teased the nipples on his chest and leaned forward to lave his navel once more while he moaned deep in his throat. His ass left my dick as he stood. I pulled his hand off his pole and swallowed him as his jizz burst from his balls and thundered through his throbbing prick into my mouth and down my throat.

He stood over me like that, his cock shoved down my throat while he came, his growl starting in his balls and working its way into a howl as it left his throat.

I swallowed every drop of him, savoring the taste of him on my tongue. I sucked him limp as he stood there, legs trembling with exhaustion and his cry now a series of whimpers as his hands clutched at the back of my neck.

So much sensation and all of it mortal, I had lived again in that moment as he filled me with his life.

He straddled my legs and directed my dick back to his hole. He rode it with renewed fever until I felt my balls pull tight.

He stopped once more, climbing swiftly off me, ripping the condom from my prick and swallowing me.

Rippling heat engulfed me and the room went dark as my orgasm started, stars dancing before my closed eyes as his tongue and lips and hand brought me over the edge. I came all over his face, his hand jerking my prick as he rubbed my balls and ass. I opened my eyes as the orgasm faded and watched him lick my dick clean.

I leaned forward to wash his face with my tongue.

While I lay on the couch, he left the living room for the bathroom and I heard the shower come on.

"You enjoyed yourself," Andrew said as he walked into the room from the bedroom.

I lay there, covered in sweat and cum and studied the man I thought I might be in love with. He was unruffled by what he had witnessed, his face as impassive as ever, his frame straight and stiff. His dark eyes seemed to cry out to me as he took in my nakedness.

"I did, Andrew. Very much."

He nodded. "I sometimes forget what it must be like for you, Thomas. Forgive me for not giving you what you need."

I shook my head, still caught up in the aftermath of good sex. "It's not that, Andrew," I told him. "You can't give me what I need and I can't give you what you really need. Not yet, anyway. I'm still unsure."

He looked towards the bathroom and, for a moment, I was sure I saw emotion there -- anger, perhaps jealousy, perhaps longing for something he could no longer experience.

"I'm in love with you," I said.

I didn't know where it came from -- the audacity to say it -- but the reality of it was out there now, for both of us to know.

He turned to look at me and nodded.

"When you're ready, Thomas, I'll be waiting for you."

He was gone. A flash of movement that left my eyes aching and wondering just what it was they had seen.

Minutes later, I got up from the couch and made my way to the bathroom and the shower it offered.

In those minutes, I'd finally made up my mind. I was going to have to ask my nameless mortal sex partner to leave. He'd been fun and, if I was to tell the truth, I was going to miss his kind of sex.

I had a lot to get ready before I called Andrew back and that didn't include mortal sex games. Love was more important and it was eternal.

In Every Vein
James Lincoln

Dusk sky, earthshadow in the east, a blue-gray thickness directly opposite where the sun had just been swallowed up.

Wheaton Medical Center stood at the end of the parking lot, a huge, imposing facility of mirrored windows and gray concrete block.

Taking my overnight bag out of the back seat and locking the car, I made my way towards the side entrance, psyching myself up to have some lab tech monitor my brain-waves and leg muscle activity and breathing patterns -- all in the name of trying to find out what the hell was wrong with me.

Of course, you know already -- look where my story is -- but I didn't. Not then.

What would appear obvious clues to you now while reading this here -- my inability to sleep at night, extreme daytime tiredness, photosensitivity, hypersensitivity to smells and sounds, loss of appetite -- were to me symptoms of some debilitating illness. Getting whiffs of strange odors no one else around me could smell wasn't evidence of heightened senses -- not to me.

Nor did a supernatural explanation immediately arise for my paleness, daytime fatigue, and digestive difficulties. Instead, a dangerously low red cell count came to mind. Or rabies. Or any number of rational medical conditions. I even suspected that I had a brain tumor.

Maybe I *was* a bit of a hypochondriac...

Which was what had brought me to the Wheaton Medical Center that evening.

I made my way inside, following the directions the doctor's office had given me. Back elevator to the third floor. Turn left. Follow the sign to the Sleep/Wake Disorder Lab.

Thinking back now, I have to smile at all the rational nonsense piled on top of something rather straightforward. I mean, what was happening to me was exactly, precisely what it seemed like: I was being visited repeatedly by a naked dead college student named Sheridan J. DuRocher. Only, Sheridan wasn't in college any more -- and he wasn't exactly dead.

God! Where did all this start?

The nightmares. Of course, they were more wet dreams than nightmares...

That first dream, like all subsequent ones, was a cruel cheat; I dreamed I woke up because something didn't feel right in the room around me.

I looked over into the darkest recess of the bedroom where the digital clock was. I couldn't make the time out, though -- only the red glows. They

seemed to be moving, but I assumed that was just the saccadic movement of my eyes in darkness.

Then I remembered that I'd busted the clock in a fit yesterday morning when I couldn't turn off the alarm.

What were those red glowing things in the corner then?

A slender shape emerged from a crouch in the shadows and advanced towards me. The red lights, twin pinpricks, moved forward and up. There were no footfalls. Silence, save my own nervous, heaving breaths.

I tried to scoot back against the pillows but I found myself unable to move. The figure hove into view, draped in the shadows bending around him and hugging his slender body.

The red glows were his eyes. He was gorgeous. Slim, but well-formed. Pale skin, as white as altar-linen. His blond bangs were long and hung in his face, over those red, gleaming eyes. He smiled a seductive, cockeyed, close-mouthed smile, and took heel to toe steps, arms at his side.

My visitor was perhaps 6'2" but seemed taller given his slender body. The lines on him were all perfect, demanding to be followed with the eyes, begging to be traced with the hands. They curved and tucked under and sleekly stretched off in all the right places. His cock was hard, thick, and long with a majestic curve to it.

His movements were -- curious. Hard to put my finger on. Fluid, graceful, but designed. Something -- *off*. It made watching him mesmerizing.

He climbed into bed with me. The mattress sagged under his weight, the springs creaked. There was something familiar about him -- something I couldn't put my finger on.

Cat-like, he crawled up over me.

Now I could feel his breath.

I couldn't speak or move. All I could do was watch as this young male beauty straddled me and began to pull down the covers, revealing my semi-nude body.

He said nothing. He moved with that sexy unnaturalness I spoke of, running a long-fingered hand over my chest. His touch was electric. Thin, elegant fingers found my left nipple and pinched it between thumb and forefinger. My cock stiffened, trying to rise up to meet him. It tented my briefs. Precum oozed into the cotton fabric.

He leaned over and kissed my left nipple gently, ever so gently. His hair, soft and silky, fell over my chest. I wanted to reach out and run my fingers through that blond hair, my hands over his pale back, but I couldn't move.

There was a sudden sharp pain. Just below the nipple.

I gasped.

His head jerked and I felt suction on my chest. His hand reached down and seized my dick through my shorts.

He began to suck on my chest beneath his tangle of hair. He sucked

rhythmically, echoed with pumping squeezes of his fist around my throbbing cane.

He began to buck, sucking strongly, jerking me. I closed my eyes and came in a huge gush inside my shorts. It was the most incredible orgasm I had ever felt.

His finger went to his side and, with a fingernail, drew blood from the skin of his abdomen. Grabbing my head he pushed my face against his wound and forced me to drink as his blood seeped into my mouth.

A wave of relaxation hit me at the same incredible magnitude as my orgasm, and I found myself unable to stay awake despite what has happening. I slipped away, falling back into sleep with a weightless, dropping sensation. The last thing I saw was him looking down at me, hair in his face, his lips smiling and blood-slicked.

The next thing I remembered was waking up in the morning. I looked down and saw dried semen. Corroboration, I thought at first, until I examined my chest. No scar. Things became less certain then.

I kept running the event over in my head at school as I taught my eighth grade PE classes, trying to figure out if it had actually happened or if I'd had a particularly vivid dream. I was wiped out after putting our middle school soccer team through its paces. I still couldn't get my visitor out of my thoughts, even after I'd decided that I'd had one hell of a wet dream.

I was carrying out the recycling box to the curb that evening at home when a week-old paper caught my eye.

There was a story I had only half-looked at the day it was reported: "Memorial services are planned today for missing resident," it began, then went on to explain that a large group was expected to attend the service held for a Wheaton young man who'd disappeared in New Orleans two weeks before. He'd gone to Mardi Gras and hadn't been seen since. The police were baffled; his parents were heartbroken.

The picture of the youth was beside the article, and I nearly had a heart attack when I saw it.

His hair in the picture was slightly shorter, but still that same blond, tangled skein. He'd been caught off-guard, flash going off in his face, surprised.

This was Sheridan J. DuRocher, my nocturnal visitor.

I was pretty sure I recognized him from school, too. He was older -- both last night and in the picture -- but I was nearly certain I remembered him from five years ago when he'd been on the first soccer team I coached out of college.

Back inside, I quickly dug out my first year roll-book. I wasn't sure how I felt to find that I'd coached Sheridan J. DeRocher in eighth grade, but I was not happy.

I remembered him. A good looking boy who seemed to dote on every word I said. I'd figured that he had a crush on me. As I remembered it, I'd handled Sheridan like I did any other fourteen-year-old and forgot him the

last day of school.

"Basically, what we do is monitor you for parasomnias," the technician told me when I'd reached the Sleep/Wake lab.

He was a short, friendly young guy with very short-cropped black hair and a killer smile that would have been attractive to me, if I weren't in the middle of a health crisis.

He wore maroon scrubs and blinding white sneakers. His skin was pale, though not as oyster-white as mine had become.

"We record your brain waves, eye movement, limb movements, respiration," he said and pointed to the computer screen. "We stick sensors on your head and near your eyes, and then belts around your chest. They send the information via leads to the computer here in this room and it's recorded, along with a video of the study." He pointed to the metal contraption beside the bed. "That supports the camera over the bed."

I nodded, looking at the monitor with a shot of a bed on it. The room I would sleep in was adjacent to the lab.

That's when it'd started, with that first dream, then seeing the picture in the paper. Each night, another visit from Sheridan, more ejaculations in his strong fist, sharp pains in the chest, seductive looks and kisses, and my whole world started to fall apart.

Maybe, I thought, it was a very much alive Sheridan; they never did find a body. But the things he did, the way he moved -- it was beyond human.

So, was I really being visited by a dead man?

"Not at all," explained the psychiatrist I was referred to after my doctor found nothing wrong with me to account for the physical symptoms I was beginning to exhibit.

"Rather a common experience actually," he said, "tied to psychological states -- misinterpreted because, while not real, it is more vivid and profound than an average dream, hence the moniker of hypnogogic hallucination -- the 'waking-dream'."

"Indeed, what you've described is a *classic* example of hypnogogic hallucination." Somehow, the way he said it, with the emphasis on classic, dismissed things nicely, my nightly ordeals squeezed into the safe confines of explanatory language, while Sheridan was reduced to something psychiatry called day residue.

"This person you hallucinate about was lifted straight out of the newspaper, even down to the red-eye effect in the photograph in the paper -- the camera-flash reflecting off of the back of his eyes and returning the color of his vessels!" This image was simply captured by my mind's eye and later swept out when the brain cleared the neural pathways during sleep.

"It sounds so -- *nothing*," I said after he had reduced everything to

scientific explanations.

"It's not nothing," the psychiatrist consoled. "These things occur in an intermediate state between sleep and full wakefulness. They are very vivid and realistic. But they are fairly standard and easy to recognize. A person is awakened in sleep by footfalls, perhaps. Something approaching…"

He studied me for a moment before continuing: "The heart beats faster. There's an enormous weight on the chest -- a suffocating, paralyzed feeling. Red eyes glare at you. The thing vanishes. Throughout history this phenomenon has been misinterpreted. It's been called incubi, succubae, witches, the Japanese Kanashibra, alien abductors. These things often have a marked sexual component as well."

I blushed; I hadn't told him my Kanashibra was jerking me off while on top of me.

"Indeed," he continued, "the word 'nightmare' is derived from the phenomenon you explained: the night-crusher."

It all made perfect sense.

I was having hallucinations elicited under emotional stress. The question, then, was what was causing this emotional stress -- something the psychiatrist was willing to explore on a weekly basis. He first wanted to rule out a sleep disorder, however -- like obstructive sleep apnea, and he scheduled me for an overnight polysomnogram.

Which was why, at 28, I was at Wheaton Medical Center, sitting in a chair in my underwear as the lab tech attached the electrodes onto my skin with some adhesive cream. They were cold and he kept apologizing after every one. So far, he'd put twelve on and it didn't look like he was anywhere near through. Wires spread out on the floor.

"Am I going to be able to move at all?" I asked. "Can I roll over in bed?"

He grinned at me. "This is more comfortable than it looks."

It took another half hour to get all hooked up. The tech tried to explain each sensor and its function -- central EEGs, occipital EEGs, thoracic and abdominal respiration -- but I didn't pay too much attention. The wires all went into a box which I carried with me.

"Yeah, right," I said.

"You'll get used to all this," he said and smiled and turned out the light. "If you need me, just call out. Loudly, though -- this microphone isn't picking up well at all. Or you could wave your arms since the camera's up there recording you."

"Thanks."

I lay there in the dark -- kind of afraid to move and disconnect myself by accident. I tried to relax. I took deep breaths. I was self-conscious about that, knowing it was being recorded. Then I got self-conscious about doing anything. I even wondered if I were blinking too much.

Calm down, I told myself. Just sleep.

After a while I managed to loosen up a bit and even forgot all the wires.

My thoughts began to drift off into peculiar directions and I knew I was fading. I went with it, relaxed.

Sinking.

Drifting.

It was ten-thirty that the EEG showed I'd hit REM sleep.

The monitor in the other room, where the lab tech sat reading a paperback, showed me lying on the bed. It showed me, and only me, every time he glanced up at it.

My eyes fluttered open, sensing him.

Sheridan was watching me, perched above me like some naked feral boy. His eyes glowed red. I knew somehow that this would be the last time we'd meet like this. This would take me to some other level. I also knew it would be different.

Sheridan leaned over and brushed aside some of my hair from my face. His hand reached out and touched my cheek. His finger traced along my contours, moved over to my lips.

I kissed his finger. Then licked it. He let it slip into my mouth and I sucked on it.

He pulled his slick finger out of my mouth and leaned down and let me kiss him. Our lips parted, our tongues found each other. My dick grew rock hard as we frenched passionately. Sheridan climbed off me completely and reached under the sheet, peeling my underwear away from my stiffness.

I let out a soft moan. He scooted down and caressed me with those soft, velvety fingers, this time delicately, not at all the hard, wrenching grasps of before. I cooed as he ran his fingers up and down the length, barely touching it at all.

Sheridan brought his lips down to it and blew on my dick. He extended his tongue and touched it lightly, so lightly; but his touch was like an electric current and it leaped.

He pursed his lips and blew lightly over the spot he had just applied his tongue to and the sensation itself was incredible.

He changed positions, curling up beside me, his porcelain
skin slightly luminous. His own dick was stiff and I wanted to touch it, but I was unable to move, held captive by an invisible bondage.

Sheridan held my dick up and studied it closely for several moments, turning it this way and that, gazing upon it with open-mouthed wonder. He seemed to be sizing me up for something indescribable, examining every subtlety of my cane. Then he slid his tongue up my hard cock in one incredibly prolonged, moist swipe.

I shuddered, not believing the intensity of the feeling, afraid I might cum before he got to the top -- wishing I would before I went crazy.

He licked his lips, then lifted the shaft up, and drew his tongue along the underside of my cockhead with a few playful darting motions. Sheridan gripped the shaft tighter and pressed my dick to his lips and slowly sucked

me into his mouth. The fattened head squeezed past his thin wet lips. He fed me into him, his lips making a tight O slid down my pulsating cane.

"Oh God!" I moaned.

Sheridan bobbed up and down a moment, then let my cock slip out. He repositioned himself on the bed for a better angle and took my cock greedily back in his mouth. He was giving me the best blow job I'd ever had. If it weren't for the paralysis that held me, I would have climbed the ceiling.

I could only lie there and take it, hands pinned to the mattress, legs unable to kick, hips only able to squirm slightly as he worked on me with abandon. My head moved from side to side, my eyes squeezed shut and then opened wide to watch.

He was taking more and more of me, inch by inch, cramming me in, trying to take me into his throat. All the while, his tongue was working around and around, getting my shaft wetter with his saliva and my own juices.

Sheridan jerked my shaft as he sucked me. The head of my dick slammed the back of his throat, pushed deeper with each thrust of his head.

Somehow I had gone past the brink of orgasm without cumming -- onto something else entirely, an incredible other level of pleasure that had lain out of reach all these years.

Just when I thought I would have the mother of all ejaculations, he rose off me and sat back.

I was near tears. I had to cum. I was in agony.

He crawled on top of me again, his hair brushing over my face, and he backed down to crouch over my dick. The tip of my slippery cock touched the pucker of his ass. He pulled up suddenly, like someone putting a foot in hot bathwater, then began to sit down on top of me.

He reached back and grabbed me and positioned my dick just so. I wanted to lift my hips and jam my rod into his tight, pale, rounded ass; but I couldn't move.

Thankfully, he continued to lower himself, and the head of my dick pressed hard against him, all slathered with spit and precum, pushing against his tense opening.

He sat lower still and then that matchless instant, when a seemingly impenetrable asshole not only lets an intruder in, but seems to become eager, occurred. I held my breath as the head of my dick slipped into Sheridan's ass as he sat down on me.

I squeezed in, burrowing, until my entire length was inside him. Then my breath escaped me in a long exhale. He sat there and didn't do anything but feel me in him. He tightened up around me and let go. Tightened and let go. His hips lifted finally and I felt the grasping ring of his ass slide up my slick cane as he lifted his butt in the air -- almost completely off me. He lingered a moment before lowering himself again.

I wondered why the lab tech wasn't coming to investigate the noises.

But I remembered the microphone wasn't picking things up well, so he probably hadn't heard. I thought that if he looked over at the monitor that he would have to see the missing boy on top of me, riding my dick. I looked at the screen and saw that Sheridan did not appear on the video. There was only me, having some restless moment with the covers in a tangle at my groin.

Sheridan slid up again, then back down on me. His fingers worked my nipples, rolling them between thumb and finger. His hips lifted and dropped, ass fucking me harder and harder. It was difficult catching my breath now as he increased his speed. He wasn't going just up and down my length now, but was wriggling his butt, and coming down at angles. I couldn't believe how tight the grip of his ass was, or how smoothly I slid in and out of his wet, tight pucker.

"I'm close," I groaned.

He lifted off of me and scrambled up my body to thrust his curved dick at my face, offering it to me, pushing the head down so it was pointed at my lips. The tip shimmered with a shiny drop of precum.

I watched as the one drop elongated in slow-motion, becoming a clear thread, landing on my lips, still attached to his cockhead. I stuck out my tongue and tasted it, savoring it. More oozed into my open mouth. Sheridan's toes worked on my quivering dick as I opened my mouth wide. One of the electrodes taped to my chin came off.

Sheridan thrust his dick at me with his fist and I raised up and took it in my mouth. Just the big, fat head, slick with precum. I explored it with my tongue, then sucked on it, then caressed it more with slippery swipes. He moaned and thrust himself forward.

His cock touched the back of my throat. He pulled back, his slick dick sliding smoothly through my tight lips, before he slid it forward again. I balanced my breathing and let him push deeper still, past the spot I wanted to gag. His hands went to the back of my head and he pulled my face up and fucked my mouth hard and fast.

Sheridan's speed increased: his frantic dick gliding in and out of my throat. His abdomen tensed as he approached climax, and I felt the head of his dick swell in my mouth. His rod convulsed and in a colossal rush he came into my mouth.

Sheridan squeezed off his entire load, stiffening his legs, tightening his grip on my head. A few more thrusts and squirts came after the initial giant torrent, spasms which racked his thin frame. He relaxed then but stayed in me as he oozed, before finally slipping out and crawled off me.

I lay there, eyes closed, swallowing still -- tasting, relaxing. My own cock was still hard and expecting to be relieved, but for now I was content to enjoy the proxy afterglow and satisfaction of bringing him to an astonishing orgasm.

A hand brushed aside some of his blond locks as Sheridan bit his lower lip, studying me intently. His eyes went down to my stiffness. I swallowed

thickly.

He kissed my stomach. He nipped lightly with his teeth. He pinched my nipple hard and dragged his tongue tip down around my navel. Another playful bite.

"Oh yes," I encouraged.

Sheridan moved lower. His hand reached over and took my still very hard cock.

He planted small kisses in a neat path downward.

Then he moved aside my dick while stroking it, and kissed his way slowly to the inside of my thigh. His tongue licked a wet spot there.

He continued to tug on my cock as his lips pulled back and his razor-sharp teeth pressed against the soft flesh of my leg.

"Ow, shit!" I grunted. His hand squeezed my dick hard as his incisors pierced skin and tapped the femoral.

It was an appealing pain. Moaning, I almost came as he siphoned the spewing blood from my inner thigh and jerked my dick up and down, fast and tight. Sheridan slurped on the rush of blood with the same rapacity as he worked my tool with his hand, and I knew the two actions were joined in more than just rhythm and intensity in his world.

It was a world I desperately wanted to join, and, as I felt myself drain into him in pulsing freshets, I could sense myself getting closer to being there with him.

[*Foolish man, what do you fear?*]

His words were from Seneca, spoken nearly two thousand years ago, but seeming to be about this very moment -- foolish man, what do you bemoan, what do you fear? Your neck, your throat, your heart are all so many ways of escape ... Do you inquire the road to freedom? You shall find it in every vein of your body.

I felt my escape approach me as he sucked, his bloody lips the wings of an embracing angel. I was pouring into him, this young man I'd once taught and who had wanted me for so long, being absorbed by him. My eyes closed as I emptied into his mouth, my cock throbbing and pulsating and straining in his manipulating, delicate fingers.

I could feel myself getting ready to blow. There were no more plateaus to reach for me; this was the end -- my sperm was rushing out fast.

Sheridan knew, increasing his hand-job and his slurping, then he removed his lips from my open wound and turned his head just as my cock spasmed and a long, hot squirt of sperm shot from my cock and into his open waiting mouth.

My hips rose as I erupted in a gush, then another came behind that, and another still, all of them with equal, if not increasing, force.

I thought for a moment my cumming would never end. There was a pause and then yet another convulsion rippled through me and I shot even more juice into him.

Sheridan pulled off after that. The last of my cum frothed out and

coated my gratified member.

"Oh -- my -- god!" I said in an elated, giddy whisper.

Sheridan sat up and smiled. Once more he dragged a nail across the pale vellum-like skin of his abdomen and a thin red crimson line appeared, welled up, and let go with a drop of his precious essence. He leaned over and I tipped my head up and let it drip into my mouth. Sheridan pressed himself against me, my lips and tongue working this slit, sucking with unrestrained lust.

It coursed down my throat, warm and thick. I grew sated quickly as he pulled off me and the slit sealed in his side. We held each other tightly. My fingers traced along his back and ran through his hair, and his fingers drew circles on my chest.

I felt myself suddenly pulled away, like when I would fall back into deep sleep after our earlier encounters, only this time it was a stronger pull from somewhere else, more potent than sleep -- beyond sleep.

The last thing I heard as a mortal was the technician running into the room in a panic, screaming to wake the dead.

Street Angel
Richard Bellingham

London is magnificent. It stretches out beneath me in all its glory, the stage on which millions of people play their parts with varying degrees of reluctance. It has a distinctive sound all its own, almost like the sussurating breathing of a living beast; a beast made from concrete, macadam, steel, and glass.

From my vantage point the ugliness of the city is invisible. The reek of a thousand car exhausts pervades the air even here, but glimmering head- and taillights move in a finely choreographed ballet that splashes pinpricks of brilliance against buildings that have survived the test of time.

I sigh in contentment as I let the sights, sounds, and scents of the city wash over me, as they invigorate me.

I am a creature of the city, just as I am a creature of the night. And below me stands my redeemer, my light. He has replaced the sun for me and his beauty burns more brightly than it ever did.

He stands beneath the streetlight with his platinum curls reflecting its sour orange light; and I feel the old, familiar desire burning deep inside of me. I can scent his essence rising over the strong, acrid odors that fume from the city's every pore, the heady musk of a youth at his physical peak. My desire burns ever brighter as I absorb every nuance of him, every subtle hint of the unique sense of him.

Only twenty summers have flitted over his body, and the fussy fingers of adolescence have been reluctant to withdraw from him. I can see the downy fuzz of a young man upon his cheeks and chin, the beanpole physique of one newly accustomed to his height.

Yet, framed by the open leather jacket, his bare torso is clearly that of a young adult. The shallow declivity of his navel rests at the center of lightly defined abdominal muscles, his round nipples crown perfect pectorals.

His stance telegraphs barely contained sexual energy, muscular thighs bulging against tight black jeans as he shifts his position. In contrast, his face is that of an angel. He is blessed with curly silver-blond hair, a flawless oval face, full lips, ice-blue eyes, and a slightly snubbed nose.

He is restless, looking at his wristwatch every few minutes, frowning impatiently. I smile to myself as I watch him from my eyrie, remembering the impetuousness of my own youth. Time has taught me patience, and I sometimes wonder if I would have learnt the lesson in my allotted span.

I stand and close my eyes, tilting my head back in order to enjoy the cool sensation of the breeze against the smooth skin of my throat. My eyelids flutter open, and I gaze up at the silver moon. I bask for a moment in the sun's reflected glory, remembering the long-ago days when I was able to stand the full light of the noon sun.

Such days are past, and nothing is gained by dwelling upon their memory. The nights are mine, and I make full use of the shroud of darkness.

I look back down upon my angel and smile as I see him looking at his watch once more.

"I am here, little one." I only whisper the words, but he hears them nonetheless.

He smiles and looks up to where I stand far above him. "Then come and get me, Dimitri."

His words are softly spoken, yet they reach my sensitive ears despite that. Beneath them lies an undercurrent of desire, his need for me eddying and swirling around each syllable.

I cannot repress a smile as I sense the intensity of his emotions, and my own desire flares to incandescence.

I step up to the gargoyle that guards the ledge on which I stand, patting him affectionately between his marble ears. I glance down as I stand at the very brink of the precipice, feeling my angel's siren call as I watch the pinpricks of light below dance their endless ballet.

I step off the ledge and fall towards him, a sigh escaping me as I feel the night air rushing around my body, spiced with the scents of the city. It billows in my clothing and caresses my skin, as intimate as a lover. Almost reluctantly, I gather the wind about myself, buoying myself up and marshaling the intimate breezes into a cushion that slows my descent, allowing me to alight next to him without a sound.

"What kept you?"

His voice is husky, soft, and yet contains a hint of mild reproach. He opens his arms to me and I enfold him in my embrace, breathing cool air against the side of his neck.

"I just wanted to watch you for a while," I tell him. "You're so beautiful, my angel."

He sighs against my alabaster skin, and his breath is almost hot enough to burn me. His hands rest against the small of my back, and he whispers quietly into my ear: "You know it embarrasses me when you call me that, Dimitri."

"I can't help that your beauty makes me say stupid things, Christopher."

My hands slip beneath his leather jacket to caress the damp small of his back, lightly stroking the smooth furrow at the center.

We draw apart from each other and I inhale his scent, so much more intense now that I am near him. He dwarfs the unpleasant stenches of the city with his youthful musk, and I close my eyes for a second to enjoy more fully his aroma.

"Let's walk."

I take his warm, slick palm in my cool, dry hand, and we walk together through the night, the unblinking eye of the full moon watching over us like a celestial chaperone.

"Fucking bent bastard!"

"No! I'm sorry, I thought ..."

The words are too far away for mortal ears to hear. But I hear them. The fear is of such intensity that I feel it from several blocks away. Raw waves of agonizing terror wash over me as I walk with my angel on the street, almost sweeping me away.

I stop in my tracks and feel Christopher's concern as the lambent flame of my desire is quenched by the overwhelming emotions that assault my mind. He looks at me worriedly, his hand resting on my shoulder, its fingers beginning to dig into me.

For my own sanity, I always hold in place a mental shield to block out the terrible emotions that resonates throughout the city. Now, I allow a tiny tendril of the fear I'd heard through, just enough to find the source. And, grasping Christopher's hand, I begin to run through the shadowy streets, feeling my angel's confused thoughts as he sprints by my side.

"Dimitri, what's wrong?" he demands, panting with exertion as he tries to match my pace, the rapid echo of his heartbeat filling my ears as his sneakered feet pound the pavement. I take pity and slow the slightest amount; enough merely to reduce the pain that running at such speed causes him. Already I am stretching him to the breaking point and, if he were to snap, my heart would shatter.

[*Someone's in danger.*] The thought I return to him is cold, devoid of the anger that I feel towards whoever is causing such pain.

If he sensed the true intensity of my anger, it would scare him. That he loves me despite what I am is the greatest gift I have ever received, and I wish with all my heart for nothing to give him reason to regret giving that gift so freely. He is mine, but only because he desires it.

By now I can hear the taunts, the whimpers, the cries of pain. Even the slight emotion that fits through the aperture in my mental defenses is enough to bring bloody tears to my eyes, and it is with relief that I close the final chink in my psyche's armor. I no longer need the trail to follow.

I stop running and bring Christopher to a halt, gently caressing his fevered brow as he attempts to regain his breath. His chest heaves and the heated scent of his body fills my nostrils.

[*Wait here,*] I tell him, planting the words directly in his mind. [*I won't be long.*]

He nods as he pants into the cool air, each humid exhalation carrying his scent to me and making me yearn for him. I wish I could take him now, taste him on my tongue, and feel his warmth inside me -- but I have a duty to perform.

I come upon them from the darkness, an avenging angel with burning eyes. The boy whose pain I felt so keenly is slumped up against one filthy wall, blood pouring from his nose and lips to stain his clothing scarlet. Hunger flares within me at the scent of fresh blood, but my anger blots it

out easily.

The sour odor of fear, as strong as the bitter bouquet of hatred. Sweat drips from their muscular bodies as they cause blood to flow from his, their fists and feet crunching into his slight body and causing whimpers and cries of agony.

I stand, unheard and unseen, behind the burliest of the brutes. He is snarling words of hatred as his knuckles become flecked with the boy's blood, as bone splinters beneath his assault.

I reach out to rest my left hand upon his broad shoulder, feeling the heat of his body beneath my cool palm. I touch him with a lover's caress and, at first, he doesn't notice me.

I clench my fingers, the digits becoming bone-white talons to dig into the monster's flesh, and with a cry of pain he sinks to his knees before me. The others hear him and turn, bloody-knuckled, to stare at me.

"Leave the boy alone." I say quietly, "Or I'll tear your friend's throat out."

I have their full attention now. Their shattered plaything is left lying in a blood-soaked, limb-splayed heap as they turn towards me, a pack of urban wolves with fangs of steel and the mercy of a blizzard.

They come for me, taunts spewing forth like bile. One of them, a slender youth of eighteen or nineteen years, shocks me by slipping under my guard and slashing out with a narrow blade, the tip of which grazes my chest as I contort myself backwards, by necessity releasing my grip on the other tough's shoulder.

They are faster, stronger, than I would have thought possible for mortals. Each alone would be no match for me, but together they work like a wolf-pack, darting in to harass their prey and then returning once more to the safety of the group.

I deal damage in return, my hands lashing out stiff-fingered to break ribs and noses, to blacken eyes and cut breath short, but the wounds seem only to energize them further.

Then I see him, my angel, shrouded in the darkness of an intersecting alley, his eyes open wide with fear. He has circled round to watch and, although I fear for him, his presence gives me all the strength I need.

I stop my dance of avoidance and stand, arms outstretched, my mind reaching out even as the biggest of them lunges towards me.

He freezes as my mind enfolds him and his companions into my psyche and, for the moment, I hold their will with my own. The knife slips from nerveless fingers, and jawless expressions of fear adorn the monsters' faces as I start to press their thoughts, crushing them with the weight of the centuries my mind has known.

A single word almost forms in my lips and in their minds, a word that would end their lives. But Christopher, so in tune with me that he almost knows my thoughts, shakes his head slowly, his eyes filled not with fear but with deep concern.

His humanity tempers my urge to seek vengeance for the shattered victim of these four brutes, and so I fill them with another word, instead.

[*Sleep!*]

They fall around me like wheat before the scythe, collapsing one by one to the ground as my mental imperatives wash over them and their minds quail into obeisance.

I look to the broken boy, whose lifeblood pours from numerous wounds, whose heart falters and trembles, and I feel a sense of hot, deep shame that I did not take vengeance for him on the perpetrators of his hurts. I glance up at Christopher, however, and his worried yet relieved smile is enough to quench the shame, to reassure me that I have done the right thing.

I crouch next to the injured youth, whose breathing grows more labored and wheezy by the second, and unbutton my shirtsleeve, rolling it up to bare my forearm. I lick my inner wrist and then bite into the skin, feeling sharp pain as my fangs lengthen and slice easily through the flesh. Blood wells to the surface of the wound and I press my wrist to the boy's lips, tilting his head back so that my blood oozes down his throat.

He suckles instinctively, his lips and tongue working on my wound to extract as much of my blood as he can get. Mewling sounds of need and pleasure come from his throat, and as he suckles on the fount of my wrist his terrible wounds begin to heal.

My blood is life – life with which the living can be healed, or the nearly dead raised as a creature of the night. This boy will live, although through this partaking of my blood he will always be linked to me. I will need to watch over him, as I watch over Christopher, and perhaps eventually he will become our friend – and lover.

After all, that is what happened when I met Christopher.

I barely sense my angel watching me. The boy is beginning to wake, and there is one more thing I must do before feeding.

I look deeply into his terrified eyes, seeing reflected within the torment he has suffered. [*You will not remember,*] I tell him.

And he does not.

He walks away, not seeing the sleeping bodies strewn around him like autumn leaves. As he leaves I slump at last to the ground, too weak even to feed from the plentiful supplies around me. The weariness of ages crushes me to the filthy ground, towards unconsciousness.

I wake to the feeling of fresh blood pouring into my mouth, invigorating me with its coppery warmth. My eyes open and I see Christopher kneeling next to me, holding the wrist of one of the monsters to my lips.

My angel has come to me, saving me as surely as I had saved the boy. I look at him with concern, fearing to see judgment in his eyes but seeing nothing but compassion and understanding.

I take all the sustenance I need from the others, enough to leave them weak but no worse, and then return to my street angel, enfolding him in a

tight embrace and kissing him upon the fullness of his sweet lips.

He groans into my mouth and his fingers tremble against the small of my back. I am warm now, and he feels that warmth as he kisses me. It intoxicates him; I intoxicate him.

[*Come,*] I tell him, [*before I grow cold again.*]

He reluctantly breaks the kiss with me, panting once again, and nods his assent. His eyes are wide, loving, desirous. He needs me, and that fact fills me with the joy I feel only when I'm with him.

It is the irony of my existence that I am immortal, but only feel *alive* when in the presence of one who will eventually die. The spark of life burns so brightly within him that sometimes I hesitate to touch him for fear of being burnt.

He lies beneath me on the bed, his eyes half-lidded as my cooling hands gently stroke the nubs of his nipples. He gasps as I bend to lick at those sensitive roundels of flesh, my tongue scooping up the musky flavor of his sweat. The fire within me swells and my fangs scrape on my tongue as my teeth extend to bite delicately into his tender flesh.

He arches his back as a trickle of his blood flows onto my tongue, gasping with the unbearable pleasure of my bite. He groans as I apply gentle suction to the tiny wounds made by my teeth, his salty blood flowing down my throat to quench my own desire. His blood, offered to me with love, burns inside me and brings me to the brink of my own orgasm.

I take just enough blood to bring him the intense ecstasy of my bite, then lick the wounds to make them close.

He looks up at me with dazed eyes, love burning deep within them. His erection strives against the crotch of his trousers and I mercifully unbutton them, tugging the zip down to allow his unfettered prick access to the air.

The strong scent of his manhood rises to my preternaturally sensitive nostrils, and I take great pleasure at it. Behind the collar of his foreskin, the pink glans is sheathed in a layer of slippery precum, and I lick every drop of the musky fluid from him.

His entire body thrills at this sensation, little shivers fluttering over his abdomen as I gently bring prepuce forward over the glans. I suckle the loose skin between my lips, drawing forth another drop of precum.

He is unbearably hot beneath my hands, and his shaft pulses with every beat of his heart.

I nip gently at the loose, sensitive skin, swallowing the sweet blood that wells up as he groans and tosses his head from side to side. That wound closes beneath my healing tongue, and I relinquish his foreskin for a moment, allowing it to slip back to its resting state. Perhaps a quarter of his slippery helmet shows beyond the collar of his skin, tantalizing me with its deep pink flush.

I lick along the length of his frenulum, nipping softly but without enough pressure to draw blood. I know him well by now and am aware that

to take blood from that band of extremely sensitive tissue is to provoke instant orgasm. I wish to prolong his ecstasy, however, making him beg for the release of orgasm.

The tip of my tongue traverses the soft underbelly of his shaft, gathering little wrinkles of loose skin. My cool fingers flutter over his flat belly, rubbing the ridges of his abdominal muscles and delving into the warm, moist hollow of his navel. My tongue reaches the shaven smoothness of his musky scrotum, the heavy balls within hanging low with the heat of his passion.

I take his sweet meat into my mouth, caressing it with my tongue as I suckle softly on him. He writhes at this sensation, his callused hand coming to rest upon my dark hair as I pleasure him. Tenderly, I sink my aching fangs into his sack, grazing the orb within with the tips. His groan at this is the loudest yet, and he falls completely still as his prick throbs and pulses, spatters of precum leaking from the tip and rolling down to gather on my tongue.

I bite a little harder and taste sperm mingling with the blood that flows into my mouth, his fingers clenching in my hair at the intense feeling. The gap between pleasure and pain is very fine, and I know that my bite brings only pleasure.

I take only a little of his manliness in this way, wanting him to spend the rest in his orgasm. My fangs withdraw and his hand relaxes, gently stroking my forehead as I lick the pinpricks on his sac closed. He relaxes his entire body as I engulf him with my mouth, taking his tip deep into the back of my throat. His prepuce unrolls as he penetrates my throat, and I feel his bare glans against my slippery inner lining.

Languidly, I begin to slide up and down on the hot flesh of his erection, taking him deep into my throat on each downstroke and suckling gently on the way back up. Precum oozes freely into my mouth, lubricating the way and making each thrust much more pleasurable. He starts to groan and thrust into me, cupping the back of my head with both hands.

I caress the heated velvet of his skin with one hand as I fellate him, the fingers of one hand fluttering over the ridges in his abdomen, lingering on his nipples. The other cups his balls, rolling them over the cool palm and squeezing very gently.

I sense that his orgasm grows near, and I draw back on his shaft until only the tip rests within my mouth. I slide my hand down his abdomen, through the silky nest of his pubic hairs, and to the base of his prick. I grip his shaft and slowly start to stroke up and down as my fangs ease into the base of his knob-end, hot blood pulsing from him and burning my tongue.

He shudders uncontrollably and groans, his entire body convulsing at the intensity of the sensation I'm bringing him. His prick pulsates in my mouth and his cream mixes with the blood that pours down my throat, satisfying my hunger at last.

He begins to regain control over his breath and his body as I seal the

wounds in his glans, capturing every last drop of blood and cream from the slick length of his erection.

"Dimitri," he whispers, "I love you."

I lie next to him and embrace him, kissing him so that he can taste the mixture of his own fluids on my tongue. I reach out and caress his mind with my own, letting him feel the intensity of the emotion I feel for him. I don't need to put those feelings into words, because he understands them for what they are.

He is my street angel, my love, my salvation.

The Gift
Michael Gouda

The streets were unfamiliar, but the scents were recognizable, and somewhere nearby would be the one who sought me out. Someone who needed me.

I needed him, too -- or someone like him -- it'd been so long. If only he'd be the right one...

Flashing neon advertisements lit the dark block of buildings with intermittent washes of red and yellow and white. A brief spatter of sooty raindrops fell from the clouds scudding across the sky. Late night passers-by stepped aside to avoid the dark caverns of doorways which were already shelter to the homeless poor.

I sniffed the air identifying the individual smells -- take-away hot dogs, onions, and chicken tikka masala. Petrol and exhaust fumes from the cars and taxis temporarily halted at the red traffic lights. Air that had been breathed in and out -- used air, tired air. But it was the air of London.

But London was home.

I had been away far too long.

One individual smell caught me and I stiffened in anticipation. So many times over the centuries, so familiar, yet always arousing: as if it was the first time. Coming closer -- the scent of one who needed me.

I saw the young man coming towards me then. I studied him, taking in the thin, pale face, the brown eyes under the curved eyebrows -- eyes which showed so much sadness.

He looked up and, seeing me staring at him, nodded. He assumed that he knew me, that I was an acquaintance whom he must acknowledge. We passed in the night without an exchange of words.

In that one intense look, however, I'd learned all there was to know about him. Alone and lonely, eaten up by an unsatisfied craving, vulnerable, and insecure. And dying. An obvious victim, I thought.

I accepted that I myself needed the young man as much as he needed me. I wondered which of us was really the victim, which the predator.

I turned to watch him walk deeper into the night. I had recognized only too easily the yearning in his eyes, a yearning which could only be satisfied with one thing. I watched for a moment more as he walked away, his body slim and elegant, his buttocks moving easily, athletically within the cloth of his jeans, his shoulders broad, his waist narrow.

I began to follow him, keeping to the darkness, avoiding the bright lights which hurt my eyes, keeping to the shadows that lay like dark pools between the orange sodium street lights.

He reached the doorway of his house, felt in his pockets for the key, inserted it, turned it and pushed open the door.

As he did so, I emerged from the darkness at his side and he started at the sudden appearance.

I smiled, teeth showing white from the shadows. "Hello, my friend," I said, my voice husky and beguiling, and so gentle that it dispelled the alarm brought on by my unexpected emergence from the shadows. "I think we know each other…"

The young man looked uncertain, anxious that he might be snubbing a neighbor, perhaps someone he had met at work, someone of influence.

"Kasimir," I said. "Surely, you remember. My name is Kasimir. Not an easy name to forget, is it?"

The young man nodded doubtfully, blushing slightly as he accepted that he had made a social solecism.

"Of course," he said, "and I'm Nicholas. My friends call me Nick," he added. "Tell me, where did we met? Was it…?"

I interrupted before he could complete the question. "Ah yes. Nick!" I said, "but can't we go in? The night has become cool." As I spoke, a chill wind sprang up out of nowhere and Nick shivered, his thin cotton shirt suddenly unsuitable for the unseasonable weather.

"Yes, yes," he said opening the door. "Please come in. Perhaps you'd like a glass of wine to keep out the cold."

He led the way into his flat. Soft lights lit up the room. There were rugs on the polished wood floor, brightly patterned Navajo designs. A large sofa was against one wall and a bookcase against another.

The books confirmed what I had already learnt from his thoughts -- Nick was interested in things supernatural. In front of the window hung a Chinese wind chime and the breeze from the opened window blew across the tuned wooden blocks,
knocking them against each other, producing a musical if slightly discordant chime. Quickly, Nick pulled the window shut.

In one corner of the room was an incense burner and the fragrant smell of joss hung in the air. Set in the wooden door of the closet was a full-length mirror, the reflection making the room look larger than it actually was. Several pictures of cloaked beings, dark against an only slightly less somber background, hung on the walls.

"I'll open a bottle of wine," said Nick. He turned to a cupboard and produced a bottle, two glasses and an opener.

I inspected the pictures, observing the cloaked figures -- their pale faces, their stark black eyes.

"You're intrigued by vampires?" I asked, as if I had suddenly discovered Nick's special interest.

The cork popped.

"It's a particular enthusiasm of mine," said Nick. "Now, you could call it almost an obsession." He paused briefly then asked, as if he were slightly embarrassed: "Do you think such creatures really exist? I mean -- outside the imagination." His eyes were bright with a strange, unsatisfied desire.

"I am sure of it."

"I wish -- oh how I wish I could meet one." He brought the glasses and bottle over to a small wooden table, the top inlaid with a marquetry design, gestured to me to sit down on the sofa and poured a measure of golden wine into one of the glasses. The smells of dried fruit and balmy Mediterranean sunshine filled the air. He picked up the other glass and started to pour.

"Why?" I demanded, almost as if the question was forced out of me, and my sudden query made Nick jump so that the wine was spilled over his other hand, the one holding the glass.

He muttered a curse under his breath and turned to look for a cloth to wipe himself. Before he could move away, though, I had seized the hand, raised it to my lips and was lapping at the spilled wine from his skin. Startled at the strange action, Nick tried to draw his hand away.

I assuaged his doubts, relaxing him. My tongue on his flesh became strangely comforting and he let his hand lie there, a passive victim, until the wine was licked away.

"Why would you want to meet a vampire?" I asked as if nothing had happened -- and perhaps nothing significant had -- though I sensed that Nick was not sure.

He handed me a full glass, and sipped his own. He sat at the other end of the sofa from me. The wine was sweet on my tongue, full-bodied and rich.

"I would like to know their secret," he said. "The blessing of immortality."

"You see it as a blessing?"

"But of course," said Nick turning so that his eyes met mine. "What else could it be? Who wants to die, to lose everything that is pleasurable? To sacrifice the knowledge you have gained over the years? To become nothing?"

My eyes were naturally as black as those of the actors in his framed photographs. I made them appear bottomless, to gaze into them was to lose oneself for all eternity.

"What if you saw what you had become as painful suffering? What if you wanted to die and couldn't?"

I never took without offering an escape, a warning. I had never once had someone take the escape I offered, but I did try.

Nick shrugged. "It would be worth it."

"Yet, the vampire has to kill so that he can live. Don't you think that he must feel guilt for such crimes?" I had not yet begun to touch his mind in order to direct him through the course of events that would follow. My conscience demanded that he have a legitimate chance to escape.

He studied me carefully, his eyes hooded. "Do you then, Kasimir?" He moved closer. "Do you feel guilt?"

I forced myself to stay calm -- though this was the first time a mortal had ever seen through me. I sensed no danger from Nick, only his curiosity.

And his burning desire to be like me. I opted for truth. It would be a novel experiment.

"Why?" he pressed and moved closer. "You don't have to kill to feed. There's nothing in the literature that says you have to do that."

"What would I do with you, with anyone, after I did feed? You would be weak for days. You'd know. You'd have some memories of it. My telling you to forget is nothing more than short-term amnesia."

"There are blood banks. People kinky enough to get off on sex while you're feeding." He snorted derisively and slid even closer. "You could even feed from a woman in the middle of her period. There's no need to kill," Nick answered firmly, full of conviction. He tasted another drop of the rich yellow liquid and let it remain for a while on his tongue before swallowing.

"This is what you'd do if I were to make you like me? Even if you could find willing victims, why would you want to give up what you have?"

"What I have?" He chuckled, his face showing strain as he quickly placed his wine on the cabinet beside him. "What I have?" he repeated, his voice rising, and began to laugh.

I stared at the tears that brimmed his eyes.

"Are you all right?" I asked quietly.

"All right?" he gulped, trying to staunch the laughter. He shuddered but managed to reestablish control over himself. "No, Kasimir, I'm not all right."

I felt the mental barriers he placed over his emotions.

"You should have asked me that this morning."

I stared at him blankly. If I went exploring his thoughts now, he would feel me.

"I went to see my doctor this morning, man. I have ninety days." He grabbed my arm. "I'm twenty-three years old and I'm going to die in three months, give or take a month..."

"Can he really be so certain?" I asked and put my hand on Nick's thigh.

"I'm a dead man, Kasimir. A lot more than you. Before..." He waved at his vampire pictures and the bookshelf. "Before I was fascinated. Now, I'm desperate."

My hand traveled carefully up towards Nick's fork over the soft material of his jeans.

He noticed, but I sensed he scarcely cared. He saw meeting me as the luckiest moment in his life. He would do anything to gain the gift he saw me carrying. In fact, the touch was exciting, arousing and, though he had never been touched by a man that way before, he did not find it in the slightest way perverse.

"I don't care," he growled. "I would join you, if you accepted me. I would become one of you."

He watched as my hand, its long, narrow fingers, grasped his ball sack and felt the softness of his cock, quickly becoming hard. I unfastened the

belt around his waist, opened the button at the top, drew down the zip exposing the white underwear and a bulge that already was large.

"Would you allow me to enter you?" I asked, taking hold of the cock through its soft cotton covering. "Would you sate my lust in order to achieve immortality?"

He was too far gone even to answer. Instead, he arched his body upwards towards my mouth as it fastened on his covered member, teasing it softly through the cloth.

I held back from controlling him; instead, I left him to experience for himself man to man sex for the first time. Still, I sought out his surface thoughts and feelings and let them flood over me. Sharing both his body and his feelings was far more exquisite than a simple sexual coupling.

Nick cried out, a wild growl that had no words. The touch of my body pressed against his was inexpressibly exciting to him -- the movements, the caresses. His body could do nothing but respond.

My proficient fingers undid the buttons on his shirt, stroking and embracing his chest, gradually moving lower, removing his clothes seductively -- the shirt, shoes, socks, stripping the jeans, the white briefs -- until Nick lay completely naked and exposed.

His fair skin was almost luminous against the red material of the sofa cover. His legs were slightly apart, his body open and vulnerable, his head lay back exposing his neck.

I stripped and lay on top of him.

Nick felt my smooth skin touch his and found it erotic and sensual. We were chest to chest, groin to groin, and he lay under the weight of me.

My hard cock, on top of his own equally aroused prick, pressed its need into his stomach and Nick felt an equal answering urgency.

I slid slowly down his body, kissing, tasting, rubbing, stroking - lingering for a time under his chin where the soft suppleness of his throat offered itself. Then moving - a little reluctantly - further down, lower, pausing to take care of Nick's nipples, his belly button, the trace of blond hair which led downwards before spreading into his bush of pubic hair, from which his cock sprouted. My tongue tasted under his ball sack, along the trail which led to his hole.

He spread his legs apart but was unable to stop the momentary, involuntary twitch of resistance as my tongue touched the sensitive entrance to him. I looked up and saw the look of apprehension on Nick's face.

"Do you want me to? You have to give me your consent," I told him. "I cannot take you against your will."

Nick had a momentary doubt, for a second he wasn't sure that this was what he wanted; but, almost as if they had a separate life of their own, his legs opened and he surrendered himself.

I put my hands under Nick's buttocks and, lifting them a little, dived into the sweet, musky darkness. At the first touch of my tongue, Nick tensed again, but was quickly overcome by a tantalizing delight that he had

never felt before.

He lay there on the sofa and enjoyed the feeling that my warm tongue produced, gliding over his hole, now with fast, brief cat licks, then slowing down, butterfly-light. Each touch was something different, each contact provoked a different sensation. Nick felt himself fast approaching a climax.

My mouth was now nuzzling at the base of his prick and Nick felt a moistened finger glide into his hole. It slid in without pain or resistance. He could feel it inside him, probing and investigating, finding the very center of his sexual being which made him groan and desire that he be invaded even further. Slowly and languorously, I washed the length of his cock with my tongue and licked away the oozing excitement from the tip.

I moved back up the length of his body, pausing just before our lips could touch. "You want me to continue, don't you?" I murmured, the sounds felt through the closeness of our mouths rather than heard. "You want me to enter you?"

His eyes met mine. There was no fear. No revulsion. Just his desire. "Don't stop," he told me. "Please don't stop."

I inserted two fingers into his hole, stretching the muscle and watched the face of the young man underneath me. I enlarged the opening gently, caressing his balls in the palm of my other hand.

Nick knew what he wanted. "Put it in me," he demanded. "Please put it in me."

But as he felt his legs lifted and sensed the urgent head of my cock pushing strongly against his opening, he tensed again.

I leaned over his body so that my breath whispered into his ear. "Relax your muscles. Just relax. Relax." The words and the tone were hypnotic.

Nick felt a growing pressure at the entrance to his arse and then my cock was past the sphincter muscle and inside him. There was a mounting fullness, a slow penetration. His body swallowed the intruder. Until, at last, I stopped. I was inside Nick as far as I could go.

"You've got what you wanted, Kasimir," Nick gasped. "You're inside me. Now, make me like you."

I bent over to kiss him on the neck and, at the same time, began to move my hips slowly in and out. Long, smooth strokes which pushed both of us up towards an erotic crescendo.

We lost the feeling of time, of place, of sound, of vision, of the external world. Nick could feel how the muscles of his own arse clamped around the invading cock to hold it as every stroke was made and the tiny rasps of my teeth on his neck.

He heard, as if from a far distance, the loud gasping breaths of two voices and knew one of them had to be his own. The tempo rose, my cock sliding freely in and out, increasing the pace, the sensation, building the stimulation until it reached the point of no return.

At that very point I bit and my sharp teeth sank into the tender flesh of his neck while, at the same time, my shaft pushed to its full extent, deep

into his compliant hole. Any pain that Nick felt as my needle-sharp teeth pierced his skin was subsumed into ecstasy as he himself came, his cock pulsating, the semen shooting over his own chest and stomach. With a cry, I exploded and Nick felt the spurts inside him. While I lapped at Nick's blood, he was filled by my semen.

"Give it to me," he told me, his voice straining as he labored to breathe. "I don't want to die, Kasimir."

I was not nearly filled but rose from his neck and brought my hand to my face. I nicked my wrist and tasted my own blood before I pressed my wrist to his mouth. I licked his blood that still dribbled from his neck while he transformed.

Afterwards, I buried my face in the hollow of Nick's shoulder, panting. Both of us lay and listened to each other's heartbeats gradually slowing and becoming regular. At last I lifted my body from his and let my cock slip from him.

Nick gasped at the sudden feeling of emptiness. He raised his head, our lips met, and he tasted his own blood. He pulled me to him, held me close, stroked my chest, and defined with the tips of his fingers the contours of my body.

"Is that it?" he asked.

"You have immortality, Nicholas," I whispered against his ear.

He pulled his head back and studied me for a moment. I watched a smile twitch across his lips.

"Would you stay with me tonight?" he asked shyly.

I smiled back. It had been so long.

"Forever and ever," I told him.

Eternity
Bill Crimmin

"There's got to be something better than this, John." I said out loud to myself as I drove down the A-1, "I hardly know I'm alive anymore."

An all-night truckers' café in the distance caught my eye and was a welcome sight. I reckoned I needed food and a gallon of black coffee to feel human again. It was the middle of the night and I was tired.

I pulled into the parking area and slid my car into a space next to a huge juggernaut. I climbed out of the car, my muscles stiff after long hours behind the wheel. A long-haired young man in a leather jacket stepped into the café behind me and crossed to a pinball table.

After ordering at the counter, I carried my mug to a table in the corner and slumped into the plastic chair. I picked up a copy of yesterday's paper and leafed through it.

Another sex scandal in the government. Inflation rising. Some celebrity getting married. And another motorway murder -- the third. I read the last article idly as I waited for my order. I took a couple of slugs of my coffee. It was hot and strong.

I felt a lot better after eating. I looked curiously around the room. The guy at the pinball table was pretty cute. I hadn't noticed that before.

His tight black jeans showed off a pert arse, and he looked as though his leather biker jacket concealed rippling muscle. His long black hair was thick and wavy and seemed to dance as he moved. I could only see his profile, but he had a manly jaw and a pair of red, full lips that made my mouth water.

He looked up then and caught my eye. I smiled as a pair of clear blue eyes seemed to stare straight into my soul.

I looked away quickly. I didn't want him to get the wrong idea. Well -- it *was* the right idea -- but it wouldn't do to be caught eyeing up another man in a place like this.

Leatherboy turned away from the pinball machine and walked over to me. He slid into the seat opposite me and gave me a smile which turned my legs to water and my cock to granite. If it weren't for the table between us, it would have poked his eye out.

"Hi," he said, "you're not a trucker, are you?"

"No," I admitted, "I'm a pharmaceutical salesman on the way back from a wasted sales trip. I was falling asleep at the wheel, so I stopped." I made a show of looking around the café. "I must admit I do feel a bit out of place."

"Don't worry about them." He said. "Their bark's a lot worse than their bite..." He paused and studied me for a moment. "My bite, on the other

hand, is deadly."

He smiled again and my cock grew an extra inch, putting an unbelievable strain on my underwear. His eyes continued to look into mine, holding me. I was hooked.

"Do you like motorcycles?" he asked suddenly.

I blinked and pulled myself from the bout of rapture I was having.

"Yes, as it happens," I said. "I used to have one myself. I traded it in when I got my job. You can hardly turn up to see customers dressed in leather and stinking of oil … I miss it," I mumbled, looking down at my hands.

"How do you fancy coming for a ride on my Harley?"

I looked up and found his eyes waiting to snare me again.

Their blueness seemed bottomless and seductive. His lips curled into a gentle smile. He wasn't smiling at me exactly, just smiling. Almost as though he were responding to a secret joke.

He licked his lips. The tip of his tongue flicked out quickly and was gone.

I was captivated. I would have agreed to anything he asked me. "I'd love to," I said, "just let me pay my bill." I began to fumble in my pocket for my wallet.

"Don't worry about that," he said, placing his hand over mine. "I've taken care of it."

His hand was soft and surprisingly cool.

My skin tingled where he had touched me. I felt goosepimples rising.

"Come," he said as he stood.

I followed him. His bike was parked directly outside the café. A huge panhead Harley. All black, except for painted red flames curling and licking over the petrol tank.

He handed me a helmet. He swung his leg over the bike and kicked it into life. It throbbed between his thighs, the roar cutting through the silence of the night like thunder.

I climbed on behind him, relishing the forced intimacy. His hard arse was between my spread legs. Inside my helmet, my breathing was loud and shallow with excitement. I held onto the grab bar and he drove off.

We turned out of the car park into the A1. His hands twisted on the grip and we were off, streaking along the highway.

The engine rumbled and roared, its power vibrating under me. It was almost as erotic as having him between my thighs. My cock was rigid. The wind caught my jacket. It flapped behind me like a sheet. The rushing air in my face felt good; just what I needed to wake me up.

Mile after mile we howled through the night. The thundering engine felt more like an animal than a machine, like an untamed beast under me. He teased power out of it and coaxed it to perform like a lover who knows his partner's body intimately.

I'd never felt so alive, so wild, so animal. I'd never felt so horny. Every

pore in my skin was experiencing pleasure. The rushing wind was a caress. My nostrils filled with the wild scents of the night. My cock strained for attention. I wanted him.

The engine slowed. He steered the bike onto the hard shoulder and stopped it. He propped it up on the side stand and climbed off.

"You want me," he said quietly as he turned to face me. It was a statement of fact, not an invitation.

I wasn't surprised that his words so accurately matched my thoughts. Just pleased that he appeared to share my need. He extended a gloved hand to me.

The moment I was standing up, he pulled me towards him. He wrapped his arms around me and held me close. His body was hard and muscular; his lips were soft and cool. His breath was intoxicating. Breaking the kiss, he took my hand and led me onto the grass away from the main road.

He shrugged his jacket off his shoulders and spread it on the ground. He pulled his t-shirt over his head, exposing his hairless, muscular chest. His skin was white and smooth, like porcelain. He pulled me down into the grass and rolled on top of me, his cock pressing against mine through the denim of our jeans. He kissed me again, snaking his tongue into my mouth.

I accepted his possession of me. I wanted him to take me, to claim my body and my soul. I wanted nothing but to become his. I knew he was the perfection I'd never been able to find.

I'd never felt this way before, but it seemed totally natural. The only thought in my mind was that I wanted to please him, to pleasure him. Reluctantly, I pulled my lips away from his.

"Fuck me, please," I begged.

What was wrong with me? I didn't bottom for anyone, but here I was offering my arse to a stranger whose name I didn't even know. My submission surprised me, but that quickly evaporated. In fact, having him in me became desirability itself.

Nothing I had ever done before seemed to apply. This was something new, something different. I felt alive, alert. I felt a part of the wild world of nature around me. Every sense was heightened. I could almost hear the air particles, feel them against my skin. I could hear small animals calling to each other as they scurried around us.

My need seemed to be part of the vast natural universe. Part of the cycle of life and death and the struggle to survive and mate. It was mad, but I didn't care. I only knew that I wouldn't be complete until he had taken me.

He ripped my shirt open, buttons flying. He undid my fly and pulled my trousers down to my ankles. He rose then and quickly took off the rest of his own clothes.

His cock was long and straight and topped by a thick bush of curly black hairs. Heavy balls hung low. He knelt and took off my shoes so that he could get my trousers all the way off.

I sat up and took off my jacket and the remains of my shirt. I wanted to

be naked. I wanted to feel my skin sliding against his as he fucked me. I wanted to experience every sensation and I didn't want anything getting in the way.

My pulse raced. My body filmed with sweat as I trembled. I looked up at him, kneeling over me.

He smiled -- the same enigmatic, secret smile I had seen at the café. He gripped my ankles and pulled my feet up and over his shoulders. He shuffled in close, pulled my buttocks off the ground, and rested them on his thighs. His thumbs parted my cheeks as he slid his cock up against my hole.

I bore down, relaxing my arsemuscles ready for the cock I wanted so much. I felt it push against my sphincter, stretching it. Then it was inside, moving slowly, millimeter by millimeter, until he was embedded inside me.

No pain, I registered vaguely, even though we'd used no lube. And I wasn't even going to think about condoms. Somehow, I knew I had nothing to fear on that score. I'd never felt so safe or secure.

He wriggled his hips, moving his fat dick inside my gut. It felt good. He flexed them back, pulling slowly from me. His prick withdrew until just his helmet was inside me. He stayed perfectly still for a moment, tantalizing me.

I wanted him to push into me again, to fill my bowel with his meat. I fidgeted under him, trying to coax his cock back into me.

He put his hands on my thighs and held me in position, and I understood. He wanted me to be still, to wait.

It wasn't easy. I wanted him to fuck me stupid. But I wanted to please him. And he wanted to be in control. I lay back and surrendered my body to him.

Slowly, he slid his cock back inside me. I felt his fat helmet pushing past my prostate. I felt it penetrating my gut. It was incredible. It was unbearable. It was divine. I lay on the grass and kept as still as I could while he claimed my arse.

He fucked me in slow motion, his rock-hard manhood sliding tantalizingly in and out of me.

Between us, my own dick was rigid. Virtually flat against my belly and drooling precum. My scrotum was tight and thick, my balls practically invisible. He wrapped his cool hand around my pole and started to stroke me. His thrusts picked up speed. He plowed my arse, wanking my cock in synchronized movements.

The scrubby grass underneath me was rough. It rubbed against my back as he continued to fuck me. Sweat dripped into my eyes. I blinked it away. I was panting hard; tensing the muscles in my belly and buttocks as my arousal grew.

He wrapped his arm around my thighs and held on tight. His other hand moved frantically on my cock.

I moaned. A ball of pleasure set in my belly. It tightened slowly, deepening. I was on the edge now. About to explode.

He began to fuck me hard, the force of his thrusts rasping my shoulders against the coarse grass. I shut my eyes. His hand pumped my prick. The knot at the base of my belly focused and broke. A jolt of pleasure shot over me, making me gasp.

Volleys of jizz splattered my chest and belly. My body shook as my dick convulsed in his hand. He thrust his hips forward, filling me with his cock. I ground my arse in circles against him, intensifying the sensations that overwhelmed me. His hand on my cock was slick with spunk. My sphincter throbbed around his rod as I pumped out the last drops of cum.

Gradually my breathing returned to normal. My muscles softened and relaxed. I opened my eyes. He was looking directly at me, smiling his secret smile.

"Did you cum?" I asked.

He shook his head and smiled. "It doesn't matter, I don't need to."

I raised myself up on my elbows, concerned. "But I want to please you," I told him. "Tell me what you like and I'll do it for you. You've given me so much, it seems only fair."

He slid out of me and lay down beside me. He leaned up on one arm and pulled me close with the other. He kissed me, softly.

"Do you really want to please me?" he asked. He looked troubled.

"Yes, I believe you do," he went on, before I had a chance to answer.

I remembered that I didn't even know his name. I opened my mouth to speak.

"My name's Adam," he said.

He'd answered that question for me, but I still had others. Who was he? Where did he come from? Did he make a habit of picking up salesmen in truck stops? I wanted answers but didn't know where to start.

"No, I don't make a habit of it," he said, "and your other questions aren't quite so easy to answer."

I gasped as realization dawned. He was reading my mind.

But that didn't make sense. It couldn't be possible. But he certainly seemed to know what I was thinking. How could I test it?

I racked my brains, searching for something obscure. The name of my parent's dog – if he knew that I'd have to accept that he was using telepathy.

"Your parent's dog is called Rags," he said, "and your address is 151 Cedar Drive, Dawlish. You lost your virginity at 16 with a boy called Nigel, and you've had mumps, measles, and whooping cough."

I was gobsmacked. I didn't know how to respond. My mind wouldn't keep up. How did he do it? If he could read my mind, did that mean that I could read his? What was happening?

Suddenly, I felt a sense of calm spread over me. Soothing fingers seemed to stroke my anxieties away. All sense of the fear that had been mounting inside me was gone. I felt relaxed. But I still wanted answers.

"Sorry," he said, "I had to do that, you were close to getting hysterical."

"You did that?" I blurted out, "You made me calm?"

"Yes. You need to be calm; otherwise, your fear will cloud your reaction to what I have to tell you. To answer your question -- yes, you can read my mind, if I allow you to. You felt it before, when we were driving and when we arrived here. That sense of wildness and belonging to nature that you experienced happened when I allowed my mind to merge with yours."

"It was incredible," I said. "Intoxicating. I've never felt so alive, so complete."

"I know," Adam said, nodding. "That's why I shared it with you. So you could taste it for yourself and decide if you wanted to join me."

"What do you mean? I have a job; I can't just leave that and move in with you. I don't even know where you live."

He laughed out loud.

"You are so naïve, John. I'm offering you far more than that. Far more than you can possibly imagine. But let me show you. Look into my eyes. Allow your mind to soften, to melt into mine. See into my mind."

I stared into those bottomless, blue eyes. They captivated me. They drew me inside him somehow, although physically nothing changed. My mind snaked inside his head and saw into his soul. I saw memories. Memories going back hundreds of years and gradually moving closer to the present.

I saw Adam on his Harley, tearing down the motorway with a young man on the back. Adam fucking the man in a field. Adam kissing the man on the neck. I felt the man's terror, heard his screams. Then blood, lots of blood. Adam driving off, the young man lying naked and white and dead in the field.

Oh, my God! Adam was the motorway murderer! I'd had sex with a murderer. I felt surprise, even mild shock -- but no fear, no recoil. My mind was still soothed by his, so I was incapable of feeling fear.

I experienced another mild shock of realization. He was no ordinary murderer. He didn't use a weapon to kill his victims, he used ... He used his teeth. And he drank their blood.

Oh, God! He was -- he was a vampire!

Recognition oozed comfortingly over me. That was what he was offering me. He wanted to make me into a vampire too.

But why? I delved further into his consciousness.

Because he was lonely. He wanted a kindred soul to share eternity with. There had been someone long ago, but he had been mortal and he'd died. Adam couldn't bear the thought of watching that happen again. He wanted someone to share his life with, forever. And he had chosen me.

"What happens if I say no?" I asked him aloud. "Do I end up here dead and bloody like the rest?"

"Nothing. I drive you back to the truck stop and let you go."

He'd let me go? When he could kill me, drink my blood and leave me?

And why didn't he simply force me to join him? I already knew that he could manipulate my mind if he wanted to. Why hadn't he made any of his other victims into a vampire if he was so lonely? Questions kept flooding over me.

"Look into my mind for your answers," he said softly.

I looked into his eyes, letting our minds merge again. I had to choose to become a vampire. He couldn't make me into one against my will. I had to want it. And there was something else; I delved further.

He wanted someone to love. Someone who would love him in return freely and unreservedly. An equal partner, not an unwilling victim. He'd sensed something in me which spoke to him, which needed what he had to offer. He wanted someone to love him, as much as he knew he could grow to love me.

As much as he could love me?

His mind was defenseless before me. I knew he couldn't lie to me, no matter how hard he tried.

"How do I know that what I felt was genuine?" I asked him. "Perhaps you got into my mind and manipulated my feelings. How do I know?"

Again, he used his mind to soothe me and remind me that I could find whatever answers I needed in his thoughts.

I searched his memories. He'd sensed my mind out on the A1 and felt something that touched him. He'd gone to the café to meet me and he'd taken me for a ride. He'd opened his mind to me while we were on the road, gave a sexual impetus to my thoughts, and softened the edges of my fear and pain.

Everything I had felt about him had been genuine; the sexual need he'd given me had been nothing more than a nudge that'd focused my desire. I had wanted him to possess me. And I knew that I wanted him again. I couldn't think of anyone I'd ever known that I wanted as much as I wanted him.

I thought about my life then. About the job I hated and had only got because my father pulled some strings. About my tatty, rented flat and my empty social calendar.

Adam was offering me total intimacy. A relationship in which nothing was withheld or concealed. And he was offering me immortality.

Did I want that?

And what about being a vampire? Could I drink blood? Could I kill innocent people? I didn't think so.

Adam laughed, softly.

"You're behind with the times, John," he said, "We don't have to kill our victims. We don't even have to feed from people, although we prefer to."

"So why? Why did you kill those men if you didn't need to?"

His mind reached out to mine again. Images formed in my brain. The three motorway murder victims had been drug dealers. They specialized in

selling heroin to teenagers. They visited youth clubs and got their victims hooked for free, before talking them into pushing the stuff at school. Get them young and you've got them for life. Even though that life probably wouldn't turn out to be very long. They had scarcely been human. They had deserved to die.

"But who are you to decide who should live or die?" I demanded. "No matter what they've done, murder is wrong."

I felt shame in his mind then. Felt the empty pang of loneliness that had led him to search for some meaning in his life. He'd thought chasing drug dealers and killing them gave his life some purpose. He justified it because it saved human lives.

"If we're to be together, Adam, I want you to promise to me that you'll never kill again."

[*I promise,*] he answered wordlessly.

[*Then, I want to join you,*] I replied with my mind. [*Take me,*] I told him. [*I want to be yours.*]

He rolled on top of me, forcing me down into the scrubby, damp grass. He leaned over me, his long hair falling in my face. The moon was behind him and it seemed to illuminate his pale body; making him glow. He dipped his head and kissed me, his tongue snaking past my lips, claiming me.

I surrendered to the kiss, exploring his mouth with my tongue. I felt his fangs then, sharp and pointed and pressing against my lips.

I shivered with arousal. Our minds were still connected. He registered my arousal and responded with his own excitement. He peppered my face with butterfly kisses, gradually moving his mouth lower. He licked my neck, wetting my hot flesh with his tongue. He kissed me at the base of my throat. I gasped. His mind yielded to me, even as his mouth possessed me. I experienced his urgent need as well as my own.

He bit me then, sinking his teeth into my throat and drinking my blood. Our bodies rocked in joint ecstasy.

I felt my life blood flowing into him, becoming a part of him, as his mind was already a part of me. My heart pounded in my ears, in Adam's ears.

I grew tired.

So very tired -- yet, I was trembling.

He sat up and brought his hand to his own throat. He used a fingernail to break his skin. Scarlet blood dripped from the wound.

He knelt closer, and, with an extreme act of will, I fastened my mouth over the bleeding cut.

I lapped up the blood, swallowing it down. I felt Adam's life force entering me, mingling with mine. I felt my senses expanding, my strength growing.

I became like him. Perfect, invulnerable and immortal.

Adam flicked the electric starter on his Harley and glanced over at me. I

smiled at him and knew his eyes were twinkling behind his shades.

[*Let's go,*] I said to him wordlessly and steered my bike out onto the motorway. Adam zoomed off after me, letting out the throttle when he hit the tarmac.

The wind rushed through my hair. My Harley's engine throbbed between my legs like a mechanical heart. The night air was pure and clear. We thundered down the motorway, the roar of our bikes tearing through the night like a scream.

Night Wings
Barry Alexander

Wind whipped through the broken windows of the old house, billowing the ragged curtains. Glass crunched under my feet as I walked over to the window to watch the approaching storm. Lightning spiked across the darkness. I turned back to the room, rubbing my eyes. I blinked and there he was.

He stepped towards me, only his eyes visible above the arm lifted to shield his features. His hair was as black and glossy as a grackle's breast. Another gust of wind rippled the cobwebs swaged from corner to corner, but it dared not touch the perfection of his hair. His steps made no sound as he walked towards me, his midnight eyes transfixing me with his gaze.

I quivered, but I tried to control myself as he came closer and closer. Slowly he lowered his arm, revealing his saturnine features: the arrogant nose, the blade-sharp cheekbones, the cadaverous-pale complexion. His full lips curled back in an obscene smile. His white teeth gleamed like freshly polished gravestones. As I watched helplessly, his fangs extended. I knew what was coming. I was powerless before him.

From the cavernous depths of his broad chest, his voice rumbled. "I vant to suck your blood!"

It was too much. I collapsed in a helpless spasm of giggles. Tears filled my eyes as I sputtered and whooped with laughter. The deserted Hollywood sound stage he'd chosen as my classroom seemed realer to me than the vampire. And Heinrich had already proved to me just how very real he was.

I couldn't help myself. He reminded me of those late night Saturday Creature Features that my buddies and I would giggle through to prove we weren't scared.

"Idiot! Dummkopf! You vill never get this right." I could almost see an opera cape swirl around him as he stalked to the farthest corner of the room, turning his back on me to show his displeasure. I was glad he didn't really have a cape; I couldn't have enjoyed the sight of his cute little butt filling out his black trousers then.

For a three-hundred-year-old vampire, he had great taste in clothes. I preferred Calvin Klein to Armani, but he looked really hot in his perfectly cut business suit. Too bad fabric didn't last as long as vampires, I'd loved to have seen him in baronial dress.

"Why me, St. Bela?" he muttered to himself. "What could I have possibly done to deserve this?"

The man had absolutely no sense of humor. Pity, because he was good-looking in a dark George Hamilton/Frank Langella kind of way. Tall, broad shoulders, and the cutest little butt. Hell, it wasn't my fault my mind kept wandering to what he'd look like naked. I never asked to become a

vampire. I didn't know how they assigned the tutors for new vampires, but I was starting to feel like Audry Hepburn parroting "The rain in Spain stays mainly in the plain." I stifled another set of giggles at the thought of Heiny playing the role of Henry Higgins.

"Lighten up, Heiny. I'll get the hang of it sooner or later."

"HEINRICH!"

His bellow was loud enough to wake the dead. But I kept forgetting -- I was dead, or undead. This whole vampire business was totally weird. I didn't feel like a vampire. I didn't even feel undead.

"How many times must I tell you? My name is Baron Heinrich von Fledermaus, a good German name, not like yours. What kind of parent would name their son Chip? What is Chip? It is nothing -- a tiny, broken piece -- it is not a proper name for a man."

"OK, OK. Maybe I'll feel more like a vampire with the proper clothes." Bicycle shorts and tank top didn't seem proper vampire attire. "I know just what I want. International Male has this great silk pirate shirt in shocking fuchsia. It would look totally awesome with their velvet colonial frock coat and wide-leg crepe trousers."

"Ach! Gott im Himmel! Unglaublich! Dummer Idiot! Verdamnter Dummkopf!"

I didn't understand most of the German he was yelling. Well, I'd heard Dummkopf and Idiot enough to understand *them*, so I got the message. Odd, my last boyfriend had the same reaction to International Male styles. He had no taste. It was one of the reasons I'd dumped him.

Some of the things Heiny told me were just plain silly. Like the thing about sucking blood. He made such a big deal of it. Sure it was a pretty color, and looked great in a wine glass. And there was sort of a kinky appeal to sucking it out of a cute guy's neck. I sure as hell wasn't going back in the closet now that I was dead -- undead, I mean.

But I had trouble believing him when he told me that soon the Blood Lust would come upon me like Vulcan Pon Farr and I would be unable to think of anything else. Puhlease! It didn't even have caffeine. It couldn't be as addictive as Pepsi.

Maybe it made some kind of weird sense, though. He said it was like being a baby only in reverse -- you had to change from depending on solid food to liquid as your body changed. He was nice enough about taking me out to eat when I told him I was hungry. We got a few odd looks when he drove his Lamborghini through the drive-up, but I didn't care. I was dying for a Big Mac. I ordered the Count Duckula Happy Meal for him since he'd never tried fast food. Guess the closest thing they had in the 17th century was the bratwurst vendor on market day. He didn't even think it was funny when I showed him how the Count's fangs popped out when you rotated his arm.

I was still hungry and talked him into stopping at the Olive Garden. We

got up to the door and my mouth was already watering. I opened the door and took a deep breath -- mmm, veal parmesan, linguini and clams, chicken scampi. I thought I'd died and gone to Italian heaven.

Then I heard a choked gasp and turned around. Heiny was leaning against the wall, clutching his chest and looking absolutely ghastly for a ghoul. His face was blotched, his hands were shaking, his breath sounded like my Chevy just before the motor died.

I had to help him back to the car. He even let me drive, so I knew he wasn't faking it. Sure I'd seen the old movies, but I never believed them. How could anyone be allergic to garlic? I'm Italian. Garlic is one of the basic food groups. Even my mother's milk was garlic-flavored.

I was still hungry, so I drove back to McDonald's, but I had to force down the Big Mac. Somehow, it didn't seem to taste as good as it usually did.

There certainly were a lot of inconveniences to being a vampire. Like that dawn curfew. But I was beginning to see some of the advantages. The Lamborghini he drove was certainly one of them. I'd have killed for a car like that when I was alive. But there were so many silly rules too.

"Why do I have to have a casket?"

"Every vampire has a coffin. It's tradition. You must have a place to rest where the sun's rays will not touch you."

"Maybe if you had a decent tan you wouldn't be so sensitive. Hey, how about a tanning bed? It looks like a casket, but you can get a tan and listen to your CD's at the same time."

I picked out a couple more German swear words that time.

Well, if I had to have one, I wanted something with style, a bit of flash. Everlasting Productions had provided the final services for some of the top stars. And since Heiny said money wasn't a problem, I wanted the best. I refused to spend any more nights in the makeshift box he'd provided.

"It's three in the morning," he protested when I insisted we go casket shopping.

"This is LA. Nothing ever closes."

The funeral director was a little grumpy when he came to the door, but he soon got over it when Heinrich slipped him a C-note for his trouble. He escorted us around his showroom with all the gracious charm of a car salesman presenting the new models.

"I can see you are gentlemen of quality with deep feelings for your dearly departed. This is our latest model. Birdseye maple with a Vercasi-designed interior of puce silk."

"I don't know, it seems awfully cramped inside. I roll around when I sleep."

"Roll around? Ah! You didn't tell me you had a non-traditional use in mind."

The director's eyes brightened and his teeth flashed like someone had just placed a lighted candle inside his skull. He was practically rubbing his

hands with glee.

"Follow me. I want to show you our LA selections."

The showroom was incredible. Crystal caskets, black lacquer coffins with inlaid mother-of-pearl peacocks, a sarcophagus with an Egyptian queen (who looked strangely like Madonna) with arms crossed chastely across her naked breasts, almost traditional models with flaming peach silk or tigerskin linings. There were models that folded out into futons, models that doubled as coffee tables, and there WAS a tanning bed model.

"And of course all of these come in full or queen size and your choice of support systems -- coil springs, waterbed, air models. Many of them also come with reading lamps and a built in mini fridge for late night snacks."

I wandered around the room, trying most of them out for size. Some were too hard, some too soft. I wanted one with a great sound system. I was torn between a luxury queen size with surround sound and mood lighting and a waterbed model with a miniscreen TV in the lid. I loved the sound system of the first but it would be great to keep up with my soaps.

"Make up your mind." Heinrich said, looking around nervously. "It is getting close to dawn."

"I'm thinking, I'm thinking."

He fidgeted. His gaze glued to the windows.

"There is no more time," he said finally. He turned to the funeral director and stared into his eyes. "You are sleepy. You must go to bed." His voice resonated with power.

"I ... am... sleepy," the man said. "I ... must go ... to bed."

Heinrich glanced back at the window again and shuddered. "There is no one here. You have been alone all night," he told the man.

"There is no one here." He turned and walked out the door. His words trailing behind him. "I have been alone all night."

I was totally impressed. It was like watching Obi Wan getting Luke past the security guards. I couldn't wait for Heinrich to teach me how to do that.

"When are you going to teach me that?" I demanded as soon as the director was gone.

"When you are ready for it. You must learn the basics first. Now get into a coffin quickly. The dawn is not far off."

Heinrich climbed into the queen-sized model. I shucked my clothes and joined him.

"What are you doing?"

"I always sleep nude." I pulled down the lid and snuggled closer to him.

"I meant what are you doing here? There are many models."

"Oh, well, if you'd rather be alone..."

I started to raise the lid, and was almost blinded by light.

"NEIN!" Heinrich grabbed my arm and pulled me back inside. The lid slammed down. "You must stay here now."

The coffin was a lot roomier than a tanning bed. To my surprise, I could

still see. Everything was sort of shapeless and gray as at twilight, but Heinrich's white shirt almost glowed in the dark. Vampire vision was no substitute for the real thing, though.

I wiggled my butt appreciatively against the satin lining. I was acutely aware of the attractive male body only inches away. Sleeping nude probably hadn't been such a good idea. Even in the queen-sized casket, I kept bumping against Heinrich -- accidentally at first, then on purpose as my cock filled and stood at attention.

I was delighted to see that my cock still worked. I'd been worried about that but couldn't quite bring myself to ask. At least it still got hard, I hoped the whole package worked. I couldn't wait for a chance to find out. But it's pretty hard to hide the sounds of jacking off when you're locked side by side in a coffin. The best I could do was roll over every now and then and feel my cock drag across satin lining or rub against Heinrich's leg.

If Heinrich noticed my erection he didn't say anything, but he must have finally got tired of all my tossing around. "If you're not going to settle down and sleep," he said, "we shall continue the lessons. You must work on your accent. No one will take you seriously. Now deepen your voice and repeat after me: I vant..."

"I vant..."

"I vant to suck..."

"I vant to suck..."

"I vant to suck your blood..."

"I vant ... to suck ... your cock!"

Silence. Maybe I'd gone too far. Picking a fight in a casket with a vampire I was stuck with until nightfall probably wasn't one of my better ideas. "Heiny -- Heinrich, I..."

"You do?"

"Do what?"

"Vat you said..."

I had been joking, but I suddenly realized I did want to do it. Heinrich was a damned good-looking man, and I wondered if what was under the front of his trousers was as attractive as the cute little butt under the back of them.

There wasn't a lot of room even in the queen-sized casket, but I managed to squirm around until I was half-kneeling, half-lying over him. Undressing him was a challenge. I had to do everything mostly by feel. My back pressed against the lid as I unbuttoned his shirt. I could feel a nice mat of hair, and I couldn't resist scavenging through the forest until I found his nipples.

"Ja! Das ist gut!" he gasped as I slurped my tongue through the tangled hair, tasting him.

I rubbed my lips over the hard peak of his nipple, then bit it gently. He jumped, but pressed closer. I sucked it until it felt swollen, then lavished the same attention on its twin.

I pulled his jacket and shirt off his shoulders. Between my legs, I could feel his cock growing and thickening. I rubbed myself against him, enjoying his hardness against mine. I unfastened his belt and unzipped him as quickly as I could. My fingers brushed against his wiry pubes. I could just feel the thick base of his cock. I had to get off him to give him enough room to raise his butt so I could work his trousers down. He toed his shoes off and helped me push his trousers and boxers off. He sighed and spread his legs, as if glad to be free at last.

I wished I could see it, but I was glad to be able to touch all of it at least. I took my time, exploring it with lips and tongue. The thick fleshy rod thrust powerfully from his groin. The tip was wet with precum.

I leaned over and kissed and tongued the insides of his thighs. Every touch of my lips made him quiver. We had all day. With his hypnotic powers, we were in no danger of being interrupted. I spent a long time getting to know his body, searching for the differences in taste and touch and scent, the different responses. Everything was different, but it was the same too.

Vampires weren't supposed to sweat, but the taste and scent of him excited me like that of no mortal man. There were no flaws on his body. No pimples, no patches of dry skin. Everywhere I touched was perfection. The back of his thighs was as silky as the skin between his cheeks. I could have got off just on the touch of skin against skin. But I wasn't about to waste a perfectly edible cock.

I slurped his cockhead eagerly, as if it were a rapidly melting ice cream cone. From the way he was squirming and moaning, I was pretty sure he liked my technique. His cock was fat, and I had to widen my jaws to the fullest to get it down, but I managed. I let it rest on my tongue for a moment, just enjoying the weight and fullness of it. He tasted so damned good. I drove my mouth down on him until I felt him nudging the back of my throat, then slowly slid off, sucking as hard as I could. His hips were dancing all over the place as I bobbed up and down on his rod.

"Gott, that is so gut!" he moaned, "But I must taste you..."

Obligingly, I crawled over his body until my dick was brushing his lips. He lost no time in going down on me. Damn, this vampire could suck!

Head to toe, we fed on each other hungrily. Just having my cock inside his mouth was wonderful, but he was a great cocksucker. He had all those little extra movements of tongue and lips that drove me out of my mind. I was whimpering with desire within seconds.

I toyed with his fuzzy balls, rolling them in my hand and working them down to the ends of their cords. He seemed to like that so much, I released his cock and sucked in one fat orb. He purred around my cock as I licked and nibbled and sucked. His legs spread and I knew it was time for a little rear action. I couldn't help smiling, I'd had my eye on Heiny's heiny since first sight, and it looked like I was going to have it before the day was over.

I grabbed the rounds of his bubble butt and spread them wide. I traced a

line from his balls up through his divide. I circled the puckered ring, teasing him, caressing the sensitive crevice and just brushing my fingers over the quivering ring. He groaned and pushed his butt at me. His hole dilated, baring the silky interior for a moment, then snapping shut.

I sucked my finger and worked it inside. He took it easily to the first knuckle. He was so tight and silky inside. I pushed slowly until I was all the way in. Then worked my finger around until I located his prostate. He bucked when I prodded the tiny gland. I caught his cock and aimed it at my mouth. Precum spurted over my lips, I licked it off, and added a second finger.

It got intense. I sucked hungrily, feasting on his flesh as I worked my fingers in his tight hole. I pumped into his mouth, wanting to drive more of myself deep inside. I could have come like that, but I wanted to stake my claim to his butt. I pulled off and crawled around so I was beside him.

I slipped my hand under his butt, and he wriggled into my palm, squirming like a cat in heat. Side by side would have been easier, but when he pulled me on top of him I didn't resist. His mouth locked on mine and his tongue rammed down my throat in search of my tonsils. He sucked face as good as he sucked cock.

He drew his knees up until they pressed against the coffin lid, inviting me inside him.

It took a bit of doing, but once I had my cock positioned there was no stopping me. I rocked forward, demanding entrance. His hole fluttered against my knob, then slowly opened. I pushed forward, inch by inch, enjoying the tight embrace of his guts around my cock. When my balls were riding his ass, he reached down to grab my ass and held me inside him while he tongued every inch of my mouth. When he retracted his fingernails from my ass, I began a slow fuck.

My butt hit the lid as I pulled almost out. I kind of liked it, it reminded me of fucking in a Pullman or the top of a bunkbed tucked under the eaves, and the quilted silk felt wonderful on my bare cheeks. I'd pull almost out, wriggle my butt against the cool silk, then plunge back inside Heiny's hot silky interior.

I could have kept going for a while but, when he started using his muscles to ripple over my cock, I went wild.

"Fichtst mir! Ja…!" he cried out.

I held onto his hips, as I flexed downward, driving my cock inside him. I plunged into him, faster and faster, unable to stop the ascent to paradise.

I thought I'd never been so aroused. But then Heinrich's lips moved off mine. He nuzzled down my throat. I felt the touch of his teeth against my neck. A tiny prick and his fangs sank into me. Fire trailed along my spine and burned up my cock.

I had never felt anything so erotic in my life. Waves of pleasure washing over me. I drowned in desire and drowned again and again. I couldn't seem to stop. My hips pumped him mindlessly as he continued to

feed on me. Then he gave a final lick to my neck and kissed me. I tasted my blood on his lips and the tidal wave crashed over me, shattering me in a million pieces.

Darkness swept over me.

I must have only been unconscious for a second. My body was stretched along his, my breath harsh and rasping in the confined space. I didn't want to move a muscle. I'd never felt so deliciously sated.

"Liebchen," he murmured, holding me close and kissing my neck. I didn't know what the word meant, but I knew I liked the sound of it a lot better than Dummkopf.

The lessons went a little better after that. But while I loved having Heinrich feed on me, I still felt no desire to drink blood.

Finally one night, Heinrich took me to a forest glade.

"Now comes the last and most important decision you will make before you are truly one of us. Look and listen," he told me. "Is not the night beautiful? Listen to its music. Look at all the wondrous children of the night."

I looked around. At first, I saw nothing but darkness and shadow. Then the clouds floated away, baring a silvery white moon. Bats swooped and fluttered across its placid orb. Luna moths danced over the pale blossoms of night-blooming jasmine. Lightning bugs winked over the pond. The eyes of nameless creatures peered at me from the shadows.

I heard the lonely hoot of an owl. The small scuttlings of forest creatures. The impossibly high squeal as dozens of bats wheeled and swooped over the glade.

"Look at them," he cooed. "My brothers of the night. Which will you choose to be like?"

As soon as I saw those marvelous wings, I knew there could only be one choice. So graceful, the way they attached to the soft furry body. I wanted those wings more than anything I had ever wanted in my life. They were to die for.

"Look! Those wings!" I gasped. "Beautiful! I must have them!"

Heiny beamed at me proudly. "There is hope for you after all! So many of us are drawn to that form. Hold out your arms, Liebchen. Imagine those are your wings, they will lift you, fly you anywhere you desire."

I extended my arms and thought of wings. I watched in wonder as I changed. My arms morphed into delicate green gossamer with just a touch of pink on the edge of the wings. My body became lighter that air. I floated, I fluttered, I swooped in and dive-bombed Heinrich's nose.

"NEIN!" he screamed. "Not the moth!"

I wasn't really listening. I hovered over the pond, dipping and turning over the reflective surface to enjoy the glorious green of my wings. Drag queens would claw each other's eyes out over them.

"Look at me, Heiny! I'm beautiful!"

"Gott in Himmel! Dummkopf!" he screamed. "Moths are irresistibly drawn to light."

Suddenly, I felt strange. Was this the Blood Lust coming on me at last? "Oh, God, Heiny, what is this strange urge?" I groaned, looking around wildly.

"Quick!" I cried then. "Which way is Vegas?"

Breakfast In Bed
Louis Carr

Footsteps in the den woke me.

I lay perfectly still, listening as the intruder entered the living room. He moved tentatively at first, then more confidently. It was definitely a him, from the weight and rhythm of his steps.

For human ears, the thick carpet would have muffled the sound, but I wasn't human.

My first reaction was annoyance. With exams over, I had the chance of a full day's sleep for the first weekday since midterms, and some idiot burglar had the gall to wake me at -- I glanced at the clock -- four in the afternoon.

As for the second reaction, my stomach reminded me that I hadn't fed in three nights. Not on the real thing, anyway. Animal blood, though a necessary source of bulk nourishment, didn't give true satisfaction.

I smiled. As far as I was concerned, this invasion translated into a free meal delivered to my door.

I noticed that he crept through the den without a pause, oddly ignoring a stereo system valued at four figures. I decided to wait and see what he was up to. Maybe he planned to ransack my office for computer equipment?

I heard him approach the bedroom. What the devil? Did he expect to find jewelry or cash stowed in the dresser?

He hesitated, just beyond the door. I caught his scent, a healthy musk untainted by drugs or tobacco -- and somehow familiar. I knew this burglar; I just couldn't place him.

I felt his shallow breathing and rapid heartbeat as he turned the knob. My stomach cramped with hunger. Faking sleep, slitting my eyes to watch him from under the lashes, I waited.

A lean young man with collar-length blond hair and long, muscular legs. I recognized him at once -- Brad Harmon, from my graduate seminar on the Tudor monarchs.

What did he want? Not revenge for his grades, since he'd finished the course with an A. He tiptoed across the carpeted floor to the bedside. The rose-tinted glow of his aura and the stutter of his pulse made my teeth tingle.

He bent over the bed. I sat up, grabbing his left wrist.

His heart leaped, and his breath caught in a gasp. His aura flickered, radiating fear.

I slowly reached over to switch on the small lamp on the night stand. Though I could see fine in the heavily curtained dimness, he couldn't. Besides, in near-dark conditions he would notice the crimson gleam in my eyes. If he hadn't already.

"Professor McNeal..." His voice trembled.

I pulled him down, forcing him to sit on the mattress. Only a sheet separated his firm thighs from my bare skin. "Brad, what the hell do you think you're doing?"

He gulped. "Are you going to rip my throat out?"

Suppressing my shock at the odd phrase he'd chosen, I permitted myself a contemptuous snort. "And get stuck with a body to dispose of?"

"So what're you going to do with me?"

"Depends on what this is all about." I projected soothing warmth to keep him from gibbering in terror but used no further hypnotic influence. Curiosity impelled me to leave his brain unclouded long enough to get a coherent answer.

"If I had an alarm system, you'd have the cops arresting you at this moment," I told him. I had sometimes considered installing one, but I'd rather depend on my own strength for defense than allow nosy police officers into my house.

He flushed a deep pink. "I didn't come here to rob you or anything like that. Yeah, I broke in, but..."

"How?"

"Patio sliding door. Glass cutter."

"Vandalism. And if not robbery, what? Assault?"

"No, man! That's not it at all!" He gulped hard. "Listen, I know what you are."

I kept my voice bland, though my grip on his wrist tightened. "I'm a very annoyed professor of history, and you are in serious trouble."

"I'm kind of surprised you don't sleep in a coffin."

Damn, just what I needed, a student imaginative enough to believe the truth about me.

"What are you raving about?" I demanded. Forcing myself to stop squeezing so tightly, I ran my thumb across the pulse point. I felt his skin go alternately hot and cold as excitement and fear chased each other up and down his nerves.

"I saw you with Kristin, after the end-of-semester party. I was the last to leave, except for her, and then realized I'd forgotten my jacket. I walked around back to the patio and watched you through the glass. Guess you thought it was safe, with the back of the house facing the canyon."

Ordinarily it would have been safe, except for the accident of Brad's trespassing.

"What do you think you saw?" I growled.

"You feeding on Kristin. No mistake -- there was blood on her neck and your mouth, after." His voice quivered. "She looked all zonked out when you sent her home. I picked up my jacket from the patio and sneaked away."

"The lighting was dim," I told him, putting every bit of authority I could muster into the words. "You misinterpreted what you saw."

"No, I didn't." His pulse slowed as the conversation calmed him. "So that's why you're so friendly with students, throwing parties and all. To you, we're a food supply."

"Sexual harassment is a serious charge."

The attempt at misdirection fell flat.

"Cut the crap, Professor. I know you're a vampire. So many things fell into place once I realized it. All those night courses you teach. You hardly ever go outside during the day, and when you do, you're wearing sunglasses -- winter and summer, rain or shine. I've never seen you eat. And I remember how queasy you looked when a couple of guys brought pizzas to class to celebrate getting through midterms." He shook his head. "No wonder you talk about the reign of Henry VIII like you lived through it."

"If you believe that, why are you here?" I was lost and knew it. "To drive a stake through my heart?"

He wasn't carrying one, and his shorts and T-shirt left no room for concealed weapons.

"God, no! I don't want to hurt you."

"Then what's the point of all this?"

He drew a deep breath, his heartbeat accelerating again. "I want you to EMBRACE me."

I could hear the capital letters.

"Do what?"

"Take me across. Give me the Dark Kiss."

"What the devil are you babbling about?"

"Turn me into a vampire," he answered with a hint of impatience.

Dark Powers! Save me from vampire groupies!

"Brad, you're wasting your time and mine. I can't do that."

"You mean you don't ... Because you only like girls?"

I dropped the attempt to argue him out of his all-too-accurate theory about me. Easier just to wipe his memory later.

"It isn't that," I told him calmly.

He was right about my tastes, though. I usually preferred female donors because of their greater sexual endurance. The average human male has one quick orgasm and then becomes useless for generating the erotic energy that flavors the blood so deliciously. Even a young man goaded by hypnotic seduction can achieve at most three or four climaxes in a night. With females, I can draw out the encounter as long as my appetite demands.

Brad brightened up. "Then you do take men sometimes?"

"I don't have any fixed prejudices on the subject. Genital anatomy is irrelevant to my satisfaction."

Of course, I'd noticed his attraction to me. To a creature who can see auras and sense emotions, his desire blazed forth every time our eyes met. Sexual harassment of a female student was risky enough, being caught fooling around with a male student would kill my career. I liked it at our quiet little university; the prospect of starting over with a new identity didn't

appeal.

On the other hand, since he'd finished the course, Brad wasn't officially my student anymore.

"So why won't you transform me? Am I too young or what?"

I sighed. "I didn't say I wouldn't. I *can't*. I'm not an undead walking corpse. I'm a member of another species. My bite wouldn't make you anything but zonked out and rather tired." I gave him a psychic nudge to discourage further argument.

His aura dimmed with disappointment. "Oh. I've got to admit that makes more scientific sense than rising from the grave." He stared reflectively into the distance. "I really liked the idea of living forever, though. What now?"

Now, I'd drink my breakfast. The ebb and flow of blood in his veins had me practically drooling.

"Now I make you permanently forget this whole harebrained conversation."

"Don't bother." He flashed a grin. "I wrote everything down in detail, all my observations and conclusions. How many times do you plan on hypnotizing me?"

"Think again. All I have to do is order you to destroy your notes."

"Don't you believe you can trust me to keep a secret?"

Since he obviously wasn't about to run away, I released his wrist. "You might change your mind and sell the story to one of the tabloids. I never met a student who didn't need money."

"Come on, Professor, why would I shoot myself in the foot that way? What college would hire a history Ph.D. with a habit of raving about vampires?"

I ran my open hand up his arm to the shoulder. The tiny cilia in my palm bristled at the moist heat of his skin.

"Nevertheless, I'd rather make sure of your silence," I told him.

He shifted position on the bed. A pool of darker crimson in his aura around the groin emphasized the growing bulge in his shorts.

"If you let me remember, I could be useful."

"Oh?" I kept rubbing up and down his bare arm. "How?"

He grabbed my hand. I allowed him to turn it over and examine it. "Hey, little hairs, just like Dracula in the book."

When he brushed his thumb over the center of my palm, I knew I should stop him at once. But I couldn't resist enjoying the tantalizing tickle for just a few seconds. Saliva pooled in my mouth. Swallowing, I said, "You really shouldn't do that."

"Why? Don't you like it?"

"I like it too much -- but you might not like the consequences." With my free hand I massaged the back of his neck. His heartbeat quickened again.

For an instant he closed his eyes like a purring cat. He opened his eyes

and let go of my hand.

"Oh, I don't know about that," he said. "Kristin looked like she was having a great time."

Before I could indulge my appetite, I had to decide what to do with him. I said in a cooler tone: "Never mind. What do you mean by useful?"

"I could become your Igor. Or Renfield. Do odd jobs, run daytime errands. Doesn't every vampire need one?"

I laughed. "Lad, you watch too many horror films."

"Seriously," he said, leaning closer. His clean, salty scent made me lightheaded. "If I figured out your secret, other people might, too. With me knowing the truth, I could keep a lookout for those people, steer them away. Misdirection."

The suggestion almost made sense. I could control Brad. The next person who stumbled on my true nature might pose more of a threat.

"And if I turn down your kind offer, what then? You'll blackmail me with your knowledge, I suppose?"

His aura flashed honest indignation. "Professor, I told you, there's no way I'd hurt you. I just don't want to forget the most mind-blowing thing that's ever happened to me."

"You're sincere now." I continued rubbing the back of his neck, teasing myself with the sensations of his hair on my palm and the blood flowing under my fingertips. "Suppose later you couldn't resist the impulse to brag to some close friend?"

His breathing became more shallow and rapid. It was obvious that he could scarcely keep from squirming. "Who'd believe me? And if you ever think I'm turning unreliable, you can always erase my memory then."

"True." Actually, not so true, since the more time he spent with me, the more deeply the facts of my nature would be etched on his brain. But he didn't need to know that. "Very well, Brad, I'll take you on trial. Not that I'll let you move into my lair, so to speak. We both have reputations to protect."

"Right." He emitted a long, shaky sigh. "Another way I could help. You'd have me around for a snack when you didn't feel like -- hunting."

I smiled at the naively forthright offer. "Aren't you afraid?"

"No. Well, not much. You didn't drain Kristin. She looked fine when I saw her the next day. And at the time, she acted like it felt incredible." He flushed a deep red, echoed in the hue of his aura.

My hand crept around the front of his neck to fondle the spot where the artery throbbed. "What are you thinking right now, Brad?"

"That I can't believe I've got a hard-on in a situation like this."

He blushed even hotter when he heard his own words. "Oh, God, did I really say that? You're messing with my mind!"

"Only a little," I said, "to relax you and decrease your inhibitions."

"Inhibitions gone, check. Relaxed, no way!"

"Then take off your clothes and get comfortable." I laughed softly at his look of shock, accompanied by an even faster racing of his heart. "You do

want me to drink from you, don't you, Brad?"

"Yeah." With trembling hands, he pulled off the T-shirt. "I guess it was in the back of my mind all along. I saw Kristin -- cum -- when you bit her. Can you do that to guys, too?"

"Let me show you." I hadn't enjoyed the luxury of a conscious, willing donor in way too long, and I planned to savor every minute. I wouldn't rush, despite the raging demand of my own hunger.

My nails skimmed over his chest, too lightly to draw blood. Timidly at first, then more boldly when I didn't object, he did the same to me. "You're cold," he said.

"Normal body temperature for us. I'll get -- hotter."

He swallowed hard as my fingers brushed his nipples. "I'm hot already."

"Yes." Heat radiated from him like an open fire; his hand practically scorched me. He stroked the inverted triangle of fine hairs that focused to a point at my navel, just above the sheet that still covered my lower body. When he ranged upward again to tweak my nipples, I couldn't suppress a gasp. With every nerve sensitized by hunger, I responded to touch almost as readily as a human male. My nipples pebbled up as hard as Brad's.

I leaned over to nibble his earlobe -- with lips, not teeth -- and trailed down the side of his jaw with rapid flicks of my tongue. He squirmed openly now, clutching my shoulders and digging his nails into my flesh. The almost-painful frisson challenged my control. Massaging his back with one hand, I licked the side of his neck in leisurely swirls, while my other hand unsnapped his shorts. Luckily he couldn't read emotions the way I could. No telling how he'd react if he could sense how hard I was fighting the urge to bite into him that very instant.

He helped to remove his clothes, then scrambled out of running shoes and socks. His cock stood erect, engorged with hot blood. Throwing back the sheet, I reclined on my side and guided him down so that we lay face to face.

"I can't wait..." he breathed.

"You'll wait until I think you're ready."

The longer I sustained his desire at its peak, the more delicious his blood would taste. I returned to licking his neck and throat, struggling against the ache at the roots of my teeth. My tongue traveled over his collarbone to his chest, flickering over each nipple in turn. The blood in the surface capillaries of his flushed skin drove me half-mad with lust.

His hips pumped, rubbing his stiff cock against my groin. The friction gave me the beginning of an erection, a rare event, since I seldom allowed my donors to touch me there. When I squeezed his buttocks, Brad reached down to explore my genitals. Though every inch of my body vibrated in response to his human scent and warmth, the clasp of his hand around my penis gave me an unexpectedly intense thrill.

A shiver raced up my spine. I let my teeth graze his chest. A few drops

of blood beaded from the scrape. When I licked them off, he groaned and tightened his grip on my shaft. My member became almost as rigid as his.

I pulled back from the temptation of his blood, determined not to end the first round yet. "Hurry!" he moaned. He moved both hands to grab my ass and pull me against him. The heat of his thrusting cock goaded mine to a delightful tension that fueled my appetite still further. "You're hard!" he gasped. "Don't you want to cum?"

"It doesn't work that way. I don't ejaculate. I share your climax." I licked each of his nipples again, then worked my way up to his throat. The throb of the pulse drove me over the edge. I pierced the skin and clamped my lips to the tiny incision. The anticoagulant in my saliva kept the trickle of blood a steady flow. I sucked avidly to relieve the pressure in my jaws.

A loud groan, half growl, from Brad. His vigorous thrusts swelled the surges of pleasure that swept over me with each swallow of his rich, young blood. I inserted one finger into the crack between his buttocks, rubbing in and out in rhythm with his pumping.

When I felt his passion rise near the exploding point, I pulled away, rolled him onto his back, and trapped his upper body under mine. He thrust wildly into the air, unable to make the contact he craved. His need spurred my hunger to dizzying heights. Now I lapped the wound instead of sucking it, making both of us delirious with the intensity of the sensation.

One of his hands grabbed his cock and started stroking. I broke his grip and pinned both of his arms to the bed. His hips kept rocking, beyond conscious control, while I continued to revel in the taste of his life.

"Oh, God!" he mewled. "Please -- my dick's about to burst..."

I knew that if I didn't allow him release soon, he'd shoot all over his own stomach. I couldn't have it wasted that way, could I? With a shudder of reluctance, I stopped drinking and licked my way down his quivering torso to his loins. My fingers probed his hole and rolled his balls within their hairy sack.

I skimmed my tongue up one side of his shaft and down the other, then up again to encircle the swollen tip. I felt the pressure within him gathering for the explosion. I closed my mouth over the head of his cock. Teasing the slit with my tongue, I pressed against the hard ridge just behind the scrotum. Heat welled up in the pulsing shaft like a surge of lava. My own penis, rubbing on his leg, throbbed in sympathy.

He shot into my mouth. I gulped it down, a salt-sweet flavor almost like blood, but not quite the same. My whole body shook with repeated waves of ecstasy, radiating from my mouth along every vein and nerve.

After licking the last droplets, I caressed Brad until his breathing began to slow. I sensed no hint of fear, even though I'd had my teeth so near that blood-suffused column of flesh. Only sated pleasure emanated from him.

I pulled myself up to the pillow and reclined on one elbow, looking down at my new donor.

"Oh, man!" He opened his eyes, looking drugged. "Man, that was

incredible! You can eat me anytime you get hungry. Uh -- how often can we do it?"

"I don't take much. One encounter per week is safe for someone as healthy as you are."

He rubbed the spot on his neck.

"Don't worry," I said. "It's as hard to notice as the puncture for a donation at the blood bank, and an enzyme in my saliva makes it heal within a day or two."

"Once a week?" He looked a little disappointed.

"One encounter doesn't necessarily mean only one climax."

A grin spread across his face.

"Just don't forget," I said, "the condition of future -- encounters -- is that you keep my secret."

"Don't worry about that! You think I'd want to share this?"

I didn't think this was the time to mention that once a week wasn't enough for me. Whether he'd have to *share* me or whether I'd take the more serious step of making him my exclusive donor was a decision for some other day.

Brad sat up, arms wrapped around his knees. "You want me to leave now?"

"Not yet." I traced his jawline with a fingertip. "After you've had about fifteen minutes to rest, we're going to do that again. Only, I'm going to screw you well and long. And then..." I paused and looked directly at him. "Renfield..." I smiled then. "You're going to check into getting that blasted patio door fixed."

Making It A Three-way
J. R. Mattingly

I'd seen him around -- Phelps Plaza, in front of the small shops at the creek separating the Buckhead section of Atlanta from the rest of the city. I'd even bumped into him at the Oxford Book Store in the Peachtree-Battle Shopping Center and we'd introduced ourselves. I'd seen him almost every afternoon sipping Viennese coffee at the Intermezzo on Peachtree.

Seth Foster was hot. Oh yeah! Blond, blue-eyed, wide-shouldered, slim, perfect white teeth, flushed cheeks, preppy as hell. This time, Seth was wearing an Emory University sweatshirt and dockers. Money too. Sweet!

Roderick and Drake would go ape-shit over him. They liked beauty just as much as I did -- and they'd each had more than a hundred years to develop some very strong tastes.

I hadn't mentioned Seth to them, yet. I'd kept him my secret, known only to the inner workings of my own vivid fantasies. I loved those fantasies, but I was wondering if it might not be time to do something about them.

I dreamed of Seth, Roderick, and myself -- together. It didn't bother me a bit that Drake was never in my dreams.

"What's up?" I asked as I neared his usual place near the fireplace of the Intermezzo, and we locked onto one another's gaze. My erection was demanding as it pushed against the inside of my zipper.

"Wondering what kind of trouble I can get into," Seth answered and I was immediately mesmerized by his full, curved lips. "Or just trying to convince myself to go home and study. You?"

"Trying to wake up and get going for the night ahead."

"A real party animal, huh?" he shot back, studying me a little more closely. "You must go to State."

"Last year. Until I found a lot more interesting things to do with my time…"

He frowned. "Not drugs, I hope."

"Hell no!" I growled. Roderick had convinced me to drop that shit fast last year. He threatened me with Drake, and I was scared of Drake. I was sure Drake wouldn't just kill me -- he'd eat my soul.

I sat with him and we chatted about everything and nothing. He kept trying to find out what I was doing since I'd left State. There seemed to be more than just idle curiosity, and I kept my life a tantalizing blank. It got him even more curious.

"Can I ask you something, Gareth?" he asked finally.

I shrugged.

"Are you gay?" he asked, dropping his voice to a whisper.

"Yeah," I answered, wondering where this was going.

"What's it like?"

The boy was ready. Right now ready. If I wanted him, I was going to have to introduce him to my masters. I smiled slowly as I visualized Seth with Roderick. But Roderick would treat him nice and I liked how I heard Seth purring.

"Are you a virgin?" I asked.

"With guys, yeah."

"Meet me back here in…" I glanced at my watch. "In three hours."

"What do you have in mind?"

"Making your wildest fantasies come true." I stood up. "Be here."

He grinned impishly. "I guess I could take in that art movie up the street while I'm waiting for you."

Roderick and Drake were vampires. I found that out last year, that night I went home with them. I'd been real coy for a week, coming on to them -- then, holding back. My usual dance. I had the best tongue and tightest ass in Atlanta and knew it. I wanted guys to appreciate me when I finally let them have me. Only, one or both of them decided they were tired of dancing. I didn't even remember leaving the bar or getting undressed. My next memory was being in bed with them -- Roderick plowing my butt while Drake was spreading my tonsils.

It wasn't until Roderick leaned over my back and started nibbling on my neck that I began to figure things out. He had such sharp teeth. And they felt big too. I got harder. Drake shot down my throat and wiggled around until he was on the other side of my neck. Then I knew.

"Just don't kill me," I groaned, humping back in time with Roderick's thrusts. "I'll do anything you want…"

Still mortal, I became their slave. I moved in a week later and dropped out of school at the end of the semester.

By the time I arrived at the house, it was totally dark. I fumbled with my keys, knowing they'd be up and knowing I was in for it from Drake. Once inside, I went right to the candlelit dining room.

"Gareth," Roderick greeted me, looking up from the table. "Drake is upset that you didn't light the candles."

"Thanks for taking care of it, sir. It won't happen again, I promise." I liked Roderick -- he was real easy on the eyes as well as being real easygoing. And he had the biggest dick.

I realized that Drake was right behind me and spun around.

"I'm the one who did your work." His grimace expressed his disdain for my existence. "You might pretend you spent at least a moment or two guarding our coffins."

"Please don't beat me," I begged, knowing Roderick wouldn't but unsure about Drake. I got down on my knees.

"Perhaps I should kick you instead?" Drake was without guilt, unlike Roderick who'd been working the Underground Railroad when Drake took

him in 1855. I understood Drake though, and, at times like this, that was what usually saved my skin -- things stayed light. "Get down on all fours, and bark for me!" Drake ordered.

"Drake, is this really necessary?" Roderick asked.

"I gave him an order," Drake said coldly. "He's mine -- you won't interfere."

Roderick's nose wrinkled in disgust as he met Drake's gaze. "Someday, you're going to go too far for even me."

I did as I was told. I dropped to the floor and faced Roderick. And barked out five short yelps. Drake laughed behind me.

Roderick wasn't amused. "You can get up, now," he told me.

They hated each other. In the year that I'd been with them, I hadn't once seen them just lay back and enjoy being together -- not once. Didn't vampires do divorce like normal people? Roderick sure needed to dump Drake.

Roderick was far more handsome, dangerous-looking, with his dark hair, and intense look. Drake sported a lighter, friendlier look. I'd learned the hard way that looks were deceiving with these two. I could spend an eternity with Roderick; Drake was -- well, he was Drake.

I poured the cabernet into three goblets. Roderick had insisted that I be allowed to join them in their libation to the evening. Drake threw a temper tantrum that lasted a week but finally gave in when Roderick wasn't buying any of it. I figured I'd better tell them about Seth; it'd distract Drake.

"I've found someone that I think the two of you would really get off on," I said directly to Drake.

His eyes flared. "Where? You must take us to him, you little fool."

"Wait," Roderick insisted. "Allow Gareth a description first." He turned to me. "This is not some common street hustler, is it? Tell us, what's so special about him?"

"I think he's a virgin, for one thing." I felt my own heart thump at the fantasy of having my chance at the boy's beauty. At watching his blood spill afterwards. "At any rate, he's young and a real cutie."

I gave them all the details. Both my vampires became thirsty with anticipation.

"I want him inside me," I insisted. Drake's laughter hurt, so I turned to Roderick. "This is important to me."

"Perhaps you might go with me to find him," he suggested. This made sense, as Drake had a difficult time controlling himself when around a tender morsel. If it hadn't been for Roderick, I would have been either dead or made that first night. "He's going to meet me at the Intermezzo," I told him.

"Drake may follow behind if he wants." Roderick gave him that look that brooked no dissent. "Let's go," he said.

"Let me have him first, if possible -- I mean if he decides he wants to." I looked to both for an answer.

"Of course," Drake agreed. "We will join you in your little adventure." He licked his lips, as he revealed those frightening incisors. "And we feed from his heart and soul. We get him off over and over again -- then we rip his neck apart."

I stepped back, into the cold safety of my friend. Roderick placed his arms at my sides. "Control yourself, Drake," Roderick growled. "There will be no killing." I felt better as Roderick gently guided me to the door.

We made our way to the coffee house on Peachtree. It was a beautiful, star-lit evening -- cool, with hints of the coming winter. I smiled but didn't say anything -- I knew how much Roderick missed the earthly, human pleasures of an evening like this.

I was eighteen when Drake and Roderick first sucked my blood. It'd probably never happen again, no matter how much I wanted Roderick feeding on me while he fucked me.

Drake wasn't about to let it happen, they risked having to make me. He wanted a slave instead. I knew Roderick wanted to, and I was sure of my desire for him -- yet, I wasn't sure about wanting immortality. I still liked feeling a cool night in the city surround me. I still liked to feel sunlight on my face.

My chest pounded when I saw Seth enter the Intermezzo. I glanced quickly over at Roderick and saw he was staring. I snapped my fingers in front of his face.

"You're the one who's supposed to control him," I told him. I wanted to pout. I wanted Roderick; I sure as shit didn't want to lose him to Seth.

"You were so right about him. He is the most beautiful mortal I've ever seen. Yes, I want this one. Go tell him you have someone you want him to meet."

"What about me?" I whispered as I stood.

He smiled up at me. "Gareth, you're Drake's as long as he lives. That was the arrangement you made with him -- to keep your mortality and your life. You didn't trust me to protect you."

I nervously walked over to Seth. "Hey, there," I put my hand out. We shook hands. "My friend would like to meet you. That's him over there, sitting by the hearth."

The attraction was mutual as far as I could see -- and I got the feeling it was equal between the three of us. We sat down on either side of Roderick.

He took Seth's hand in his. "I am Roderick."

We led him to believe that Roderick and I were lovers, and ready to play.

"So, what're you guys doing the rest of the evening?" Seth asked.

"Why don't you join us for a glass of wine?" Roderick asked. We walked on either side of Seth, taking him home.

I chose a merlot. Roderick stroked Seth's hair. I had my hand on his leg. I mentally measured the outline of his hard-on, and my guess was about seven inches. This was going to be fun.

"Great place," Seth said as we sat on the sofa. "What's behind that door?" He pointed towards the basement. Was Drake playing with the boy's head already?

"The cellar. We'll take a look if you'd like," Roderick offered. "We have some wonderful antiques -- actually, I've thought of something down there that I want to give you."

"Really?" Seth made a production of studying Roderick's crotch and then mine. The three of us rose together and we moved to the door. As Roderick turned the doorknob, I felt the icy presence of Drake. Roderick hit the light switch with his long, sinewy, fingers.

Seth stepped down between us without even hesitating. The old, wooden steps creaked beneath our weight. He was sure ready for the night's adventure. He had no escape -- either he was dead meat or a slave. Or, perhaps, they would make him into a third companion and I'd have yet another master.

Seth and I kissed while Roderick fondled us both. Seth knelt and Roderick grabbed his hair to guide his face towards my bulging crotch. He undid my button-fly and pulled my pants down to my knees without any direction from Roderick. He licked my balls on his way up to my long, hard shaft. He dove on my cock then. The hot wetness of his mouth had me ready to blast off.

I didn't want to shoot so soon. I wanted to stay in the dance. I raised him to his feet. "I should be doing this for you," I told him, leaning into him to steal a kiss while I unzipped his pants. Getting down on my knees, I pulled them down to his ankles and licked my lips at how thick his dick was. Oh yeah! I wanted him in me. And I knew I'd better hurry if I was going to get it. Drake was just so good at fucking up even the most foolproof of wet dreams.

I stood back up and smiled. "Fuck me," I told him, stealing another kiss before I turned around and reached down to grab my knees. Roderick was sucking on his neck -- lightly, not yet breaking the skin -- from behind. Seth wasn't slow on the uptake at all; he was in position before I could reach around and spread my cheeks.

"Oh man!" he groaned as he slid into me. Only a year ago, I'd never let anybody take me bareback -- until Roderick took me that first time. Now, I couldn't imagine it any other way.

Seth could fuck. My hard dick, dribbling precum, bobbed from one thigh to the other as he plowed my ass. My sweat dripped on the floor under me. I gave myself up to what he was doing to me with his dick and rode the pleasure trails like I did when it was Roderick behind me.

I heard Roderick growl and Seth gasp. I looked over my shoulder just as Seth's cock seemed to grow an inch in length and two in girth. I smiled

when I saw that Roderick had begun to feed. Seth started pounding me good, lifting me up on my toes with each thrust. I reached behind him and grabbed his asscheeks.

Seth moaned and pushed deeper into me -- staying there for long moments. I glanced over my shoulder again and saw Roderick wiggling his big cock into the blond's ass, even as he kept lapping at his neck. "Yeah," the boy purred. "Sweet Jesus, yeah!"

We started up again, this time in a three-way with Seth in the middle. He took direction well. He pushed into me when Roderick plunged into him. He felt almost like an extension of Roderick. I wanted it to go on forever.

My balls were tightening fast. My breathing was ragged and my eyes glazed. I didn't even have anyone feeding on me. I shuddered, my cockhead thickened as it bounced from one thigh to the other. I blew thick ropes on the floor, my legs, and even on my chest. I hadn't even touched my dick. Seth's cock was still working my ass, as was Roderick's working his -- but slower.

I looked back at the others. Seth was lying on my back, his butt high in the air, and Roderick was standing up behind him, giving it to him. I was only getting the ripples of the riptide lashing through Seth's ass. It was enough. I reached between my legs and took my still hard cock in hand, stroking it in time with the boy's thrusts. I had well-defined pleasure trails and I rode them again as I began to climb towards another orgasm.

Seth mewled. He panted. His chest slid over my sweaty back. Roderick's every thrust pushed into me. Seth's dick got thicker, harder, inside me. I threw myself into overdrive. I came just as his first hot rope splashed into the walls of my gut. Roderick howled as he came too.

We led him into the second room of the cellar. Seth gasped when he saw the two polished black wooden coffins side by side on their pedestals.

"What's this?" he demanded, looking from one to the other of us. His heart beat loudly. Even I heard it. It drove vampires mad -- Roderick had told me once. He tried to turn, but we had a firm hold on his arms.

Seth's eyes widened at the sight and sound, of the opening container of death. Drake was making his grand entrance. All naked and golden and hard. His dick was almost as long as Roderick's but thicker.

Seth stared at Drake's equipment as he took one step towards him and then another, his eyes glassy. He wanted it and I was willing to bet that Roderick wasn't controlling him now. Drake kissed the front of his neck; and Roderick came up to kiss the back. I bent down with my back against the side of coffin -- in front of Seth.

He was hard again, pulsing as fangs made new openings at his throat. His cock found its way into my begging mouth. I took it slow and easy. My face pressed against his belly.

"Oh, man!" Seth groaned. "Do me!" his voice crescendoed. "Yes! Take me!"

"What if you don't come back?" Roderick teased.

"I don't care," he moaned and I knew Roderick held his mind like a vise. "I'll go anywhere you want to take me."

I had him down to the pubes and I didn't let go. His cockhead was buried in my throat, and my lips were buried in his short curlies. I gargled, and Seth pranced in excitement. I felt the nick of fangs against my neck and knew it was Roderick. Drake still lapped at Seth's neck and he moved behind him.

The boy pushed deeper into my throat as Drake slipped into him. Seth stood on his toes, quivering. Roderick's lips left me as his fingers came up to caress my neck. I saw him tear open his wrist and knew Seth was about to become immortal.

Roderick's arm shot up the chest of the boy we'd brought home from the Intermezzo. [*Drink*!] he commanded as Seth unloaded everything he had down my throat. Seth's legs shook and he started to lose his balance. They were taking him close -- closer than I'd ever been. I gripped his butt to hold him in place.

"What...? No!" I heard Drake cry as he realized what Roderick was doing.

Roderick chuckled. [*Too late.*]

I collapsed in front of Seth, my lips sliding along his shaft until just his knob remained in my mouth. I couldn't keep my eyes open. I felt Roderick in my mind. [*Sleep little one,*] he told me. I blanked out good.

When I woke, daylight peeked through the boarded-up windows of the cellar. I didn't see Seth and my masters were closed in for the day. I went upstairs and made coffee. I thought about what I had while I was having my caffeine fix. It was a pretty good guess that Seth was in Roderick's coffin.

I had the perfect opportunity to get rid of Drake. The plan poured from my head in four part harmony. It was all there. All of it -- like I'd planned killing him forever. And it was perfect. So clear. Like crystal.

I went back to the basement. I ripped the sheetrock off the inner window frames. I found the stake where I'd known it would be. If Drake had seen any part of my plan in my thoughts last night -- thinking of what he'd have done to me make me shake.

But I wasn't shaking. Man, I was stronger than I'd ever been, but I wasn't surprised. I knew I was the only one who could rid us all of Drake. It was up to me -- and me alone. It was my duty even -- to Roderick and to Seth. To me too. I was a rock.

I stepped over to Drake's casket. Taking a deep breath, I threw open the lid.

Immediately, Drake's eyes flew open to the sunlight that poured through the windows. I stepped closer, the stake in one hand and a sledge

hammer in the other. He looked at me. The tableau lasted only a moment. Both the stake and the hammer slipped out of my hands -- I just opened my hands and they fell. Drake yanked the lid back down.

I stood there frozen, staring at the closed coffin -- images of Drake draining me and tearing me apart. I couldn't stop shaking.

My spine snapped back into place. Yeah, I was dead meat if I waited around until dark. But I wasn't going to be that stupid. The plan was still a perfect one. I didn't even need to stick him. I knew with complete certainty that the sun and fire killed a vampire just as dead as an wooden stake did.

I ran back to the supply room and found the heavy chains that they'd used when they moved to the house. I didn't even wonder how I knew about them or the stake either.

I wrapped the chains tight around the coffin. They kept trying to slip off but I finally got them in place and locked them. I felt Drake trying to get into my head but, somehow, I was resisting him better than I had in the year I'd known him. Purposefully, I used another chain to drag his coffin up the flight of stairs and through the house to the back door.

I could hear Drake's muffled shouts. He banged on the lid. I felt his fingers grabbing more and more of my brain but I fought it. I was almost safe. Roderick was almost free -- Roderick and Seth. And me. We almost had the life we all wanted. I only had a little more I had to do.

The sunlight alone might have killed Drake, but it was best to be sure. I dragged the heavy box all the way to the huge barbeque pit in the back. I thanked the gods above that my vampires had insisted on having a high privacy fence. Drake was cursing me now while he still banged on the lid.

"Relax, Drake, I'm just trying to help you," I told him. I picked up the firestarter and found myself pointing it at me instead of the coffin. "Not nice, master," I growled at Drake. I squirted the stuff over the coffin, emptying the whole can. I picked up the matches and struck one. I pitched it and the coffin belched into flames.

I no longer felt Drake touching my brain. It was almost like he wasn't there any more. The splintering of the lid scared the shit out of me. He glared at me, his jaws wide open. The sun hit him then. He screamed. Then the fire touched the old satin and the whole coffin was burning. So was Drake.

"Your wine, gentlemen," I offered as Roderick and Seth entered the living room. I took a long, slow drink to calm my nerves. I looked deep into Roderick's eyes. They shone with a new brilliance. "I hope you aren't too upset with me."

Roderick only smiled. "Upset? I am eternally grateful." He took my hand in his, and kissed me. "You carried out my will to exact specifications."

"Be with us," Seth prodded.

"Yes, do," Roderick echoed. Both were pressed close to me, one on either side. "You belong to us now. You belong *with* us."

"I..." I had been going to refuse. Because Drake wanted me to be his slave -- as a mortal. Only, Drake was dead.

I looked from Seth to Roderick.

Each took an arm and I was raised an inch or two off the ground. I shivered when I felt the pricks of both of their fangs. They sucked on both sides of my neck. I was hard, and a wet spot soaked through my pants. The sharp sucking at my neck was bliss.

Seth unzipped me and slipped his fingers inside my shorts. I smiled as he began to massage my bone. Roderick squeezed my left nipple. He pulled at the ankh there, and I winced. Seth's fingers teased my crack as he worked me out of my clothes. My hand pulled Roderick's large cock out of his pants. My other hand wrapped itself around Seth's love toy.

"Let's go find a bed," I told them, pulling away and exerting my new-found equality.

"Let's take turns with him," Seth suggested as we all three settled on the bed in my room. I rolled onto my side to face the blond beauty. Roderick entered me as I dove for Seth's hard, throbbing dick.

I was close even as I felt Roderick's pubes scratch the slopes at the bottom of my crack. My balls were tight against my shaft. I was lightheaded and breathing hard as I swallowed Seth.

Roderick's lips nuzzled my neck and I got harder. My heart beat loudly in my ears. I felt faint and instinctively knew that I either died tonight or they made me. I drifted down into oblivion as Roderick pummeled my ass and lapped at my blood and I hummed my love around Seth's cockhead in my throat.

I came to again, with Seth inside me -- his torn wrist at my mouth. He slipped out as easily as he slid in. And I sucked at his blood greedily.

Amsterdam
Simon Sheppard

Late afternoon, when things change.

Tall, maybe six-five. Thin, almost skinny. Not bad-looking, but short of handsome. Just his type. The thin man looked at him and stroked his crotch.

At this time of day, the Web wasn't crowded. Maybe two dozen men, most stopping by on their way home from work. For a drink, a quick fuck, shelter from the raw February wind. All sorts: older guys still in good shape; younger guys with hungry eyes; tired men significantly past their prime. A chubby guy with a North English accent joking with the barboy. A Japanese tourist still gripping his indecipherable guidebook.

Everyone in the bar's rear room was staring up at the video monitor, where a blond hunk shoved his latex-gloved hands up the butts of two kneeling men with wide-open assholes. Everyone except the thin man, who was staring not at the monitor, but straight at him. He felt his crotch swelling against his winter camouflage pants. Staring straight back, he grabbed at his thickening dick.

The thin man walked to the stairs and went up towards the darkroom, never looking back.

He gulped down the rest of his Dommelsch and headed for the stairs. Just above his head, the blond hunk was still punch-fucking a stretched-out hole.

Up the stairs, opposite the direction of the Exit arrow, white diagonal against black wall. Out one door, then back inside through another. At first the darkroom was impenetrably black, but in seconds his eyes had adjusted. The dim shape of the thin man was leaning against a wall directly in front of him, waiting. For a few long seconds, nobody moved.

The thin man turned, walked down a dark hallway. He followed. At the end of the hallway, a room with a toilet on the left, a still darker room on the right. The thin man leaned against an invisible wall. They were inches apart. They could feel each other's hot breath. The thin man reached down with both hands, grabbed both dicks, squeezed.

He put his hand around the thin man's narrow waist. Slid his hands beneath his shirt. Scabbed-over nipples.

Amsterdam, he thought, must be the tit-work capital of the world.

The thin man let go of his cock and raised his hands behind his head.

He slid his hands to the thin man's belt buckle, started to undo it.

The thin man pushed his hips forward and moaned.

Freed of jeans and briefs, the thin man's average-sized, uncut dick stood stiffly out. From somewhere down below, the muffled beat of neo-disco.

He grabbed the thin man's cock with his left hand and stroked, sliding

foreskin over dickhead. His right hand found the guy's ass and gave it an exploratory slap. The thin man groaned for more. He grabbed the thin man's hips and turned him around so he was facing the wall, hands still behind his head. He started slapping the guy around in earnest now, each whack of hand against flesh echoing through the darkroom. The thin guy writhed appreciatively, pushing his butt out for more. When he reached around for the thin man's cock, it was dripping wet.

He shoved the man over to a bench and forced him down onto his knees. Not "forced," really, since the thin man quickly lowered his head to the bench and hungrily shoved his butt in the air. Even in the room's near-darkness, the white flesh of his ass glowed softly. A dark crack down the middle. The smell rich, slightly revolting, rose to his nostrils like an aphrodisiac.

The action had gathered a small crowd: a couple of the older guys, the Japanese tourist. He'd built a rhythm, whacking one butt-cheek, then the other, then a slap right down the moist, hot crack. Somebody's hand reached out to the bottom boy's ass.

Rude motherfucker.

He pushed the hand away, reached between the skinny thighs and grabbed hold of hard dick.

WHACK! The thin guy pulled away. He pulled him back by the dick. Slapped him again, hard.

"Pull your pants up and follow me to a hokje."

He headed down the hall to one of the small, dark cubicles with locking doors. The thin man followed him in. He closed the door and clicked the lock shut.

A few minutes later, the lock clicked open. The thin man walked out alone. The Japanese tourist, still hungry, hesitated for a minute, then walked in. Tripped over something on the floor. Something heavy and soft. Bent down, peered into the darkness. Opened his mouth and screamed.

But by then the thin man was gone, fading into the gray drizzle shrouding the Sint Jacobsstraat.

Late afternoon. I'm walking down the Sint Jacobsstraat, across the Damrak to the Warmoesstraat, past Mister B and the Argos, over to where the tourists feed the pigeons on Dam Square. I stop for a paper cone of frites. I'm not hungry, of course, but the hot fried potatoes with mayonnaise get the taste of blood out of my mouth.

Amsterdam is a brown city. A brown, old city. And I was old when these buildings were new. A tired, cold city. As I am tired and cold.

I've been careless. Leaving that boy in the bar back there. Unforgivably careless. In all my years, my centuries, I've never done such a thing. They're going to get me. Now they're going to get me. And I don't care.

He walked into the Argos. Past the chains hanging from the ceiling, the

Satanic animal head hanging by the bar. Just past midnight, not yet crowded. Down the steep, familiar stairs to the darkroom in the basement. Plenty of guys hanging around already. That one, the one illuminated by the light from the stairway, he looked interesting. Faintly familiar. Tall, maybe six-five, and thin, almost skinny. Sharp cheekbones, eyes hidden in shadows; he would do.

He walked over to the thin man, looked up at his face. The thin man's expression gave nothing away. He reached up, stroked the man's hair. The thin man put his hands behind his head and leaned back against the wall. As though he was waiting to get blown. Or slapped. He reached down, undid the guy's zipper. Already hard.

"Come to a cabin," he said, in English, to be safe. The leaning man didn't move. He repeated it, in Dutch, but there still was no response. He slapped the guy's hard dick.

The tall, thin man writhed in pleasure, and he did it again, harder.

"Yes," the man said. "Ja."

He grabbed the thin man's dick and pulled him into one of the wooden cubicles, locking the door behind them. He unbuckled the man's belt, pulled his jeans down to his knees, then ran his hand up a thin, solid inner thigh till he felt the soft, warm ball sack against his fingers. He flicked a forefinger at the man's balls. The man moaned and shoved his crotch forward. He slapped the man's balls with the palm of his hand.

"Good?" he asked.

The man nodded.

"Poppers?"

Another nod.

He shoved a small brown bottle under the man's nose, then took a hit himself.

Within seconds, they were tearing at one another, kissing so hard that he could taste blood in his mouth. He unbuttoned his fly, pulled out his dick, grabbed a cock in each hand, and stroked. The thin man grabbed him by the throat, tracing his veins with cold fingertips.

My hands are on his throat. My lips are on his neck. I want to strike, I'm ready to bite down. I can taste him. I can taste him already. And then he moves his hand from my cock to the back of my head, presses my face into the hot hollow of his neck.

In a husky voice he whispers, "That's it. That's right, fucking kill me, man."

I'm overcome, not by feelings of lust, but of sudden, irrational tenderness.

It's so unexpected. Unasked-for. I don't want to leave him there. I don't want to leave him at all.

I run my tongue from his neck, along the hard ridge of his jaw line, over his stubbly chin, back into the warm, sweet cave of his waiting mouth.

The thin man, Theo, hurried from the bar.

"HEY, WAIT UP." It was the boy who said he wanted to die. Theo hesitated, then turned around. In the dim light of the cold, windy street, the boy seemed fragile.

"Where're you off to?" The boy spoke Dutch with a Slavic accent.

"Home."

"Mind if I come along?"

"What's wrong with your home?"

"Okay, okay -- sorry." The boy turned to go. The seat of the boy's jeans was thoroughly ripped-up. The flesh of his ass looked their bicycles.

"I live over by the old docks."

Despite his hunger, all Theo wanted to do was sleep, sleep with this boy in his arms.tender and pale.

"You really want me to kill you?" Theo's voice was tender, too. Tender and pale.

"I want you to take me home with you."

"My bike's over there."

"Mine, too."

They unchained.

"Let's go, then."

And they pedaled off into the black, raw, welcoming night.

It's morning now. The boy is curled up, asleep beside me.

How did this happen, this compromise, this need? How could I have let him get this far, come into my apartment, into my life?

Christ, I'm starving.

Milos woke, stretched like a cat, smiled at Theo. "Coffee?"

"None made."

"I'll do it. You just stay there."

Milos's skin was translucently pale, revealing blue veins coursing with blood, when he threw off the covers. Milos climbed out of bed and walked off to the kitchen.

Theo couldn't take his eyes off the boy's ass, the way skin and muscles shifted as he moved. The boy was fleshy, not plump exactly, but fleshy, as though he were happy with his body, at home in his body. Milos's dick was still hard as he switched on the coffee maker.

"It'll take a few minutes. Come back to bed."

I could do it now, Theo thought. I could do it right now.

Milos bounded back towards the bed, his dick bouncing crazily. He kneeled by the side of the bed, grabbed Theo's wrists and guided the thin man's hands to his throat.

Theo's hands slipped around his neck.

Milos bent to kiss his lips.

"Squeeze harder," he whispered into Theo's mouth. The grip grew tighter.

He wrapped his hands around Theo's hands and pressed them into his flesh. His dick had gotten so hard it almost hurt. His breath was coming in gasps now. Blood pounded in his head.

Theo was out of bed now, kneeling on the floor, kneeling between Milos's naked thighs, his knee pressing hard into the Slavic boy's soft balls and hard dick. He pressed Milos's head back till the boy arched his back, groaned, fell backwards against the cold floor.

Theo threw himself onto Milos's squirming body, dick against dick, hands still around his new lover's throat. He took Milos's lower lip between his teeth, bit down hard, made blood flow. The dark, metallic taste filled their mouths like a sudden shock. They came, both came, brutally, desperately, ecstatically. Theo loosened his grip, stroked Milos's beautiful face, wiped the tears from his eyes.

"I'm hungry," Milos said.

"You're welcome to the kitchen, but I'm afraid you won't cabinets, Theo reached for the remote and switched on the TV. A too-handsome blond man was reading the news. "Police are still searching find much to eat."

While the naked boy was rummaging around in the hollow for the killer of a man who was found murdered in the dark-room of a popular gay leather bar this week..."

None of this is simple. I wanted it to be simple, the relationship of predator and prey. Instead, I have this, this boy here, someone to -- God, I don't know, look after? -- just when I've become so tired, so fucking weary. Just when I've begun to sow the seeds of my own destruction.

Unless, of course, he himself is part of the process.

On the third morning, they were lying entwined in each other's arms when the doorbell rang. Theo struggled out of bed and pulled on a thick woolen robe.

"Mind if I come in?" Pieter asked when the door opened. "It's freezing out here."

"It's not a convenient time, Pieter. I'm sorry, but you could have called first."

"Who's this, then?" Pieter's pale blue eyes were fixed on Milos, who'd gotten out of bed and was standing a few feet behind Theo, naked, one hand loosely cupped around his dick.

"Pieter, this is Milos." Theo's voice was dead. "Milos, Pieter."

"Is he one of us then? Have you had him yet? No?" Pieter walked over to Milos, reached for the boy's ass, and kissed him on the cheek. "Well, don't worry dear, he will."

Pieter turned on his heel, walked out the door, and was gone.

"What did he mean, 'one of us'?" Milos asked while he was pulling on his pants, preparing to go out in search of breakfast.

"Perhaps I should tell you," Theo said. This has gone on long enough, he thought.

I told him. I told him everything. He didn't say a word. I don't even know him well enough to be able to read his face. So I don't know.

He's out now, gone to get some breakfast for himself. He's lucky that his hunger can be assuaged so easily. Has he gone to the police? No, I doubt it. Will he be back? I have no way of knowing. Do I even want him to come back? Outside the windows, the gulls are swirling above the half-frozen canal. Do I even want him to come back?

It was already early afternoon when Theo heard the click of the key in the lock. Milos locked the door behind himself and just stood there, the chilly light playing on the angles of his face.

For a moment they watched each other in silence. Then Milos knelt at Theo's feet, reached into a little bag he was holding, and pulled out an old-fashioned straight razor. He opened the gleaming blade and held it against the skin of his forearm.

Looking deep into Theo's eyes, he drew the razor across his flesh, leaving a gleaming red line in its wake. He offered his wound up to the tall, thin man standing above him.

Theo leaned down, put his lips to the blossoming flow, and nursed gently. As he sucked at the upwelling blood, he felt the boy's body shudder, tense, then shudder again. It was not till he drew his lips from the wound that he realized that Milos had used his free hand to unbuckle his jeans and take out his cock. His half-hard dick, shiny with cum, still rested in his fingers.

"Had enough?"

For now," Theo said. "For now."

Milos pressed his hand against the gash to stanch the flow.

"I love you," he said.

Theo stared out the window at the flocks of gulls diving, wheeling, diving again.

Sometimes I think back to the great days of Amsterdam. Down by the Montelbaanstoren, desperate men with nothing to lose boarded ships that would take them to the edge of the world. I would watch them sail off, and wonder how they felt as they looked back at the cozy brown city they might never see again. Maybe the way I do when I look into this Slavic boy's eyes.

Another day passed. Theo was feeling faint with hunger. He offered Milos some of the hashcake he'd bought at the gay koffieshop, waited till the boy was asleep, then slipped out and bicycled to the Web.

He found a boy that was to his liking, very young, short and slight, with a nose ring and a dazzling smile. It was easy to get him to go to the dark room, easy to get him into a cabinet, easy to pull the clothes from his body until the boy stood naked before him, thin almost hairless, with a small, almost delicate hard-on.

Delicate, that's what he is, Theo thought as he slipped his hands around the boy's thin neck. He knew that this was stupid, doing this here, so soon after the other one. Even so, he pulled the boy closer, till he could feel the boy's body heat, till the skinny young boy began jamming his hard little dick against his leg.

"Please let me suck you," the boy gasped, reaching for Theo's crotch. The naked boy kneeled. Theo watched as the kid opened his fly, gulped down his cock.

A thousand miles away. The skinny boy seemed to be a thousand miles away. A bony white shape in the airless gloom. Skinnier even than he was. But not, despite his voracious cocksucking, anywhere near as hungry.

In a few short moments, Theo's hunger was sated.

Milos's heart. I lie here undreaming, watching him sleep. Deep within him, within his fragile, mortal body, his heart pumps, steadily, erotically, sending life through the network of his veins. His heart, his secret heart.

I want to reach inside him, into his soft ass, slide my hand up into him until I grasp his heart, feel its mindless beating. Hold his life in my hands. Feel the coursing of his lifeblood against my fingertips.

But do I want to love him? Do I want him to love me?

"The police were around to my place, asking questions."

"They haven't been here yet."

"They will be." Pieter was sprawled in Theo's living room, sipping strong black coffee. "You're the one, aren't you, Theo? You're the one who did it. Stupid of you."

Theo stared at the square of moonlight on the floor.

"You've ruined a good thing, brought trouble to the rest of us, too." Pieter's pale blue eyes shone in the semi-darkness.

"You're angry, then?"

"Not really angry, Theo. But if trouble comes, I won't be there for you, none of us will. You do understand, don't you?"

"Of course I do."

The front-door lock clicked open. Milos walked in, arms loaded with groceries.

"Ah, I see the dream boy is home," Pieter sneered.

"Why do you hate me, Pieter? Is it because you're jealous?"

"How wrong you are, boy. I knew Theo long before you arrived on the scene, and I'll know him long, long after you've gone."

"Why, then?"

"Because Theo is acting like a damn fool, and you're a part of that. You're a threat to him. A threat to us all. You think you understand. Maybe you even think Theo loves you. But you understand nothing, nothing at all. You're just a little fool, a young, young fool."

"I think you've said enough." Theo's voice was flat, expressionless, lacking passion, maybe lacking conviction. "I think you'd better go now."

"Maybe I'd better. But when this all comes crashing down, you'll remember what I've said. Though it will be cold comfort to you then, Theo." Pieter smiled grimly. "You may not believe this, but I wish with all my heart that I turn out to be wrong."

He was at the door, wrapping a long woolen cape around his shoulders. "Take good care of Theo, little boy. He's in trouble. Big trouble." He opened the door. The cold night blew in. And then Pieter was gone.

I haven't been able to sleep. I walked the frozen streets till dawn, till mid-morning. My wanderings have led me here, to the Rijksmuseum. To the long hall that leads to The Night Watch, hordes of tourists squinting at Rembrandts. Over here, to one side, almost ignored, hangs The Jewish Bride. It's an astonishing painting, one of Rembrandt's finest. A light seems to glow from within the couple, he placing his hand upon her breast. Over her heart. Their hands meet in unutterable tenderness. The light remains undimmed, through all the years since it was newly made.

And this tenderness, it makes me want to weep. Only I can't weep. Because I'm closed off, forever cast out from the tenderness of this couple, this simple love. And so I can't weep, because I can't feel. Not like they feel. And so whatever else I'm trying to feel is turning to bitterness, to anger. I can see why that man took out a knife and slashed The Night Watch. If I had a knife…

If I had a knife…

"Where have you been?" Milos asked. "The police were here looking for you. They said they'd be back later."

Nothing can kill me, because I'm not alive. Not in the way other people are. Not in the way Milos is, warm, feeling, hot blood coursing through his veins, blood that he kneels to offer me. His heart is a work of art, a work of art of unutterable tenderness.

When I told him I had to go, he said he wanted to come with me. To escape.

"There's no place to escape," I said.

He stripped himself naked for me. His dick was already hard. He begged me to put my hands around his neck. To squeeze hard.

His heart is a fucking work of art.

When the police arrived at the apartment by the Oosterkerk, they found the door ajar. They called out; no one was home. They pushed the door

open. In the middle of the living room floor was a pool of blood -- three, maybe four feet across. It had been shaped into the form of a heart, a wet valentine. The outer edges of the heart were drying to a duller brown, but the center of the heart was still shiny, wet, red.

On the wall above the heart, someone had thumbtacked a post card to the wall. A reproduction of a painting. A Rembrandt: The Jewish Bride.

So fucking tired. So fucking weary. So very, very old.

Graveyard Shift
Jon Thomas

"Oh, yeah, Cris! Suck my fuckin' dick, man!" I panted at the blond bobbing on my Italian sausage in my dream. "C'mon, man, I gotta cum!"

Just as I was reaching the point of no return, the PA system announced: "Trauma team to Stab Room 3. Seven minutes." I jerked awake to find myself lying in bed in the on-call room and my hard cock tenting the front of my scrubs. The voice seemed to become more insistent. "Trauma team to Stab Room 3. Seven minutes."

"Shit!" I swore. "Why do I always get paged when I've got a good dream going?"

I reached for my shoes and saw it hadn't been a completely dry dream. There was a prominent dark spot against the surgical green of my scrub pants.

I quickly changed into a fresh pair before heading out, bleary-eyed and blinking, into the brightly lit chaos of the Emergency Department of Hennepin County Medical Center.

That my sex partner in the dream had been Crispin Carter was enough to make me cringe. I might have the hots for him, but he was still my supervisor; and I was up for the last evaluation of my residency in the next couple of days. I didn't want to imagine what Dr. Cris Carter would do to me if he knew I was fantasizing him going down on me.

I forced the rebuke from my thoughts. "What've we got?" I asked as I made my way into the stabilization room.

"Multiples from a rollover MVA on I-94. At least one critical, three majors," said the charge nurse on duty. "Say, Vinnie," she continued with a smirk and a raised eyebrow in my direction, "did you lose your stethoscope down the front of your scrubs again, or are you just happy to see me?"

Following the direction of her glance, I looked down and discovered that my cock was still making a noticeable bulge in my crotch. Blushing, I pulled my white lab coat closed over it before replying. "Sweetie," I sighed, "you know I love you; but the only thing I notice about a woman is her mind -- and possibly her bag, if it matches her shoes."

The one thing I truly loved about my job, though, was that I could crack jokes with the staff in my campiest, swishiest Donald Maltby imitation, they could rib me about showing up to a 3 AM trauma page with a hard dick, and nobody so much as batted an eyelid -- except in jest.

All was not perfect in my life, however. Not only did I have a serious case of the hots for Dr. Carter, I worked for him. And he was putting off my final evaluation to the last minute. Lately it seemed like he was going out of his way to avoid me. I'd been telling myself that I was just being paranoid, but I was getting less sure of that by the day.

Topping that off, I'd begun to notice a certain uneasy feeling on the back of my neck. Invariably, I'd look around and find Cris Carter watching me from someplace. That'd been going on for several months now.

If my Aunt Margherita was to be believed, there was a touch of malocchio about anyone who provoked that reaction. Though malocchio wass literally translated 'evil eye,' my aunt always said that it didn't mean people who had it were necessarily bad. They just had a touch of what we'd call psychic or paranormal abilities. Zia Margherita maintained to her dying day that I was one such person, though I'd never taken that stuff seriously.

Still, whenever I felt the hair rising on the back of my neck, I'd come to figure Dr. Carter was staring at me. I also had to fight down an overwhelming instinctive urge to make the sign against evil influences at him.

My shift finally ended at 7:30 that morning.

Even after 24 hours on duty, I was too wired to be able to get to sleep right away. Part of it was the adrenaline rush that always came with a really good trauma case. But mostly it was the aftereffects of the dream I'd had in the on-duty room.

When I got back to my loft apartment in Minneapolis' Warehouse District, I took matters into my own hands. Since I had a full day off before I was due back on duty, I could afford to take some time for a proper wank.

I was naked five seconds after the door closed behind me, my dick already swelling towards its full 8.5 inches. In no time at all, I was sprawled on the couch with a ratty old towel underneath me, pulling my heavy foreskin back and forth across the sensitive knob of my cock in time with the thrusts of my favorite dildo in and out of my asshole.

"Fuck, yeah," I panted as the flaring head of the dildo raked over my prostate. I shuddered at the wave of pleasure that followed. "Gimme all of that blond doc dick! C'mon, Cris: fuck me harder! I want everything you've got in my hot hole!"

I popped into the zone, that magical place where the sex is really hot and everything's going just right. The rhythm of my fist working the foreskin back and forth over my cockhead was in perfect synch with the thrusts of the dildo in and out of my hungry hole. My balls tightened in their sack and my head lolled back against the cushions.

For a few moments, it felt as if the column of plastic inside me had transformed into a living column of flesh. My fingers became light, feathery caresses touching my neck and upper back, then moved around to my sensitive nipples.

"Yeah, Cris," I gasped, my throat parched raw from my heavy breathing. "You're pushing all the right buttons. I'm so close. Fill me up, stud, and ride me on home!"

I pushed the dildo to the hilt inside me and surrendered to the molten tide that flooded through me as it hit bottom. Giving one last tug on my

rigid cock, I imagined that the volleys of spunk landing all over my chest and belly were his, not mine.

When my orgasm was over, I barely had the energy to clean my toys and myself before collapsing into bed for 12 hours of blissfully sound, dreamless, uninterrupted sleep.

* * *

Dr. Crispin Carter glared at the personnel file lying on his coffee table. It bore the label "Vincenzo Biondo, M.D." and was the last of the files he'd had to deal with over the past week. He'd waited until the last possible day for submitting the residents' final evaluations before tackling Vinnie's.

Professionally, Dr. Biondo was one of the best physicians he could remember working with. He chuckled when he realized that was quite a long list of doctors, as he'd begun his studies in Paris with Laennec in Napoleon's day.

The problem with evaluating Vinnie had nothing to do with the medical qualifications of the man. The problem was personal: several problems, really.

First, he found Vinnie quite attractive. More than that, he had begun having very strong feelings towards the young physician, and that worried him. It was always dangerous when one of his kind fell for a mortal. While he had hardly been celibate, it was the better part of a century since the last time he'd truly been in love. He had little idea of how the game was played among mortals at the beginning of the 21st century.

More disturbing -- because he could not be certain what it meant -- was that, lately, Vinnie rarely left his sight.

A number of times in the last few weeks, Cris had caught the young doctor looking in his direction with a curious expression on his face. He'd been afraid those glances meant Vinnie was aware of Cris' interest in him and found it unwelcome. Or, worse, that the resident had other, more dangerous suspicions about him.

He'd finally resorted to touching Vinnie's thoughts yesterday morning.

Cris' questions had been definitely answered and he was left in what he was afraid would become a perpetual blush.

Vinnie had still been asleep in the on-call room just before the MVA hit them in Stab. Room 3 when Cris had sought to touch his thoughts. He'd been hit with an overwhelming surge of intense lust that drew him right into Vinnie's dream.

He'd been able to taste the young doctor's hardness moving between his lips, and smell his musk as he pleasured him in that most intimate of all kisses. Cris' body had tensed along with Vinnie's as he'd drawn close to the brink of his orgasm.

Still more intense had been the fantasy that Vinnie indulged in last night at home. Despite the fact that Cris was for all intents and purposes

dead to the world at the time, the mortal's mind had still called to his over more than 20 miles in the throes of passion.

Interesting and exciting as those speculations might be, all Cris knew for certain was that Vinnie wanted him and that he wanted Vinnie. Cris had no idea of the man's intentions, and was unsure even of his own. Only, he wanted more from this particular mortal than a quick fuck, no matter how gratifying.

"Do you have any questions?" Cris asked at the end of the evaluation. The question was essentially a formal noise to signify that the interview was over, so he was surprised when it provoked a response.

"Yes, I do, actually," Vinnie said. "Do you dislike me?"

"Dislike you, Dr. Biondo?" Cris asked, quirking a puzzled eyebrow. "Whatever gave you that idea?"

"The last couple of weeks it seems like every time I turn around, you're staring holes in my back from across the room. A couple of times, the look on your face was enough to boil water with." Vinnie frowned.

"I've been offered a position on the staff here after completing my residency, with a promise to make it permanent if I pass my boards. But if I've done something to offend you or if for whatever reason we aren't going to be able to work well with one another, I'll regretfully decline the offer and look for work elsewhere."

Cris thought that it probably wasn't the best place for this conversation. But neither one of them was on call, and he knew they were unlikely to be interrupted. Besides, Vinnie looked like he really needed some resolution.

"I like you a great deal, Vinnie," he said. "You're a superb physician, you work well with your colleagues, and you have the diagnostic instincts of Virchow himself. The reason I've been staring holes in your back, as you put it, is that I've been trying to figure out why you've been following me around for the last few months, staring holes in *my* back."

Cris smelt Vinnie's fear rising, along with the musk of his lust, and he fought back a smile at the thought of it. It pleased him to see the deep blush suffusing Vinnie's coloring as he sought to frame his reply. His thoughts were so intensely colored with emotion that Cris had to strengthen his shielding to keep them out.

"Well you see, Dr. Carter..." he started, haltingly.

"Call me Cris, Vinnie -- you're no longer my student, and we're in private."

"Cris, then," he said, clearly thinking over his choice of words very carefully. "It's just that, well..."

"You seem to have come to the end of your Latin, as my mother used to say. Shall I help things along a little?"

He nodded.

"You find me attractive, yes?"

Vinnie's eyebrows disappeared into his hairline and his mouth worked silently for a moment before eventually stammering "Y -- you knew?"

"Not until a few days ago, at least not for certain. But when one hears one's name being called out in the middle of the night, and when the person who did the calling comes into the Stab. Room with a huge tent in the front of his surgical scrubs that *isn't* a misplaced stethoscope, it's not that hard an ailment to diagnose -- no pun intended." He grinned as the young doctor turned crimson.

"I'm sorry to have given you the impression that I disliked you, Vinnie," he continued quickly. "Quite the opposite, in fact. I hope I'll have the pleasure of working with you for many years to come."

He rose to signify that the meeting was over. Vinnie's shame was evaporating, leaving only his strong desire beating against Cris Carter's mental battlements.

Keeping himself under tight control, he contented himself with shaking Vinnie's hand warmly at the office door, and resting his other hand companionably on his shoulder as the young man left.

* * *

"Damn!" I growled as I left Dr. Carter's office after my evaluation. He hadn't wigged out when he found out I had the hots for him. That's something, at least. But I'd give anything to know how he really feels about me.

That continued to simmer at the back of my mind all through my shift. It didn't help that we had one of our rare quiet days, leaving me plenty of time to stew and brood. Still, the combination of pre-evaluation anxiety and an eight-hour shift left me absolutely drained. I was running on fumes when I got back to my apartment. I drew the blinds and barely had the energy to undress before falling heavily into bed.

There was a dream waiting to claim me the moment I closed my eyes. Cris and I were naked, sprawled side by side on my huge bed in the loft. The rose-and-purple hues of sunset over water flooded through the floor-to-ceiling windows.

We were making out: I was erect, but Cris' soft cock reposed on the creamy skin of his inner thigh.

"You must not be as excited about this as I am," I teased him, fondling his 'nads gently.

"Self-control, my young friend," he replied. "I don't want this to be over any time soon."

He broke our embrace and began to work his way down my body. My neck and earlobes benefited from his oral attentions as his cool hands roamed lightly over my chest and abdomen. Occasionally, he'd grip my

erect tool and stroke it a few times, but never enough to do more than keep it hard.

His lips moved to my chest. He nuzzled and bit at one nipple while pinching and rolling its companion in his fingers; then he switched sides and began again. His free hand roamed my body and brushed all of its most sensitive spots.

I was beginning to catch fire, and I hoped he'd give my cock some sustained attention before his manipulations elsewhere had it shooting off on its own.

I reached for him, but he gently pushed my hand back to the bed at my side. "Not now, Vinnie," he mumbled around a nipple. "This is for your pleasure. Mine will come later."

Running his fingers rhythmically downward over my abs, he skirted my cock and pushed my thighs further apart. As he nuzzled in the cup of my navel, his fingers began a magical dance up one leg from knee to scrotum, across the musky dampness beneath my balls, and then down the other leg. When he'd come to the end of his reach there, he'd reverse course and begin again.

In no time at all, I was panting like a bitch in heat and the precum was oozing steadily down my cock knob to pool briefly in my navel until Cris lapped it up.

Finally, he moved his head still lower -- I thought to begin sucking me off, as I'd been begging him to do for the past five minutes. But after a perfunctory lick from my balls to the tip of my spear -- a lick that nevertheless sent fireworks shooting up my spine -- he turned his head to nuzzle at my left thigh.

When nuzzle turned to nibble, I thought I'd died and gone to heaven. It felt like a long, slow, effortless orgasm, except my cock wasn't pumping out any juice apart from the precum that had been flowing since Cris began playing my body like a familiar instrument.

A brief instant of light-headedness was replaced by a warm lethargy that enveloped me in warmed silk from head to toe. A blissful sigh hissed from between my teeth, at which Cris looked up at me, his lips a dark coppery hue and a slight flush tingeing his pale skin a coral pink. I was pleased to see his foreskin pulled back from an erection only slightly shorter than my own.

"So you liked that, did you?" he smiled and licked his lips with a fetching grin.

"The most super-galactically mind-blowing sensation I've ever felt in my life, sexual or otherwise, and on top of that I haven't even shot my wad yet?" I waxed eloquently. "Damn right I liked it! Now why don't you put those lips to an even better use on my cock for a while, and then plant that thick sausage of yours where it'll do me the most good?"

"Actually," he replied, "I was hoping you'd do the honors this time."

"Just let me catch my breath for a moment," I told him. "But I'm usually the one getting fucked, not the one doing the fucking."

"Me, too," he said. "But I don't mind changing for the right guy."

"Got a condom for me?" I asked, looking around the room and spying none.

"You're clean, Vinnie," he said, gazing deeply into my eyes and spreading himself to allow me to kneel between his legs. "So am I. I don't want anything to come between us. I want to feel your warm flesh moving inside me with no barriers, and your essence filling me up when you finish."

Cris held my gaze and his eyes seemed to say "Trust me. It'll be all right."

I accepted a bottle of lube that appeared in his hands as if by magic, and used it to prepare us both.

His tunnel was smooth and tight as I pushed a finger in past his rosebud. He moaned softly as another entered, then another. When I could comfortably fit three inside of him at the same time, I decided he was ready for the real thing. I pulled my fingers out and wiped them on the towel that lay beneath us. Again, Cris whimpered, this time presumably at finding himself empty.

Looking up at me, he whispered, "Do it, Vinnie. I'm ready for you."

I gave a few tugs on my erect dick, then lined up its head with the entrance of his chute. A grunt escaped his lips as I worked the tip past the tight sphincter and into the clenching warmth beyond.

"Are you OK?" I asked, seeing his face screw up into a grimace as the full width of my tool began to stretch him.

"I'm fine," he replied. "Fill me up with that thing. I can't wait to feel all of it deep inside of me."

As gently as I could I pushed the remainder of my cock inside him until I felt my balls against his smooth cheeks. I held myself there, barely twitching back and forth, until I felt his hole relaxing around my girth.

"Yes, Vinnie," he panted as I began to move in earnest inside of him. "Do it! Nail me hard and deep!"

I was happy to oblige him. His chute gripped every square inch of my dick in a gentle embrace of living silk. If this was how Cris' ass would welcome me each time I fucked him, I knew I could easily grow to love the role of top to his bottom.

I was soon rabbit-fucking him, pulling almost all the way out of his hole and plunging back in as far as I could. The swollen nut of his prostate raked back and forth across the flared rim of my cockhead with every stroke. Beneath me, Cris was virtually limp on the bed, his head rolling from side to side as waves of pleasure coursed through him. He was moaning and grunting constantly, precum oozing from beneath his front curtains, the foreskin now having slipped forward once more over the head of his cock.

"You feel so good inside me," he grunted. "Yes. Yes, just like that."

"I'm nearly there, Cris," I panted between thrusts.

He locked his gaze with mine at the exact moment my orgasm began. I saw a long sequence of similar scenes in his sky-blue eyes, stretching endlessly into the future -- and knew I hoped for nothing less.

My jizz flooded his tight hole. The soft, rhythmic slapping of his foreskin back and forth over his smooth knob became a long, low moan as a series of rippling contractions began deep inside his body. His spunk erupted over his naked torso and abs.

I collapsed on top of him, exhausted. He kissed me and whispered: "Sleep well, dearest Vinnie." He pulled away and wiped us both clean. I floated languorously, my eyelids growing heavier each moment. The last thing I saw before sleep overwhelmed me in my dream was the copper glint of the firelight off his fangs as he smiled sweetly down at me.

Five hours later, I woke up, my head swimming. "What the fuck!" I groaned. My day off and I couldn't even get caught up on my sleep.

I remembered the dream then and reached for my rigid cock before I was awake good.

The hair on the back of my neck began to bristle; and, before I knew it, I was getting a full dose of malocchio.

I let go of my dick and sat up. I listened hard, looking for anything that sounded off. The apartment was quiet -- just the usual noises from the appliances and some muffled sounds from the street below. Everything seemed normal.

I lay back, reminding myself that I'd never put much stock in that evil eye stuff. I started running the dream of me fucking Cris through my mind.

I sat up, my eyes bulged as I got to the end. Cris'd had *fangs*! More than that, He'd been biting me during our foreplay.

I damn near pulled a muscle throwing the bedclothes off of me. Heart pounding, I checked both of my inner thighs closely for anything remotely resembling a puncture wound.

I didn't find anything, but my pulse didn't start to return to normal until I saw that I still had a reflection in the bathroom mirror. I headed to the kitchen to make doubly sure -- the six heads of garlic there had no perceptible effect on me except to make my stomach rumble. I finally accepted those fangs had only been part of one weird-assed vivid dream when my fingers didn't shrivel up and fall off when dipped in holy water.

I settled down then. "Don't be such a drama queen!" I told myself sheepishly as I climbed back into bed. I mean, really -- vampires? A vampire *doctor*? Next thing I knew, I'll be voting Republican and advocating supply-side economics.

Sleep had almost reclaimed me when another revelation hit. In my dream, Cris had been the one leading *me* in the dream. Maybe both of our subconscious minds had been working over time. Maybe there was something to malocchio after all.

I sat up and reached for the phone. "I'll just give him a chance at me away from the office," I told myself and smirked.

I pulled out the Emergency Department's phone directory and found his unlisted home phone number.

"This is Dr. Crispin Carter," the voice came down the wire, "and you've reached my voicemail. Please leave your name, number, and a detailed message; and I'll return your call at my earliest convenience."

"Cris, it's Vinnie," I said after the beep. "Listen, I don't know what came over me that I didn't ask you about it earlier today, but I'd like to buy you dinner or something to say thanks for all your help and guidance this last year. Let me know when you're free and you pick the place. Call me at home or catch me at the hospital. 'Bye."

Let's see what he says to that, I told myself after I'd hung up. I lay back and closed my eyes. "Just so long as there aren't any real fangs," I mumbled to myself.

Dog In The Manger
Tom Millios

Jamie had walked his new dog, Alexandra, around the block and was taking the stairs up to his floor for that extra bit of exercise. His mind was devoid of any real thought beyond the pleasures of a hot shower and the wank that would go with it.

The moment he reached the fourth floor and stepped into the corridor his pleasant mood instantly evaporated. His hand gripped the banister hard. Halfway down the hall, there was a door slightly ajar. His door. Jamie's heart seemed to drop to the pit of his stomach, then bounce up to become stuck in his throat. It was suddenly hard to breathe.

The toy poodle pulled the leash from his hand and pranced right down to the door. She stopped and looked back at him as if to demand that he come along before disappearing into the flat.

He told himself that he had left it open by mistake. It was the only explanation. If someone was in the flat, the dog would be barking her head off. He had a hard time believing it, though.

He remembered his mobile phone then -- and where he'd left it. He wished he'd brought it with him when he'd taken Alexandra for a walk. He'd have phoned his friend from police college the moment he found the door open. Matt was training to be a police officer, he'd know what to do. Only, his mobile phone was in the bedroom on top of the bedside cabinet.

Jamie tried to hear past his breathing as he entered, trying to focus on any sound coming from the flat. What if someone was inside? Waiting for him? His heart pounded in his chest, though it felt as if it had moved up to lodge in his throat.

Hair bristling on the nape of his neck, he took another step into his flat. Slowly. Very slowly.

The dog lapped noisily from her water dish in the kitchen. Then silence. She barked, calling him to bring out the dog biscuits. Jamie chuckled and relaxed slightly.

He knew where she'd be all right. She'd be sitting patiently by the cupboard where she'd already learnt he kept the dog biscuits. As soon as he got to the kitchen, she'd be watching him mournfully until he gave her a treat.

It was obvious that the dog didn't sense anything wrong. Jamie was certain that meant his home was safe now.

He turned and pushed the door shut. He stood for another minute waiting to make sure that the dog was not making any unusual noises. He heard the lapping of the water again and was certain things were OK. He locked the door this time, making sure both locks had engaged.

In the kitchen, he reached for the kettle before noticing it was full and steaming.

The hair on his neck bristled again. He stared at the kettle. His heart began to hammer. He was sure that he hadn't put it on before he left to walk the dog.

He glanced at the wall phone and wondered if he'd have time to call the police before whoever had let himself into the flat could kill him.

"Sorry," a voice said from the short hallway that led back to the toilet and Jamie's bedroom.

Jamie froze. He tried to swallow the lump in his throat as he turned slowly to face the voice. It was Matt.

"You left the door open and I let myself in," the black-haired man said as he entered the kitchen.

Jamie was relieved to see his friend standing there looking at him. It felt normal. Safe.

"Hi," he said, swallowing his heart. "Your ears must have been burning. I was just thinking of you."

Matt crossed the room to him. He took Jamie's shoulders and pulled him close. He kissed him on the cheek. "Thought I'd pop in for a coffee," he said.

Alexandra came over and sniffed his leg curiously.

"You went ahead and got the dog, I see," Matt said, not sounding happy at all.

"I am so glad to see you," Jamie mumbled, letting himself relax in Matt's arms now that he was safe. His face pressed against Matt's breast.

"Hmmm…"

"I thought someone had broke into the flat when I came back from walking the dog and found the door ajar."

"I should have waited outside," Matt said and frowned as the dog pawed at his trousers leg.

The door hadn't been open when Matt arrived, of course; but the blond didn't know that. Jamie'd got pissed often enough the past couple of months and Matt had made sure to help him home. Jamie'd never question his friend being inside his flat. Matt had left it open, hoping for just this reaction from Jamie.

Matt'd fancied Jamie since he first bumped into him in the pub at the end of the street a couple of months ago. It wasn't a gay club -- not exactly -- but this whole area of London was predominately gay. The pub simply reflected the people it catered to.

Matt had got a bit wild trying to impress the guy until, in desperation, he told him that he was training to be a police officer. Jamie had clearly been impressed. Things between them, however, had immediately lost that steely hardness that characterized the sexual hunt, becoming warmer -- friendlier.

It'd been two months already, and Jamie hadn't yet invited Matt into his bed. Things had not developed as Matt had wished them to, although he hadn't given up. He still had a trick or two up his sleeve, if it came to that.

Jamie, on the other hand, was almost sure he didn't want a serious relationship but, at the same time, he was rather fond of Matt and his good looks ... So, he flirted with him. They were good mates, and Jamie did not want to risk losing their friendship for the sake of a one-night stand. Still, if he was to tell the truth, he wanted it to happen properly with Matt -- if it happened at all.

Matt had picked up on the blond's mixed signals but didn't understand them. He didn't understand much about the modern world around him and wished for the millionth time that he hadn't hid himself away for so long after the Great War. True, he'd been grief-stricken when he learnt his lover had been one of the last men killed before the Armistice; but he'd known even then that he'd get over the hurt. Instead of being rational, though, he'd bought up most of the property in this section of London, turned it over to a proper property managing company, and gone to ground for 82 years. He was rich as Midas, and the world at the beginning of the new millennium was hardly recognizable as the same place he'd been happy with his last lover nearly a century ago.

He thought Jamie was playing hard to get. Or that he was incredibly naïve. Possibly he hadn't worked out yet that Matt wanted more than just sex. A very long-term relation, he hoped.

"You fancy me staying with you tonight?" he asked Jamie, "I'll keep the monsters away."

The dog seemed intent on ripping the leg of his jeans into strips. Matt pushed it away with his foot. [Shoo!] he commanded. She left then, looking back at him suspiciously. [Lie down!] he told her when she was beside the sofa.

"What, tonight?" Jamie asked in surprise, pushing away from Matt. He blushed when he felt his cock lengthening to show its interest. "No way. I'll have a coffee, but then it's my bedtime. I need my beauty sleep. Tomorrow's still Friday, and I still have to earn a living."

"I think you've had enough of that." Matt was thinking of beauty sleep and was serious. He couldn't imagine Jamie being any more handsome.

Jamie wasn't about to be serious. "Do you mean the coffee?" he asked.

"No way. I mean you're one of the handsomest men I've ever known." There was a prolonged silence in which Jamie could not think of a suitable reply.

"Too kind," Jamie finally said. "Drink your coffee, luv, and then I have to get that beauty sleep." He laughed. "I turned 28 not many months ago -- I'm sliding further into old age with every breath I take..."

"Maybe some other time then," Matt said wistfully.

"I appreciate you coming round," Jamie told him, consciously softening the rejection now that he realized it was there. "I'm glad you came." He smiled at Matt. "Perhaps we can do that new club tomorrow night -- the one that everyone's talking about."

"That would be nice," Matt said and quickly leant closer to kiss Jamie's cheek. He stood up. "I'll see myself out."

"Damn! Damn! Damn!" Matt grumbled out loud as he glided down the stairs to the ground floor. He almost didn't see the nosy old cow from the next floor down in time to put his feet on the steps so that he'd look like any other normal man walking down a flight of steps. He nodded to her and ignored the reek of her suspicion as he passed her. He wondered if he could refuse her a new lease on her flat when renewal came around.

He wished he could figure Jamie out as he stepped out of the building. The man certainly seemed interested, and he lived an openly gay life. He should be up for a bit of nasty. But, for two months now, they'd somehow always managed to slide past the moment when things were supposed to happen.

Matt frowned as he reminded himself that he had only himself to blame. He turned to look at the glass doors back into the building. It had been Matt himself who'd decided within minutes of first meeting Jamie that he'd stay out of the blond's mind. They could have been shagging since that first night -- if Matt hadn't decided to be so noble that he was stupid. They could have been building something that would last forever.

His gaze moved up the building to the fourth floor, and the blond's flat. He pursed his lips when he saw that Jamie had apparently turned on every light in the flat. "You're mine." he whispered. "You just don't know it yet."

He looked around quickly and found he was alone on the pavement. He grinned and began to rise towards Jamie's fourth floor windows.

Jamie poured himself a glass of Merlot and sat on the sofa. Using the remote control, he was flicking through the channels until he came across the old Lugosi *DRACULA*. He remembered being fascinated by the story as a child. His parents had not let him watch the film, but he had got the book out of the library.

He wondered if someone who fed off other people's blood could really exist. As the vampire on the TV bit into an attractive starlet's neck, he picked up his glass and drank his wine. He offered a toast to the Transylvanian Count on the screen.

He dipped his finger into the wine and let it drip back. He looked at his half-filled glass, sighed, and finished it off in one more gulp. He wished Matt hadn't left. Maybe a shag now and then wouldn't destroy their friendship, after all. His cock again began to lengthen along his leg again.

He couldn't believe he was thinking about sex while watching Bela Lugosi. Now, if it were Matt with the fangs, Jamie thought it wouldn't be so bad. He grinned as he began to think of ways that a bit of nipping might be quite sensual.

Matt sat on the window ledge and watched his blond friend watching *DRACULA*. He wanted to see Jamie naked. And hard.

On the sofa, Jamie leant back and opened his flies. He started to reach into his boxers to pull himself out but hesitated with his fingertips in his pubes. His face was slack for a moment before his tongue sneaked out to wet his lips. He stood up grinning as the Count turned into a giant bat and pushed his trousers and pants down to his knees roughly.

Matt nearly swooned when he saw the nine inch battering ram that was Jamie's tackle. "I've been missing that?" he whispered to himself. "Bloody hell!"

It was at that moment that he decided he wasn't going to be satisfied with just looking at a naked Jamie as he tossed off. No. *He* was going to have all of his blond friend -- and it was going to have him starting that night.

Jamie pulled his shirt over his head and toed his shoes off before stepping out of his trousers and pants. Dressed only in his socks, he lay on the sofa and wrapped his fingers around his rod.

Matt waited and watched as Jamie's speed increased. He was unsure if he should appear before or after Jamie had got himself off. As Jamie's hips flexed, pushing himself into his fist and pulling out, Matt opened his flies and pulled out his engorged cock.

"Matt, suck me!" Jamie groaned from the sofa. "Deep throat me! Yessss…"

"Shag my arse, Jamie!" Matt hissed as his mind generated for him the feelings he hadn't known for almost a hundred years.

Jamie was still lying on the sofa, sated and half-asleep, when Matt let himself into the flat later. His chest was covered with his jizz. The blond's cock was still tumescent but wasn't hard, his foreskin covering all of his large knob except for the piss slit. He looked good enough to eat, but feeding on Jamie was the farthest thing from Matt's thoughts. The credits for *DRACULA* were running on the telly.

Matt left his own clothes in the flat's tiny foyer, just inside the door and stood beside the sofa, savoring the blond's nude perfection. Jamie had invited him inside the first time Matt helped him home from the pub and had never rescinded the invitation. It'd been no problem at all to enter the flat and lock up after.

Alexandra growled low from the other side of the sofa but made no move towards Matt.

"Nice," Jamie mumbled.

Matt's gaze moved up the blond's body and stopped at his shadowed face. He saw the glint of Jamie's eyes and knew that he was studying him. "You like?" he asked.

"Yeah…" Jamie reached out and caressed the arsecheek closest to him. He grinned when Matt went instantly hard and pushed back against his hand. "Very much."

"Perhaps I should help you to your bed -- for that beauty sleep you were talking about earlier..."

"I was thinking of something a bit more rigorous, Matt."

"So was I..." He chuckled. "I just didn't want to sound too gross."

Jamie sat up, his hand moving to grasp Matt's. "I want our friendship to last," he said softly. "I want sex, too -- especially now that I've seen all of you. Only, I'm not sure I can commit to a relationship..."

Matt lifted him to his feet. "We've got all the time in the world to work things out, Jamie." He leant closer and his lips touched the blond's. "One thing I am sure of, though, is that having sex with you isn't ever going to affect how I feel about you," he said before he kissed him.

"How far do we carry this?" Jamie asked later, after he'd broken the kiss.

"Whatever you are comfortable with. Although a good shag would be preferred."

"You loser!" Jamie cried and pushed Matt away playfully. "Won't any one else have you?"

"I love you."

"You serious?"

Matt was totally embarrassed he had come out with it.

"You are, aren't you?"

Matt did not deny it. Now he had said it, he didn't want to take it back; yet he could not bring himself to repeat it. Let Jamie deal with it how he wanted.

Jamie studied him for what seemed to be forever. Matt had never felt as nervous as he did standing naked before the man he knew he loved, not even when he'd been dying at Waterloo and the old gypsy offered him life.

"Kiss me again," Jamie said finally. He was still grappling with surprise at Matt's declaration of love; but the main thing he was feeling was that he wanted the comfort sex with a good-looking man would bring him. And Matt was a good looking man.

"I'd love to," Matt told him. "But only when you're ready."

"I'm ready," Jamie grumbled. "Stop talking and kiss me." He pulled Matt to him. As their tongues met, his hands massaged Matt's arsecheeks. They ground their cocks against each other as their tongues dueled. Jamie's bollocks tightened and he knew he was close.

"I want you," Jamie gasped, pulling away from the kiss. One hand still cupping Matt's nearest arseglobe, he took his friend's hard cock in the other and led him to the bedroom.

The dog followed them and stood in the doorway as they moved into each other's arms at the side of the bed and again began to snog. She growled low in her throat.

"Don't worry about her," Jamie said, chuckling, as he broke the kiss. "She's not used to anyone sleeping with me yet.

Matt wasn't worried. [*Lie down*,] he commanded Jamie mentally. [*Stay hard and wait for me.*] He fully intended to take care of the damned dog. Permanently. He caught Jamie's concern for the creature, however, as he was leaving his mind.

So, I won't take care of it the same way I was going to, he told himself as he started to advance on the door and the animal standing there.

The dog stopped growling when she saw Matt coming towards her. She began to shiver when he reached her. Matt picked her up and pulled the bedroom door closed behind him. Matt could think of only two ways of quieting dogs, and he wasn't going to ruin things with Jamie by killing her. He held the mouth of the dog firmly shut and brought the neck to his mouth. He bit into her neck, his fangs pushing through the fur and breaking the skin, and sucked until the dog stopped shaking.

She was panting hard when he put her on the sofa. He placed one of the large cushions under her to make her more comfortable. Her wound was already healed. The dog would be OK after a couple of days of resting up.

He wiped his mouth and licked curiously at the remains of the dog's blood. It wasn't as tasty as human blood, and he wouldn't choose to live off dogs unless he had no other choice.

Jamie was lying on his back, his eyes half-closed and his hands at his sides when Matt re-entered the bedroom. Matt stood beside the bed, studying his friend's body and especially his tackle. It definitely was longer and thicker than any he'd seen or taken. And the helmet looked to be the size of a billiard ball, its skin pulled back into a collar behind the bell-end.

Matt bent to kiss Jamie again, teasing himself by play-biting the blond's lower lips while his fingers encircled Jamie's erect cock.

Jamie's arms reached up and pulled Matt even closer towards him. He stroked his back and ran his fingers slowly down the outline of Matt's spine.

Just this touch of Jamie's hands on his bare back made Matt feel as though they were melting into each other. He drew back and placed Jamie's hands at his sides again. He ran his fingers from the neck down his torso, across to each nipple, circling each one and then spreading the whole palm of his hand down his stomach to the top of his bush.

He could not resist bending down to kiss the top and then running his tongue down the whole length, following the stalk onto the balls. He was convinced even more that he had made the right choice.

He straddled Jamie's body, a leg on either side of Jamie's waist, and gazed down at him from above. Very slowly, he bent down to kiss Jamie's neck. He pricked the skin and tasted the clean tang of the blond's blood.

He had definitely made the right choice in a lover. There were no STDs and no drug residue in Jamie's blood. He sat back on his haunches and felt behind him for his friend's cock. Holding it against his arse crevice, he raised up on his knees until it was pressing against his back entrance. He willed his anal muscles to relax and slowly began to lower himself on it. He

gasped as the huge knob popped through his sphincter. He could feel each and every vein on that dick, the hardness of the flesh, as it worked his arse.

Jamie's hands moved onto his thighs as Matt continued to lower himself, then onto his arsecheeks to pull them open. He sighed when he was completely inside Matt and his hands moved up his back to his shoulders, pulling him back down for a kiss.

They lay that way for several minutes: snogging, Matt's pole pressed into Jamie's tummy, Jamie's big cock buried in Matt, his pubes tickling the backside of Matt's bollocks. Finally, Matt ground his bum against the blond's crutch.

He broke the kiss and snuggled his face against Jamie's neck. "That feels so bloody good!" he moaned. "Fuck me…"

Beneath them, Jamie's hips began to flex, pulling his cock almost out of Matt before pushing it all the way back in. Matt's fangs again scratched the blond's neck, breaking the skin before sinking deeper.

He had learnt to do this in the years in the years after Napoleon was sent to St. Helene -- ever so gently that no one knew he was puncturing them to drain blood from them. He could simply take what he wanted and the man would then be on his way, none the wiser. His partner just thought he'd received a lover's bite, and the marks would be gone by morning.

With Jamie it was different. When he had first set eyes on him in the pub, he knew he wanted to spend the rest of his life with him. Every thing he'd learnt since only served to convince him further that, together, they would be totally invincible. Only, he couldn't make Jamie yet. His friend would have to agree to that, before it could happen.

"You are so beautiful," Matt said out loud, forcing himself to stop feeding. Jamie's hands caressed Matt's back and buttocks as he shagged him. Matt's lips found Jamie's and their tongues again dueled. He swept Jamie's hair back and caressed his cheeks, his arms, his sides as they kissed and Jamie's dick moved in and out of him.

Matt felt the hot spunk rising through the balls, the shaft and then spurt out from Jamie's knob, now deep inside him, into his own body. Without having touched himself, Matt came at this point as well, covering Jamie's chest. He closed his eyes in ecstasy and breathed in the smell of the sweat, the spunk, and could not resist bending down to lick some so that he could taste it as well.

He settled on top of Jamie and listened to his heartbeat. They fell asleep in each other's arms, Jamie's dick still inside Matt. He knew that, when Jamie awoke, he would want Matt as much as Matt had wanted him.

Jamie awoke the next morning to find that Matt had already left. He grinned at his morning hard-on as he stood. "Well, lad, you just might get a real work out this weekend -- if Matt's willing," he told his tackle and, giving it a stroke, started for the shower. He definitely hoped that Matt was willing. He could get used to the man's kind of loving quite easily.

The dog looked to be totally knackered when Jamie came out of the bedroom tying his tie. "Want a biscuit, girl?" he asked and she only twitched her tail in reply. He stopped and studied her closely. "You're trying to give me some sort of guilt trip, aren't you?" he asked finally and moved on to the kitchen where he quickly set out her water and food dishes.

"You'd better get used to sleeping on the sofa," he called to the dog as he picked up the box of dog biscuits and returned to the living room. "At least, I hope you have to. I hope Matt wants to make last night a regular event."

The toy poodle whined but allowed him to give her a biscuit. Her tail twitched twice.

"You've got fresh water and tinned food to help you get used to the idea of losing your bedmate," he told her with a laugh as he started out the door.

By Sunday evening, Jamie had lost all fear of having a relationship with Matt. If he was honest, he was in love with his black-haired friend. The sex they shared was good as well, better than he could ever remember it being. He was actually getting sore down there, he'd shagged Matt so often the past several nights.

There was only one problem Jamie could see with pursuing a relationship with Matt -- one quite small, really. His friend had left the bed before dawn each morning and simply disappeared. He didn't use the toilet, he didn't use the shower, he didn't eat. He just disappeared.

That simply wouldn't do -- not if they were going to live together.

They'd both have to get up and go to work, of course. Bills did have to be paid. Couples worked on making their flats lovely. They painted and sewed and -- well -- they wove their lives together. Dawn disappearances on weekends, and being gone until nightfall, left a lot to be desired.

They were going to have a talk when Matt arrived -- if he arrived. That was something else that Jamie didn't like: not knowing for certain when he'd see Matt again.

At least, the dog was up and about again -- as spry as she'd been last week, she was.

He sat on the sofa beside the dog and sipped a glass of Merlot, waiting for Matt.

Matt appeared in the foyer.

One second, nothing was there; the next, Matt was there smiling at him. Jamie was sure that he hadn't heard the door open. The dog growled, its hair seeming to stand on end.

Jamie decided that he was hallucinating. It was impossible for people to enter rooms without opening doors, wasn't it? "I'm glad you decided to join me," he said and rose. "Want a glass of wine? Or maybe something to eat?"

"I want you," Matt told him and entered the room. "I want to make love to you."

The dog hopped down and sped across the room to nip at Matt's ankle. "What the...?" he growled and kicked the poodle across the room. Alexandria had drawn blood and, looking over at the animal, he saw that she was now licking her lips. Matt's eyes became little more than slits as he realized what had happened.

Jamie looked from Matt to the dog and back, unsure if he should be angry about Matt kicking his dog or concerned because Matt had been bit. He suddenly felt calm, the tension building in him seeping out of him.

[*She'll be all right, Jamie,*] Matt told him mentally, keeping his thoughts comforting. [*I'm sorry I kicked her -- it was just reflex.*]

Jamie looked over at where the dog had landed. She sat there quietly but seemed to be all right, except that she was looking back at him strangely. Almost hungrily, like *he* was a dog biscuit or something.

"Let's go to the bedroom, Jamie," Matt said, a strange sense of urgency in his voice that nearly pulled Jamie out of the calm that had come to hold him.

Matt shut the door behind them as Jamie continued on to the bed. [*Strip!*] he projected at the blond, besotting him with enough lust to power a Roman orgy. His own clothes flew off him as he crossed the room.

Jamie entered his arms, his lips locking with Matt's as their cocks began to grind against each other. He held onto Matt's neck and pressed himself hard against his body.

Matt's fingertips traced across Jamie's back and down his spine to cup his arseglobes as he directed them to the bed.

Jamie felt himself falling backwards but Matt's strong hands had come up to hold him by the shoulders. He knew he was safe. His legs spread and rode his friend's hips as he lay back on the bed, still holding onto Matt. It wasn't until Matt's knob slipped past his balls and began to press against his entrance that Jamie realized where things were going.

"I've never..." he mewled, breaking from the kiss.

"Never?" Matt asked in a surprised whisper. "With an arse like yours?"

"Every lad's taken one look at my kit and bent over."

"You'll love it."

"Won't it hurt?" Jamie worried, even as he surrendered.

"It won't -- I promise." Matt reinforced his words by sending another rush of lust through the blond.

Jamie locked his lips on Matt's, his tongue pushing through the man's teeth to duel his. Matt showed his friend's mind how to relax his anal muscles and began to push slowly but steadily against his entrance. Jamie's arse opened easily, welcoming Matt's dick inside.

Matt broke the kiss when he was fully buried in Jamie's bum and began to trace his jaw with his lips. He began to move inside the blond and Jamie moaned. Matt's lips moved onto Jamie's neck and his teeth broke the skin just enough to get a trickle of blood. Beyond the door, the dog growled.

Jamie was quickly entering realms he'd never known existed. He held Matt's face to his neck and ground his hips against the invader in his arse. His own cock was hard, oozing precum and bouncing across his belly.

Matt tried to ignore the dog's continuous growl beyond the door as he kept up a steady rhythm in Jamie's arse and licked at the trickle of blood he'd opened up on his neck. Dogs were stupid creatures, any way. The bloody thing would never figure out that she could simply walk through the closed door -- all she'd have to do is visualize the bedroom and she'd be in the room with them.

"Fuck me!" Jamie groaned, his body beginning to shudder beneath Matt. "I'm close ... Oh, shit! Fuck me!"

Matt felt as if a vise had suddenly clamped down along every centimeter of his dick. Jamie was breathing raggedly when Matt felt the first volley of his friend's jizz hit his chest. He held still, letting his friend experience his orgasm.

"Jesus!" Jamie cried through clinched teeth as a second eruption shook his body.

Matt kissed him, lying across his chest as Jamie's body shuddered spasmodically for several more minutes.

"You didn't cum, did you?" Jamie asked finally.

"Not yet..."

"Give me a few minutes to recover..." He reached up and brushed Matt's hair out of his face. "And you can shag me again."

"You like it then?"

"Definitely..." Jamie heard the dog's low growling then. "She wants in." He lowered his legs and grimaced as Matt's cock pulled out of him. "I'll be just a minute, I promise," he said and slid across the bed.

Matt lay back and watched as Jamie padded to the door. He stroked his hard cock languidly.

The dog smelled Jamie's blood as the door opened, growled once, and sprang. He fell back in shock as her jaws clamped on his neck. He could only gurgle as his windpipe collapsed. He tried to push her off him but she would let go.

Matt flew from the bed before Jamie could hit the floor. He grabbed the dog and threw her down the hallway. He heard the thud as the dog hit the wall. Kneeling, he could see the damage to Jamie's neck and knew he had only moments to live. He brought his wrist to his face and tore back skin; then shoved the wound against the blond's gaping mouth. [*Drink!*] he commanded, even as he sensed Jamie's consciousness retreating.

"What happened?" Jamie asked as he pushed himself up on his pillows.

"Your dog attacked you."

"Jesus!" Jamie groaned. He brought a hand up to his torn neck where the wound hadn't fully healed yet. He looked at Matt. "I was dying, wasn't I?"

Matt nodded but said nothing.

"How did you save me then?"

"I fed you some of my blood."

"Like a vampire or something?"

"Yeah."

Jamie stared at him so hard his eyes bulged. "I'm a vampire too then?"

Matt nodded again.

"I can't be!" he sat up with preternatural speed. "Vampires can't go out during the day, and I've got to work."

"I'll take care of you, Jamie."

"How? You're a student at police college, Matt! The rent on this flat is more than a police officer makes…"

Matt sighed. "I lied, Jamie. You seemed so interested in policemen and … Well, I own this property -- the whole complex. I have enough money for both of us."

"What about my dog?" Jamie asked after several moments of silence.

"She's a vampire too -- remember how she attacked me the moment I arrived tonight?"

Jamie nodded.

"She drew blood. It only takes a drop or two."

"What am I going to do with a vampire dog?" Jamie groaned.

"She'll sleep during the day, like we will." Matt shrugged. "We'll walk her at night and be careful what we allow her to feed on."

Several more moments of silence followed as Jamie worked through his new situation. "I suppose I'm going to have to get used to this, aren't I?"

Matt nodded.

Jamie grinned. "Come to bed then and let me have the second course. I think having you shag my arse will help me get used to it faster."

The Great Nothing
Ruthless

The day died in a welter of blood colors. Crimson spilled across the horizon as the sun slipped below the pine forests of the Maritimes. Pink shadows stretched out across the sand and touched the ocean.

I walked slowly along the beach, the wet sand masking my footfalls. My chest hurt and I gasped for breath. It was my first day in St. Andrews and I'd been walking since mid-day. First, through the small tourist town and, now, along the shore north of it. The last of the people walking the beach retreated and the wind blowing in from the sea began to grow cold. Deep, numb exhaustion had invaded my body. Curiosity had become mindlessness. Pain had become a dull ache, easily ignored. My steps had long since become mechanical. I walked on. When the blackness of night finally closed around me, the beach was deserted.

The sea sighed and murmured to itself in the dark, like a man going to sleep after a long day. Muttering on the stones, the water stirred, rolling over easily. Curls of fog made ghosts over the water and seeped towards the beach. They lingered where the water lapped against the shore but vanished when I came near them.

The fog ghosts made me think of guys drifting aimlessly in the night, making secret meetings with each other. This was the kind of place guys would go to meet other guys, I told myself as my cock stirred in my jeans. In the summer after dark there were plenty of places to go among the dunes, and there were plenty of excuses to take a stroll with an eye out for a pick up.

I was surprised at the appearance of the thought and stopped where I stood. I had been comfortable without thinking. Now I realized that I'd pushed myself too far; I was bone weary. I sat down and faced the dark, murmuring sea.

I was surprised too at the nature of the thought. I hadn't had a sexual thought since the doctor delivered my death sentence back in Montreal. I certainly didn't want to be horny this close to the great nothing I knew awaited me. It'd be just my luck for it to come over me right in the middle of a good fuck. I'd never get off and the poor guy in my butt would find himself fucking a dead man -- not a pretty picture.

Two more fog ghosts disappeared ahead of me.

I began to cough. "It's too cold now for that!" I growled out loud to myself between breaths. It was late September. The wind that blew in from the ocean had a touch of winter in it. The tourists were long gone. I was alone.

And fucking horny!

Two guys walked the water's edge close together, coming towards me.

They were shoulder to shoulder, so close that they might almost have been holding hands.

As they drew alongside me, I saw they were young. They had short-cropped hair and wore navy uniform, just a couple of sailors heading back to base. They weren't cruising. Their heads turned in unison and I felt them study me. They garnered my attention enough that I stopped coughing.

They were together and I had no one. If either of them had been alone, I might have spoken up, but we exchanged no words. They walked on and I held my gaze on the sparkle of white caps beyond the water's edge.

I took a few deep breaths before I looked back towards St. Andrews and the navy base beyond. The sailors weren't to be seen; the beach stretched empty. There was nowhere for them to have gone, no cover on the flat expense of sand. Gone. It was as if they'd never been.

I stared. Had they been particularly vivid fog ghosts? Or was I beginning to hallucinate, fading even faster than I had thought I was. I pulled my knees up and wrapped my arms around them.

It was just before dawn when I left Montreal. I hadn't looked at the driver when I boarded the bus. I handed him my one-way ticket to St. Andrews, Newfoundland, and shuffled down the aisle to the back of the Greyhound. I didn't look right or left. And I didn't look when we pulled out of the station and started east.

Been there, done that -- that was Montreal for me, the city where I'd been born and lived all my life. The city that had been home. Just one more part of my past. Like sex. Like life. Like my dreams. It would all be gone soon enough -- because I had no future to make any of it relevant.

I felt nothing as dawn streaked the eastern sky. I had one to ninety days to live. Ninety if I stayed in Montreal, let them feed me ever larger doses of morphine until I had to be hospitalized. A few days or thereabouts if I continued to react like an irresponsible child to my cancer. There was no more emotion in me. I put one foot in front of the other and took the step. That's all I had any more -- one step after another -- until I couldn't move any more. Until the great nothing finally claimed me.

Me with cancer. It was almost funny -- if I'd had the energy to laugh. I was a thirty year old, 5 foot, 11 inch, 160 pound Quebeçois with black curly hair and olive-complexion -- I didn't look sick. I looked good enough to pick up at any club. And I was going to die -- soon.

I sold everything I had, gave away the rest, and quit my job. I left Montreal with a thousand dollars in my wallet and death waiting around the bend for me.

I'd never been to the ocean. I'd never wanted to; I preferred the slopes to being a snowbird driving for days to spend a week in Florida. The sea *was* the epitome of death for me, ready to swallow a man alive. It was the physical representation of it. That was why I was en route to St. Andrews. To meet the endless nothingness that was my future.

I had to face death -- its personification, at least. I had to make myself get used to it -- because I already had one foot through the door beyond which I would cease to exist. And the other one was sliding out from under me.

I bought provincial papers at the bus' first stop and read them without interest. I arrived in St. Andrews at twilight two days later. A cab took me up the shore to the tourist home I'd already rented a room in.

My gaze was fixed on a froth of white water that ran along the sand and almost reached my feet. The ocean had the hush of breathing. It sighed in steady rhythm. It seemed almost alive, but I knew better. I wondered how cold the water would be.

I sensed a sudden darkness yards up the shore and turned towards it. It became the shape of a broad-shouldered man strolling leisurely towards me.

"Hey there," I said when he was almost upon me.

He drew a little closer and stopped. He had a thin face with a strong jaw, and a glimmer of white from his teeth -- the sort of man I'd have picked up in a second in the old days. I figured him for thirty. His gaze traveled over me and checked me out -- from my fatique jacket, salt-stained jeans, my crotch, my empty hands and my face.

"Hello," he said back, his voice deep.

"Is this beach a place where guys go cruising?" I asked without thinking. He was so sexy that I spoke without considering how direct I was being.

He grinned, his teeth gleaming. "Were you looking to meet someone?" he asked as he sat beside me.

"Not really." I shrugged. "It just seemed the right kind of place, so I wondered -- that's all."

"It can happen here." He looked me full in the eyes when he said it. His steady gaze turned his words into strongly suggestive ones. I let myself slip just for an instant into fantasy.

In the might-have-been, I would have pulled his shirt and trousers open and pressed my body against his warmth. His cock rising to meet mine, our lips touching and seeking and tasting, the salt of his hard masculinity in my mouth...

I smiled ruefully and turned away to face the ocean again. It wasn't going to happen. It was never going to happen for me again.

The man stayed. He was silent, but his presence beside me was as palpable as the endlessly moving sea.

"You from here?" I asked finally. "Or a visitor, like me?"

"I live here." His deep voice had a trace of an accent, nothing strong, but something that wasn't Canadian or even American. "I have a place on the road near to the church. And you -- where are you from?"

"Nowhere now," I told him. "I got on a bus a few days ago in Montreal and started traveling. I've run out of land so I can't travel any more -- that's

just as well, though, because I'm almost out of money too." I had a thousand dollars left; but I wasn't going to mention that. I hoped it would be enough.

"What's your name?" he asked.

"My name's Charlie," I said. "What's yours?"

"Seredy," he said.

The white tops of the waves turned over, a frosty phosphorescence that vanished as the dark water evened out, sliding into the blackness of the great heaving mass of water. There was a low swell on the sea. The mist was a grayness that darkened until the air and the water seemed to become one. The waves rose, sighed, and subsided. In the heavy night air, I felt the mist forming beads of cold on my hair and clothes.

"D'you ever think," I said a few moments later, "how unbelievably deep, how heavy the ocean is? All those billions of tons of water, what a weight it is and how cold. Tons and tons and tons of water?"

I looked back and he nodded. I looked away again at the dark restless water.

"The great nothing." I said bitterly. "The land ends and the ocean goes on forever, cold and empty water. It has to be cold, nothing but coldness -- and so vast I can't even stretch my mind to picture how big it is."

"You're thinking morbid thoughts tonight," he said. He wasn't asking.

"Yeah," I agreed.

"Are you here to kill yourself?" he asked. His warm, deep voice was as calm and conversational as if we were talking about what a misty night it was.

"No," I said. "I'm too afraid of death to do that."

He moved closer beside me. I felt his breath on my neck, easy in and out, breaths as slow and steady as the waves rolling over in front of me.

"I saw a couple of Navy guys on the beach a while back," I said. "It made me think about that accident they had a week ago down at the base. I read about it in the paper. You heard?"

I looked at him over my shoulder and he seemed curious.

"They were testing some pressure chamber, part of the submarine development program and six guys got trapped," I continued. "All those guys, they suffocated in there together." I shuddered. "Hell of a way to die. They found one lot of them at the outer door of the pressure chamber. They'd been clawing the door and they'd clawed their own faces, fighting for air, struggling, trying to stay alive.

"But there were two other guys; they were buddies. They went into the inner chamber, instead. They found them side by side. They cut each other's throats; they were lying there as peaceful as if they were asleep -- except for the blood."

I gave a small harsh laugh. "Imagine that, being so scared of dying that you kill yourself."

It didn't shock me at all that I'd just put into words what I was beginning to think of for myself.

"Maybe they preferred it that way?" he suggested. "Being together?"

"Maybe they did," I agreed. I'd have liked to have someone with me when the great nothing came; but there wasn't a chance of that happening. But choosing my own time, choosing the way it came -- that had a strong appeal to me. It would put me in control of something I had no control over.

Beside me, Seredy moved. I didn't look up. I felt his breath on the nape of my neck and knew he was kneeling behind me. I longed to lean back and have him hold me. Just one last time. Somebody. The warmth of flesh.

Me, belly down in the sand and him, thrusting into me while his teeth clamped a moist pleasure pain on the back of my neck. And even though it wasn't going to happen, I savored his closeness and the image.

"I guess you think I'm loony," I said. "Rambling on about this morbid stuff at a stranger. I'm just trying to figure it all out."

"Life and death and love and God and the ocean?" he suggested.

"Yeah," I said. "Just imponderable shit like that."

Seredy moved. I thought for a moment that he was about to touch me, because I felt his breath burning on my neck below my ear, but when I turned my head he was still kneeling a pace back.

It had been an illusion. My senses were going; I was hallucinating. It was not going to be, and it ached too much to think about what I was never going to have again.

"I guess I'll head back to town," I said. "It's too cold to sit around, babbling like a lunatic on the beach."

"You can't stand the cold?" he asked, then nodded. "That's because you're sick. You're not well." He stated it, didn't ask it. He must have seen it in the hollows of my face, the exhausted stance of my body.

"Yeah," I agreed. "Too sick to be out on a cold night." Bitterness was in my voice.

"Seriously sick," he said.

"I'm dying." I said. "The chemo nearly killed me, and it was all for nothing anyway. I've got cancer. They couldn't make it go away. I've got a few days they say, maybe weeks." I looked out at the dark ocean. "My life can probably be measured in hours now."

"Then you should go back to your room," he said. "Go back and live your last few hours in warmth. If you stay you could die tonight on this beach."

"That's right," I agreed. "That's sensible."

I shook myself together, pulling my jacket close. Caution and reason spoke to me again. Go back. That was right. I climbed to my feet, looking back over my shoulder at him.

Seredy continued to watch me. I turned my back on him and looked to where the town lights glimmered distantly in the night. They were blurred, like I was seeing them through glass. They were tiny lights. I put my head down and started to walk.

I was still bone-weary as I left him, but I felt better, somehow. Seredy

and the flicker of horniness that he had woken in me made me feel more alive.

When I looked back a few moments later, I could still see him. He hadn't vanished like the two ghosts had done. He seemed bigger, somehow. His shoulders seemed to have grown massive, until he looked sinister and mishappen, like a hunchback -- like he had grown great black wings and folded them around himself.

The sand under my feet shifted. I turned back towards St. Andrews. Step by step, I was being sensible, going back to the empty little rented room. Four walls, harsh lights, and silence instead of the breathing ocean, the dark, and the seeping cold.

I walked slowly towards the town and the tourist room that I had rented. I thought of life and of sex. Of having a warm body under my own and moving with it, of digging my fingertips into the firm muscle of another man's butt and pulling him into me. Of the wiry feel of his hair and the distinct smell of stranger sweat and stranger skin, exploring it with my mouth. It had been so long, I couldn't help but think of sex after talking to a guy like Seredy.

The two sailors appeared out of the mist, coming towards me. One nodded as they approached, the other smiled. Then, they were past me; and, when I looked back over my shoulder, there was nobody there.

The rim of the sea glimmered where the waves licked near my feet. The land and the sea were both quite dark. The town lights seemed to have vanished. The only man-made light was from the naval base a few miles to the south.

Those far-away floodlights made a white glow in the sky, a nimbus over the point softened by fog. Somewhere out on the water a ship's horn wailed. It had a lonely, frightened sound. The foghorn at the base answered it. They were out of cadence like two lost people calling for each other in the dark.

I continued to walk, putting one foot ahead of the other.

I woke the next afternoon and didn't remember having gotten back to my room. My leg muscles were sore, my chest was a mass of pain. I wished that I had brought morphine from Montreal. I realized that, subconsciously even before I'd left, I'd planned to kill myself like those two sailors on the sub had.

I'd surrendered to the finality of death and only sought to speed it along -- on my terms. To establish my control over it.

But the sea had proved last night not to be some sort of personalized death. It had been alive; it hadn't been the great nothing. Then, there had been the two sailors and Seredy. Part of me didn't believe they were real; but an even greater part of me wanted them to be. They seemed almost to represent the two forks in the road before me. The sailors as ghosts, pale

reflections of life once I died; Seredy as life itself.

I didn't understand it but, inside myself, I knew it was true.

I wanted Seredy -- for as long as I could have him.

I got up and dressed. I knew I could find the spot where I'd seen him last. I also knew I'd never be able to walk that far again. I didn't have five miles in me any more. I called a cab and waited outside for it.

The sun was just kissing the trees behind me when I started onto the beach from the road. I sat down in a hollow where the sea grass grew in a thick semicircle that faced the water, maybe five feet above where the high tide would reach. I was within yards of where I'd seen Seredy the night before.

I prayed that he would come looking for me again. I wanted the life that I knew he could bring out of me for as long as I still breathed.

I was cold by the time the sun set half an hour later. I was losing the internal argument I was having with myself, too. I'd made too much of a chance encounter. Not enough oxygen getting to my body from the few lung cells I still had. Cancer cells spreading through my body instead of oxygen.

Yeah, I was feverish, all right. I was clutching at straws and seeing them where none even existed. I had to be.

I made to push myself to my feet, disgusted at myself. But it was too much work to go back. I closed my eyes. The air moved cold on my cheeks, frost prickling my nose. Cold.

If I lie down, I thought, I'll get colder. No one was waiting for me, so no one would look for me. If I didn't push on to St. Andrews now, I might catch my death of cold. If I did, I could die in a rented bed.

I told myself that I'd only rest for a little while. With my jacket pulled snug around me, I quit worrying about it. I lay back and listened to the foghorns crying out, searching for each other in the dark.

"Charlie?" Seredy's voice came warm and rich and sudden, only a few feet from me.

"Christ!" I cried and sat up.

He took the last few steps towards me. I noticed his empty hands as he sat down beside me. The dim planes of his face and his thin sensual mouth were close by my shoulder.

"You decided to live after all," he said.

"As long as I still have breath," I answered.

"That doesn't seem nearly long enough," he said.

"What?" I choked.

"Last night, you wanted to know if this beach was a cruising spot," he said, ignoring my question.

"I wasn't cruising you," I lied. "I was just curious."

"You're gay?" he asked.

"Yeah."

He took me by the shoulders. I sighed as his lips touched my neck. He kissed the pulse in my throat and his lips were warm on my cold skin. I surrendered to his lips and he moved up to my mouth.

"It'll be warm enough here," he said. "With the heat from two of us."

His lips plucked at my mouth. My cock had swelled into a hard-on that strained uncomfortably under my fly. It didn't take his hands long to slide over my thigh and find it. He kneaded it first through the cloth.

"Let me..." he muttered.

"Yes," I groaned.

His hands felt hot enough to burn when they slid under my clothing. He closed his fingers around my prick, squeezing and setting up a throbbing which made me thrust towards him.

He knew my nerve endings better than I knew them myself. He knew when to pull, when the note of a growl at my ear made an answering groan come from me. I felt the thickness of his hard-on bulging against my leg. I kissed his mouth feverishly, all the while rocking my hips to slide my cock in the circle of his hand.

My shirt came open. He slid my jeans down somehow without my realizing it. I was craning my hips up towards his working hand. I was trying so hard to get his pants open that I hadn't paid heed to what he was doing. It felt so right.

I fumbled eagerly until I got my hand inside his trousers. His cock was a thick log with full balls below. His cock pointed right up his belly. It was so hot.

He laid me back on the sand to tug my jeans out of his way. His lips trailed down my belly. I was unbelievably horny. I wanted more.

One of his hands slid below my balls and began seeking and pushing on my asshole. He kneaded my opening. His other hand thrummed on my cock. His lips felt like an explosion of heat when they closed on the head of my prick. I grabbed his head to pull more of him onto me.

His tongue licked and flickered over the head of my prick. My whole body trembled. I wanted him to suck my cock so badly. I wanted to slam it into his willing mouth and fuck his face until my cum jetted and he swallowed every drop.

He sent his wandering hands on a fresh assault, playing and probing and jerking on my prick.

I wanted to fuck his face, to cum without caring, to live as I once had lived. But I also wanted to share. I wanted him as much as I wanted him to have me.

I panted as I twisted around to reach him. My chest hurt. Somewhere in my mind, I feared the onslaught of a fit of coughing. I gripped his cock and brought it towards my face. The nerdy part of me that had worried about coughing now worried that I'd die in the middle of sex.

I might, I told myself, but I'd have lived until the last moment. My lips touched his knob, pushing his skin back.

"You don't have to," he said as he spread my legs.

"If we do this – we're equals. I want you, too."

"Equals?" He raised an eyebrow.

"That's right," I told him. "Whatever I let you do to me, I do it to you. If you fuck my ass, then I'm fucking yours, too."

"All the better." His lips curved and his face had become a hungry smile. Then his mouth came down on my cock again and his strong, eager hands were swarming over me.

His mouth was hot and tight, sliding up and down, squeezing until I was thrusting, hard and driven. I couldn't get enough air. I came harder than I ever had before.

I gasped. I was in pain, every point of my body making itself known. My orgasm crashed over me endlessly.

He took me by the waist and turned me. He placed me on all fours before him. I stifled a whimper, bracing myself, knowing what was coming. I felt the wetness of his ready prick against my asscheek.

His hand came down to prepare me first. He used his own spit to wet my asshole. Then he guided his prick to my hole and began to push.

It was pain, a wonderful pain. And I pushed back against him, impaling myself on his thick, stiff cock. I pushed back while he held the cheeks of my ass wide. The pain of his entrance robbed me of breath. But I was beyond pain.

It was a good feeling. I pushed back inch after inch. His cock butted into me deeper and deeper. A sudden sensation, unbelievably good, racked me when the blunt head of his prick slid over my prostate. I felt more alive than I could remember.

Groaning, I continued to push myself on him until I felt the wiry curls of his pubes against the insides of my cheeks.

"Fuck me!" I cried to Serady, to the living sea, to life itself. "Fuck me, for God's sake! Make me live! Fuck me hard!"

He started to pound me. Every stroke knocked a gasp out of me. The heat of his body blazed across my back. The sensation of the fucking was so strong that I was only dimly aware of the warm, callused tips of his fingers playing with my cock.

Stroke, stroke, stroke. Harder. Deeper.

"Oh God! Do it!" I cried.

The force of his strokes battered me open. He was buried up to the wiry softness of his crotch hair -- then he drew back until only the tip of his big prick was inside me before he slammed it in again.

I panted like I was running. Pain started to become a part of me. Of my existence. He slammed into me so hard that the intensity made me collapse helplessly into the sand.

Seredy was near to cumming. At the last moment, on an outstroke, he took my leg and flipped me over. Now I was on my back, with my legs in the air and his gigantic body looming over me.

He held my ass off the ground by the knees as he returned to pounding into me.

I realized I was losing it. Life. Living. Even as I lived it. I sprawled in the sand and couldn't breathe. His strokes were deep and fast, bottoming out, hammering.

Seredy made no sound when he came. He opened his mouth and the dim light from the navy station caught his teeth and made them gleam when he gaped in a soundless cry. I felt his cum flooding me, not heat, but a shooting, liquid fullness. I felt his cock throb. He poised -- dark, frozen, and somehow terrifying -- as I began to fall away from him.

The sea's murmuring dimmed. The vision of him blurred. I gasped, trying to pull air into my lungs, as I thought I saw him bring his wrist to his mouth.

I faded. I could feel consciousness fleeing from me. I told myself that, at least, I'd lived until the last. It had been worth it.

I collapsed into myself as he dropped his torn wrist to my lips. I retreated into myself, knowing that I was dying as my body sucked greedily at Seredy's last offering.

[*I've got you, Charlie. It's okay,*] Seredy told me.

A long time passed. I realized that my chest no longer hurt. That I could breathe easily. That I was -- *hungry!*

I woke. Brought out of the nothingness that had held me by the incongruity of feeling alive, when I knew I'd died.

It was night still and the sea was again whispering to itself. Moonlight, cold sand, and long seagrass made themselves known to me.

Seredy.

He looked at me with compassion. He reached out and took my hand and helped me rise to my feet.

I looked out at the sea.

"You won't die again, Charlie; I've made you reborn," he said. "Do you understand?"

I understood. I had gone into the great nothing. But beyond the great nothing there was the whole world of night and eternal life to explore. A thousand stars studded the dark vault of the sky, twinkling, infinitesimally small. I felt like I could rise up into that glittering height.

"Where...?" I looked at him and understood finally. "Will you be with me, Seredy?" I asked.

"Only if we're equals, Charlie."

Chosen
Chad Stephens

I lived directly across the street from my old high school where they filmed the Buffy the Vampire Slayer TV series. The brown stucco administration building was abuzz with activity. It was almost midnight and I was sitting on the porch watching the shoot, dressed in just my shorts and sandals and bored as hell. The moon was full, bathing the area in an eerie light.

The parents were out of town at another Amway convention, and I had the house to myself. Alone. I hadn't found a hunk on the beach I wanted to bring home, and I'd spent half the afternoon looking. My dick throbbed at the lack of attention.

I finally noticed a dark-haired man standing just outside all the commotion at the school and looking right at me. I felt instantly drawn to him. It was weird, in a funny sort of way.

A shiver ran down my spine. I wanted to break eye contact and couldn't. I focused my concentration and tried to tear my gaze away.

"Interesting, isn't it?"

My head snapped back like I just hit a brick wall or something. He was standing in front of me, and I was face to face with him. I didn't remember him crossing the street.

"What the hell?" I cried.

"Perhaps," he said, smiling. He was intensely sexy. He stood about 6'2", a few inches taller than I. His medium-length hair was black and curly; his deep, rich cocoa brown eyes sort of sparkled in the night. His clean-shaven jaw was square. His smile revealed a set of beautiful white teeth, framed by killer dimples. He couldn't have been more than a couple of years older than me.

My dick jumped back to attention. I had never felt so attracted to anyone in my life. The chemistry was so electrifying I was fighting myself to keep from touching him.

He held out his hand. My hand clasped his like a magnet. His long, thin fingers joined with mine, erotically charged. I felt the tenting effect in my shorts.

"Uh -- hi," I stammered. "Another season of Buffy, huh?"

"Buffy?" his voice was smooth, mellow, and oh-so-sensual.

"My name's Chaz Johnson," I babbled.

"I'm Leigh, Charles."

"It's Chaz. The folks didn't give me a real name."

Duh, what a stupid thing to say. I wanted to slap myself.

"Just Chaz then. And don't slap yourself."

Did I say that out loud? I didn't think so. I stared at Leigh.

"Let's take a walk," he suggested.

I followed him out to the street and we turned towards the beach.

Leigh was wearing black jeans, black boots and a blood-red silk shirt, open a few buttons to reveal a sexy triangle of dark hair on his chest. I couldn't take my eyes off of him. At the beach I plopped down on the sand and he sat next to me. His leg brushed against mine.

"Are you working on that show?" I nodded in the direction we'd just come from.

"I'm here to see you," he said.

I couldn't help staring into his eyes. He was so damned handsome. What else could I do?

"Do I know you?" I practically croaked.

"You will," he said and smiled.

He leaned into me, our cheeks touched ever so slightly. His breath whispered across my hot cheek as our lips met. He opened his mouth and drew me in. His tongue was cool and sweet. The tips touched, moist and sensual, as we explored each other's mouth. His teeth were smooth and his incisors were long enough that I became aware of them.

Leigh enveloped me in his arms. I wrapped my arms around him and held him close. I could feel his strong back under the thin silk. I had an almost uncontrollable desire to tear his clothes off and have sex right where we sat. It was as if I wanted to crawl into his skin.

The intensity of my feelings was scaring the hell out of me. His lips broke from mine, nibbled a bit on my ear, and planted light little kisses down my chin, across my neck and over my bare, hairless chest. His tongue played against my hard nipple. I shivered. We broke apart. My cock was rock hard and oozing gobs of precum.

"Are you cold?" he asked as he unzipped my shorts.

"Like, are you some kind of actor or something? You're so hot. I mean. Well -- you know…" I couldn't finish. I knew I was blathering and figured it was best just to shut up.

Leigh remained quiet, unnerving me even more, as he opened my shorts and pulled my briefs down to free my cock.

"It's all right," he finally said. "I'm here for you."

"Meaning what, exactly?" I asked, looking down at my exposed crotch and my treasonous dick throbbing away in anticipation. "I mean," I continued, "it's like you're reading my mind. Anyway, do you know anything about vampires? That's what they're filming at the school. Ever watch that Buffy show? Not very believable, huh?"

Leigh's hands traveled up and down my arms, slowly, ruffling the hair like a light breeze would do.

"What do you know about vampires?" he asked softly and pulled both my shorts and underwear down past my knees.

"Just what I see on TV and the movies. Some are quite hot, especially that Angel guy. But they can be pretty scary, too."

"Not to worry," he started nibbling again on my ear. His hands caressed my bare legs. His silky smooth fingers lit up my thighs with charged tension. I spread my legs. Leigh grasped my cockmeat. I sucked in my breath at his touch.

I held onto him and allowed my hand to graze across his bulging crotch. I could barely breath.

"Do you -- you know -- want to go back to my house?" I asked. "I mean, there are vampires here and all."

"And there'd be one in your house, too."

"I don't understand," I managed to squeak out, even as I stared at him. Leigh massaged my exposed cock and balls.

The intensity built in me. I couldn't move. I could feel my cum juices churning, ready to escape. I had no control over my feelings; sensations soared through my body. I turned my head to see Leigh's handsome face and saw his beautiful mouth exposing those large incisors I'd felt before.

"I have a gift for you," he said.

At least that's what I thought he said.

Before I knew what was happening, Leigh had sunk his teeth into my neck. It was almost as if I could feel my blood coursing into his mouth.

Ugh!

Then my cock exploded with an orgasm unlike any I'd ever had.

"Just remember," Leigh whispered as he drew back, "you don't have to kill."

"What did you say?" I mumbled in a trance. I watched as he bit his wrist and then pressed it against my lips.

"I'll return when you're ready," he said when I licked him clean.

I zonked right there on the beach.

I awoke in my bed the next afternoon. It was overcast, but I still felt like I was getting too much sun -- that feeling where you know you're going to start peeling any minute.

What a dream I'd had, I said to myself as I pushed myself out of bed.

At least, I hoped it was a dream.

Okay, some of me hoped it was just a dream. Another whole part of me wanted it to be real.

I felt really weird. My senses seemed to be on overkill. I padded to the mirror and stared at my nude body, squinting against the brightness. My blue eyes and the blond curls that fell to my shoulders were there, just as my eight inch salami was. I examined my neck and saw two small bruises fading before my eyes.

Naw, I told myself. That shit ain't real. No fucking way!

I couldn't get Leigh out of my mind, though. Who was he and where did he go? Was he real? Was this all an erotic dream? I knew Leigh couldn't be a vampire. They didn't exist. And they died so easily when Buffy hit

them with a wooden stick. They seemed pretty stupid, too. But Leigh was hot! And smart. He had to be an actor with that show. Yeah, I was sure of it.

Everything was so bright that I had to find my dark sunglasses.

I got dressed and stepped gingerly outside. I headed to the main Torrance library. I didn't crumble into a pile of dust when I went outside, so I figured I wasn't already dead meat -- not that I believed in vampires for a minute.

I had them on the brain, though. If there *had* been a Leigh and he *had* done something to me, I had to find out what was going on with me. Things definitely weren't right.

I was also feeling extremely horny, as usual. But it was different in a weird sort of way. And there was that icky feeling of taking too much sun that stayed with me as I walked. And how bright everything was, even though it was overcast.

"May I help you, sir?" the cute young male librarian asked. He stood behind the front desk. About twenty-five years old and a little short of six feet, he was kind of smooth skinned and very clean cut -- the kind of guy you expected to find working in a library.

"Do you -- uh -- have a book on vampires?" I asked.

"A book? We have a lot of books. Any one in particular?" He continued to watch me.

I removed my sunglasses and fixed my gaze on Tim. That was his name. It said so on his name tag. He met my gaze and seemed to grow even whiter.

"I said I'm looking for something on -- you know -- vampirism. Perhaps with a list of the symptoms. How about a vampire book for dummies?"

Tim couldn't take his gaze off me. It was making me extremely uncomfortable.

"Is something wrong?" I asked, suddenly thirsty and hungry at the same time.

I gazed deeper into Tim's eyes. He wasn't moving. He stood perfectly still. I couldn't even tell if he was breathing. "Should I call 911 or something?"

Tim said nothing. He just sort of smiled stupidly. I waved my hand in front of his face. He didn't even blink. I leaned across the counter and touched his shoulder. Nothing.

I shook him slightly. Still nothing.

I scanned the library and saw that the place deserted. I leaned further over the counter and grabbed Tim's crotch. I could feel his cock and balls all scrunched up and growing.

What the heck! Before I could stop myself, I walked behind the desk, bent down and unzipped Tim's pants. I pulled his slacks and white Jockey shorts down and his hardening cock just sort of sprang out. Not bad for someone in a coma. I knelt in front of him and took him in my mouth. But, as nice as his equipment was, I wanted more.

I had an overwhelming desire to lick his neck. I stood up, opened his tie, and pulled his collar away from his smooth neck. My mouth went for his exposed neck. My newly overgrown teeth easily broke the surface and I drank Tim's hot, sticky blood.

My heart beat rapidly like it was going to burst. I felt a rush of energy coursing through my body, more than any power bar provided. Yum!

[*You don't have to kill.*] It was Leigh's voice in my head. I quickly looked around the large room. There was no sign of Leigh, but I could feel his presence.

I looked back at Tim and saw the trickles of blood moving down to his collarbone. The bruises on his neck. There was no doubt in my mind that I'd done that to him. I was on the verge of a full-on panic attack when I looked down and saw his man-meat still jutting up at me, rock hard.

I couldn't resist. After all, I was still gay, even if I may already be a little dead. Thank goodness Tim had enough blood in him to maintain an erection.

I knelt and took Tim's cock back into my mouth. I could taste his precum and sucked it up, kind of like washing down the blood. Again, yum! In what seemed like only moments, my nose was buried in his pubes and he was squirting jizz directly down my throat.

I anxiously straightened up, put my sunglasses back on and went back to the front of the counter.

Tim shook his head and looked at me as if for the first time.

"May I help you, sir?"

My heart speeded up almost audibly. I was afraid that Tim would realize what I had just done and come after me. I avoided his eyes. "Where are your computers? I want to go on-line."

"Through that room over there." Tim pointed to a glass enclosed room. He glanced down and noticed his exposed cock. His face turned bright red. I nervously scampered away.

Sitting in front of a computer, I remembered that I was computer illiterate. Yet, somehow, I seemed to know what to do. I could see my reflection on the computer monitor.

That's a good sign, I told myself. If those Dracula movies were right and I was a vampire, I wouldn't cast a reflection. At least, I knew that I was still part of this world.

A rapid search led me to more vampire web sites than I had ever imagined. I entered a couple and got some basic facts.

I was so freaked out by what I'd found out that I turned the computer off. I was scared shitless. I was afraid of dying and at the same time I was afraid of living forever.

I decided the best thing to do was leave the library, go to the beach and forget any of this ever happened. I'd probably wake up soon and find out this was all a bad dream. It had worked for Dorothy in Oz.

[*Relax. Everything will be fine.*]

- 128 -

My attention snapped back to the blank screen before me and fixated on the pale reflection of Leigh that was now there. His arms seemed to reach out and wrap around my shoulders. I never felt so safe and loved in my entire life.

What the hell was that all about? I hardly knew this man.

[*Ah, but that's not true,*] he told me, his lips not moving.

The strength of his gaze was just as disconcerting as it was last night -- but there was a difference now, some kind of a connection that hadn't been there before.

"Where the hell did you vanish to and what the fuck did you do to me?" I couldn't help blurting out.

Leigh smiled at me and I melted. He exuded sex in a way I found irresistible.

[*Can you read my mind?*] I asked without actually saying the words. I thought of the song from the Superman movie.

[*You know I can. With practice, you'll be able to as well.*]

"Why do I feel like I've known you for years?" I asked.

[*I've been watching you for several years now,*] he continued telepathically.

"I never saw you."

[*Of course not. I had to be sure you were the one.*]

"The one what? I don't understand what's going on with me. Did you see what I did to that guy behind the front desk? I fucking sucked his blood!"

[*How did that make you feel?*] he asked.

A smile played across my lips. Was there a tinge of jealously hidden in those simple words?

My eyes rounded as the thought hit home. How would I know that?

"I don't know," I said. "Kind of powerful, but also out of control. A little guilty. I hate that. I never feel guilt. I'm even having all these strange thoughts. Am I going crazy, Leigh?"

[*Not at all,*] he told me. [*You just need a little more time, Chaz. I'll explain everything when you're ready.*] Leigh removed his hands from my shoulders.

In spite of my confusion and even fear, I knew one thing for certain. I wanted Leigh and I wanted him real bad. It was like he was a part of me.

I stood up and turned around, only to see that I was alone. "What the fuck," I grumbled as I started for the door. "Leigh did it to me again!"

Redondo Beach was pretty deserted for a mid-summer evening. I was still getting my heart to slow back down to normal.

There were a couple of hunks playing volleyball, but I resisted the urge to suck their throats. I mean, what happened to just wanting to suck cock? It was all so freaky.

I reached the Redondo pier. It was low tide so I had no trouble walking under the original old wooden structure. A dirty sign posted on one of the huge pilings stated 'Danger -- Beware of Rocks and High Tide'.

I found a large, flat rock that didn't look too dangerous and perched myself on top.

I watched as waves crashed towards me, one after the other. Three or four footers. I wished I'd brought my surfboard.

A hand touched my shoulder and I freaked -- instant panic. If I turned around, I'd see Tim, the librarian, there, accusing me with his eyes. With big holes in his neck.

"I told you I'm not a vampire," I groaned.

"Yes you are," Leigh said.

I snapped my head around to lock eyes with my nemesis. My heart raced again but with an erotically charged intensity now. Even my fingers seemed to tingle. Maybe I was just having a heart attack. After all, I wasn't used to all this stress.

"What is up with you, coming and going like a ghost or something?" I grumbled. "Why did you leave me alone in the library? First you screw up my life and then you leave me to fuck it up even further."

"I'm sorry." Leigh put his arms around my waist. "Really, I never meant to cause you so much pain." He turned me towards him and kissed me gently on the lips.

Leigh was not playing fair.

I parted my mouth and caressed his tongue with my own. I leaned back against the nearest piling, wrapping my arms tightly around his waist. I was not going to let him get away this time.

All my anger seemed to disappear, seeping into the growing evening. Damn, I'd really wanted to tell Leigh off. But being next to him felt so right. Our bodies were connected in an ocean of passion.

My cock pulsed stiffly in my shorts, pressing hard into Leigh's thigh. He was again wearing his black jeans, but this time he had on a simple black tee shirt.

My mouth broke free of his and traveled over his entire face. I wanted to taste all of him. His cheek, his jaw, his closed eyelids, his ears. A quick tonguing of Leigh's ear sent a shiver through his body. I smiled. I knew he wanted me, too.

I grabbed onto his firm asscheeks and pulled him tightly against my hard-on.

After a moment, he pulled away, smiling at me. I couldn't help smiling back. "You're right. I do owe you an explanation. And I do want you, much more than you know."

"Well then, let's do something already." We were completely alone, except for a few seagulls watching us from nearby pilings. The roar of the ocean filled my ears. The sea spray was invigorating.

I untucked Leigh's shirt and pulled it over his upstretched arms. My

tongue made a path from his throat down to his hard, brown nipples. I wrapped my lips around the firm flesh and sucked each one. His head reared back, his beautiful brown eyes partially closed.

I continued downward until I reached a thatch of hair below his belly button. I tasted his skin as I dropped to my knees. I unbuckled his belt and unsnapped his jeans.

Unzipping his pants I allowed them to fall to the sand. I removed his shoes and socks and Leigh stepped out of them. He wore a pair of bright red, silk boxers. I could see his large cock straining for release.

I stood quickly and stepped out of my shorts. The seagulls squawked, seeming to voice their approval.

[*You're gorgeous.*] Leigh thought at me.

I was hearing his thoughts. I was sure of it. I smiled. My eight-inch cock stood straight up. I pulled his boxers down and he stepped out of them. Kneeling in the sand, I took his thick, hard cock into my mouth. I could taste his precum. I took the purple engorged head into my mouth and held it there for a moment. Then I plunged the entire cock down my eager throat. My nose brushed against Leigh's dark, curly pubic bush and I breathed in his scent.

I pulled back and repeated the motion again and again. I massaged his firm asscheeks and pressed his body tight against mine. My breathing was short and furious. I allowed his cock to escape from my mouth and tongued his hairy ball sack. I took the two orbs into my mouth and tasted them. Once again I let go and slid my tongue slowly down his thigh.

Leigh broke away from me and knelt down before me. His brown eyes seemed to pierce deeply into my blue ones. I couldn't believe this sexy hunk of a man was naked before me. I tentatively touched his firm, square shoulders. He pulled me into his embrace and held me. My hands massaged his full head of curly black hair, then grasped his body tightly against mine. Our cocks touched together, seemingly embracing on their own. I smiled.

Leigh smiled back at me. He stood up and held out his hand to me. I took it as my lifeline. He guided me back to my rock. I climbed up and lay back. The cool, flat stone was unable to suck the heat of my passion from me.

He nestled his tongue against my firm balls. I could feel his cock against my leg as he leaned into me. It felt so warm, so right. He took my cock in his hand and massaged the slick head as he tongued his way between my open thighs. Leigh pierced my puckered hole, pushing his finger firmly inside.

I moaned. I knew Leigh was loving this and I knew this was what he wanted, almost as desperately as I did. I felt both happy and a bit frightened.

He pushed his finger deeper into me while pressing his mouth hard against my inner thighs. Then he took my cock into my mouth and slurped up my precum. Back and forth he went until I could bear it no longer and spewed load after load of cock juice into his mouth.

After I'd quit spasming, he let my spent dick go and stood. He stepped back and studied my cock resting on my belly.

"I want to fuck you," he told me.

I looked into his brown eyes. I felt like I had just passed some kind of test.

I reached into my shorts and pulled out a condom. "I'm always prepared," I told him. "Even if we're the living dead, we still can't be too careful."

I pulled the condom onto Leigh's pulsating member while he raised my legs onto his chest.

"Whoa!" I cried. "I'm going to need lube to take that thing!"

"You won't," he told me as he lined himself up. I felt a tingling inside my head.

He plunged into my fuckhole in a single motion.

I took it all, moaning ever so slightly. Fullness but no pain.

I could hear his heart beating wildly. Weird, but very, very erotic.

His cock pushed in and out of my tight butthole, but he never once broke eye contact with me. We were one, complete.

I was hard again. My passion built with each thrust, harder and harder, deep into my very soul. My eight inches jerked and jumped across my belly and back again. My balls tightened. I reached out and grabbed his asscheeks, feeling them flex under my fingers.

[*Hold it just a little longer, Chaz. I want to cum with you,*] he thought at me and began to pound my butt hard, pistoning in and out of me. I strained to hold my eruption back, watching him watching me, still one with him.

He pushed into me hard, spearing my guts. His cock expanded in me, and I went over the top. The muscles all along the walls of my chute clutched at him, squeezing his cock. He groaned and I felt the heat of his jizz filling the tip of the condom buried inside me.

Exhausted, Leigh fell upon my chest. Our lips met and parted as we held tightly on to each other.

"So what the hell have you done to me?" I asked finally when I could breathe normally again.

Leigh smiled. "I've given you the gift of life so that we can be together this time."

"What do you mean 'this time'?"

"We were lovers almost a hundred and forty years ago..." He smiled. "Your name was Charles then."

"What happened?"

"We were in the First Massachusetts Regulars at Manassas -- the first battle. Your platoon didn't make it back when we retreated. I didn't care if I lived or died then. After the war, I was stationed in New Orleans. That's when I became a vampire. It seemed like I've been searching for you forever. And, when you have eternity to deal with, forever is truly a long, long time."

I rested my head upon his chest. Leigh put his arms around me. It felt so right, but I didn't want him to know how much I was beginning to care for him.

[*Too late, I already know.*]

"This mind reading thing is gonna be a bit tricky getting used to," I said. "How the hell am I gonna keep any secrets from you?"

"You're not." Leigh smiled at me.

"Damn!" I grunted. This was going to be an interesting eternity.

Hunting Season
Jay Starre

I watched him sleeping in his bed from the window. So peacefully --
the sleep of a man who hadn't yet learned the frailty of human life.

It was early in the hunt, though. I wouldn't move any closer yet. I'd
merely watch -- and contemplate how I would take him.

His sleep turned restless as my thoughts turned lascivious; his body
ground against the bed. The sheet slid down his chest to rest at his hips,
exposing him to the warm mountain breeze wafting in through the window.

He turned onto his stomach, managing to kick off the sheet completely
and revealing his smooth body in its entirety.

His broad shoulders tapered to a narrow waist that swelled into a pair of
buttocks that were as full and pale as the moon behind me. But, then, I had
chosen him partly for his looks.

His asscheeks began to flex, slowly and unconsciously, as he fucked
the mattress. I wondered if his restlessness was due to my proximity. If part
of him sensed me watching him.

I could project my thoughts to any mortal, but most failed to hear
anything but the most emphatic command. Their receivers were dull, so to
speak. This one seemed to be aware of me, even in his sleep. I decided to
test him, his receptivity.

It was one of the tests he'd have to undergo, anyway -- if he was to
make it through this hunt.

I gazed at his pristine ass, blemish-less and taut. I imagined my hands
on it; my long fingers sliding across the expanse of perfect flesh, then
kneading that ass, then moving towards the deep crevice, and finally sliding
into that valley and searching out the buried slot, hot and moist.

Another moan from him was followed by a languid undulating of his
ass. His cheeks rose up, as if feeling my imaginary fingers. He was very
suggestive. A good sign.

[*Open up for me,*] I told him. [*Spread your thighs and let me touch you.
Let me feel your secret pulse. Let me reach inside you and enter your soul.*]

The moan became a stifled groan as he buried his face in his pillow and
shoved his butt in the air. His asscheeks parted as his thighs spread wide to
expose the puckered, hairless button that led to his inner being.

[*Feel my finger on that pucker,*] I told him from my perch on the
window sill. [*Feel it tickle and tease you, then slide inside you. Feel it
prepare the way for something bigger, something fuller.*]

He responded with a squirming intensity that thrilled me to the core.
His hard white butt rose higher, the small hole between his nether cheeks
twitched and then gaped open as if, at that moment, my finger actually was
penetrating them.

My own cock rose up in eager response. I stroked it as I mentally threw more commands at my unconscious prey.

[*Feel my manhood as it stretches and fills you. Feel it sink into your guts, feel it throb through your whole body, feel it bang your prostate and massage your sphincter. Feel my power, feel my strength. Taste what it's like to be mine!*]

He lifted his ass high in the air and spewed a load of jizz over his sheet. The sight of that quivering asshole and that hard cock pulsing as it sprayed was too much for me. I had to flee or fall victim to my own desires.

I rose and flew to my small cabin nestled in the circle of cliffs beyond town, not more than twenty miles from Calgary. I changed back into human form the moment I'd alighted on the pine table in the center of the main room.

He'd been so amenable to my will! I'd only suggested, not forced him, to visualize himself in such a sexual situation. I'd never come upon such willing responsiveness before.

I wondered if he was the one, after all. He was certainly beautiful. But I'd learned too many times that beauty of form often has little to do with beauty of being. It had precious little to do with willing responsiveness as well.

Was he the one? Would my hunt for a mate reach its culmination with this man? I smiled at the delicious idea of it.

I'd have to let him show himself unwittingly to me. He'd already exhibited two of the qualities I needed in a mate but, alone, they wouldn't be enough. There had to be more to make a relationship last an eternity.

With a forbearance that was unlike me, I waited.

Summer in the Canadian Rockies slipped into autumn, then snow blanketed the world as winter fell.

I observed him from a circumspect distance. I told myself that the hunt had gone on far too long. I wasn't going to see in him what it would take to try a relationship. He was only going to be dinner or a night of abandoned wantonness -- or both.

He laughed a lot. He played football with his friends. He drank with them in Calgary and in the village. He went home with several. But each time was only a hedonistic night with a friend and he left the next morning. He enjoyed life.

I hoped. And put off riding the hunt through to its end.

It was a busy night in the small mountain resort town just outside Calgary. The slopes were open for skiing, and the streets were alive with Canadians and foreign tourists alike. People thronged the restaurants and pubs.

I enjoyed the flavor and the cacophony of languages I picked up with my incredible hearing.

I entered the pub, sensing that he was already there.

He approached me first. Either it was fate or he was merely sensitive to my roaming thoughts.

"Hi there," he said. "Nice night, eh?" The blond grinned brightly as he moved between the bar and me.

"Beautiful. And you're beautiful as well," I replied honestly, to hell with anyone who overheard me. My own smile was quieter. I wasn't given to overly boisterous displays.

"Thanks! I haven't been called that before! Hot, maybe. And cute." He wiped his hand on his jeans and stuck it out at me. "I'm Kevin. And you're...?"

Was he the one? I ached at the feel of his thigh pressing against mine in the crowded room.

I decided to be blunt. Some small part of me wanted to frighten him away, to save myself from my own lustful predations.

"I'm Sean," I introduced myself. "And you are cute and hot, as well as beautiful."

"You're probably Irish, too -- with red hair like that and a name to match!" he told me, diving into the pick up scene with abandon. "Hot too."

He studied me a moment longer, and a frown touched his face. "You seem familiar, Sean. Have we met before?"

"No, I don't think so," I answered with surprise. "I live north of here in a cabin on Whitecap Road. I'm a writer and quite reclusive most of the time."

I was being as honest as possible. My journals were very important to me.

"You do ski, don't you?" he continued. "I'm a ski bum myself. I don't do much but ski and teach skiing." Kevin chuckled at himself and put his hand on my arm.

I inhaled his breath, the slight odor of beer and the warmth of his blood-filled lungs exciting me. I was not certain how to proceed. I did not trust my desires.

"Yes I do, cross-country," I said.

"Great," he cried, "let's get out of here and go for a ski! There's a full moon. We'll ski to your place." He set his beer stein on the bar and looked at me expectantly.

I followed him to his small apartment in the jumble of new condos crowding the edge of town. I observed the way he walked, confident yet languid. I decided that he wasn't lazy, otherwise we would not have been about to ski five miles at night. But he was unambitious.

I nodded. That was the perfect word to describe Kevin.

He grinned at me as he rummaged through his messy foyer and produced two pair of skis, boots and poles.

"These will fit you. I figure you're just about my size."

My thoughts were in turmoil. The warmth of his flesh was palpable as

he brushed against me in the foyer. I could barely control myself.

Did I want to have sex with him or feed on him -- or both? Or had I finally decided that I wanted to make him? All three, all three, I screamed internally.

"This'll be awesome! No one ever wants to do this kind of shit," Kevin babbled as we went back out into the night.

He knew where Whitecap Road was. I followed his lead. Snow blanketed the sides of the highway, enough to ski comfortably.

I had learned the sport as a lark and, although I could fly at will, I found the near-silent and rhythmic swishing of cross-country skiing hypnotic and soothing. I stared ahead at his pumping ass and broad shoulders. I recalled that ass naked, writhing and parted.

"Let's stop up in the trees a minute," he spoke into the quiet of the night.

The town quickly fell behind us. The road we had chosen was deserted. We were alone. He turned and faced me as I moved close. His smile under the moonlight was welcoming. Our skis crossed as I halted inches from him.

"You are so damn hot!" he said. "Something about you, something mysterious and quiet and weird, excites me."

Kevin leaned across those inches and nuzzled my ear with his lips. "I want your body. I want you to fuck me," Kevin breathed into my ear.

His gloved hands reached out and embraced me. His mouth found mine. His tongue slipped past my lips.

It was a simple matter to trick him so that he did not notice my fangs as his tongue explored my mouth and tonsils. It was not a simple matter to control my own passion.

I opened his trousers and shoved them and his underwear to his knees. I reached behind him and cupped his delicious buttcheeks in both my gloved palms. I pulled him closer, pressing my erection into his belly. We did not speak.

I prodded his naked butthole with a gloved finger, teasing it and finally violating it as he ground his body against mine and devoured my tongue with his sucking mouth. His hands dropped to my waist and insinuated themselves into the waistband of my trousers, tearing them open and fishing out my stiff prong. He groaned into my throat, continuing to grind his cock against mine.

The full moon floated over us, a sentinel. Although totally focused on the enchanting physical sensations of our impromptu groping, a part of me was disengaged, doubting.

I realized why, the intensity of the moment explanation enough. I was not going to feed on this lad, to suck his blood in a thirsty midnight feast. I had made my decision without consciously doing so.

I wanted more than just to feed. Much more. I hungered for a mate. I wanted to make him, as my own maker had done to me in the early part of

the last century.

I had been alone for almost ninety years. I had fed, I had enjoyed sexual jaunts with handsome men, but I had not made another vampire. Never. Beginning only in the last decade, I had become more and more fixated on the idea of doing so. I wanted a companion.

So I had started a hunt. I had met with no success. I had lusted after young men, burly and strapping handsome men. But none had stirred me to love. Not one.

Until now. Kevin's light touch on my cock, his abandoned grinding against my penetrating finger and his throbbing erection rubbing against my own belly were proof to me of lust. I could yield myself to that lust. Or I could strive for more.

"Let's go to your place," Kevin gasped as he disengaged abruptly from my arms. "I want more. I want you in my arms, I want your hard cock up my ass as you kiss me and love me."

We held each other as we untangled our skis.

"Beware," I told him as we started again along the road. "There's more to me than you realize," I warned.

"You're either an angel or a devil," Kevin laughed as he pulled up his pants and moved off ahead of me. "Either way, I feel like I trust you."

Trust me? The view of that incredible butt rhythmically grinding ahead of me was like a lure calling me to my own downfall. How could he trust me or I trust him? I was a vampire. This was not a secret I revealed without cause. Could one trust with such a deep secret?

The moonlight illuminated the snow in an eerie fashion, and the trees that surrounded the road flowed by in a magical dance. Kevin's hair gleamed in the moonlight. I was falling deeper in love with every passing moment.

An hour later, we'd reached my cabin. Together, we'd made a fire in the hearth, and the room was becoming cozy and warm. Kevin slowly stripped as I watched He grinned and slowed down. His pulsing erection testified to his desire.

"Fuck me, Sean," he told me, his voice soft after he stood before me naked, his hands spread at his sides. "I've never wanted anyone like this. It's almost like I was promised the greatest sex in the world with you and this is where I collect."

He smiled again, something almost impish. "I'm not a virgin or anything, but I haven't done it more than a few times. Your cock's pretty big, so you're gonna have to lube it."

He sat down on the bearskin rug and lay back. "You have condoms, don't you?" he asked, his naked limbs flushed by the blazing heat of the stoked-up fire.

"Of course," I answered. They were a necessity for any kind of sex life with mortal men.

I fetched the lube and condoms and came back to stand over him, studying him for a moment. My heart was full, and over full. Could his soul be as sweet as his physical form?

He rose to his knees, reaching to undo my zipper and unbuckle my belt. His eyes were on mine as he pulled my pants and underwear to the floor. My hard cock thrust up into the air between us. He laughed in his throat as he swooped down over it and swallowed with eager swiftness.

"Yes!" The moistness of his mouth was incredible. He reached around my waist, cupping my butt and pulling my crotch to his face as he snuffled and slurped on my cock.

It was fantastic. I barely managed to remain on my feet as the power of his lust enveloped me. He sucked like he was starving and my cock was his first meal in days. He took me past his tonsils and choked and gagged but continued to bob and slurp with unreserved enthusiasm.

He pulled back and looked up at me, his fist still holding me. "Fuck me with this thing! It's huge! I've never seen a boner so damn long!"

Kevin got on his hands and knees, his head craned around to gaze up at me trustingly. His creamy thighs were parted, that butt spread and the winking hole exposed. His shoulders bunched with tension.

"Fuck me, Sean. My ass is yours."

I discarded my clothing. When I was naked, he grinned at me and whistled. I was muscular, although lean. Hairless, except for the reddish fur at my crotch, I was pale but pink from the glow of the fire. His eyes told me he appreciated my own special beauty, the ethereal glow of a hungry vampire that few mortals ever witness. His eyes shone their lust.

I fell to my knees behind him and thrust my cock up the valley between those lush butt mounds. I wrapped my pulsing cock with the condom and squirted lube all over it. It grew even more as I did so. Kevin would feel this poker way up inside him. It would fill him as no other had or ever would.

He grunted and mewled and raised his creamy buttocks up to meet my entry. His palpitating anus stretched and welcomed me with eager surrender. He cried out as my shaft penetrated the spasming sphincter and into the tunnel beyond. It was as if a massaging fire clamped over my cock as I shoved it deeper. I held his taut buttcheeks with both hands as I fed him more and more of my shaft. Kevin shoved backwards and swallowed me, as eager as I to merge, to meld into one.

The length of my shaft was buried in his warm butt. He was mewling and begging me to fuck him. His eyes were moist as he gazed into mine with total trust.

I leaned forward and covered him with my body. Our naked flesh was as one. My lips touched his neck and opened, allowing me to touch his naked flesh with my fangs. I caressed the vein there with my tongue, then I bit.

"Yes! I want it, take me! I want to be yours!" Kevin cried out as his blood spurted into my mouth.

I tasted him as my cock pummeled his willing bowels. He writhed and moaned and wiggled with languid enthusiasm, giving himself up to me entirely. I suckled on his life-giving blood more slowly, pacing myself. When he cried out in orgasm, his hard cock spewing on the skin beneath us and his pliant asshole convulsing around my penetrating shaft, I allowed him to slide into unconsciousness.

We lay together there on the bearskin rug all that night before the crackling fire. He tossed in fevered dreams for some time while I contemplated my options.

There was no question I wanted him. I wanted to have him as my partner, my lover for eternity. That's what I'd decided as we made our way up from town.

But what would he want? Would he be willing to give up his life of fun and carefree hedonism?

He awoke as I lay beside him gazing at his perfect body. For a moment he was confused, then he seemed to recall what had gone on before. "You fucked me." He grinned and wiggled his butt against my crotch.

His grin became a frown. "And you did something else."

His eyes widened and his face went blank.

"You're a vampire," he said quietly.

There was no hint of fear or condemnation. It affected me more than everything that had gone on before. It was enough.

"Yes, I am. And I seek a partner." I looked at the fire. "I've been hunting you every since I first laid eyes on you this summer. I love you."

"Damn!" he growled.

"What?"

"You played with my head back then, didn't you?"

"Played with your…?"

"Back in June -- I had the most incredible wet dream … And you were the one fucking me raw in it."

"It was only that one time -- I was watching you and decided to see how susceptible to suggestion you were…" I realized what he'd just said. "You recognized me?"

He nodded.

"I've come to love you, Kevin."

"I think I love you too," he said and turned on his back so that he was looking directly at me. "But we should talk some more. Can you wait a little longer before I decide?"

His honesty touched me.

"Of course, I can," I grumbled.

An impish grin grew on his face as he rose and straddled me. With his own hands, he pointed my stiffening bared cock at his quivering sphincter and impaled himself once more.

"I love your dick, I love how deep you go!" he moaned softly. "I love the way you look and talk and feel, Sean." Kevin sighed as he lowered

himself completely into my lap and grunted with the fullness of my stiff boner thrusting up into his heated guts. "Let's not think of anything else right now."

He rode me, tossing his head and crying out. His naked chest glistened with sweat as he fucked himself wantonly on my shaft. I reached up and pinched his nipples, causing him to pant and lean forward with his mouth wide open. He was without inhibition, as was I. We made a good pair.

He fucked himself to another orgasm, this time without the aid of my fangs in his throat. I had fed and was full of life and flushed with love. There was no moment so joyous as when he erupted once more, his seed splashing in a fountain to spray my heaving chest. Even after he came, he did not relent.

"Fuck me more!" Kevin groaned. "It doesn't matter that I shot! Something has happened to me!"

It was true. His face was flushed and fevered. His pale blue eyes gleamed with desire, and with love. It was beyond the physical, it was beyond the metaphysical.

It was my turn to surrender. I orgasmed inside him over and over as he rode me, sucking my jizz out of me as if it was my blood and he was the vampire.

We became one that night. Although it was months before he joined me in surrendering his mortality, it was that night we truly became soul mates.

In Like Flint
Peter Eros

Flint has a narrow, handsome face. His eyelids droop and his lower lip swells. It's not just that he's sexy – that goes without saying. He's the penultimate statement of sexiness.

He has a voice that's rich and velvety. He talks fast and, when he talks about sex, his speech accelerates. He's got the easy gait of someone who's been turning heads for years.

Flint rides a Harley and swaggers with the sexy roll of a cowboy coming into town after a long cattle drive. His mane of lustrous hair falls over his face, flicked back regularly with a toss of the head or a fondling into place with a slender hand.

Since his arrival in DC almost two years ago, his name has been bandied about with a mixture of curiosity and speculation that credits him with an uncut prick to die for as well as anal and oral skills that'd make any cock twitch. He's reputedly also accommodated some of the largest dicks in town.

I lust for him with every atom of my body.

I'm Jason Lyons -- tall, blond, built, and an avid sexual opportunist. I've got a whole set of unfulfilled yearnings where Flint's concerned. I'm tantalized by his beauty and his air of mystery. Like everyone else in DC's gay world I know who he is and am sure that he has a dark secret I'd like to share.

I've placed myself in his path at every opportunity, openly playing the tempter. I just know somehow that involvement with him is my future. I've got it bad where Flint is concerned.

We've glimpsed each other many times at dance clubs and raves, even in glory-holed loos and secluded park thickets – during those fallow periods when affluent johns aren't providing me sufficient income or action.

From acquaintances I know that Flint has inquired about me. He knows that I'm a trainer at my gym as well as a hunk for hire, with a prick as substantial as his own model is reputed to be and glutes maximally developed for power play. Also reported to me is his approval of my disdain for drugs and those who use them.

We finally connected at the DC Eagle. I was dressed in brief cutoffs that provided flashes of my gonads and a nipple-revealing tank top. When Flint studied me with admiration, I was caught between disbelief and obscene relish at his interest.

Even my chest hair was aroused as he nodded towards the exit. I followed. Damned right I did! With my eyes locked on the hot, winking hollow of his ass, my whole body enveloped in a bubble of hyper-

stimulation.

He pulled me to him the moment we were outside. We kissed at the top of the steps, our bodies grinding against each other. We each slipped a hand in back of the other's shorts, anticipation in our fingertips as we stroked hard glutes down towards the dark, hidden entrances. His mouth mauled my jugular and he gasped and grunted his pleasure as, despite my apprehension about embarrassing hickeys, I returned the favor.

He inquired about my HIV status when we started down the steps and looked pleased when I told him. He led me to his Harley and said that he was clean also.

On his hog, Flint raced me across town and his basement apartment in one of the old subdivided mansions overlooking Rock Creek Park. The feel of the throbbing Harley between my legs intensified my chronic crotch-itch.

We pulled up behind the house and parked in front of the entrance to his basement apartment. We entered a long, low-ceilinged living room with a kitchen nook at one side, beyond which lay an ornate bedroom.

Flint didn't waste any time getting undressed. I didn't either, stripping off my muscle shirt and dropping my cut-offs. I wanted him on top of me, wanted his broad shoulders pinning me down as he ground away in my guts.

Flint pushed me down onto the bed and fell to his knees, taking me in his mouth as I grabbed the back of his head. He bobbed and sucked, easily accommodating my prick deep. His mouth and throat rhythmically stroked my cock while his fingers found my butthole.

In no time, jerking and throbbing, I cried: "I'm cumming!"

Flint swallowed most of my load before sliding up my body to kiss me. Then he lay back, exhaling with a sigh of contentment, as I moved to suck his jaw-stretching shaft.

I reached around to his ass, massaging the cheeks before inserting spit-slicked fingers inside him. I was conscious of the beauty of his body. How much more beautiful his body was than mine. Even his face was more beautiful, less a mask.

"Jason, I'm gonna shoot! Ah, fuck…!" he gasped as he thrust all nine inches of his cock down my throat, my face buried in his thick nest of pubic hair. I gagged a bit as he began to spew but managed to swallow most of his cum. After I had cleaned off his dick, sucking and tonguing the folds of skin, Flint eagerly licked away the jism that had smeared my face.

He slid from my grasp and swaggered to his well-stocked bar. I watched the ripple of his legs, the pumped glutes, with a glimpse of genitals swinging between his thighs, the broad shoulders, the muscled neck, the mop of black wavy hair, all an erotic turn-on that re-charged my prick.

"Bloody Mary?" he asked.

I nodded and looked around at his scarlet-walled bedroom. The king-size four-poster bed I sat on with its intricately patterned red silk bedspread dominated the room. The walls were covered with drapes. On the back wall

was a glossy black wardrobe. On the wall at the foot of the bed was a life-size, provocative and sharply focused nude oil-portrait of Flint.

He placed my drink on the bedside table and leaned in to kiss me. I kissed him back, longing for him to fuck me.

But Flint wasn't in a hurry to get sexual again so soon. We kissed and canoodled as he questioned me about my past.

I was an orphan until I was shoved out on the street ten years ago, at age eighteen, with no marketable skills or assets except my well-formed body. I chuckled when I told him how soon I was attracting gentlemen willing to initiate me in my body's marketable potential. Flint nodded sympathetically.

"I guess I was an easy mark, grateful for any attention from those men," I told him. "But most of them were warm and often thoughtful."

"Sounds as though you were fortunate."

"Yeah, I learned a lot in a short space of time, enough to know that I craved sex with other men. And I was tough enough to hone a self-planned escort niche for myself, without any pimp cramping my style or skimming my earnings."

"Enterprising!"

"Lately, I've been thinking about things," I said quietly. "I've been trying to figure out what to do with my life. Maybe, you wind up doing what you're meant to do. Maybe your path chooses you, you don't choose it."

Flint caressed my cheek and kissed my eyelids.

"I'm sorry that I've avoided you all this time, Jason, but I had to make sure that you and I clicked in the ways necessary for a partnership to evolve. I had to satisfy myself that your commitment to me would be as serious as your commitment to yourself. Life with me is a truly life-altering experience."

"You mean...?" I stared at him, my face inches from his, hoping I was understanding him right.

"I hope you'll be my life partner."

I sat back, studying him. "You haven't told me anything about yourself."

"Now that's a long story -- one that I'm not sure you're ready for, yet. But we are more similar than I willing to let myself believe. We're both determined and totally ruthless when it suits our purpose."

I looked at him in astonishment and he grinned.

"When you're ready, I would like to fuck you. I do want to be inside you. Will you take me?"

An itch flared hot and bright inside me. I glanced down at his hard dick. I knew exactly what would scratch it best. "Please!" I nuzzled his ear. "Flint, I've been dreaming about this for a long time."

He tore open a condom and slid it onto his prick. Pushing my ankles over my head, he began to nibble my pucker, spitting and probing with his

tongue. He lubed his fingers and used them to open my sphincter. He found my prostate and stimulated it with his forefinger before he decided I was ready.

I cried out as he eased his huge pole into my chute. He pulled back a little before ramming it all the way up my ass.

"Oh yes!" I groaned, feeling his pubes up against my asscheeks. I closed my eyes as his lips found mine. My senses were overwhelmed with the smell and the taste of him.

He began to grind his cock in and out of me and my heels settled on the small of his back, pulling him into me. The bed creaked with his plowing my ass. His cock got harder and bigger as he worked my hole. His lips left mine and trailed along my jaw to find my neck.

He shoved himself all the way into me, his pubes scratching my ball sack. He raised his head and growled as spurts of hot cum flooded the rubber. My fuckchute clamped down on his tool. My whole body convulsed and my cock erupted on its own.

Flint fell on top of me. Still embedded to the hilt, he returned to sucking on my neck.

A moan rose to my lips but Flint was quick to swallow it, his firm lips locking over mine once more as my tongue rose to duel with his.

His schlong softened and slid with an audible plop from my ass. Flint fell to one side and vacuumed my torso with his mouth, sucking each of my nipples to erection. I felt his erection begin to grow against my thigh again. That damned itch flared up my butt again.

But I had to pee. I pushed him aside and pulled myself to the edge of the bed. I caught a glimpse of his mouth and the extra long incisors I'd not noticed before as I found my feet.

I glanced in the bathroom mirror, checking my neck for hickeys, and noticed a slight dribble of blood from a couple of small punctures, but no noticeable bruising. I touched them gingerly but felt no pain, only a pleasant throbbing.

When I came back from the bathroom, Flint pulled the condom off as he stood. He kissed my sweat-slicked hair as he passed me, the condom dangling from his hand. In the bathroom doorway, he dramatically turned and emptied the contents into his upturned mouth as his fingers squeezed out every drop. He grinned and smacked his lips.

I lay on the bed, light-headed but tingling all over with gratification. As I raised my arms and stretched, Flint returned. He lay beside me and tweaked each nipple.

Nibbling my ear, he murmured, "Before I spill the beans about myself, I'd like to know a little more about you, Jason."

I shrugged, unsure where he was leading.

"I need to know that you can go all the way with me. Can you share my heart and I yours? If you commit to me, there can't be any barriers between us."

I sat up and faced him. "I figure I won't get tired of what we just did for at least ten years," I told him grinning. "We're both gay, and we both escort…"

"You won't need to sell yourself again -- and I won't." He smiled, a hint of mischief there. "I intend to stroke your body until it feels strange to you when I'm not touching you," he said. "I'm going to give you pleasure and torment. I'll wake you with my tongue or my fingers or my voice telling you all the ways I'll have you when you ask it of me…"

His face lost all expression then. "I'm a vampire, Jason, born as a human in the long dead city of Ur in Sumer and bonded to my first vampire master at age twelve."

Certain that he was funning, I asked: "Do you mean that I'll be a vampire too?"

"Jason, it remains only for you to drink my blood for that to happen. In thirty-five hundred years you're the only one I truly wanted to share the future with." He snorted. "You're also strong and can help me allay my fears. Sometimes, I am still that boy of long ago -- needing a strong arm to hold me."

Still figuring this was some kind of joke, I asked: "Aren't vampires creatures of the night?"

"We are. You'll have to give up the day. You'll be a creature of the night forever. That's when we'll feed and play."

He kissed me tenderly on the lips, my nose and my eyelids. He licked and nuzzled my ear, then slid down to my neck. My body remembered what he could do to it; I cuddled against him and murmured: "Take me, Flint!"

He smiled at me. "It's time for you to fuck me," he said.

I knelt between his spread legs. His cock throbbed in my hand. I raised his legs and explored his manhole, with my fingers leading the way and my tongue in hot pursuit. My cock got harder and bigger as I slurped and probed his hole. He looked down at me and said: "Fuck me. Give it to me."

I reached for a condom but he shook his head. "Bareback's better, Jason. Just do it."

I lubed my cock in a flash and was soon pushing my tool deep into his butt. In no time I was pounding into him.

Flint brought his hand to his face, seeming to cover his mouth with it. He groaned and then raised his hand to me. "Drink," he said as the palm of his hand touched my lips.

My whole being was centered in my cock pumping in and out of his ass. I didn't think as my tongue reached out and began to lick his hand. It was wet and there was a slightly copper taste but, mostly, I tasted Flint as I lapped at his blood.

His ass clamped down suddenly on my tool. He raised his head and roared as his cum shot out of his bouncing prick.

I was balls deep inside him and started to flood him with my manjuice.

He scooped up the splatters of his cum with his fingers and sucked

hungrily. I slid out of him and lay down next to him, leaning over to snack on what remained. He rolled over on one elbow and looked at me.

He smiled and said: "Jason, you are one hot fuck! I reckon I need you to move in here with me. The sex is fantastic. I just hope you'll love me, too. It's been a very long time since I've had someone to share my life with."

The thought that I needed someone to love as well had begun to perk in my mind. The night's culmination of two years of lusting after this man had made me feel the huge emotional gap at the center of my life. I'd reached the point where I wanted a lover, not just a fuckbuddy.

"I need real commitment, Jason, for all time," Flint said, his voice almost strangled. "I have no desire to share my life with someone unless we become one. I think you and I can do it. Move in with me."

I'd always shied away from commitment before. I'd always been afraid of it before. Part of me wanted to get dressed and run at that moment. I didn't know much about him at all.

And I wanted to stay naked and cuddle with him forever.

"Maybe we can try it for a while," I agreed cautiously.

He grinned and reached out to touch the tip of my nose with his fingertip. "I've been watching you the past two years, Jason -- just like you've been watching me. We already know a lot about each other. If we work at it, we'll make it."

He cradled my face in his hands. "You belong to me," he said. "No one else. Only to me – and I to you."

He leaned towards me, his lips touching mine, then crushing them as his tongue sought to pry open my teeth. My arms went around his chest as I opened my mouth and surrendered to the tongue duel he demanded.

Later, I woke with a start and realized that I'd been dozing, safe in Flint's arms. He reached between us, parting my thighs, adjusting our positions. His erection leapt in my hands, the crown expanding from its sheath.

I shifted and raised my leg over his hip.

He made me feel complete. Our sex was the best I'd ever had. And it was now. I could go over my doubts tomorrow.

I looked over my shoulder at him as he plunged into me bareback. His eyes burned into mine. He flexed his pelvis, pulling from me slowly, letting me feel the whole length of him. He pushed back into me with the same slow movement.

It was too slow. I turned so that my side was pressed against his front, my heel dug into his butt, pulling him into me.

"Do you like the way I fit you?" he asked as he again buried himself in me.

He watched my face. He began to pull out again and my sphincter contracted hard, trying to keep him within me. I bit my lower lip as a bolt of

heat shot through me. His fingers became a fist riding my dick.

He began bucking and his tongue caressed my ear. I writhed within his embrace as his pace increased. He watched my eyes, wanting to wait for me.

Everything within me was rising, exploding. Releasing with such power that I could only gasp and hold onto him.

He pounded into me over and over. "You're mine," he growled as he stiffened, driving himself against me.

A great shudder rippled through him as he came. His grasp tightened around my cock before he collapsed against me. My muscles spasmed as we experienced each other's orgasms. I raised my head to nuzzle him and my fangs pierced his neck.

I couldn't believe that I'd nourished any qualms about our union. The promise of coupling like this dispelled all doubts.

Later, we lay in each other's arms and I watched the puncture wounds on his neck disappear. I still wasn't sure about this vampire stuff. I didn't feel any different than before -- except that I was one sexually satisfied had his. Tear, yes -- but puncture? Then, there was Flint's healing without so much as a trace of my bite.

Flint rose and began to dress, saying he'd drive me home. "You'd best sleep in tomorrow; my men will collect you in the evening."

I could barely keep my eyes open as he drove me home. My eyelids were drooping as I fell into my bed. I thought I felt his lips brush across my brow before I slipped into the sleep.

I awoke soon after sunset the next day and was surprised that I had slept so long. It took the first mug of coffee for me to remember the vampire stuff from the night before. There was something about vampires not being able to go out in the day. That worried me -- my job at the gym was a day job. And I wanted to keep it. While I made good money as an escort, I needed the job at the gym for credit card applications.

I wondered what else I was going to have to give up. Maybe Flint and his dick weren't worth the cost, after all.

I was pulled out of my doubts by a knock at my door. I quickly found a pair of cut-off sweats, put them on, and opened the door. To two good-looking young guys. Before my dick had a chance to get interested, they told me that Flint had sent them -- to move me.

I'd forgotten that he'd invited me to move in with him and that I'd accepted. Things suddenly were looking up. Maybe Flint and his dick *were* worth the cost, after all.

Within two hours I was settled and sorted -- and back in bed with Flint. I was fucking myself silly straddling him, his huge cock pounding up into my guts. I didn't have a doubt in my head. Flint and his dick were *definitely* worth a few momentary dislocations.

My cock skipped across his abs, happily leaking precum wherever it

landed on him. Orgasm rode every nerve in my body, threatening overload. "I'm close!" I gasped.

"Shoot it, Jason," he ordered. His hands rose to ride my thighs, his thumbs caressing my balls.

I threw my head back and howled as I rode Flint into the heat of forever. His fingers wrapped around my spurting prick and began to milk it.

Exhausted, I rolled off him. He pulled me to him, pressing his body against mine, and lay beside me.

"I'm going to have to work," I told him when I finally had my breath back. Some of my doubts were back, too.

"Why?"

I pulled back to look in his face. "I don't have a whole lot of money saved up and, now, I can't be a trainer at the gym." I frowned. "I guess I'm going to have to put a lot of effort into really building my escort business..."

He smiled and pulled me back to him. He held me there, caressing my cheek with one hand and brushing my hair with the fingers of the other. "Jason, did I ask you to live with me?" he asked quietly.

I nodded.

"And I asked you to be one with me, didn't I? To share my life with me?"

I nodded again.

"Then, don't worry about money. We have enough to live on comfortably forever."

I felt his dick begin to grow against mine.

"Think you could go for another round?" he asked.

I grinned and moved to straddle him.

Thresholds
Mark Apoapsis

Monday evening:

I was happy, though, that Neil was having dinner with me. I was shy about asking other guys to hang out with me. I'd met Neil last year, however. We were in the same line of work, and he enjoyed some of the same stuff I did: kayaking and beaches, hiking and camping. When I ran into him after the last session for the day, I asked if he had any dinner plans.

"No," he said. "Do you know of any good restaurants around here, Jon?"

"What are you in the mood for?"

"Pizza. I've been drooling over the picture on that ad in my room ever since I checked in."

"Pizza sounds great. Where is it?"

"The ad says they'll deliver to the hotel, so why don't we just do that?"

We went up to his room. Rooms, actually. The hotel was one where everybody gets a small suite, with a living room separate from the bedroom, so you don't have to put away your dirty socks before inviting associates over for a business meeting. Of course, Neil hadn't yet accumulated any dirty socks and didn't seem concerned with letting another guy see his untidy bedroom. He left the door open.

I was really tempted to order the Garlic Lover's Special. I'm one myself, but I hardly ever get a chance to indulge that pleasure with David. I agreed to the Deluxe Vegetarian Neil proposed.

It proved easier than I'd imagined to relax with Neil over pizza and beer. We both had an offbeat sense of humor. He liked morbid jokes, and I love irony -- so we made a great pair.

"Did you know that people's hair keeps growing after they die?" he asked from out of the blue. I think it was his way of testing me, seeing if I was easy to freak out.

"Tell me about it," I said. "Just try getting a corpse to go to the barber regularly." I was rewarded by Neil laughing.

His room was on the fourteenth floor and, when he stepped into the bathroom to rid himself of some of the beer, I asked if he'd mind if I went onto his balcony to admire the view. I wasn't about to stroll through another guy's bedroom without permission. Neil told me to feel free.

I'd already admired the view from my own room on the eighth floor, but that was the sunset, and there was something magical to me about nighttime: I associated it with romance and fun. The small balcony was basically part of one long ledge, separated from the neighboring balconies

by iron fences that I could have easily climbed over if I were reckless enough to risk my neck on that kind of thing.

The unseasonably warm night air felt great. I unbuttoned a couple of buttons on my shirt – I'd noticed Neil doing the same earlier, but hadn't followed his example – and when he emerged from the bathroom, I left the sliding glass door open as I rejoined him.

He wore a wedding band this year. I'd suspected he was straight, but the ring dashed my fantasies about a chummy weekend of camping or jogging along the beach. Last year, it could have been just us two guys; now he was unlikely to leave his wife behind. In another few years, he'd be saddled with children.

We had more beer, and it wasn't long before I made a trip to the bathroom and Neil made a second one. As soon as he shut the door, I heard a tapping on the sliding glass door. Puzzled, I walked into the bedroom. Silhouetted against the background of city lights, a male figure stood on the balcony. Slim, fairly tall, longish hair -- he looked familiar. No, it couldn't be ... My jaw dropped.

"Mind if I come in?" David asked.

I slid the door open the rest of the way and stepped out with him. "What the hell are you doing here?" I demanded -- but not very forcibly. I was happy to see him.

"It was only an hour's flight. Worth it, if only to see the dumbfounded look on your face, man."

"How'd you know where I was?"

"Once I found the hotel, I hung out until I saw you on the balcony here."

"You scared the shit out of me." I knew he enjoyed that.

"If you don't want me around, man, I can split," he said, and swung himself over the railing, dangling by both hands.

"Damn it!" I cried out, lunging forward to grab his wrist and the collar of his denim jacket, and haul him back up. I knew he was strong enough to pull himself up easily, but it still freaked me out whenever I see him pull a stunt like that.

When I had him standing back on the balcony, I clung to his shoulders for a minute, my heart pounding.

He threw his arm around my neck, and I knew he must be able to feel the pulse beating at the base of my throat. "I love getting your adrenaline flowing, Jon!"

"Now's not a good time. Let's go inside." I wondered if he knew it wasn't my room, or cared.

Neil came out of the bathroom right after we walked into the living room. I knew I should introduce them and apologize for inviting David into his room without asking, but I'm not very good at that kind of thing. And how could I explain David?

While I was dithering, David stuck out his hand and said, "Hi, I'm David. I'm a friend of Jon's."

Why ddid it always look so simple and natural when he did it? David was never awkward with strangers, even when it came to making suggestions that ought to be awkward. Thirty years of experience hadn't taught me that skill. I doubted fifty would.

Looking only slightly puzzled, Neil shook his hand and said, "I'm Neil. Nice to meet you, David. Have a seat and join us. Did you just get here?"

David took off his jacket, revealing the full glory of the bright colors that had been peeking out. It was one of his hand-tie-dyed T-shirts, and it looked older than he did: threadbare and ragged from hundreds of washings. He's got a big collection of them.

"Yeah. I -- like -- just flew in."

"Want some pizza?" Neil asked.

"No thanks, man."

"I guess they fed you on the flight," Neil said.

"Oh, I never eat…" David paused. "Peanuts," he finished with a hint of a smile.

"Have some beer, then."

David started to say something, but I shot him a don't-push-your-luck look and he said, "No thanks. I just dropped by for the company."

I wondered if Neil assumed David was here on business too. Maybe he thought David was my co-worker. After all, 'friend' doesn't imply the lack of some other relationship. But David didn't exactly look the part. With his youthful good looks and his tie-dye shirt, bell-bottom jeans, and sandals, he looked like he'd just stepped out of Woodstock. He could pass for 20, even 18. If his soft brown hair was brushing his shoulders, that would have completed the picture, but he'd recently gotten it cut to a more modern length.

Neil and I finished the beer and pizza as the three of us chatted amiably. Neil seemed completely charmed by David. My bladder was full to bursting again, so I reluctantly excused myself. I had flushed and had my hand on the doorknob when I heard heavy breathing and moaning through the door. Feel the knob, I quipped to myself. Is it hot? I would recognize David's moans anywhere, even muffled against flesh. Especially muffled against flesh. He was obviously doing to Neil … Well, not exactly what I wanted to do to him, but close enough.

But I couldn't just do whatever the hell I felt like. Not like David could. I'd seen it happen before; I shouldn't have been surprised.

I could picture exactly what was going on. The thought of my lover's mouth exploring the half-naked body of my straight friend was giving me a painful erection. I pulled my pants down and freed my cock. I used some hand lotion from the convenient little bottle provided by the hotel. If Neil noticed it later, I figured he'd understand. Once my breathing was normal, I threw the wad of tissues into the toilet and flushed again.

They were still going strong out there. I laughed softly to myself: David was right -- I did have too many thresholds, and they were all self-imposed. I forced myself to turn the doorknob. It wasn't like I was barging in without warning; they should have been clued in by the toilet flushing again. Resisting the urge to knock, I pushed open the bathroom door and stepped out.

They were doing it standing up, right where we'd been having pizza. Neil's shirt was lying in a heap on top of the beer bottles, and the T-shirt beneath had landed in one of the empty pizza boxes. His pants were around his ankles. His well-muscled chest had less hair than I'd pictured, but what little he had nicely fringed his pecs. His bulging biceps gave the illusion that he was stronger than David, whose head he held cradled against his chest with his right arm while his left hand massaged David's back through his tie-dyed shirt. Neil's wedding ring was clearly visible, but it'd taken more than a little piece of jewelry to scare off David. Unlike me.

Neil's head was thrown back, and his eyes were closed in pleasure. David was working his way down the wispy trail of hair that led into Neil's boxer shorts. David paused here and there to suck gently. He began to peel the soft gray boxers down until they hung up on Neil's erection.

"No," Neil said softly. He tried to push David away, to no effect. "No. Please."

David usually sleeps in his shorts, and today was no exception. I pulled them off, exposing his semi-erect cock. Pulling the covers off the bed so that his naked body lay completely exposed before me, I knelt down at the foot of the bed and began sucking on his big toe, holding his foot firmly in both hands. Then I worked my way up, ending up lightly licking at the bottom of his balls. He was stirring by this point, but still unable to resist. I ran my tongue up the underside of his half-erect shaft, eliciting a soft moan.

I took him firmly by the shoulders and flipped his unresisting body back onto his belly. I caressed his perfectly shaped ass, so white that I was sure he'd never once exposed it to the sun in his entire short life as a mortal. I massaged it, admiring how young and firm it still felt. I looked at the clock again: still plenty of time, if I skipped breakfast.

A minute later, I climbed naked onto his prone body, leaning my weight onto his shoulders. As always, he groaned sleepily as I entered him. I slid into him with the long practice of thousands of lazy mornings like this. He was still just as tight as if he'd never done this in his life. He groaned louder and clutched at the pillows, half awake now, with each decreasingly gentle thrust. I'd learned over the years that I didn't need to hold back; he never felt sore by the time he wakes up. I thrust deeper and deeper, wrapping my arms tightly around his chest, until I'd emptied my juices into him.

As I relaxed, I rubbed his nipple with one hand and ran the other up his arm until it found his hand. He grasped it, and fell back into a deep sleep.

It felt so good to lie there that I was in danger of falling back asleep myself. I managed to get up before that happened. Tucking the covers protectively around my sleeping lover's naked body, I went to get a quick shower and hoped there was time to grab a bowl of cereal downstairs.

I was a few minutes late for the session and wound up in a seat at the back. During the break, Neil came up to me at the coffee urn.

"I saved you a seat up front, if you'd like to join me."

"Gee, thanks," I said, a little surprised he was still speaking to me now that he'd had a chance to reflect, in the cold light of day, on what David had done to him last night.

"I missed you at breakfast this morning."

"I -- uh -- slept in." I felt the blood rushing to my face as I thought of how David and I had spent the night. "David woke me up when he came in, and -- um -- it was a while before I…"

"Say no more," Neil said with a knowing look, clapping me on the shoulder.

I would have said more – said anything! – to get him to keep touching me. When he turned away, I surreptitiously adjusted myself before following him to the seat he had saved for me.

Tuesday afternoon

Neil surprised me again by asking if I'd have lunch with him. I arranged to meet him in the lobby, explaining that I wanted to stash my laptop in my room. Really that was an excuse to check on David, make sure the Do Not Disturb sign was still on the door, and maybe have a word with the maid.

As I was getting my key out, two young guys emerged from the room next door. Really cute: one with black wavy hair, one blond, both with a little bit of a beard. I smiled at them and they smiled back. Reminding myself that they really were a decade younger than me and that our age difference would look a lot bigger to them than it did to me – and that they were probably straight – I tried not to fantasize about sawing through the wall separating our bedrooms. Anyway, I had my own guy who looked every bit as young as them. I went in to check on him.

Neil's only regret from the night before seem to be that he hadn't let David go further. He was clearly interested in pumping me for information about David. And I didn't mind being pumped, as long as it was Neil pumping me.

"I felt totally relaxed with him," he confided, "like the way I feel after an hour in a hot tub and a long massage. Know what I mean?"

"Tell me about it," I said.

"How long have you two been -- together?"

"Eleven years."

"Wow! Good for you. And you don't mind that we…"

"Not at all. I liked watching the two of you enjoy each other."

Neil grinned at me shyly. We continued our meal in silence. Then he said, "I never would have thought something -- something like that would feel so good." He paused thoughtfully. "I guess there must be some biochemical reason it feels good."

"Sure, just like there's a biochemical reason it feels good to have sex with your wife," I said. "Evolution saw to that. Does that make your feelings any less real?"

Neil blushed, and I kicked myself for being so blunt. And for reminding him that he was married.

When I came back with my laptop, Neil had defended my seat from all interlopers, and despite my gaffe he was as friendly as ever all afternoon, offering to bring me coffee when he got up to refill his own cup.

"What are you doing for dinner?" he asked at the close of business.

I stared at him stupidly.

"I'm sorry," he said. "You and David probably have plans. I'm not trying to…"

"No, that's okay," I assured him, surprised to see him being the one to feel ill at ease. "David won't expect to see me until after dinner."

"Well, great, then. If you're sure."

"Absolutely," I said. I'd have asked David first, but I'm not good at that, and I'd feel underhanded about being the one to ask, when my motives were so mixed up.

Tuesday evening

I took a second shower before dinner – not a cold one, as my better judgment suggested – and shampooed my hair this time. While shaving, I studied my towel-wrapped body critically in the mirror. Not nearly so young as when I'd met David. I wasn't quite as muscular as Neil, but I was in good shape. I spent a lot of time at the gym – and not just in the steam room ogling the towel-wrapped bodies of other men, though that did provide a good incentive.

The hot mist rising up behind me reminded me of that steam room. There was something so erotic about the way its tendrils curled around my bare shoulders…

I was so startled when cool hands suddenly grabbed my shoulders that I nicked myself. Damn! When would I ever learn? I hated it when he did that.

"You asshole!" I said, looking at him out of the corner of my eye. "Look what you made me do!"

"I'm looking, I'm looking!" David said.

In the mirror, I watched a crimson trickle run down my neck as I felt his hands caressing my chest. Even the smallest cut on the face bleeds so freely. When the trickle reached my chest, David turned me around – he was still naked, I saw – and slowly played his tongue up and down my chest, lapping up the precious drops. He worked his way up my chest and neck, finally licking at the source, which immediately closed up.

He was useful that way; sometimes when I nicked myself without his help, I'd wake him up and make him lap sleepily at my face until it was all better. Sure beat the hell out of sticking little pieces of toilet paper on my chin.

"I love the way you taste when you're startled," he whispered. "With or without the menthol." And he started nibbling at other, menthol-free areas of my skin. The towel around my waist dropped to the floor. He scooped me up in his arms and lifted my cock to his lips. He sucked me off expertly, knowing just when I was on the point of orgasm and stopping just short of climax. Finally, he pushed me past the point of no return, but just as I would have ejaculated, he bit down on my engorged cock and drained it of blood, making it instantly go limp.

Afterwards, even though I was running late for my dinner with Neil, I stayed to watch David shave. I touched his face to show him where he'd missed a spot. Thanks to that delay, I got to see the cute guys from next door waiting for the elevator. This time they gave me a funny look.

Wednesday morning

I hadn't had a chance to talk to Neil since last night. He'd eaten with a bunch of other people; he'd invited me to join them, but I didn't feel comfortable horning in. Then we got separated and didn't get seats near each other for the afternoon session. I decided to take a break in the mid-afternoon. The topic was something of little interest to me, and I didn't get to sit next to Neil. And I wanted to get David back for sneaking up on me while I was shaving last night.

In the bedroom, I opened the curtain ever so slightly, and a narrow beam of indirect daylight poured across the carpet. David had been sleeping on his back with the covers pulled about halfway up his chest. Now he'd rolled over onto his side, leaving his naked back exposed to me. I stripped to the waist myself, then crept over and pulled the covers down, got my arms under him and rolled him onto his back. He resisted weakly in his sleep, but I lifted him off the bed and moved him to the floor, with his feet next to the shaft of sunlight. When he still didn't wake up, I picked up my T-shirt, which I'd tossed on the floor, and held it up so that it reflected a little sunlight onto his body.

He groaned, and his eyes opened. "You wouldn't!" he whispered hoarsely. But I knew he relished being totally at my mercy.

Grinning, I grabbed his bare feet and dragged him across the carpet. He gasped as the stripe of light played up his legs. When it had passed harmlessly over his shorts and suddenly hit his belly, he whimpered.

I dragged him a little further and watched him squirm as the light fell across his chest. I sat him up, got behind him and wrapped my arms around his chest, sometimes shielding him with my arms, sometimes allowing the beam to hit his skin, just to feel the shiver running through his body. His chest was slowly getting a pink stripe across it, as though I'd whipped him with a wet towel. I knew from experience that this would disappear within an hour.

When I decided he was pink enough, I dragged him out of the sunbeam and checked my watch. I still had plenty of time to play before I needed to go back downstairs. And there were endless possibilities. Things I hadn't done to him in years.

Wednesday evening

Neil and I had dinner plans, so I tried to catch him on his way out of the conference room. When it was clear that I'd missed him, I went to his room, but there was no answer to my knock. I waited a while, then finally went back to my room to see if he'd left a message.

As soon as I walked in, I heard soft, suggestive sounds coming from my bedroom. David rarely brings anyone home, but he'd clearly brought someone to our room.

They hadn't bothered to shut the bedroom door. I almost didn't enter anyway, but I thought I recognized the other set of moans.

Sure enough, it was Neil. David had him pinned to the wall, holding the bigger man's wrists over his head with one hand while his mouth wandered all over his torso. Neil's bare feet were actually a few inches above the carpet. David had him completely naked this time, and I had a nice view of Neil's exposed armpits, his taut stomach, and his half-limp cock dangling over his balls. With his free hand, David was stroking Neil's crotch.

David had taken off his own shirt and sandals, or maybe he'd allowed Neil to remove them.

"I take it you're not quite ready for dinner yet, Neil?" I said to announce myself.

"Those fascist dress codes," David agreed, without turning around. "No shoes, no shirt, no shorts, no service."

Neil smiled sheepishly at me. "David is having dinner first. On me."

"But I saved room for a second course," David added.

"May I take your order?" I joked.

"Far out." David looked over his shoulder, his hazel eyes burning seductively into mine. "Strip," he ordered.

I was shy doing it in front of Neil, but when David talked that way I could never resist. They both watched me take off my shirt and drop my

pants. I was going to at least leave my shorts on, but David stared at me until I took them off and stood naked before my friend and my lover.

David used his free hand to pin my wrists to the wall. Now Neil and I were strung up like two naked prisoners in a dungeon. David alternated his attentions between us, but it hardly mattered; I got off on feeling Neil's reactions to my lover's mouth all over his body at least as much as I enjoyed the familiar sensation of it exploring my own body.

I loved the wonderful lazy feeling that slowly spread through my limbs and made me want to lie there all day while David did whatever he wanted to me. Although he might be a creature of the night, he affected me like a day on a warm sunny beach. Beside me, Neil was experiencing the same thing, until we were both putty in his hands. David finished by teasing each of our cocks with his tongue. Neil didn't protest.

David lay us on the carpet, with Neil's face on my chest and his arms trapped under my back, while he bit into Neil's ass cheeks. As he wriggled in response, I had to hold Neil's head tightly against my chest to keep his rough cheek from rubbing my nipples raw.

Just when I thought David was done with us, he lay us side by side and bit me beneath the collar bone, letting the blood puddle, then bit Neil on the forearm and held his arm over me.

Neil and I lazily watched our blood mingle on my chest. "Guess we're blood brothers now," Neil murmured. He put his arm around my bare shoulders and leaned against me a little to watch David lapping up our blood.

All this intimacy was having an effect on me, on top of the usual effect of David's attentions. I was used to David bringing me to the edge, and then half the time leaving me to satisfy my own needs once he'd satisfied his own. With his casual gesture of affection, Neil was teasing me the same way without meaning to. And I wasn't sure that Neil would be comfortable with my getting myself off while he was beside me. At least David enjoyed it when I shot my load over his chest.

I went so far as to rest my hand on Neil's hairy thigh, my fingertips just inches away from his balls. He didn't flinch. I watched his bare chest rise and fall. He was breathing deeply with some suppressed emotion.

"It looks like your friend could use a little help, there, Jon. Why don't you get him off?"

I felt Neil tense a little, and he turned his face away.

I said, "I'm not sure that would be a good idea, David."

"What's your problem, man? You know he wants it."

"I need him to say so."

But Neil wouldn't meet my eyes. I knew he wanted a hand job, even a blow job. But he couldn't bring himself to ask for it, and I couldn't bring myself to touch his cock if he didn't.

"What's the big deal?" David demanded. "He digs you. Why can't you just move your hand a few inches?"

"Why couldn't you go to that dance with me last month?" I countered.

"Just not my scene. They shouldn't hold those things in churches. Religion is the opiate of the masses, man."

"Yeah, right," I said. "And why can't you cross someone's threshold until they invite you?"

"OK, I guess that was a cop-out. But I have an excuse. What's your hang-up, man?"

I couldn't explain myself, any more than David could. But I knew how much I enjoyed feeling Neil relax against me, as he realized I wasn't going to violate his boundaries.

Thursday, late morning

The next day, Neil was warmer than ever to me. He invited me to lunch, just the two of us. I agreed, and arranged to meet him in the lobby after I dropped off my laptop and checked on David.

As soon as I'd let myself into the room, I knew there was something wrong.

I dropped my laptop on the floor and rushed to the bedroom door, which was still closed. I opened it to find my worst nightmare realized: bright sunlight was spilling into the room from the partially opened curtain. Illuminating the bed. It was empty, which scared me even more. For the split second it took me to see the form crumpled on the floor on the near side of the bed.

I rushed over to David. He was curled up tightly, in the scant shadow cast by the bed, hiding his face. His naked back was bright red and hot to the touch. I heard him whimpering softly from the pain.

Cursing under my breath, I went to close the curtains. I noticed that the sliding glass door was open then. I'd left it unlocked so that David could come and go that way if he wanted to, but neither of us was stupid enough to leave it open. There was too much danger of the curtains billowing. I tried to imagine the maid having come in, walking right past a person on the bed, opening the curtains, and fleeing when the screaming started. That scenario didn't make a whole lot of sense. But neither did the idea of someone entering from outside. We were on the eighth floor.

I told myself the how of it didn't matter. What mattered was that David was badly hurt. I slid the door closed and locked it, then closed the curtains carefully.

I lifted David back onto the bed as gently as possible, but he still cried out in pain. I laid him out on his back and gasped when I saw the true extent of the damage. His chest, which had gotten the full brunt of the sunlight, was badly burned: raw and red and blistered all over. There was a blackened streak slashing across his chest, bordered by grayish flakes of skin that were peeling off – like a bad sunburn, except that these flakes turned to dust at a touch.

I imagined how close he had come to his whole body turning to dust like that and began to shake.

I quickly pulled myself together, telling myself I wouldn't do David any good by having a breakdown.

"You're gonna be all right," I whispered to him. I had no idea whether that was true, but it was the first thing that came to mind.

At least I knew what I could do to help, if he wasn't beyond help. I took off my long-sleeved shirt, leaving on my T-shirt. Lying down on my side, I gently draped my arm across his face, with the soft flesh of the crook of my arm against his lips.

For a few seconds, nothing happened, and I started to panic. Then I felt his dry, chapped lips working at my skin. Then his teeth. It hurt much more than usual – but not half as bad as seeing him like this did.

I was slipped into a pleasant torpor, only to be jolted out of it by the shrill ringing of the telephone. I rolled over and answered the phone, vaguely aware that my arm was still bleeding.

"Hey. It's Neil. I'm in the lobby. What's keeping you?"

I sat up slowly, and black spots swam before my eyes. I looked down at David, who was staring up at me.

"More?" he whispered hopefully. "Please?"

I forced myself to look away from those pleading eyes. "Would you mind coming up here, Neil?"

"Why? Is something wrong?"

"Yeah."

"I'll be right up," he said decisively.

My arm was still bleeding, so I pulled off my T-shirt and tied it around my elbow. I swung my feet over the bed, waited until the clouds of black spots cleared up again, then tried to stand up. It took me two tries, but I managed to get on my feet, and I was leaning against the front door when the knock came.

Neil took one look at my blood-stained makeshift bandage and asked, "Did something happen to David?"

I nodded and started to explain, but my vision faded out, and the next thing I knew, I was leaning heavily into Neil, who was holding me up, his hands on my bare back and biceps. He slung my good arm over his shoulders and half followed, half carried me into the bedroom.

"Holy shit!" He ducked out from under my arm and bent over David. "What happened?"

"The curtains and the sliding glass door were open," I explained. "I don't know how they got that way."

"Heavy," David whispered.

"He says the situation is serious," I translated.

Without a word, Neil stripped down to his T-shirt and offered David his bare arm. David sucked on it gratefully.

"I wish we had a blood pressure cuff," I said after a minute. "Do you mind if I monitor your pulse, Neil?"

"Go right ahead, buddy. Thanks."

I took his free wrist and felt his strong pulse under my thumb, and stared into his eyes. I would have liked to lay my head on his chest and listened to his heartbeat, but I couldn't justify going that far.

After a few minutes, I noticed Neil's eyes losing their focus and his pulse getting weaker and more rapid. "Lunchtime's over, guys," I told them.

When Neil didn't move and David continued sucking thirstily, I pulled at Neil's arm. He resisted weakly.

I got the bleeding stopped by pressing a wad of tissues against his arm for a few minutes.

"C'mon," I told Neil. "We all need to rest for a while." I helped him to his feet and we supported each other into the other room, like a couple of drinking buddies staggering home together.

Neil made me sit down on the couch while he got us each a glass of water. "I guess lunch will have to be room service," he said.

"Yeah. Let's rest a few minutes first."

"Yeah."

"Sometimes," I reminisced as we sat together, "David would suck me slowly for an hour and then bring me coffee and juice and cookies in bed."

"Sort of like the Red Cross, huh?"

"So he tells me. I wouldn't know."

We did call for room service, and we each ordered a hearty lunch. Neil answered the door. I still didn't feel like putting a shirt on.

After lunch, I checked on David, who seemed to be resting comfortably and actually looked a little better. We sat down on the couch together to rest some more. Neil wound up falling asleep on my shoulder.

I must have fallen asleep myself, because the next thing I knew, I was awakened by a thud. Neil had fallen to his hands and knees on his way back to me.

"Please tell me you didn't give him another drink without me there to make sure he didn't suck you dry."

"He's feeling more himself now. He stopped on his own. Even licked the wound closed." He held up his arm, which was free of any obvious sign he'd been bitten.

"Is he rational now?"

"Well, he's a little delirious, I think. He said something about seeing a cat on the balcony."

I held out my hand and helped him up onto the couch with me. "You should have woken me. Don't do anything stupid, okay?"

"I just don't want him to die," Neil said, his voice breaking.

I was already holding onto his shoulders. I pulled him close, and we hugged each other so tightly I could feel his heart working to pump whatever blood he had held back. The thin cotton of his T-shirt was all that

separated my skin from his. But I was thinking mostly about David, and wept softly at the thought I might lose him. Neil stroked my hair and pressed his lips against my cheek.

We held each other for a long time. My lips were inches from Neil's ear, and there were a lot of things I would have liked to whisper to him. "It feels good to hold you." "I'm worried about you." "I wish I could get even closer to you." "I like the way you smell." But I could no more force any of those words past my lips than David could force his way into a man's room uninvited. I had so many feelings for Neil that I didn't dare expose to the light of day.

After a while I reluctantly disengaged myself from my friend's arms and went to check on my lover. He looked better, like a man recovering from a bad sunburn. His eyes raked hungrily over my bare torso and then fixated even more hungrily at the bloody T-shirt I still had wrapped around my arm. I untied it and pulled it off, and lay down beside him. When I arose several minutes later, my skin was clean and unbroken after a thorough licking, though the room spun around me as I stood up.

After dinner – room service again – we helped David into the bathroom and laid him down in the tub, but left the drain open and turned on the shower as we gently scrubbed him with a washcloth. He had begun to itch all over, a sign that his skin was healing and trying to shed the layer of dead skin. Or "undead skin," as Neil insisted on calling it. Neil's T-shirt got soaked, and he peeled it off.

When we were done, David was shiny and pink, with tender new skin replacing the sunburned areas. But he was still weak as a kitten, and I could count his ribs. We carried him back to bed, and Neil and I lay down on either side and took turns holding David's head against our chests and letting him sink his teeth into muscle tissue and sip slowly.

He seemed lucid, so I asked him if he remembered what had happened to him.

"Like I said before, I saw a dude on the balcony. Young guy. Thin. Blond. Scraggly beard."

"He's staying in the room next door," I said, nodding in that direction.

Neil looked angrier than I'd ever seen him. "Someone did this on purpose?"

"Not necessarily," David said weakly. "He looked surprised."

"He'll pay for this, whoever he is. Let's pay a visit to your neighbor, Jon."

"Neighbors," I corrected. "There are two guys next door."

"So? There are two of us. We can take 'em."

"We're weak with blood loss," I argued.

"They'll be too, once we get done with them," he growled pushing himself into a sitting position on the bed. "One way or the other." Using the wall for support, he got to his feet.

He staggered out. I had no choice but to follow him, or he'd have taken on both guys himself. Weak as he was, he'd surely wind up locked in the hotel room at the tender mercies of the men who had hurt David.

The blond answered the door. Neil slammed his shoulder into it, knocking him down. He picked him up by his shirt front and shook him angrily. "What were you doing trying to sneak in my friends' window?"

The kid looked scared. He couldn't have been more than 19 or 20. He managed to kick Neil's feet out from under him. Neil fell to his hands and knees. When he started to climb to his feet, looking woozy. The younger man was about to punch him in the stomach, but I grabbed his arm, then wrenched him into a full nelson. Neil recovered and socked him in the jaw. He went limp in my arms. I unlocked my hands from behind his neck and supported him by his armpits.

Neil was still in a rage. He punched the unconscious man in the stomach.

"Hey!" I protested. "Was that necessary?"

"We need to teach him a lesson. He damn near killed David." He grabbed the guy away from me by his shirt again and flung him to the ground, then glared at him as if deciding whether to wait for him to wake up before kicking him in the ribs.

"I know, but beating him up won't solve anything."

"What are you, a pacifist?"

"Not really. But David is."

"Then at the least we should do is strip him naked, carry him back to your room, and string him up by his ankles for David to drain at his leisure."

"I guess I can go along with that."

"Good." He knelt down and ripped the unconscious kid's shirt open, revealing a smooth chest, and began fumbling with his belt.

"Can I come in?" David asked. He was standing outside the door, which we'd left wide open. Fully dressed and looking fit. Was it nighttime already?

"Is this the guy you saw?" I pointed to the kid, who was beginning to stir.

"Yeah."

Neil growled and lashed out at the guy's bare chest with the belt in his hands.

"Neil!" David said, shocked. "Cool it!"

"Neil," I said, laying my hand on my friend's shoulder. He pushed me away and pulled the younger man's pants down to his knees.

"What are you doing?" David asked.

Neil grabbed the guy by the balls through his briefs. "What were you doing trying to get in the room next door?"

"First ask him where his friend is," I suggested. The bedroom and bathroom doors were open; I walked over and glanced around to make sure we weren't about to be ambushed.

"Leave him alone, guys!" David pleaded.

"I don't know where he is," the kid mumbled groggily. Then he cried out; Neil must have squeezed. "I left him down in the bar trying to pick up some girl. Please, don't hurt him! He didn't do anything. It was all my idea."

"What was?" Neil demanded.

"To sneak a web cam next door. We had a bet. We heard some wild sex going on last night. I thought it sounded like two guys."

"Well, you were wrong. About the sex part."

I guess Neil still didn't think of getting his blood sucked by David as 'real' sex. I wondered where he drew the line. And whether he'd let me approach it.

"And you were going to record us?" Neil asked, angrily. He stuck his hand up the leg hole in the briefs to get a better grip, and squeezed until the guy screamed.

"Get in here, David!" I said.

Almost faster than I could follow, David was in the room and holding Neil's arms pinned to his sides. Nice to see he had some of his strength back.

"Mellow out, dude!" He looked down at the kid, who was edging away and pulling up his pants. "What's your name, man?" he asked gently.

"K -- Kevin," the kid stammered. He tried to rebutton his shirt but found that the buttons were all gone.

"I'm David, and my bro here is Neil. He's flipping out because you almost killed me today."

"What? All I did was open your balcony door. I didn't even come in! I didn't mean to hurt anybody!"

"I know, man." He turned to me. "Would you two mind splitting for a while? I need to rap with Kevin."

Kevin probably didn't know that rapping was something white boys could do, but he seemed less threatened by David than by us.

"Are you sure you're all right now?" I asked.

"Thanks to you two, yeah. Maybe you should both get some sleep. Neil, can Jon crash in your room? Our sheets are kinda gross after this afternoon."

Neil readily agree and I gratefully accepted. When we left, David was sitting with Kevin on the couch, nuzzling his neck, and Kevin's shirt was spread wide open again. I wished I knew how he did that, so I could copy him.

"I wonder if the sofa makes into a bed," I said.

"I'm too tired to deal with that. C'mon, the bed's plenty big enough for us both." Neil put an arm around my shoulder and propelled me into the bedroom as if I couldn't make it across the threshold under my own steam. As if I were David. Or a virgin bride.

He was right about the bed, of course. It was king-sized. We could both sleep on it without touching. Neil stripped to his shorts without another word, and I followed his example.

"You're going to fall off the edge like that," he observed, once we were under the covers. "I don't bite."

I rolled toward him. "Neither do I."

He scooted close to me and rested his chin on my shoulder. "I know," he said, sounding almost disappointed. His mouth was so close that I could feel his warm breath on my neck. Daringly, I reached out and brushed my fingertips against his chest hair, not quite touching his skin.

"You have no desire to suck out my vital fluids."

"Oh, I wouldn't say that," I said lightly, but my heart was pounding.

"Trouble is, my wife has no such desire, either."

"If you'd asked me..."

He laughed and grabbed my head, pinning it against his chest, tousling my hair playfully. "You need a shave, buddy."

"So do you."

"But I'm not the one who's gonna be sucking you off."

He meant it!

"You don't fool me," I scoffed. "You like a little pain with your pleasure." Besides, I was not going to let him close his eyes and pretend I was his wife. I started rasping my way toward his crotch. He moaned; Neil's bites had left his chest more sensitive than usual. "You have two choices: my chin, or my tongue, on the way down."

"Tongue!" he whispered.

I licked my way down, using the trail of hair as my guide. By the time I slipped his shorts off, he was fully erect. I repositioned myself between his legs so my tongue could get at the sensitive underside. He wriggled so much I had to rest my forearms on his thighs to hold him down. When I finally took him in my mouth, he gasped so loudly that I wondered if anyone had ever done this for him before.

"Can I shoot in your mouth?" he asked in a mewl a few minutes later.

I lifted off of him and looked up at his face. "If you do that, I swear I'm gonna rub my cheek right against your balls."

As I expected, he made no attempt to warn me when he was getting close. After swallowing every drop of Neil's load, I made good on my threat. He let me torment him for a minute or two, and when he couldn't take any more, he grabbed me by the armpits and dragged me back to a face-to-face position, then wrestled me until I was underneath him. We fell asleep that way, wrapped in each other's arms with Neil's weight on top of me.

We slept a few hours, but I woke up before dawn. I couldn't sleep knowing that David was with a guy who had almost killed him. I got up, and Neil woke up when I rolled him off me. He insisted on coming down with me.

David was still next door, and let us in. He had Kevin and his dark-haired buddy totally naked, arranged on the carpet in a very compromising position. They looked to be maybe half-conscious as they held each other's hard dicks.

David held up a tiny web cam. "Either of you computer-heads know how to work this thing?" he asked. Neil volunteered. "All right, dude! You shoot and I direct," he said handing the web cam to Neil.

"Have fun?" David asked in a whisper as he moved beside me. I nodded. "We'll have to make sure the dude knows he has a standing invitation at our place whenever he can make to the east..." He studied me for a moment before shaking his head. "I'll make sure he knows it. If I leave it up to you, we probably won't ever see him again."

Night Friends
Mark Wildyr

Let's get a couple of things straight, okay? I'm smart, good-looking, sexy as hell -- and straight!

Did you get that? I'm a man -- all man, all five feet eleven inches, one hundred seventy pounds of me.

But I've got this funny quirk. I carry a hell of a package, and I get a kick out of teasing the fags with it. So, you're apt to find me in a gay bar letting them drool -- and even paw a little. Just by spreading my legs at a table I've outed so many queers that when they refer me as an 'outie,' they don't mean my belly button.

I'm as comfortable in a queer joint as any of the faggots there. Everybody in the place knows he's not going to get anything except a grope or two. I could go home with anyone in the joint, but I don't -- although I've met up with a couple of out-of-towners after leaving the club on two or three occasions.

Getting your cock sucked isn't a big deal. Kinda enjoyed it to tell the truth, but I'd never admit it to another soul if my life depended on it. The one time I fucked butt I kinda got into it, but a woman's pussy seems more natural. Strange -- a girl's mouth isn't made to suck a big cock, and a guy's butt's not made to take a hard one up it. Personal opinion only.

There's one bar in this town called the Low Brow where the line blurs between straight and gay. Patrons of both persuasions frequent the place, and it's sorta become a regular for me. I can go in, claim a vacant booth, lean back, stretch my legs, and before you can say jack-shit, there's somebody on either side of me and a couple of brews on the table. My money's no good there -- not as long as I let them feel me up.

The waitress had my mug and was setting it down on the table of my usual booth almost before I could get comfy. She smiled a quick one and jerked her head towards what was probably an old queen waving from the bar. "I'll be damned!" she groaned and beer sloshed onto the table.

I followed her gaze into the dark corner beyond the bar. "Who?"

"Antonescu. I thought he'd gone for good a year ago."

"Is he trouble?" I could only make out an outline of a man in the corner.

"Naw. He just sucks the life out of any party -- he's a damn vampire."

I watched her jiggle her hips away and knew whoever she'd seen was on his way over.

"Ariel Antonescu," a tall, slim -- refined -- man announced, holding out a manicured hand.

I stumbled to my feet. "Chad Quarles," I said, accepting a cool, steely shake. I wondered how this Ariel Antonescu had managed to reach me so fast.

"May I join you for a few moments?" he asked, a slight accent evident. I'm no good at accents, so I had no idea where it originated.

"Sure. Free country," I told him, taking his measure as he pulled out a chair. Early thirties, probably about five years over my own twenty-eight, a 'look-down-the-nose' kind of haughty elegance, an ethereal handsomeness that was nothing like the let-me-run-my-hand-through-your-hair-you-good-looking-stud look everyone said I projected. But he was no porcelain doll; there was a suggestion of power about him.

"Thank you," he settled himself and waved to the waitress, making a circle with his forefinger towards the table. She nodded her understanding and moved off to fill his order.

The man flat wore me out! He sat with me for an hour, keeping a steady supply of beer flowing while we talked about everything and nothing. He didn't ask one single personal question beyond my opinion on things, and I realized later that he provided no details of his background. But talk, we did! About city, state, national, and world affairs. About the merits of hounds over setters, a pump shotgun over an automatic, about every damned thing on earth.

At last, he rose, thanked me for the company, and then paused. "You're different," he said quietly. The way he said it wasn't a come-on, a criticism, or even a compliment. It was just a statement that defied contradiction. "I think we shall become very good friends." With that, he walked towards the men's room while I leaned back in my chair, exhausted.

Two of the younger queers scooted over and had a field day feeling my cock and balls because I was too worn out to put a rein on them. When one started working on my zipper, I roused enough to get out of the place, staggering as I made for my car. I never staggered, even when I was blasted on my ass!

The next morning I was my old self again. Being a real estate broker gave me an opportunity to move about as I pleased and kept me in enough coins to pursue the role of a carefree eligible bachelor. Frankly, I enjoyed my life. During that week I sold a good property, had a Friday night date, and fucked her half the night. By Saturday, I was again ready for the Low Brow.

I didn't realize that I was looking for Antonescu until I saw him sitting alone in the dark corner of the lounge. It threw me for a minute when I saw that all the cigarette smoke in the room was slowly collecting in his remote corner, but I drifted with the smoke right to his table.

He stood and shook my hand. "Mr. Quarles, so nice to see you again," he said in his well-modulated voice. He gave the 'Qu' a little flip so that my name almost came out 'Karls.'

"Call me Chad. Everybody does."

"Antonescu," he said, giving me to believe that's how he preferred to be addressed.

We settled down to comfortable patter like anyone else on a Saturday night in a dive filled with working guys and queers. He monopolized the conversation, but he kept it so interesting that I didn't notice. The guy was a whiz at history. He had his own spin on things. Sorta quirky. No, that's not right; it was more like he were relating the events as a bystander.

Usually, I claimed my table near the bar and waited for the procession of supplicants to come by paying homage to my package, each wanting to touch it like they were fingering the Blarney stone. I spent the entire evening at Antonescu's table tucked into a rear corner. Nobody came near us. Not only that, by midnight, I was done in, whipped, totally enervated. Antonescu, apparently saw my distress and expressed concern.

"Think I'll pack it in early tonight," I told him, puzzled over my condition. I wasn't sick or anything, just drained.

"I'm concerned for you, Chad," he said, syllables accented a little differently. "Are you certain you are not ill?"

"Naw," I waved a nerveless hand that flopped a little like it was drunk. But I wasn't drunk.

"Let me help you to your car," he said, his voice soft.

"Naw, I'll be all right," I mumbled.

"I insist," he said, clasping my upper arm in an amazingly strong grip.

"Don't understand..." I mumbled by way of protest as we exited the place. I heard the sudden silence behind us broken by a rush of excited conversation before the door closed. Shit! They'd all think we went home together!

"I would be glad to drive you home," he offered.

I experienced a sudden glow of friendship for this strange, attractive man. "Naw. I'm feeling better already -- do me a favor..." I said, peering into eyes that were mere pinpoints in the darkness. "Go back inside and have a beer, will you?"

He threw back his head and gave a laugh. "I will, my friend. I will protect your reputation if you will do one thing for me in return."

"What's that?" I asked, experiencing something foreign to me as I took in his fine, patrician features. What the shit? Was I interested in this guy?

"I understand you are a realtor. I am considering buying a home. There is one in particular I am interested in seeing. According to the sign, it is a multiple listing, so I would like you to show it to me."

"Sure. Name the time and place."

He gave me the address and suggested Wednesday night.

I frowned at him. "At night?"

"Is the time an inconvenience?"

"No. It's okay. You want me to pick you up?"

"Meeting me there would be satisfactory."

"Wednesday night at eight it is!" I repeated the address to his satisfaction and kicked over the motor.

"Now," he said with a trace of a smile in his voice, "I shall return to the lounge and rescue your reputation."

I spent an inordinate amount of time Sunday thinking about Ariel Antonescu, wondering what was so different about the man. Okay, so he was handsome and educated and charming. So was the guy in the office next door to me, but I didn't spend hours thinking about him and wondering who he really was.

Maybe it was the air of mystery around Antonescu. The thing that confounded the hell out of me was that by the time I reached that conclusion I was nursing a hard-on. Deciding I was too lazy to go scare up a date, I spread my legs and took out my cock. I was proud of old Buster. He was big and stout and served me well when it counted. Many a girl had made a fuss over the big buy.

Closing my eyes and summoning a picture of the last one I'd fucked, I began to pump it. With my other hand, I touched all my hot places, the belly right above my cock, my full, wrinkled sac, the flesh behind my balls. As I got close to take-off point, I moved to my nipples, rolling first one and then the other between my fingers until the little dickens were sore. All of a sudden my nerve ends discharged, and I struck a gusher.

Cum pumped into the air and splashed back onto my body, coating me in the slick, whitish fluid. I finished the orgasm with short, spastic jerks, and rested with my gooey hand around my rapidly collapsing cock and an arm across my eyes.

As I lay panting, I realized that Antonescu had popped into my mind just before I shot my balls. Weird! I spent the rest of the day catching some Z's and getting things ready for work.

Monday was crazy, and Tuesday wasn't much better. I spent Wednesday morning closing on a nice four bedroom, three bath, and didn't get around to looking up the listing for the place he wanted until almost closing time. A quick call to the listing agent confirmed it was still on the market and gave me a realistic idea of the owners' expectations.

There were no cars in evidence when I pulled up before the large adobe, the darkness broken by only a small electric lantern atop a lamppost in the front yard. The house was isolated, and the closest street light was two blocks away.

Deciding to take a quick look, I closed and locked the car and strolled up the curved flagstone walk. As I gained the porch, all my senses kicked in.

A presence hovered near. My mouth went dry, my skin prickled. I'm not a jumpy man, but sweat trickled down my back even as my blood turned to icicles.

"I hope I did not startle you," came the rich, cultured voice. "I arrived early and was enjoying the night view. That's one of the things I like about this property."

I relaxed. "Didn't know you were here. Didn't see a car."

His hand flickered in the moonlight. "I parked down the road a bit. I wanted to see what lay beyond the house."

"Not much, frankly."

"Yes," he said. "Another thing in its favor. May we go inside now?"

Once we were inside. Antonescu donned a heavily smoked, wrap-around pair of shades and made a slow, methodical round of each of the rooms.

Within thirty minutes, he turned to face me. "I like it. It will serve me nicely. Do you think an offer of three hundred thousand would be accepted?"

"I don't know," I answered frankly. "The listing agent says they're motivated."

"Motivated," he repeated softly. "That means they are anxious to sell. Perhaps I should lower the offer."

"Motivated, not crazy," I said quickly. It's listed at three hundred fifty and is worth every nickel."

"I think I shall walk through once again," he announced.

I tagged along behind him, noticing that he removed the shades, but did not turn on the lights we had carefully snapped off as we left each room. The darkness didn't seem to bother him as he absently noted that this or that piece of furniture would fit here. When he reached the master bedroom, I hesitated at the door, reluctant to enter for some reason.

Antonescu halted in the middle of the room and turned to face me. He was swaddled in darkness, the pupils of his eyes picking up errant shards of light and reflecting them back at me. He stood waiting silently.

I had an unreasonable urge to flee, but my feet were rooted to the carpet. I swallowed hard as something swirled around me in the darkness, caressing my body and gently propelling me into the room. My shroud was warm and comforting, and in some manner emanated from the dark, still form standing in the room.

Puzzled by my helplessness, uncertain of what I wanted, I moved to him, reaching a tentative hand to his breast. The moment my hand touched the soft, expensive suede of his jacket, I suffered a desire so intense that my sudden erection threatened to burst the seams of my trousers.

Strong, gentle hands pulled me into his embrace. His lips brushed my neck before they moved to my jaw, my cheek, then to my mouth. The intensity of his kiss robbed me of all strength. I slipped to the floor, his arms easing my fall. He lay beside me, long, tapered fingers exploring my face.

"You are truly a handsome man," he whispered. "So desirable. So male -- yet, so vulnerable." He bent to kiss me again while his hands loosened

my shirt, my trousers. As if in a trance, I lifted my hips as he shoved my clothing to my knees.

It was as if no one had ever handled me before. His touch sent sparks throughout my body. He moved down my torso, exciting every part of me as he went. My nipples strained for his mouth. It seemed as if his tongue washed my sternum, not merely the skin that covered it. My navel fluttered to his moist touch. Then he was in my pubic bush, twining his tongue in the hair, emitting small grunts of pleasure. My sac drew up at his caress, eager to deliver its load.

I made to push him away, but his mouth closed over the pulsing, dripping tip of my impatient cock, robbing me of my will. I was his, and he knew it. Slowly, inch by inch, he swallowed my cock, drawing the entire length into his throat. Nobody had been able to take it all before.

His hands toyed with my balls and thighs, my chest and belly as he moved his head up and down on me. I sprawled across the carpet, helpless before my desire -- *his* desire. My moment arrived. Cum spewed up out of me, filling his mouth, his throat. Never had I cum as I did then! I thought it would never end and, when it did, I was exhausted, unable to move.

Antonescu, on the other hand, was charged with energy. He gazed down upon me, enchanting me, holding my attention so that he was almost naked before I realized it. Uncertain over his intentions, my fear rose, rousing me to protest.

"Be easy," he cooed in a calm, sure voice. "This is an act of love, Chad -- my own St. Chaedda. Can you not feel the love between us?"

I fought to raise some protest, some feeling of revulsion, of outrage, but it would not come. I lay naked beneath him as he rose and straddled my body. He sat on my groin, his flesh firm and smooth and exciting. Then he pressed his erection against my spent cock.

"You are wondering what it would be like? What it would be like to taste me as I tasted you? It is incomparable," he said teasingly. "Do you want me as I wanted you?"

"I...no. N...yes," I heard my timid voice speaking without my consent. "Yes!" I cried more harshly, with genuine feeling. And it was true! I wanted his cock! I wanted to taste it, inhale his aroma. What would his balls feel like? His cock?

He slowly slid up my torso, his ample cock gliding over my skin. Almost against my will, I opened my mouth to his offering. And I began to suck the first cock of my life!

He was big, and I had trouble, but he was also patient and worked himself into me slowly. Gradually, I learned to relax and accept more of him.

"That is the way," he said quietly, encouragingly. "Take it. Suck me, St. Chad. Take my essence. Take it and mix it with yours, make it powerful!"

I heard him only dimly. My world had shrunk to the thighs penning my shoulders, a pair of balls on my chin, and a big cock drilling my oral

passage. But, at that moment, that was what I wanted. I forgot about queers and straights, reputations, women's pussies! I *wanted* his cock, his cum, his attention. I *wanted* to be the center of his universe. I *wanted* to be needed, desired, made love to -- by him!

Antonescu pulled out of me and fell with his lips on mine, his tongue thrusting deep into my mouth. Despite his exertions, his breathing was not particularly labored, whereas I puffed and sucked air like a steam engine.

"That was your first time?" It came out something between a statement and a question.

"Y -- yes," I stammered, feeling ten years younger than my true age, like a fumbling adolescent anxious to please rather than the mature, sexually experienced man I was.

"You were magnificent," he said, his hand stroking the tangle of hair between my nipples. "Your manhood is like a bar of iron. Your semen is thick and strong. A man's seed."

"Doesn't it all taste alike?" I asked in my ignorance.

"No, not at all. Some is too musky, too bitter. Some is virtually tasteless. Yours is strong, but sweet. Ideal!"

I frowned. "You suck a lot of cocks?"

He rose on an elbow and gazed through the darkness into my eyes. "Only those attached to men I care for."

"Come on," I tried to make light of it. "You don't even know me."

"I know enough. I know that I'm attracted to you above all other men. I know that I want you again and again. I know that I want you to save yourself for me -- only for me!" His voice gained in intensity. "Do you understand?"

"Wait a minute!" I protested. "I'm not queer! I like to fuck women. I'm a man!"

He lay a strong hand over my mouth. "That you are! A real man! If you were not I would have no interest in you. But you learned something about yourself tonight, St. Chad. Admit it! You liked what we did. You'll like what we do in the future. You will come to love me, Chad Quarles! You will see."

"Wait a minute!" I scrambled to my knees, prevented from rising by the trousers tangled around my ankles. "This is a one-time thing! I'm not gonna…"

He stilled my protests by taking my flaccid cock in his mouth. Despite my words, I placed my hands on his broad back and felt the muscles beneath the skin. I roved his spine, swept my hands up to his armpits, and got hard as crystal! His hands felt everything I had. I flinched when he probed the crack of my ass, but relaxed and allowed him to play. Then he came up, pulled me to his breast, and dropped onto his back. I fell between his parted knees.

He raised his knees. My cock probed his buns. He parted them with his hands, and the crown of my penis touched his sphincter. It was the most

exciting, powerful thing I'd ever experienced. I penetrated him. He locked his heels behind my butt and pulled me into him in one long thrust. "Fuck me!" he cried. "Fuck me like the magnificent animal you are."

Inflamed by his words and the moist silken channel sheathing me, I began to thrust. I lost my head, went crazy, passed out -- something. I fucked for half an hour, pummeling him, stabbing him, riding him!

As I sagged against him, the man beneath me grasped my hand and moved it to his cock. "Beautiful!" he sighed. "Worthy of a real man! I have not been fucked like that for -- a long time! Now show your love! Make me cum!"

I pumped his long shaft no more than a dozen times before he shot his seed. He was barely through his orgasm before he grasped my hand and brought it to his lips. He licked his semen from my fingers.

Suddenly repulsed, I pulled out of him and yanked my trousers up over my prick. Leaving my shirt unbuttoned, I fled the house, guilt and revulsion -- and a strange finger of fear -- puckering my back as I roared off into the night.

I was skittish the remainder of the week. Every time the phone rang, I jumped. I flubbed a perfectly straightforward sale on a small two bedroom, and was a wreck by the time Friday afternoon rolled around. What little calm I had managed to restore to my shattered life evaporated when the receptionist handed me my mail. I knew before opening the expensive, cream-colored envelope with no return address that it was from Ariel Antonescu. As I unfolded the letter inside, a certified check fluttered to the desk. I picked it up. Fifty thousand dollars! The guy had been serious. He'd even doubled his outlandish deposit.

Every time the phone rang, I jumped. I flubbed a perfectly straightforward sale on a small two bedroom, and was a wreck by the time Friday afternoon rolled around. What little calm I had managed to restore to my shattered life evaporated when the receptionist handed me my mail. I knew before opening the expensive,

Grabbing the phone, I reached the listing agent phone before he left his office and gave him the offer on the house. He was impressed by the news that I held a sizable deposit. The man, whom I knew slightly, promised to call me at home on Saturday with an answer.

My hand was shaking as I hung up, and I sat in the nearly deserted office finally allowing myself to think about what I had been blocking from my mind. I'd been sucked by this weird guy. And I'd sucked *him*! Sucked a man's cock! Willingly! I didn't try to avoid it! What the fuck did that mean?

I groaned aloud with the next realization. I'd fucked him! I'd stuck my cock up his ass! Shot off in his butt. It had been the best, most exhilarating sex I'd ever had! What kind of hold did this guy have over me? Who the fuck was he, anyway?

The waitress that first night had called him a vampire. I knew she didn't mean it literally. She couldn't have. There's no such thing, after all. Despite that, I entered Dogpile and typed in 'vampire' as the key word.

The material claimed there were modern vampires among us today. It did not speak of legions of the undead stalking the unwary or horrible creatures turning themselves into bats and flying away into the night. It reasoned that vampires shared a physical existence on the human plane, yet are not quite human. They appeared eccentric to others -- to mortals. Eccentric -- like Antonescu.

A vampire had an extraordinary capacity to absorb, transform, and manipulate something called 'pranic energy' or life force. Among the prime sources of such energy are fresh blood and a man's semen. Like Antonescu!

A vampire had psychic ability, absorbing vibrations from everyone, becoming an involuntary vortex, draining all energy. Like Antonescu sucking the life out of everyone in the bar, leaving them numb and lethargic. Like Antonescu draining my energy and leaving me exhausted. Like Antonescu drawing even the smoke in the air into his vortex!

A vampire was selfish and sought to control others. Like Antonescu telling me he wanted me for himself alone.

A vampire functioned in the night because of photosensitive eyesight and an upside down internal clock. Like Antonescu wanting to meet me only after dark, wearing shades as we turned on lights in the house to inspect it.

A vampire might or might not take blood, but if he did, it was to gain energy. Like Antonescu licking my neck, giving me the creepy feeling that he had been about to bite me.

A vampire might travel through other dimensions. Like Antonescu arriving at the show home without a car.

A vampire might have tremendous sexual energy, exchanging this force with another, who was attractive to him. Like Antonescu sucking my cock, making me suck his, and coercing me into fucking his ass.

One sentence sent chills down my back and ice into my bone marrow. *A vampire may establish a long-term relationship with a single person who derives satisfaction from being a psychic servant...!*

The doorbell rang around ten Saturday morning. It was a florist delivery van with two-dozen red roses. That spooked the hell out of me! There was no card, but there was also no doubt about who sent them. At noon, another van delivered a huge fruit basket and a box of expensive Belgian chocolates. What the fuck was this guy doing? Wooing me?

Of course! That was exactly what he was doing. He had proclaimed his love verbally, although I'd almost missed it. Now he was sending tangible manifestations of his devotion like an old-fashioned lover.

It was nearly evening when a third messenger delivered the small box. I leaned against the closed door and tore off the wrappings with shaking hands. It was a ring box. Inside lay a huge signet of blackest onyx with a large Gothic 'A' outlined in gold and inlaid with diamonds. Below the initial was a small, blood red ruby. It was beautiful in an archaic way. A small note was included.

"Forgive me for acting like a love-struck swain, but it appears that is what I have become. It is true, St. Chad! Antonescu loves you deeply, hopelessly, timelessly. The ring has been in my family for centuries. Please accept it as a symbol of my love. Pray God that it will adorn your hand when next I see you!"

It was signed Antonescu.

The telephone startled me so badly that I dropped the ring box. The golden circlet rolled across the floor and came to a rest in a shaft of sunlight pouring through the window, it's diamonds flashing fire, the ruby dark and mysterious.

It was the listing agent for the property Antonescu wanted. His offer had been accepted. I put down the phone not certain how I felt about that. It meant I would have to face him again. It also put a handsome commission in my pocket.

The phone shrilled again with my hand still on the receiver. I lifted it gingerly, already aware of who was on the other end. My hello was shaky.

"Good evening, St. Chad. I hope this has been a good day for you."

"Antonescu," I gulped. "Uh -- yeah, it's been okay so far. I just got a call. They accepted your offer. The property is yours. Do you need to arrange financing or..."

"No, that is not necessary. But I want to see it again. Can you meet me there tonight?"

"Too late to back out now," I half-joked. "I've got fifty thousand of your dollars."

"I have no interest in backing out. But I want to view it through the eyes of an owner. With you."

"Look," I said. "You've got to forget what happened the other night. I lost my head or something. Come to the office and we'll do the paperwork."

"Bring it to the house tonight," he said in a low, seductive voice. "We will walk through my new home and then make love to one another. Antonescu will make you feel as you have never felt before. I will give you experiences you never imagined. Tonight at eight."

It took a second to realize that the phone was dead in my hand. How could the fucker talk to me like that? How could he expect me to -- to...

I fell back in my chair and dropped the phone. Because he knew I wanted to see him again, fuck him again, see if it was as good at the first time. Damn! I did want to fuck him! Wanted to suck him! Wanted to feel his tongue on my cock. Oh, God! What was happening to me?

The fact that I willingly went to meet a man I believed to be a vampire in a remote lonely spot at night did not lessen my fear. My new knowledge heightened that fear. Heightened my senses, my awareness, my anticipation.

Although I arrived early, I knew that he was already there, hovering somewhere out of sight in the early darkness watching me, measuring my mood, savoring what was to come. As I opened the door to the house, he confirmed his presence.

"This will be a night to remember," he whispered in my ear. I froze, unable even to flinch in surprise. He molded his body to my back, his strong, gentle hands enfolding me and sliding down to cup my manhood. I was already erect, and had been since I parked in the drive. He nibbled at my neck, sending shivers down my spine. I moved into the entryway and turned to face him without even snapping on a light. He closed the door and leaned against it.

"Have I told you how handsome you are?" he asked. "How beautiful? Men are so much more beautiful than women, do you not agree? Women are dainty, exquisite. Men are more forthright, have a stronger presence."

I swallowed hard. "Do women attract you?"

"No one," he said, avoiding the question, "attracts me as you do. You are the most beautiful man I know. And I have looked for you all over the world."

"Looked for me?" I asked, startled.

"Yes, my St. Chad. I have searched the continents of the world for you. And I find you in this rustic corner of the New World. But the search was worth it." The tone of his voice changed. "I need you, Chad. This minute!"

I stood as if in a daze and allowed him to strip me completely. He pushed me to the soft, carpeted floor and teased my erection with his tongue.

"I like your manhood. Big, pulsing with life, filled with dark, rushing blood. I like the big glans, the stout shaft, the smooth satiny skin…"

Abruptly, he ceased talking and claimed my lips in a kiss. Without bothering to undress himself, he tasted my flesh from head to foot, pausing to examine, touch, and lick everything that caught his interest. In the meantime, my excited prick beat in the air, precum leaking from the tip and sliding over the glossy head.

At last, he licked the clear, slick lubricant from me and closed his lips over my crown. His tongue flicked against the bottom, puckering my flesh, causing me to imprison his head between my legs.

"Suck me, you fucker!" I growled. "Go down on it all!"

Antonescu would not be rushed. He swallowed my length, but came up and moved to my balls. Lifting my legs, he trailed his tongue to that place behind the sack that drives me wild. Pushing my knees to my chest, he moved lower. His teeth grazed my asscheeks, his tongue flicked in my crack. I shivered in delight.

Spreading my legs as far as they would go, he pressed between my buttocks, his tongue probing, poking, seeking. I jumped when it reached my sphincter, I almost fainted when it pierced the puckered muscle. Oh, God!

He thrust it in me, out of me, licked, stabbed. He fucked me with his tongue.

I stood it as long as I could, then lowered my legs, grabbed his head, and pressed it down on my cock. I held it there as I pumped my hips, driving myself down his throat. Losing control, I spasmed, my nuts blasted -- fucking exploded!

And when it was all over, I was drained of semen and energy alike. I lay sprawled across the carpet while he removed his clothing and draped himself over me.

"What…did you…do to me?" I panted, my chest heaving against his. My nipples toyed with his as I gasped for air.

"I love you," he answered simply. "That is what I do to you. I love you."

"How -- why?" I didn't even have the strength to ask questions coherently.

"Why? Because you are a very interesting man. A man who had lived this long without discovering who you are. Teasing those poor souls in the bar when all the time you needed a man yourself. I felt the need to show you, and in the process, fell in love. How? By being me. Antonescu."

I was breathing easier now. "And who is Antonescu?" I asked, taking an inordinate amount of pleasure in the feel of his long frame lying atop me.

"Are you feeling stronger now?" was his non-answer.

I grasped him around the waist and rolled over. I kissed his lips, tasting myself on them. I kissed every part of him as lovingly as I had ever touched any woman. I discovered pleasure in his firm muscles, his corded arms. He had the clean, musky odor of a man in heat, and I washed it from him with my tongue. I paused only briefly as I reached his hard prick. Then I took it between my lips and tried to emulate his maneuvers with my tongue. He gave an appreciative groan.

I forgot everything except the beauty of giving him pleasure. I sucked him as if I'd sucked a hundred cocks, without choking, without gagging. I found a rhythm and stayed with it until he whispered something in a foreign tongue and filled my mouth. I slurped at it, drinking his essence, feeling the magic of it warm my insides and restore my strength.

Power! The thought reverberated inside my head. The power of his seed! The power of his love! The power of his body! He'd given it to me, freely, unreservedly.

We lay in one another's arms. I knew what was coming next, but I didn't care. I drew warmth from the curve of his back pressing against my chest, the pressure of his buttocks against my groin. My cock began to part his flesh.

I fucked him as we lay on our sides, a more gentle coupling than the first had been, and even more precious. My ejaculation engulfed me totally. As I lay softening inside him, I realized that he had not cum, and that brought a suspicion of what lay in store. I didn't care. I would accept him.

At length, I rolled over on my stomach. He moved between my legs, his strong hands caressing my buns.

"Beautiful," he murmured. "You offer me yourself freely."

Antonescu pulled apart my buttocks and stroked my crack with the slippery tip of his cock. The thing throbbed against me, eager to taste me. He began slowly, as if to savor the moment. His crown centered against my pucker string, and the muscle parted for him. The head entered my channel in a flash of fire. I cried out.

"Relax," he cooed in my ear. "The pain will soon be gone. And you will know the joy of having Antonescu inside you."

He eased the rest of his long cock inside me carefully. As my tissues stretched to accommodate his presence, the pain faded, replaced by an incredible feeling of fullness.

As though awaking from a dream, I realized that a man's cock was inside me, stroking my prostate, sending flashes of pleasure, sparks of ecstasy from my bowels throughout my nether regions.

And I accepted that I loved the man inside me.

As the love spread through me, lust followed close behind. Soon, I was moving my hips, meeting his thrusts, pulling away from him as he almost came out of me, and then smacking sharply against his groin as he lunged. He fucked. I fucked. Growing increasingly savage, we butted against one another, sweated, snarled curses, fought to go deeper, ever deeper!

Hard again, my cock rode the soft shag of the carpet, sending sparks through my balls. When he came, I felt the warmth of it, the strength of it. I came again, helpless to control it. I spewed my seed all over his carpet. Heedless of the mess, I pressed my shivering, shaking butt hard against him until the storm passed and he collapsed on top of me.

Spent, we remained as we were. Finally, he turned me over and lay with his cock against mine. Black eyes that seemed to carry their own inner light studied me carefully. His flesh was warm and comfortable against mine. I was content.

"Do you know who I am?" he asked at last.

I wet my lips and nodded mutely.

"And still you came to me. Was it because you love me?"

I nodded again.

"I must hear the words," he insisted.

"I love you," I rasped through a dry throat.

"I believe you," he said, a faint smile exposing his small white teeth. "Yes, St. Chad, I believe you love me, just as I love you."

The Right One
Murray Brown

The last lengthening shadows of day were fading into night as I left my new condo.

I walked through the gentrified Charleston neighborhood of renovated Victorian mansions and upscale cafés. I liked to feel the warmth of a crowd, any crowd. Charleston crowds are the best, full of men with improbable names out of novels and ditsy women scented with French perfume.

Even a vampire can get lonely.

Two men, obviously a couple, fiddled with herbs in a flower box at a second story window, sharing their day's experiences with each other. Just ahead, a model-thin woman jerked on the leash of a terrier and the dog growled in protest.

Maybe I could get a pet ... I shook my head immediately, before the thought could take hold.

Yeah, the next time I'm desperate to feed, I'd snap Rover's little neck. Wouldn't that be sweet?

No, a pet wouldn't help at all.

Jamming my hands into the pockets of my tight jeans, I walked towards the art film theater that had helped me decide to move into this neighborhood. I loved art film theaters and houses with high ceilings.

What I really wanted was sex. I was always horny when I woke up and, this time, I'd slept eight years. I shook my head to dispel the thought.

When I thought of sex, I thought of Edward.

Beautiful, *vicious* Edward. The vampire who made me.

I shuddered. Edward had had lots of lovers, one at a time. He'd littered Charleston with the corpses of men foolish or lustful enough to succumb to his good looks and charm.

Edward had lived to kill.

He usually killed his partners. He left them in alleys or shoved them off the Ashley Cooper Bridge.

"Jonathan, you're lucky I gave you the dark gift," Edward had often told me, "instead of me leaving you to go out with the tide off the Isle of Palms." He'd used almost the same words every time for more than a century -- just after he'd slammed himself into me.

I didn't kill. I wouldn't. It was too much of a fundamental difference for our relationship to last. We hadn't survived a month together the first time.

I learned to feed without killing. Edward had told me that wasn't possible. I shook my head to banish the memory of him. His dictums of what could and couldn't be.

If I told the truth, I was afraid of sex -- and had been for the 140 years I'd been a vampire. I lived with the fear that, in a fit of passion, I'd lose

control, bite too hard, tear too much. That I would kill.

As Edward had killed.

I didn't want to harm those I wanted to make love to.

Edward had made sex something dark and dirty, an act laden with death and evil. "We all play with our food, little fool!" he'd ridiculed me often in that month.

When I was awake, I jerked off often and spent evenings in crowds to ease my loneliness. Crowds provided the illusion of company, of companionship.

At the theater, I bought popcorn and a soda, trying to blend in with the crowd of moviegoers.

I wished!

I snickered as I tried to imagine being like them again, being mortal.

I had never blended in, not even when I was mortal. I had been a giant to the Charleston of my youth before the Civil War. I was still taller than most in the new millennium. With ebony hair and glittering, green eyes above high cheekbones, I had never blended in -- whether mortal or immortal.

I was always alone -- until Edward. And after him. But I was always drawn to him, like a moth to flame. When the need became too much, I went back to him. For the sex. In the forlorn hope that we could finally love each other.

It was just as well. I was too dangerous for anyone else to know.

Putting the useless popcorn beneath my seat, I leaned back and listened to the thoughts of the people around me.

A young woman worried about her math class. An older lady was trying to decide if she should re-upholster her sofa. There was a jumble of other thoughts, sweaty teen-agers wanting to do the nasty. Lonely men dating their second choice and wondering if they should've stayed home and just jerked off.

I'd hated it at first -- hearing people's thoughts. The women who thought they could change me. The men who mistook my apparent youth for ignorance and thought they could exploit me. The idiots who thought that any degree of difference -- the color of a person's skin, the god they worshipped, or the gender they fucked meant they were less than human.

I'd come to love hearing thoughts when I needed to feed, however. They helped me to avoid nasty errors. I would never harm an innocent person. But the idiots . . .

I drank their blood with a vengeance. I'd even broken my own commandment to myself with some. I drank those dry -- the child abuser, the hate criminal, even the occasional self-righteous preacher whose sole contribution to humanity was the hate he spread. Only when I needed to feed, though.

As long as evil endured, I would not go hungry.

This was the first time in almost forty years that I was leaving my mind

open.

I had read the romanticized versions of the vampire mythos -- I knew that blood drinking was supposed to give a burst of sexual ecstasy to the vampire as well as his prize. I'd never experienced that -- not with Edward or the few others I'd known since becoming a vampire.

Blood drinking was a necessity. And, for me, sex was just a memory. A memory that teased and tormented me, a memory that swelled my cock and dared my heart.

I was frightened of sex -- as scared as one of the undead could be of himself. What if I moved through the shadowy night and found a man I wanted -- not one I wanted to feed on, but wanted in that desperate, once familiar way? Would I love only to kill?

Like Edward.

I fed with careful control. I didn't know what would happen if the lust that still burned within me was let loose.

Edward had taught me well. I doubted myself. I feared what I could do most of all. I would read a man's thought and go home alone.

I smiled to myself as I took a seat in the theater; I liked it when a man wanted me. I knew I inspired quite a bit of longing. I could have a good wank hooked into the thoughts of a hunk that wanted to fuck me to oblivion.

Another part of the vampire mythos was crap, too -- the bit about no sexual desire that some writers put in -- the blood drinking as a substitute. What a load.

I awoke night after night, my dick throbbing, aching, ready to shoot off at the merest thought, the briefest sight.

Immortality was eternal hell. Fuck being undead. I'd dump it for undresses with the shades up, I told myself, thinking of the exhibitionist across from my bedroom. He'd put on a good show last night, my first night in the condo.

[*Oh, really? Can't you do better than watching your neighbour and beating off, girl friend?*] The voice was catty but held a tinge of real amusement. [*Why don't you leave the theater so we can talk?*]one last fuck. Frankly, being a vampire sucked.

The theater lights dimmed. I adjusted my vision. I didn't even snicker at the bad pun I'd made.

My memories drifted to a young man from years ago -- from almost forty years ago. A man I'd met shortly after I'd broken off with Edward the last time. A beautiful young man -- a body like a Greek god, a smile like sunrise. A man I'd surrendered to Edward that last time I saw him.

[*So, being immortal sucks, does it? It depends on what you do with the time, honey. There are all sorts of interesting ways to pass the years...*]

The voice spoke inside my head. It was a rich tenor voice with a strong Southern accent. A voice like a fine single malt Scotch or a slow jazz piano. The voice was vaguely familiar, pulling at me from over the years.

I groaned to myself. Great! I was now a crazy queer vampire who had been celibate for more than fifty years. What else could go wrong?

A man three rows down was obsessing about his taxes -- would these damned mortals never shut up?

[*Jonathan, why do you think something has to be wrong? Maybe it's time for something to be right for a change.*]

The voice was still inside my head -- soft, seductive, but somehow strong.

I shifted in my seat as the movie started. I scanned the theater; no one was thinking anything remotely like the voice.

I stared at the screen, forcing myself to concentrate on the opening scene. I frowned; it was another insipid French comedy. I exhaled with a small snort of disgust.

I might as well go home and hope the man across the alley undresses with the shades up, I told myself, thinking of the exhibitionist across from my bedroom. He'd put on a good show last night, my first night in the condo.

[*Oh, really? Can't you do better than watching your neighbour and beating off, girl friend?*] The voice was catty but held a tinge of real amusement. [*Why don't you leave the theater so we can talk?*]

This telepathy, this game playing -- it was just like Edward. But he was dead. Some sharecropper had found him nibbling on his son's neck. A sharecropper who had a broken, jagged ax handle plunging into Edward's back before the vampire who made me could uncouple from the boy and defend himself. Edward had gotten what he deserved, 140 years late as far as I was concerned.

I watched the screen for a few more minutes, trying to get into the comedy. The voice I was hearing wasn't Edward's. But I knew it, even if I couldn't place it.

[*You win,*] I finally projected towards the voice and rose from my seat. A blonde woman dissolved in a puddle of lust as I squeezed past her. An older woman in pearls with her boy toy date glanced appreciatively at the way my jeans molded my package. The boy toy checked out my bulge from beneath lowered eyelashes.

I stood alone outside the theater, hearing cars rushing down roads miles distant. The conversation of the kids at the concession stand came in clearly. The voice in my head was silent.

Stood up by my own damn psychosis, I told myself and chuckled.

I brushed my hair off my forehead. A block away, the staccato click of boots on pavement came closer. I felt a tightening in my groin, a burning deep in my belly. I knew with preternatural knowledge that something was about to change.

[*Take a walk down King Street.*]

"Well, sure. I'm just thrilled to obey a voice inside my head," I said out loud. The sidewalk seemed deserted.

[*Which way should I head? Near where the King Street Knife and Gun Club was or farther up near the Battery?*] I projected.

Not receiving an answer, I started towards the Battery. I was angry at myself for surrendering to what I figured was a full-blown psychosis bred in my sex-starved brain. Behind me and moving away with every step I took was the site of the Knife and Gun Club that had once been Charleston's premier gay bar in the fifties and sixties.

Heedless of the cars waiting at cross streets, I walked through the night like a man with a mission. I winced as I recalled the night in the autumn of '60 when I'd last seen Edward at the Knife and Gun.

I had been sitting in the bar talking to a recent Citadel graduate with the trademark burr haircut and perfect posture of the military college. I had thought the young man seemed more mature than most recent graduates. He had looked right into my eyes as if he wanted to know all about me.

I'd sensed the presence of another vampire before I saw Edward. Seeing him, I leaned closer to the young man, making it clear I wasn't interested in anything but the youth beside me.

"Engineering sounds fascinating," I told him. "So, you won't be joining the army or anything? You'll be working for Carolina Power and Light?"

The graduate nodded. "I'm really looking forward to designing dams. I find the challenge of conceiving an idea and seeing it come to life in concrete fascinating."

He sipped a Bourbon and Coke. He leaned closer to me, obviously attracted. "Hey, we're all on some kind of power trip -- mine just involves real electric power."

The newly minted engineer blushed at his own bad joke.

I laughed and moved closer. I could feel the warmth of the young man's breath on my cheek. My dick throbbed in appreciation of the man's clean-cut handsome looks.

I was having more fun than I'd had since becoming a vampire. I was ready to give up my near celibacy and take a chance on my ability to control myself with a mortal. I wanted the Citadel graduate that much.

"Like that dam for the Tennessee Valley Authority and the Hoover back in the thirties," I mumbled.

"Oh, I'm man enough to erect really large ones," the graduate joked.

A cold hand settled on my shoulder then, a hand as cold as the grave. Edward.

"Aren't you going to introduce me to your new friend, darling?" he asked as if we were a couple. We'd not seen each other since the end of the war with Spain and Teddy Roosevelt had come back from Cuba to run for Mayor of New York -- when I had finally refused to see him again.

The engineer moved back, looking from one to the other of us. "Are you two together?"

He blushed. He seemed to fumble for words but kept looking at me.

"But, of course we are," Edward told him smoothly. "What has

Jonathan been telling you?"

He turned to me. "Have you been naughty, dear?"

He'd looked back at the Citadel graduate and ensnared the young man with his eyes, even as he asked his rhetorical question.

The youth was hypnotized by Edward's piercing vampire stare.

"There's always room for one more," Edward said softly, seductively, to the Citadel graduate.

[*Back off!*] he projected at me.

I had backed off. The young man left with Edward. I was powerless. I knew what happened to mortals who looked into Edward's eyes.

I had really liked the young man.

Depressed, I slept for fifteen years after that encounter, through a near nuclear war, a Presidential assassination, and the first man walking on the moon. I'd awakened to find that the trust I set up for myself had prospered obscenely. I was in control of more money than I could possibly spend.

I was alone and horny. Too many times during the seventies I wondered if the Citadel graduate had survived his night with Edward. I grew to believe even more strongly that I'd be just as bad as the vampire who made me if I ever gave into my sex drive. I didn't want to hurt anyone.

I walked on, distracted now, confused by the memory. The friction of denim against my crotch stimulated me, however.

I walked past several large galleried houses. Lights glowed amber behind thick wavy glass. White curtains fluttered in the slight breeze. I stopped, entranced by the grace of a large white antebellum mansion that looked like a wedding cake perched in a garden lush with night blooming jasmine.

[*Up here,*] the now familiar mental voice said. [*Come on, look up.*]

The voice came from the galleried porch of the house that I
faced.

I looked up and saw him in the dim light. A muscular man, broad shouldered and narrow hipped, silhouetted against the indoor light. I saw a square-jawed young face, large gleaming teeth behind full sensuous lips, deep-set gray eyes that glittered with vampire lust.

[*Don't you remember me?*]

A Citadel class ring glittered on his hand.

I was speechless.

[*That's what comes from not getting out much, darling.*] Humor touched the words, gentle and curious, even desirous. The voice chuckled. [*You end up at a loss for words -- come on up, honey.*]

The engineer from the Citadel, looking not a day older than he had thirty-eight years ago, motioned towards a spiral staircase in the garden.

I moved up the stairs as fast as preternatural speed could carry me.

"I thought..." I said as I reached him.

"I know what you thought. I knew that night that you weren't strong enough to protect me from Edward."

He grinned broadly. "I was one nasty girl when he started in on me --
it's just as well, though. It took me two weeks to get rid of him." The
engineer arched a brow. "By the way, my name's Rhett. Mama was a real
romantic."

He held out his hand in a camp little gesture.

My thoughts were jumbled. Continuing the charade, I bent and kissed
Rhett's hand as though the engineer was a southern belle. "I'm pleased to
make your acquaintance, Mr. Rhett," I drawled.

"I hope you're pleased enough to make up for lost time," he answering,
pouting with exaggeration.

"Well," I countered, "I live only to please, my dear."

Looping his arm though my arm, Rhett led me through the French
doors into a large sitting room. The room was an eclectic mix of his taste
and family heirlooms; a silk oriental rug graced the floor. Set within an
antique cabinet nestled a state of the art television. He pulled me down next
to him on a silk brocade love seat.

"Now, sugar, you just tell Rhett what you've been doing since last we
met."

I noticed he had a dimple in his cheek. Unlike most vampires, his skin
retained a slight olive cast.

"Not much," I confessed. "Mostly sleeping."

I let my arm move from the back of the love seat to
encircle his shoulders. "I felt bad about what happened."

Rhett looked deeply into his eyes. "If I had not been made into a
vampire, would you have fucked me? Would you now?"

I didn't answer. I couldn't. I was once again in the Knife and Gun Club
with Rhett, drooling for him. Trying to convince myself that I could have
sex and not kill. Wanting him.

"You'd have simply kept on wanting me but slunk back to your lair to
jerk off in that solitary splendor you've been living," he said, answering his
own question. "We both know there wouldn't have been a chance in hell
you'd have had sex with me while I was mortal. You'd have been too afraid
of killing me."

He shook his head slightly, his fingers touching my cheek.

"Haven't you learned to feed without killing? Of course, you have.
Well, darling, we can have sex without killing, too. All that death junk was
just a lot of hooey Edward used to enslave his fledglings."

I nodded slowly. I'd known what he was saying since I was made. I'd
known it, but I had never been able to live it.

His fingers slowly moved in circular patterns around my shoulder
muscles. His eyes locked with mine, his tongue flicking out to lick my lips.

"I wouldn't have hurt you," I told him and tried to believe it.

"I know. But you wouldn't have fucked me then, either. I understood
that then, even though I didn't know what you were." He grinned. "Now
you will. After Edward turned me, I spent years looking for you."

He laughed. "And you've been right here under my nose the whole time."

I faced him, a resolve controlling me that I'd not known since the year South Carolina took Fort Sumner and I became undead. I cupped Rhett's face in my hands.

Flooded with heat and my heart hammering in my chest, I realized I could do as I liked. I could kiss, lick, and suck every inch of the delicious man-flesh in front of me without worrying about losing control and rendering an innocent victim dead or undead.

I covered his mouth with my lips. My tongue thrust into Rhett's mouth, free at last of my inhibitions.

He moaned and wound his fingers through the shaggy hair covering my collar.

I deepened the kiss as I slipped my hands beneath his tight T-shirt. My fingers moved across Rhett's washboard abs before they journeyed up his ribs to caress the large aureoles. I
rubbed my thumbs across his erect nipples while I sucked on his lower lip.

He moaned and squirmed, drawing closer against me with each movement.

I lay on Rhett, covering his solid body with my own lean, long-limbed frame. I never withdrew from the torrid kiss that held our lips locked together. Another moan escaped Rhett as I continued to suck and nibble his mouth.

He reached between us and unfastened my jeans. Clumsy in his frantic haste, he jerked the denim down. My cock sprang out of the confines of my clothing as if it had a life of its own. Rhett's hands encircled it, pulling the foreskin onto my shaft.

I tweaked his nipples as he stroked my dick.

Breaking the kiss, I moved back just inches. As one hand traveled down Rhett's toned chest and across his trim waist, my other hand shoved my trousers to the floor. I fumbled to unbutton my shirt.

Rhett made short work of his own clothing. "We have all night," he told me as he pulled me back to him. He licked and sucked the sweet flesh at the base of my neck while his hands continued to move up and down the length of my dick.

"All night," I repeated as I grabbed his ass, squeezing and kneading the flesh. I pressed my groin against Rhett and we rubbed together in a frenzy of want and need.

He sat up and I sat back on my knees. Rhett turned around and braced himself against the loveseat with his arms. His position elevated his ass; he bent his knees so he was half on the silken cushion.

I slowly licked and kissed a path down his spine, enjoying the tremors my kisses generated. I cupped his butt in my hands, massaging the flesh, rubbing the cheeks together as my mouth got closer to his glory hole.

I licked a path down along the valley between Rhett's asscheeks and,

with a spit-dampened finger, I plunged inside. He inhaled suddenly, stiffened, and then relaxed into the rhythm of my probing finger.

"I'm loose enough, honey," Rhett purred. "Give it to me now. I like it fast and hard."

I positioned myself and slipped my hands around Rhett's hips to grab his shaft. I plunged into him; he rocked back against me, claiming all of me.

"I've dreamed of this ever since that night at the Knife and Gun Club," Rhett said through clenched teeth. "I've wanted you since the moment I saw you there. Do me good, honey."

I pulled my cock all the way out leaving just the tip of my penis pushing against his entrance. With a control I barely remembered having, I rubbed the crown lightly up and down the crack of his ass.

"Don't you tease me, honey!" Rhett growled. "Put that big old hairy thing back in me."

I started to fuck him then. Hard and fast. Rhett's growls of pleasure filled the air, joining my own groans in an anthem to eros.

I was close and drawing closer to the maelstrom of orgasm. I was cumming too soon. I wanted more. I had to have more. I slowed my pace.

Bracing himself with his forearms, the corded muscles standing out sharply, Rhett pushed back against me, looking back at me over his shoulder.

"Don't stop now! Please, oh please, fuck me," he moaned.

I shoved the entire length of my tool into him again. I buried myself in him, leaning against his back, I bit Rhett's neck. It was just a love bite. It didn't break skin. I erupted deep in his body.

Rhett twisted around to face me, pulling me down to him so that he could nibble my neck.

"See, lover," he said smiling, "there's nothing to worry about." He licked my neck, giving the flesh teasing little nips as he came in torrents, rubbing against my crotch.

Sweeping back my hair, I smiled for the first time in a century. "I'm beginning to see some benefit to immortality."

"Only some?" Rhett grinned wickedly. "I have a lot of ideas for how to spend eternity."

"I have a few of my own," I answered before giving him another long hot kiss.

"Those ideas better involve only one other man, sweet boy," he said sternly and placed the tip of his finger on the tip of my nose. "You see, Jonnie boy, there's something you don't know about vampire sex -- when one of us spends years hunting a lover he turns into a very jealous vampire."

He nuzzled my collar bone, he rubbed his hands across my chest. "I need to warn you that unless you're ready to be a one-lover vampire there's gonna be some real bloodshed."

I kissed him again, pulling him close in a show of preternatural passion. "No blood shed," I told him. "You're all I need -- forever."

The Right Of It
Daniel Ritter

He's getting older.

I watch him sleeping as I get ready to leave. I need to be underground before sunup. I dress quietly, trying not to make a noise, but he wakes anyway.

"Going already?" he asks, rubbing his eyes.

"Yes."

"What a shame." He rolls onto his back, his hands behind his head, grinning at me. The sheet has slipped to his waist and I can see him hard under it. I consider sucking him off; no time. Damn! He knows what I'm thinking, though. He lowers the sheet and strokes his cock while I put my shoes on, making me frantic. Take him up on it, and it will be the last blowjob I ever give.

"What are you trying to do to me?" I ask, my voice low.

"Give you something to look forward to," he says.

I fall on the bed, onto him, and kiss him hard, hard enough to cut his lip. I capture the blood with my tongue, taste a bit of him. "You are such a fucking sexy bastard," I tell him.

"Get out of here," he says, smiling. "I want to be able to see you tomorrow."

One last kiss, and I'm heading down, down the stairs, down to the subway tunnels, emerging briefly in the pale light of earliest dawn and then to the cathedral. I nod to the sexton and continue in, looking like a morning penitent but really heading for the crypt and for the one coffin that isn't sealed -- mine. I open it, crawl inside, and prepare for sleep.

I met him thirty years ago. Originally, I had nothing on my mind but food. A vampire didn't get hungry often but, when he did, it was a hunger unlike anything a mere mortal ever experienced. This was Longing with a capital L, and even knowing the consequences for the victim didn't make the slightest bit of difference. You had to eat. So I was walking the streets, looking for someone healthy enough to make a decent meal, someone like him.

He was tall and a bit dark. He'd told me later that there's a bit of Native American in him. He was leaning against the brick wall of the bar looking like he should be smoking, but he wasn't. Good. I hated nicotine. Made me dizzy. I knew the place. I went there from time to time when I was looking to satisfy other hungers. He was staring blankly out into the night, thinking. I leaned against the wall next to him.

"Nice night."

He nodded. "Yes."

"Waiting for someone?"

He shook his head. "No."

"Looking for someone?"

He actually noticed me then and looked me up and down. "Maybe. Do you have something particular in mind?"

Yes, food. "I might. Want a drink?" Let him think this was something ordinary.

"No," he said, "I'm not thirsty. You?"

Not for alcohol. "No, thanks. Want to take a walk?"

"All right."

We went side by side and silent down the street to an alleyway that led into a courtyard. Peace and quiet, unless someone else had gotten the same idea first. We were lucky. Nobody had.

In spite of my hunger, I was starting to think of things other than food. He was a good-looking man with a nice, sexy ass packed perfectly into snug, black jeans and his biceps bulged out of the sleeves of his T-shirt. The bulge at his crotch was just as impressive. It seemed a shame. But as I came closer, he saw something in my eyes and started to laugh. It threw me. "What?"

"I know what you are," he said. "I don't believe this. I've been picked up by a fucking vampire."

"How did you know?" I asked, surprised. Most people don't even believe in us.

"Years ago, I spent some time in Brussels. I was just a kid then. I met a guy who worked night shift in an old opera house, at least that's what he said. Turned out he was a vampire. Don't know why he never bit me."

"You were a child," I said. "We don't feed on children."

"Cool," he said. He looked me up and down again. He was no weakling, but I could snap his neck with a flick of my wrist. "I guess this is it then."

"Nothing personal," I said, although I was having second thoughts. I was starting to like him.

"May I have one last request?" he asked.

"What is it?" I asked, expecting that he'd want to write a letter to his mother or something. That was what they usually asked, if they had time to think about it.

"I'd like to suck your cock." I could hear his breath quickening, see the blood darken his face. He was entirely serious.

"You would?" I asked. Horny was overtaking hungry, something that never happened, and I was no longer sure what I wanted. He had a sweet mouth, the only soft feature in an otherwise hard, angular face.

"I would. That's what I came here for. If I'm going to die tonight, I might as well die happy." He put his hand on the growing bulge in my jeans. "Nice," he said, his voice low and his breath quick. I could smell the

sharp tang of desire on him. "Very nice. Just a little taste? You can bite me when I'm done."

I swallowed and nodded. "All right."

He dropped to his knees in front of me, unzipped me, and fished my cock out. His fingers were cold but his lips were not. He covered the head with his mouth, his tongue trying to dig its way under my foreskin, and I groaned and tangled my fingers in his hair. He was good at this, damned good.

His other hand dug into my pants for my balls, stroking them in counterpoint to his dancing tongue. He was taking his time, but I had the feeling he was prolonging the blowjob for its own sake. This was a final pleasure, not a plea for mercy.

He pushed my foreskin back with his lips, tonguing the head of my cock, pressing it against the roof of his mouth. I started thrusting and he let me in little by little until his lips closed around the base of my cock and I could feel the vibrations of his moan deep in his throat.

I forgot all about food. I lost myself completely in his mouth. He was greedy, talented, his lips unbelievably tight as he sucked me. He pulled my pants down over my ass and dug his fingers into my cheeks, pulling me into his face, burying his nose in my pubic hair. God, he was good! I felt my balls tightening, knew I was going to come any second.

He knew it, too. Two cool fingers traced a line from my asshole to the base of my testicles, drawing the semen upward out of my body and into his mouth in frantic, joyous spasms.

He rested his head against my belly for a moment, then he dressed me carefully and stood up. "Do your worst," he said, grinning and wiping his mouth.

Fuck that! I could find someone else to eat. I yanked him against my chest and kissed him hard, tasting my cum on his tongue and listening to the pounding of his heart. It made me ravenous, dizzy from hunger. I bit his lip and sucked at the blood, just enough to hold me for a little while. It was so hard to stop but my dick was still humming and wanted an encore. He stood perfectly still, waiting, trusting something, certainly not me. What? He fascinated me.

"Do you have a place?" I asked.

He gave me an address.

"I'll be there in an hour," I said.

I found a hapless bum and drained him dry, then went to a seedier part of town where once-expensive shops had been turned into warehouses and then into apartments. His building had an old-fashioned cage elevator and I took it to the fifth floor. His apartment was Number 2, an old, battered green door with cracking paint. I pressed the button. The door opened seconds later.

"Come in," he said. His lip had swollen where I bit him.

I did. It was a big place, a single, large room with cathedral ceilings and one hell of an echo. Off in the corner, there were a few rooms defined only by partitions, bathroom and bedroom undoubtedly, but the rest was wide open.

I took off my boots, set them next to a pair of running shoes on the mat next to the door and followed him. There were window seats below seven feet of leaded glass overlooking an incredible view of the city. Beside one was an instrument case. Bassoon. No wonder he had such a fantastic mouth. Double reeds demand a lot from a player's lips. It also helped explain his cavalier attitude towards death. Musicians aren't generally the most stable people on the planet.

"What do you think?" he asked.

I pressed my body against his back, running my hands up over his tight abs. "Very nice," I murmured into his neck.

He ground his ass into my crotch. "I didn't really think you'd come."

I growled in his ear. "I want to cum like that again."

He snorted, disgusted by the pun, but his breath was quickening. "Insatiable, aren't you?"

"Damned right. Turn around." I yanked him around hard, letting him feel a bit of my supernatural strength. His eyes widened with a trace of fear and a much larger dose of lust.

"What's your name?" I asked.

"Eric. What's yours?"

"Hans-Dieter."

"German?"

"A long time ago."

"How long?"

"A few centuries."

He laughed. "I guess this is what they call having a thing for older men."

I laughed with him. "Much older."

He was standing so close that I could hear his heart beat, hear the blood coursing through his veins and the air filling his lungs. There was the faintest trace of alcohol on his breath; he'd had a shot of something when he got home. He wasn't as cool as he wanted me to think.

"We've established that vampires like having their dicks sucked," he said. "Do they like having their asses fucked, too?" He unbuttoned my shirt, baring my chest to his chilly hands.

"Vampires like that just fine," I said.

On his bed, we wrestled like puppies. He kept pushing at me, making me shove back, as if he wanted to feel what I was. His cock was about medium length but thick and meaty and, like most Americans, he was circumcised. I traced the scar with my finger, felt him jump at my touch.

He'd brushed his teeth when he got home, and I tasted a fine layer of mint over anticipation when I kissed him. His body was young and hard. He

was in his mid-twenties at a guess and I'd seen a weight bench in a corner. His touch went from feather-light to hard grappling, but his hands were always cold even though the room was almost too warm.

Truth? Vampires love having their asses fucked, at least this one does. Barring furniture accidents and sunbathing, I'm immortal and a thousand times stronger and quicker than everyone else. Nothing hurts me; nothing touches me, except maybe a bassoon player's tight mouth in an empty courtyard.

Maybe once in a century, it gets like that, where I can lie back, my legs spread and pulled to my chest, watch a young man grease his straining cock, knowing exactly where it's going to go, knowing that he knows everything and doesn't care. I felt his fingers probing my waiting hole. Damn it, would that boy's hands ever warm up? His cock was hot and hard, though, and he eased it into me slowly, his face opening and relaxing as he sank to the hilt.

It was the only time I got to be helpless, when the taker got to be taken. He screwed just like he sucked, playing a bit before he settled into a slow, steady rhythm.

I was as entranced by his face, by the sweet agony that played over it, as I was by the heat radiating from my ass. He wrapped his hand around my cock, working the skin over the head in time to his own strokes, and I lost myself in that maddening mix of satisfaction and ever-growing desire.

I thought I'd break apart on him. He was growling, getting frantic, his hand and his hips jerking harder until, with a low agonized groan, he emptied his balls into my rectum. Just as he had done before, he rested for a moment, then dipped his head down and jerked me off into his mouth.

I found out later that he has a circulation disorder called Raynaud's Phenomenon that made his hands and feet cold a great deal of the time no matter what temperature his surroundings were.

That night, I found a scar on his abdomen and he told me that he had died on the operating table six years earlier while having his appendix removed. That was why he had so little fear of me. He understood death.

And that is why he will not let me make him, bite him and suck him just to the edge of death, to that point where the body lives but the soul flees. At one point, I let myself admit that I loved him and asked if he'd stay with me. He only smiled and said no.

"I don't know why you agreed to become what you are," he said.

"It was the Plague," I said. "I didn't want to die, so I took the chance when it was offered."

He shook his head. "You're a fool, Hans-Dieter. Death's not so bad."

"Is it all true, the white light and everything?"

"Kind of." He looked at me wistfully in the moonlight. "I wish you could die."

"You do?" I asked, surprised. "Why?"

"Same reason you want to bite me."

"Let me, please!" My finger on neck felt his pulse.

"No," he said sadly. "I like living, but I don't want to live forever. When it's my time, I want to be able to go. Besides, if you bit me, do you really think we'd stay together forever?"

I sighed. He was right. Once or twice, long ago, I'd fallen in love only to fall out again after too long. It's a rare romance that lasts even a normal human lifespan.

"What makes you think it would work if we both died?" I mumbled.

"Nothing else matters when you're dead," he said, his face pensive. "Nothing else matters anyway, but you only really know that when you're dead."

I would never find out. I'd traded my soul for immortality. I had to go on living because the only alternative was oblivion.

He leaned up on one elbow. "You fucked up," he said, but his eyes were gentle and one of his hands played over my belly. "You live a half-life and now you're stuck with it. Nothing on earth, not even you, can convince me to do that."

He bent down and kissed my neck, a reminder of my nature and my foolishness. "I'm going to miss you like hell, though."

"If I hadn't become a vampire, I wouldn't have met you."

"Yes you would have," he said as his nose burrowed into my armpit.

"You can't know that."

"I do know that," he said and I almost believed him. His hand, warm for a change, wrapped around my cock, squeezing me firmly.

"I could do it anyway."

He looked sharply at me. "Do, and I'll make your life hell for the next two thousand years."

I wanted to, but I couldn't. Instead, I got to watch him age.

Several days ago, after he found some gray hairs, he called me his Arwen. I laughed and called him Aragorn. He asked if I wanted to see his magic sword. "Handed down from father to son," he said, grinning.

Only, it wasn't funny anymore.

I've lived for over six hundred years without him and I suppose I will go on living when he's gone. But sometimes I wonder if he has the right of it.

At the time, faced with certain death, I chose immortality as those I knew and loved fell hideously ill and died even as I rejoiced that I had been given a second chance. I never believed what the priests said about heaven, so I never thought that I might have been giving something up. Until Eric.

In my crypt, I hear the sounds of the world waking as I drift off. I'll go to him at sunset as I have every night for the past thirty years. I've listened to his concerts, hung out with him in bars and coffee shops, shared late dinners and channel surfed with him. I've fucked him, been fucked by him, then watched him as he slept, unable to sleep myself. Musicians tend to be

nocturnal, but not so much as vampires. I have been there for his nights, but not for his days. He's right. It's a half-life.

Had I not been hungry that night, I would never have seen Eric slouched against the rough brick wall of the bar. But, because I did, I will one day see him nailed into a coffin that will never open again.

Anniversary
Davy Jones

I

"I'd like us to go out tonight, Vlad," I told him.

"We can do that, Wayne," he answered. "Where do you want to go?"

"I'd like to dance at the Man Connection."

He winced. "Such a crude name – and such a bad part of town, too. Must we?"

"I'll go by myself if you don't want to go."

His dark brown eyes got big, "No, I don't want you to do that. We can go -- if that will make you happy."

THAT was expecting a lot, but I just nodded. He stepped up to me, wrapped his arms around me, and rested his head on my shoulder.

At first I stood there stiffly, but he always seemed so vulnerable when he did this, so I finally wrapped my arms aro, he smelled nice – I ran a hand through his fine black hair. Aund him and he sighed contentedly. He was warm, he was softlmost six inches shorter than me, he seemed so frail.

It's all an illusion, of course. My boyfriend is a vampire. He's not really young and sweet – he's been dead at least 600 years – and he is definitely not frail.

But I can't handle that reality – not much of it, anyway – and, master of illusion that he is, he's very careful to hide as much of it from me as possible. He sighs again and rubs his nose against my chest. I squeeze him tight for a moment, then kiss him gently on the head.

"It's still early. We have at least two hours before we should arrive, no?" Vlad ran a hand across my stomach. He felt my body respond to him, and made a happy-sounding noise.

"Yeah, go ahead. Probably better to do it now anyway."

He got to his knees and undid my belt, opened my pants, and freed my erection. His hand on me felt wonderful – he knew exactly how to pleasure me – and he took his time, stroking my balls, lightly rubbing my hole.

He switched to sucking me. This used to freak me out – even if I couldn't see his fangs, I'd still know they were there somehow – but he was actually better than any boyfriend I'd ever had about not scratching me when he sucked on me. And he was awfully good at it, which made up for a lot.

We'd have been together a year tomorrow. I closed my eyes and thought back to it.

II

Night comes early in the Northwest in December, but the ski resorts near Seattle have huge floodlights and working guys like me pay extra for "night skiing." It's kind of eerie being out in the woods after dark flying across the surface of the snow – especially the way the lights make everything look unreal.

So that was where I met him for the first time. Maybe around 6 PM, as I walked up to the line for my lift ticket, I saw this beautiful young guy in a blue North Face ski jacket with his hood down. As I took my place about two people behind him, he seemed to sense me looking at him, and he turned and smiled at me. I was lost. When he got his ticket, he stood to the side and waited for me.

"Hello," he said with a thick accent. "My name is Vlad."

"Uh -- hi, Vlad." I stuck out my hand. "I'm Wayne."

He smiled. "Very pleased to meet you, Wayne."

"I haven't seen you before."

"No. I am new in your city. Are you a – how do you say – a regular here?"

Now it was my turn to smile. "I'm here five or six days a week, and we don't call me a regular; we call me a ski bum."

He looked very serious. "That sounds like very bad word for very nice guy."

God I loved that accent!

I laughed. "It just means I ski a lot. Are you a big skier?"

"I have some experience, but this is my first time here. Would you like to show me around?"

Would I!

"Sure. What are you comfortable skiing?"

"Can we start with only the blue? To warm up? I can do the black, but not right at first. Is it okay?"

Actually I felt relieved he wasn't a total beginner. I mean, I could teach him and all – even though I wasn't an instructor – but I liked the idea of just skiing together a whole lot more.

"Sure. I like to warm up on blues myself. Follow me."

We schussed down to the nearest lift, got a quad all to ourselves, and let the machine haul us up the mountain.

"You know, if we were REALLY cool, we'd be riding, not skiing."

"But I think we are riding?" He seemed puzzled.

I laughed. "No, I mean snowboard riding. We're both on skis. Cool dudes – especially teenagers – they ride snowboards, but everyone just calls it 'riding.'"

"I have seen this snowboarding; I think it is not for me."

"Oh it's not so bad. I go both ways." I paused to see how he responded to that, but he just smiled. "I just felt like skis tonight."

We reached the top of the lift, dismounted, and played tag down one of my favorite runs.

Throughout the evening, I'd flirt with him on the lift up, and he'd smile or flirt back. I got bolder. I started patting his thigh to respond to a joke he'd made. He starting feeling free to touch me too, although not quite as overtly. It was wonderful. The time went by all too fast.

He'd taken the bus, so I offered to drive him back, and we chatted in the car. We quickly established that we were both gay, both single, and both interested in serious romantic affairs. He seemed to share my love of literature, and had read an amazing amount of it in English. I suggested we stop at my place so he could see my library; he agreed with a smile.

"I think most Americans do not have so many books!" He seemed to approve very much.

I stepped up behind him and put my arms around him. "I'm not like most Americans." I kissed him on the neck. For some reason, that made him laugh, but he leaned back into me and made a contented sound.

I led him into my bedroom and we casually undressed each other. He had just enough definition to look nice, but nothing to suggest he spent a lot of time at the gym. His upper body was so smooth it surprised me and I spent some time running my hand over his chest and stomach, then embraced him strongly and kissed him forcefully.

We rolled onto the bed together, grinding our erections against each other, and then continued our mutual exploration. As I'd expected, he was uncut, but he had the I led him into my bedroom and we casually undressed each other. He had just enough definition to look nice, but nothing to suggest he spent a lot of time at the gym. His upper body was so smooth it surprised me and I spent some time running my hand over his chest and stomach, then embraced him strongly and kissed him lightest, most delicate foreskin I'd even seen. I stroked it gently.

"Am I doing this right?"

"Yes, Wayne. That feels very good." He smiled again. After a bit, though, he motioned me onto my back, got between my legs, and took my cock into his mouth.

It wasn't just that he had good technique – his sheer enthusiasm was contagious. I couldn't ever remember being so excited from a blow job before.

He'd bring me close and then stopped to kiss me some more, then he'd continue sucking. I wasn't sure how long he prolonged it – it seemed like an hour – but when I finally came, it was like my whole body was involved, my back arched, my dick on fire, convulsively squeezing out shot after shot of what felt like gallons of cum. Vlad swallowed it eagerly.

Completely drained, I fell back onto the bed. I'd never had an orgasm that left me almost unable to move before. Vlad looked down at me with eyes bright and a really happy smile.

"Wayne, that was perfect. Just perfect." He leaned down and kissed me on the neck. Didn't bite me – just kissed me.

I started to reply, but realized I couldn't talk. He stroked my cheek and stared into my eyes.

"I need someone like you, Wayne. Someone to take care of me. Someone I can trust."

Starting to get my breath back, I said, "I really like you, too, Vlad." I smiled up at him, and he smiled back. He lay on top of me, resting his head on my shoulder.

I held him there drowsily, then suddenly remembering myself, said, "Vlad, I haven't taken care of you yet."

"Oh but you have." He snuggled closer. "And so much better than I'd hoped for too!"

"What?" I was still out of it, and I wondered if he could possibly have jerked himself off while he was sucking me.

"It's complicated. Let's just enjoy being together for now."

We snuggled together and I dozed off. No surprise, between the exercise on the slopes and the exercise in bed I needed some rest.

"Wayne, you need to wake up."

"Mmm?" I was disoriented at first. Then I looked at the clock. "It's just 6:00 AM, Vlad. What's the matter?"

"I have to go, Wayne, but I want to be sure I see you again." Still naked, Vlad was standing next to me, one hand on my chest, gently shaking me.

I smiled. "I want to see you again too." I rubbed his arm. His hand went to my erection. "Are you sure you need to leave so soon? Maybe I could return the favor for last night?"

He put his hand on my cheek and kissed me softly on the lips. "I would very much like to do that, but I must hurry. Can I meet you here tonight at 6:00?"

"Uh, wait a minute, you don't have a car." I started to climb out of bed. "Where do I need to drive you?"

He smiled. "I don't need the car, I only need you to invite me back."

I gave him a puzzled look, "Of course you're welcome back, Vlad."

He got a very happy look on his face.

"One more thing."

"Yeah?"

"Promise me to save yourself for me tonight."

"Save myself?"

He looked distressed, then sighed and said, "Don't masturbate today, okay?" I looked down at my erection – I'd been thinking of doing just that – but I promised him I'd wait for him.

Then he opened the door, stepped out on the back porch – still stark naked – turned into a rather large bat, and flew away.

III

As Vlad got further into his blowjob, I lay back on the bed, spreading my legs to make it easier for him. It felt just as wonderful as always – better, maybe, since he'd learned exactly what made me respond and made it last for ever.

He licks me, sucks me, touches me in just the right ways, and I'm his helpless slave until he's done. Somehow, he manages to incorporate undressing me into his routine without missing a beat. As he stimulates my naked body, he takes me right up to that bright tingly place where I know I'm going to cum but I'm not sure when, and he keeps me there. Tonight, he has a finger inside me, and, like everything else he does to me, it feels so wonderful.

Finally I crossed the point of no return but, having delayed my ejaculation so long, Vlad guaranteed that even the final build up seemed impossibly prolonged. The orgasm was huge, gushing, and uncontrollable. He took it all into himself, as though some of my life were flowing out of me and into him.

As, of course, it was.

As usual, I lay there utterly spent, and he stood there recharged. He undressed himself, showing me that beautiful body, slipped a condom over his erection, lubed it up, and eased himself into me. He smiled and stroked me tenderly on the cheek as he slid into me.

This part of our lovemaking is always surreal to me. I'm dazed, half-awake, and I can hardly move. He doesn't do it every time – maybe just once a week or so – but when he wants me that way, he just takes me – I can't resist or even object. Not that I would.

IV

All that day I'd wondered if I'd dreamed it. Only the fact that his clothes were still in my bedroom convinced me that I'd at least had SOMEONE visit that night. And as the day wore on, I wondered if he'd be back. I wondered if I WANTED him to come back.

But thinking about him made me hard, and I was still trying to keep my promise to him.

Darkness came, and when 6:00 PM came around, I nervously stood by the door to the porch. Sure enough, I saw a flash of movement, and then a naked Vlad knocked on the door and asked to be let in.

"I dunno, man, I've never done this before."

"Wayne," he sounded hurt, "can I come in before your neighbors see me?"

Now that I knew exactly what I was letting in, you might think I'd be less concerned about the neighbors, but I opened the door and let him in

anyway. He asked about his clothes, and I handed them to him wordlessly, then watched while he dressed – all but the shoes and socks.

"Thank you." He stepped over like he wanted to kiss me, but I moved away.

"This totally freaks me out, man. Are you a vampire or something?"

He looked sad. "Yes, Wayne, I am. Does that mean you don't like me any more?"

He looked just as beautiful as he had the night before, but I felt torn between strong desire and real fear.

"I'm afraid you'll bite me," I whispered.

"Blood comes from semen. It can be enough."

"Uh…" I mumbled, "I think we learned in biology class that that's not really true."

"It is ancient wisdom, Wayne. Trust me."

"But won't it turn me into a vampire? Or eventually kill me?"

He smiled. "That is not how you become a vampire. With some simple precautions, I'm sure we can keep that from happening." He got close to me, and this time I didn't push him away. "And you are so full of life and so strong," he rested his head against me, and I put an arm around him. "You can share some of yourself with me." His hand went under my shirt, and I was lost. We quickly got naked, hugged, kissed, stroked each other, climbed into bed together.

But when I watched that mouth going towards my cock again, I freaked out and pulled away drawing my knees up to my chest.

"Wayne, I promise, I will not bite you."

"I just can't help thinking about it." My erection was already wilting and my balls were trying to hide.

"Wayne, look at me." He opened his mouth wide. Perfect teeth, healthy pink gums. No sign of fangs.

"Uh, so how do you do it when you need to?" That wasn't very clear, but he seemed to understand.

"To drink the blood? I have the fangs when I need them, but right now that is not what I want." He looked up at me imploringly. He put a hand on my cock and started trying to coax it back to life.

What the hell. I'd been horny on and off all day. It didn't take a lot to charm my snake back out of the basket. This time, when he lowered his head, I didn't flinch. Well, maybe a little.

But, as before, he quickly swept me up into an intoxicating state of arousal. My heart was pounding, my breathing was heavy, and it seemed like my whole world consisted of nothing but my pole and the feelings radiating from it.

Once again, I blew a load so hard it felt like my insides were coming out. Once again, he sucked it down greedily, and once again I was totally spent.

As I lay there unmoving, he stroked my hair gently and cooed to me. He kissed me on the cheek. Finally he lay beside me and just held me while I recovered. He was still very erect and I could feel him pressing against my side.

"Man, that's really something else," I said weakly.

"I'm glad you enjoy it. I think we can help each other out this way."

"But don't you want me to do something for you? I feel bad about that."

"What you do for me is very wonderful, Wayne." He snuggled against me.

"But you're still hard."

"Oh. That's something else that passes from you to me."

"So you want me to do something?"

Vlad sat up and looked at me very seriously. "I would like to enter you sometimes, if that would be okay with you."

Now normally, I'm a top. I'm not fanatical about it, but I generally like to be the one in control. With Vlad, though, I was so clearly NOT in control, that it seemed rather natural to let him take me. Anyway, I consented, partly because I was still so weak it was about the only thing I could do for him.

It surprised me a bit, though, when he put the condom on.

"Can vampires get AIDS?"

He gave me a serious look as he got into position to mount me.

"No. But if we don't do this, it will eventually make you a vampire, and you don't want that."

I didn't try to push him away, but I felt a cold sweat as he pressed himself against me. That condom was the only thing protecting me from turning into a vampire?

On the other hand, like everything else he did, this felt really nice. I'd been fucked before, of course; but maybe I was never properly relaxed for it. Where his member touched my hole felt warm. As the pressure increased, he whispered sweetly into my ear, and I felt myself relax more to welcome him and the warm feeling spread to my stomach and my loins.

So, although Vlad wasn't the first guy I ever let inside me, he was the only one who managed to make the entry not only painless but actually pleasurable. As he started thrusting in and out, the warmth spread through my whole body. His grip on my ankles and the ease with which he repositioned my body gave me a hint of just how much strength he really had. Somehow, that seemed very sexy too.

He didn't make a lot of noise when he came, more sharp, short breaths – gasps almost – but I knew from that and from the extra force he used as he took a few last hard deep strokes inside me. He gently pulled out of me and lay on top of me. I wrapped my arms around him and we rested together.

"I think we were meant for each other, Wayne." He breathed lightly into my ear.

He moved in later that week.

V

"I'm still planning for us to go out tonight, Vlad."

"I know you are, and we will go." He gave me a comforting squeeze.

He needed to drain me at least once a day, and that generally wiped me out for an hour or so. Whether he fucked me or not, he always climbed into bed with me and held me while I recovered. Sometimes we'd chat. Sometimes I'd sleep. If we did it late enough, I'd sleep straight through.

But it played hell with our social life. His schedule was already severely limited the time we could spend together – especially in the summer when the nights were short. Losing part of every evening to sex and recovery didn't leave us a lot of time. We hadn't even been skiing yet this season.

Lying there naked in his warm embrace, I stretched a little, then snuggled up to him and heard him sigh contentedly. Determined not to fall asleep, I started chatting with him about recent events in the news.

Vlad and I always had great conversations together. In all his years, he'd had time to read very widely and he'd seen enough history to have a different perspective on current events. Since I'm a news junkie and a big reader too, we never lacked for things to talk about.

Great conversation and great sex – if a little too intense – but I'd started to wonder if that made up for all the other things.

VI

Moving a vampire into my house wasn't the easiest thing to do. First, we had to do all the moving ourselves, since it had to be in the middle of the night. Between his strength and a U-Haul, that wasn't as bad as it might have been. The worst part was the coffin, especially since we didn't want to spill any of the dirt out of it.

I hated to think of him sleeping in that thing, though.

Anyway, we put it in the crawlspace under the house. That sounds worse than it is; this crawlspace was six feet high, had a regular door into the basement, and even had a ceiling light. Vlad liked it because it had a dirt floor. At his insistence, we changed the lock on the door so he could lock it from inside.

"Are you worried I'd try to hurt you during the day when you're vulnerable?"

"No, Wayne," he squeezed me affectionately, "I know you wouldn't do that."

"So, why go to this much trouble?" We'd both been working at this almost all night – we had no more than another hour to finish this, and the instructions for replacing the lock were confusing.

"I don't want you to see me while I sleep."

"You watch me sleep all the time."

He smiled and stroked my hair, "Yes, but you look very beautiful when you sleep." Then his smile faded, "I can't make you a good illusion when I sleep."

"Illusion?"

"Just a few small ones . . . Ah! This is how it goes!" The new doorknob slid into place and worked perfectly.

"So tell me about these few small illusions of yours."

He looked at me very seriously. "I don't want you to see my true vampire form."

"I can handle it."

He shook his head, "I don't think so. Not yet. Please say you will be okay with this."

I sighed, but nodded. He smiled, hugged me again, then stepped into the crawlspace, closed and locked the door, and turned out the light. I heard the coffin lid close.

I went upstairs to watch the dawn, then climbed in my own bed and slept until noon.

VII

Somewhere around ten, we climbed out of bed and showered together. We soaped each other up and scrubbed ourselves, while enjoying the hot water. Then we dressed to go out.

I generally like simple clothes -- like blue jeans and a polo shirt. Vlad favors more stylish outfits, with European names I don't keep up with.

I had to admit he looked spectacular though in an all-black outfit so tight it looked like he'd been poured into it, set off by a light gold chain around his neck. "Now I feel very plain. People are going to wonder why you're dating me."

"You look beautiful to me, Wayne."

"Well, I don't look beautiful to me." I rummaged through the closet looking for something better – not that there was a lot to choose from, and I couldn't fit into any of Vlad's clothes.

"Maybe you should let me help you pick clothes."

I stopped. "Right," I snorted. "As soon as Nordstroms has another night sale."

"Well," he hesitated, "sometimes the stores are open at night."

I sighed. "Forget it. I'll go like this."

We got in the car and I drove.

VIII

Life with Vlad soon showed itself to be at least as complicated as sex with Vlad. In the winter, he'd greet me in the mornings and join me for breakfast (not that he ate anything) and a shower. He'd turn in about the

time I left for work, but he'd be up when I got back. It made for an almost normal life.

At the height of summer, though, he couldn't get out before 11 PM, and by the time I recovered from sex with him, I'd need to sleep – and he had to go back in his coffin by 4:30, so I hardly saw him at all during the week. (I'd stay up all night on Friday or Saturday though -- just so we could be together.)

Trying to get him a drivers license was the worst. He really wanted one, but how do you get a birth certificate for someone who'd been dead 800 years? Vlad's last fake ID made him 60 years old – nothing anyone would believe any more for a minute. Fortunately, the people who make fake IDs preferred to do business after dark, and Vlad somehow managed to come up with a birth certificate that made him 22. But he wanted a real drivers' license, not a fake one.

So I drilled him in driving – only night driving, of course, and then, when the days got short enough, we went to the DMV so he could take the test. They accepted the fake birth certificate, and he passed the written test easily. I was really worried about his driving test for fear the examiner would notice that Vlad didn't appear in the rear view mirror, but there were no problems there, either.

But we still couldn't get him the license because the picture wouldn't come out.

IX

We had to park uncomfortably far from the dance club, but I didn't mind the walk. The winter air invigorated me. As usual, Vlad didn't seem to notice.

The man at the door carded him and, as usual, complained about the lack of picture ID. But he let us in anyway. Washington State had finally given him his license, but in place of a photo it said, "Valid Without Photo." I wondered how many of those there were.

So we danced. Then we rested – or at least I did – and downed some beers. Then we danced some more. The beers may have been a mistake; I'd wanted to make it to midnight – to dance through to our first anniversary – but I found myself getting sleepy. When we took a break again, my head drooped onto his shoulder.

"Wayne, I think you need to rest. Let's go home now."

"Mmmm?"

"Come on. This has been fun. I'm glad we came, but you need to sleep now."

I let him guide me out of the place on his arm.

The cold air woke me up a bit. I felt irritated that I couldn't stay out late because I'd given Vlad too much of my energy.

"I'm tired of you using me," I growled.

"Wayne?"

"I know it's some vampire magic you've got that makes me do things you want me to do."

"That isn't exactly right."

I shook myself free of his arm.

"I see it all so clearly now," I said, getting into being peevish, and made a wrong turn and headed down a blind alley. "Whatever you want me to do, you can touch me or whisper to me, and all my resistance fades away," I continued. "You use me when you want me, and I can't do anything about it."

"That is not strictly true, Wayne..." He stopped and looked around. "This is not the way to the car," he said.

"So you admit to using magic on me?" I said, still peevish and not really paying attention.

"Hey, faggots!"

We looked up and saw three large men standing at the entrance of the alley, trapping us inside. They carried baseball bats.

"We saw you love birds making nice out on the street," the leader continued, tapping the bat against the palm of his hand. "We thought you needed a lesson." The other two aped him and tapped their bats against their hands.

Vlad and I backed down the alley, and they followed us until we reached the end. Now I felt real fear clutch at my heart.

Vlad stepped between me and the goons. "What do you want?" he demanded.

"The Earth doesn't need people like you on it, cocksucker."

Vlad laughed, and I heard this change from the sweet happy laugh that had always charmed me so much into a much deeper, frightening thing that went on and on. It seemed to unsettle the goons.

In a deep, deep voice, he said: "So remove me then. If you can."

Even before he fell on them, I saw the looks on their faces change from smug and excited to absolutely terrified as Vlad revealed his real self to them. At first, I thought he only wanted to scare them away, and from behind, I didn't have the best view of what he did, but I saw the hand that wasn't a hand any more sink its claws into the nearest one. I caught a glimpse of the red eyes. And the fangs. I heard the leader scream. I heard them all scream. I heard myself scream.

I sank to the ground, put my face against my knees and put my hands over my ears, but I couldn't completely hide the sounds. The screams got high pitched and suddenly cut short, one by one. When silence had fallen, I heard a sound like water running down a drain. Or like a straw makes when your drink is almost empty. It went on forever.

"Wayne," I heard Vlad's sweet voice, "we need to go."

I just crouched there, eyes closed tight. I felt him pick me up, and I clung to him. He carried me back to the car, set me in the passenger's seat, buckled me in, and drove away.

Part way home, I opened my eyes, and looked over at him. I guess I expected to see blood on him or something, but he was immaculate. When we got back to the house, I stumbled up the stairs, into our bed, and wept.

"May I come in?"

He sat down and tried to comfort me, and, after a moment's hesitation, I let him. Already my mind was drawing a distinction between *my* Vlad and the beast I'd so briefly seen. With my head in his lap and his arms around me, I calmed down fairly quickly.

"Well, there's one good thing to come of this, anyway."

I looked up at him. "What could that be?"

"I won't need to 'use' you for several days now." He sounded sad. "You won't have to feel so put upon."

"Vlad, I'm sorry I said that."

"No, I know what you feel, I think. Usually, you really do want to make love with me. Sometimes, I admit I help you. But believe me, my magic can create the desire for sex, but it cannot create love. Sometimes, I have thought that you loved me..." He trailed off.

I rolled on my back and looked up at him. I smiled. "I do love you, Vlad." Then I softly said, "My lover *and* my protector."

He smiled back, radiant, "I love you too, Wayne. And I have not loved anyone for a long, long time." He held me close and we didn't speak for a while.

Then an idea occurred to me. "So these next several days – when you don't need my cum..."

"Yes?"

"Can I have a turn at fucking you for a change?"

He looked surprised, then grinned slyly and kissed me on the cheek. "Happy anniversary," he whispered as his lips neared my ear.

The Hunting Trip
Jordan Baker

I've never been an evening person. Getting up before midnight seems futile somehow. I never get anything done those first few hours after sunset.

I know it's juvenile, but I love to spend those first few half-awake hours snuggling under the covers and reliving some of my better lays -- or perhaps daydreaming about future ones. This evening, it's the latter.

I was thinking of the pale young man with long, lustrous black hair I'd encountered at a gas station the night before.

That's really all it takes, a glimpse of someone new, and my mind is racing.

I closed my eyes and imagined my hands running over the smooth, firm flesh of his chest, my lips toying with his nipples and tracing designs over his stomach. In this particular dream, I'd turned him on his side and was caressing his ass, gently running my fingertips over its opening as I took his cock deep into my mouth. His all too mortal organ burned against the coolness of my tongue, and I bobbed my head faster as he began to swell and pulse with impending orgasm.

Just as this fantasy man gave his first gasp of orgasm, I slipped my middle finger into his ass and pulled him tighter against my mouth. His body convulsed as salty jets of cum began to flood my throat. Digging my nails into his buttocks, I crushed his hips more firmly against my face until my nose was buried in his pubic hair.

We lay there together, drained of all energy, until I felt his hand massaging my cock towards orgasm. He was leaning forward to kiss it when the alarm rang a fourth time. Jolted from my dream fantasies, this time I smacked the clock with enough force to crumple the brushed aluminum casing like tissue paper.

Rising before midnight, I grumbled, is uncivilized.

Out of habit, I dialed the bank's time and temperature number. I'd once gotten my buttons confused and set the damned clock for a.m. instead of p.m. When I threw open my window curtains, the resulting explosion burned me to my last inch of skin.

It was 6:15 p.m. -- brief moments after sundown and time for all good vampires to be at work. Too bad I wasn't working these days. I'd lost my job on the graveyard shift at the chemical plant for 'habitual tardiness'.

I know what you're thinking. I should have gotten up earlier or showered the night before or some other nonsense. But look at it from my point of view. Have you ever been late for work because you stopped by McDonald's for coffee and some idiot was working the drive-through? Or worse yet, one was in line ahead of you picking up breakfast for his entire department and requesting separate bills?

Hmm?

Well -- imagine that, instead of cruising by the drive-through, you had to fly to a nearby town, find an unsuspecting loner wandering the streets in the dead of night, make sure there are no witnesses, drink his blood, and convince him it didn't happen -- all without staining your work clothes or leaving any clues.

You can imagine my chagrin when the foreman informed me there was no reason why I shouldn't be able to eat and get to work on time.

"Other people do it every night, Richard," he said.

Well -- I'm not other people. I've tried to explain that several times, but even on the rare occasion when management listens, it fails to understand.

So, I ripped his throat out and used him for a midnight snack. It was the first time I'd killed a man in a century.

I must begin economizing now that I'm unemployed.

I'm celebrating my new found freedom with a little hunting trip. It's Mardi Gras in New Orleans, which means tourist season is officially open and I plan to bag my limit.

I can't really store up the blood -- it grows cold far too quickly. However, tourists tend to carry large amounts of cash -- not to mention jewelry, camera equipment and other goodies. Common robbery is distasteful but, alas, sometimes necessary. A good week in the French Quarter can pay for a year's lodgings and entertainment.

The trip from my home in the Ozark Mountains to New Orleans was instantaneous.

Vampire's don't really fly, you see, it's more like visualizing a place and being drawn to it. The time spent is negligible. The downside is that we can only travel in this manner to places we've been before.

Thus, in the days before air travel, we were a shabby lot, haunting the areas we'd grown up near, rarely getting more than a night's travel from the spot of our death.

Thank god for air travel and window tinting!

In this case, I knew exactly where I was going -- the Thibodeaux family crypt in Lafayette Cemetery.

It's a lovely little marble dwelling in one of New Orleans' more scenic graveyards. My friend, Justin Thibodeaux has been traveling in Europe the past several years and offered me the use of it for any hunting trips I might take.

Ordinarily I'd have booked a suite at the Mont du Leon or even the Marriott, but I enjoy roughing it when I hunt. It helps me get back to the basics -- predator, prey, loot.

When I arrived, the crypt was clean enough, but incredibly musty. I doubted Thibodeaux used it much. Last I heard, he still lived in the family mansion out on Plantation Row.

The first order of business, therefore, was to throw open the crypt doors and air the place out a bit. The cemetery gates were chained each night at 7 p.m., so my actions would go unobserved.

I suppose I didn't hear anything because I was singing as I unpacked --
"Whiskey in the Jar" of all things. So, throwing the doors open, I cheerfully
bellowed, "the devil take the women for you know they can't be easy..."
and found myself face-to-face with a dark-haired youth sitting on the
ground in front of the crypt.

After a moment of staring at one another in surprise, he sang, "Mush a
ring a muh dool ah ma dar."

Together we finished the chorus, "whack-fol-the-daddy-o, whack-fol-
the daddy-o, there's whisky in the jar."

"Are those the right words?" he asked after another awkward pause.

"Damned if I know," I shrugged. "I always thought it was a bunch of
Irish nonsense. Too lazy to find words that really rhyme so they just made
something up."

Again that awkward silence.

I took the opportunity to study the young man. He was attractive
enough in a feminine way. Lustrous black hair cascaded to his shoulders,
providing contrast for his pale skin and piercing blue eyes. His body was
slender and well-made, but for some reason he was dressed in what
appeared to be an outfit of deep purple velvet ... and a matching cape.

At the moment, he was reclining on the ground, his back pressed
against a tombstone. By the light of a candle perched precariously atop the
same stone, he'd been writing on a paper tablet when I appeared.

I noted he was studying me, no doubt finding me to be a much less
exotic creature. A youngster myself -- perpetually 24 physically -- I was
dressed rather simply in jeans and a white cotton work shirt. This was, after
all, a camping trip. It had been a while since I wondered what I looked like
to others.

My features are still handsome, I suppose, although not so finely
modeled as those of my young acquaintance. Dirty blonde hair, green eyes
and an average frame. I look like what I'd always been -- a cossack. No
matter where I travel, the mark of the horse warrior is forever stamped onto
my features.

My new friend seemed intrigued. In fact, he seemed too interested in
me as he finally stood.

"How did you get in there?" he asked. "I couldn't budge those doors."

Why not be honest? He probably wasn't going to live much longer
anyway.

"They lock from the inside," I answered.

"Yeah, but how did you get in there to unlock them?" he continued,
missing the point.

"Six guys put me in a box and carried me inside back in the 1700s." I
grinned. "I don't remember the service very well, but I think it was
raining."

"No, seriously, how did you get in there?"

I stopped moving towards him. Either he was dumber than a box of

rocks or he bore investigation. I tend to give everyone the benefit of a doubt, so he got the grand tour.

"C'mon," I shrugged. "I'll show you around."

"Cool," he said.

"The crypt is owned by a friend," I said. "He's letting me stay in it while I'm down here on a hunting trip."

"God, that's so cool," the kid replied. "I'm staying at a Motel Six with a couple of friends. It must be awesome to actually camp out in one of these. What clan are you in?"

"Clan?"

"Yeah, in the game. What clan are you a member of? We might be allies."

"Or we might be enemies?" I suggested.

"Not likely," he snorted. "Politically, maybe, but vampires always stick together against the mortals."

"The mortals…?" I let my voice trail off as the youth studied the corner where my things rested.

There wasn't much there, a duffle bag with spare clothes, a few books and my CD player and headphones.

"You don't have any candles or lanterns," he noted. "And no food."

"I don't need light," I explained, "and I normally just pick up something to eat in town."

"You really get into this role-playing, don't you?"

"I haven't the slightest idea what you're talking about," I confessed. "By the way, do you have a name? Mine is Richard."

"In the game, I'm Lord Athelstane, bard of sorrows," but you can call me Jim," he said extending a hand.

"Hi, Jim," I said, taking his hand. "Tell me more about this game. It sounds fascinating." Actually, I found myself fascinated with him, more than I had been by any man in two hundred years.

For the next several hours, Jim introduced me to the world of *Vampyre: The Gathering*. It seems some woman had created a market for vampire chic with a series of books. Now college kids were dressing up like Vincent Price and parading about her home town with fake fangs and capes. I didn't quite follow the bits about die rolls and saving throws, or why some people could pretend to be werewolves or mummies, but the implications of the rest were quite clear.

I could hunt here with impunity.

Endless streams of pale young men and women would deliver themselves to me, thinking we were playing a game. Unfortunately, they'd all be dead-broke college students who were stacked like cord wood in shared motel rooms.

Not exactly the kind of thing I needed to further my financial goals.

"Check this out," Jim said, pulling my attention back to him. "I've been practicing for weeks."

With that statement, he took a sip from a silver vial, then palmed a disposable lighter and breathed across it, sending a column of flame in my direction. Instinct and panic overtook reason and I leaped to the other side of the coffin. If he hadn't been laughing so hard, Jim would have realized no mortal human could have moved that quickly.

"You should have seen your face," he giggled. "Man, you freaked."

"I was burned rather badly a while back," I explained, dusting myself off. "I'm afraid I don't see fire as being particularly funny."

"Hey, I'm sorry," he apologized. "I didn't know."

"No problem. Hey, do you want to see something really scary?"

"That sounds fair," he said, "but keep in mind I'm really hard to scare."

So I transformed.

Not into anything as gauche and cliched as a giant bat or werewolf. I wanted there to be no doubt in his mind this was real.

I scanned his thoughts for that one nameless dread we all keep locked away in our subconscious, that one thing we would never admit to ourselves -- and became it. Bending light like balsa wood, I molded the darkness around me until I was invisible, a smooth, dark surface on which to play back the personification of the youth's most horrible night terrors.

I didn't know what he'd seen in those shadows, but he crumpled to the ground in tears. I didn't feel much like a winner as I listened to his ragged sobs.

I felt embarrassed that I had hurt him. And shame. "Bloody hell," I sighed, kneeling to stroke his hair. "I'm sorry. I just meant to get you back for scaring me."

I noticed he'd wet himself then. Choking back a chuckle, I made my voice as soothing and hypnotic as possible as I began stripping away his clothes.

"Let's get you out of this ridiculously faggy outfit," I suggested. "My things should fit you. Then when you've calmed down a bit, I'll walk you home."

Jim's hard-on became evident as I removed his clothing. My hand inadvertently closed over it as I reached for his underpants. For a moment, there was silence, then Jim swore softly and resumed crying. It had a different tone now, though. He wasn't scared anymore, just embarrassed.

Cursing myself mentally, I remembered how many times during the evening I'd commented on the effeminate nature of his clothing and the overall "gayness" of dressing up in a cape and parading about the streets.

From my birth on the steppes of 16th century Russia to my current life in 21st century Arkansas, I'd always been more comfortable among rednecks than any other group. It's probably a sign of my own prejudice that "feminine" homosexuals make me nervous.

I simply didn't realize he was one.

I must learn to stop shooting off my mouth.

"Shhhh," I whispered, still holding him and returned to stroking his

hair. "It's all right." I felt a tenderness towards this boy, and that too was all right. It was something I'd missed for too long and not even known it.

He struggled against me initially, embarrassment turning to anger, but I held him tight. Turning his head so that our faces were only inches apart, I whispered again, "It's okay, really."

We remained frozen like that for what seemed an eternity, our eyes locked, studying each other's souls. Then, slowly, inexorably, we drew closer until our lips met in a tender, exploratory kiss.

There was a gentleness in Jim, a sweetness I had never encountered. At first we simply played with one another, taking turns trapping our lower lips, darting our tongues against each other as if fencing. Then gradually, the intensity grew and we began to kiss in earnest, drawing deeply upon one another as if our life's breath was to come from the embrace.

Meanwhile, our hands explored. Jim's body was firm and smooth with just fine down covering his arms. I raked my nails across his skin, sending shimmering waves of gooseflesh cascading across his body. He moaned softly as my tongue flickered over his small, hard nipples. He cried out loud when my lips -- and then my teeth -- followed.

I thought he would pass out when my hand grasped his cock. My fingers curled around his balls and tickled them, bouncing his testicles in the curve of one hand as the other grasped his shaft and began stroking it gently.

It had been ages since I'd felt such heat. The skin along his cock seemed alive as Jim ground his hips slowly in time with my hands. His movements became more urgent and I increased the tempo and pressure of my own efforts.

Pressing him against the cool marble floor of the mausoleum, I pressed my lips to his and drank in his warmth. Soon his cock began to spasm and his balls emptied, semen spurting over both of us as he climaxed.

Jim collapsed on the floor, covering his eyes with a forearm as his breathing slowly returned to normal. I used the time to remove my cum-stained clothing and turned back to Jim, my naked body gleaming like ivory in the candle light..

"What are you?" Jim finally asked.

"What you play at being," I told him simply.

"Am I to become one of you now," he asked, his voice quavering between bravery and wistfulness.

"Not from a hand job," I snorted.

"But you could bring me over if you wanted to?" he persisted. "You could make me a vampire -- a real vampire?"

I studied him. Make him like me? I had actually enjoyed myself -- and not once thought of his warm blood coursing through him. "It depends on what you mean by real," I shrugged. "But yes, I could make you a creature like me. But it's not like the stories. At least not all of it is."

"How much is true?"

"You'll have to give up sunlight. Crosses won't bother you, but garlic will. No one knows why. It doesn't kill you, but it makes you sick as a dog. Of course, the scent of garlic always made me sick when I was mortal. You can eat anything you like, but it won't taste like it does now. It'll seem flat, lifeless. Except for blood. That will always seem to sparkle in your mouth."

"But you live forever?"

"No. You live until something kills you," I said.

"Carelessness is the leading cause of death. Oversleeping in an unsecured area. Getting trapped somewhere where the sun can't be avoided."

"I don't get it. How could that happen?"

"We drink human blood to survive, Jim," I explained. "Some of us still kill. Don't think of it any other way. We hunt down human beings and feed off their blood -- and their money. Both are felonies. If you get caught, you will go do jail and jails don't provide vampire-friendly environments. An overnight stay in the drunk tank is capital punishment as far as we're concerned."

"Oh," he said, the full import of it sinking in.

"That's right," I chuckled. "For good or ill, you have to be a flawless serial killer. And you have to deal with making a living and paying taxes. The paperwork is unspeakable, but if you don't do it, you could end up with a 10 a.m. appointment with an auditor. Blow off enough of those and they will come and get you. Again, that's a death penalty."

Silence stretched like a fine, thin wire connecting us. Just as I was expecting it to snap so that Jim could float painlessly away, he spoke.

"Is it worth it?"

"Yes," I said simply. "Because the alternative is..." My voice trailed off as I gestured at the neatly arranged drawers of coffins in the crypt's walls.

"Then you'll make me a vampire?"

"If you wish," I sighed. "And if you'll follow tradition. You'll have to remain with me for a few years while I teach you the ins and outs. It's important to all of our kind that fledglings understand the importance of being thought of as a myth -- of leaving no proof of our existence."

"And if I'm not willing to follow the rules? Or you decide I'm not going to be able to cut it after a few months of training?"

I refused to meet his eyes, choosing instead to study my nails.

"You'll leave no proof of my existence," he said.

I nodded.

"I already know what you are," he whispered. "You don't have a choice. You've got to turn me or kill me, right?"

Again I nodded. "So you tell me," I said, "is it worth it?"

"No other side-effects?" he asked.

I grinned.

"It's easier to demonstrate than to explain," I shrugged. "Suck my

dick."

"Excuse me?"

"You asked a question..." I smiled. "If you really want the answer, suck my dick."

Jim grinned as he crawled over to me and cupped my balls in his hands. He didn't notice the coolness at first, or the cue ball feel of undead flesh. It became more obvious as my erection grew. His fist pulled my skin down onto the shaft; his tongue was electric when it began to lap at the head of my penis. Again that wet heat that's become so lacking from my existence threatened to overwhelm me.

His lips created a vacuum around the head of my cock. His tongue fluttering over my slit tickled and I pulled away; but, grabbing my ass in both hands, he pulled me back, taking my cock deeper down his throat. I gave in and allowed Jim to set the rhythm for our lovemaking.

He was an expert cocksucker, always seeming to know exactly when to let things cool a bit and when to heat them back up. It seemed like hours that he played his lips and tongue over my shaft, bit and chewed my foreskin, and tongued my knob. Finally, he seemed to come to the conclusion that it was time to finish things off.

I knew when he made the decision because he squeezed the shaft of my cock against the roof his mouth with his tongue and began bobbing his head furiously. I was unable to hold out against this new assault and let myself go.

My cock spasmed as it pumped against Jim's face and I could sense from the way he'd stopped moving he was preparing to swallow. Moments later, my orgasm subsided and I looked down at his perplexed face. My softening cock was still trapped in his mouth.

"What happened?" he asked as he let me go.

"I came."

"But you didn't really," he said. "I mean, nothing..."

"No body fluids, I interrupted. "Cum is really just concentrated blood when you get down to brass tacks."

"No, it isn't," Jim said.

"Well, the doctor I spoke with about the situation said it was."

"You told a doctor you were a vampire and couldn't cum?" He looked incredulous.

I shrugged. "He was an 18th century Russian alchemist..."

"That's a joke, right?"

"He was the best in his field at the time."

"You haven't considered asking someone with a more modern outlook?" Jim asked.

"They'd want a blood test, now, wouldn't they?"

"Vampires can't cum," Jim asked.

"We cum. I feel the same sensations. I just don't produce fluids. I suppose if I were to cum right after feeding, I might squirt blood."

"You've never tried it?"

"Do you feel like fucking right after a big meal?" I asked.

"No, but I think I could find a few spare moments of eternity to experiment a little."

"Then you've made up your mind?"

"Given the alternatives, I don't see much choice."

"Then I suppose we should drain those balls of yours one more time," I suggested.

"Why? Is that part of the transformation process?"

"Not really, but since you might never be able to do it again, I thought it was the prudent thing," I grinned. "Besides, I'm still horny."

The decision was made, we spent the hours before dawn trysting in the crypt, exploring one another's bodies with our tongues and hands. I was glad that he would be with me.

Just before sunrise, he broke from our embrace and, smiling at me, lay on his back.

"Fuck me while you're doing it," he told me. "I want it to be love making between us, Richard."

I climbed between his legs, lifting them to my shoulders. "You're sure?" I asked as I placed my dick at his entrance. He nodded and I began to slip into his warmth.

"Feels good," he mumbled and bucked up to take more of me.

I thrust my cock to the hilt in his rear end then, bending over him and drinking Jim's blood as I made love to him.

"Yeah," he crooned. "Fuck me, Richard. Make me yours."

As I fed, I jacked his cock, moving slowly in him.

He moaned. He thrust against me. His was a pleasure I'd not felt in many mortals before. There was a joy to him now that our union was complete. It was there in his surface thoughts as my movements in him became shorter and faster. His fingers gripped my asscheeks hard, guiding me in my possession of him.

His joy, his pleasure, communicated itself to me as we made love. It became my own. He was food. He was a good fuck. And he was a lot more. As I pulled my face from his neck, I rose onto my knees and pushed deep into him.

Full, I made a tear in my wrist with my own teeth and pressed the wound over his lips. We climaxed together as he began to drink deeply of me.

He slipped away into oblivion as the day began.

I smiled and closed my eyes, letting him sleep. When night fell, I would begin teaching Jim a whole new game -- one far removed from die rolls and saving throws. It was a rite of passage in all cultures, I realized, stroking his hair as he slept.

Tomorrow, I'd take Jim on his first hunting trip.

Hillbilly Blood
Vic Howell

I pulled off my t-shirt and sat on the two-seater, careful not to get splinters in my butt. The wood was old and dry in great-granddad's shitter. I was more than a little surprised that the seat hadn't fallen through the moment I put weight on it. I wondered how long it'd been since anyone had even been in the thing.

I had a wicked hard-on and had every intention of taking care of it.

My jeans bunched at my ankles as I started to stroke the thick seven inch baby between my legs. I imagined warm, wet pussy clutching at my dick as I pounded my pud.

I spit into my palm, rubbed it over the wide mushroom knob of my cock and began really going to town on old Henry down there. My other hand absently rubbed my hard abs and moved up to my nubs. I moaned as my balls started to tighten. Sweat and precum lubed my dick.

The ancient privy rocked under me. Groaning. Moaning under the fully-grown pine trees that hid it. I waxed my johnson as the outhouse creaked around me. Just a little more...

A crash yanked me back to reality. I stared at the growing summer twilight through the now gaping hole that had been the door moments before, my fist frozen in mid-stroke.

[*You better come out of that shithouse, Sammy Taylor,*] a voice I'd never heard before told me.

I didn't realize it was inside my head.

I hesitated. I wasn't sure I could handle the embarrassment of being caught jacking off.

[*Get your butt out of there, boy. Now!*] the voice commanded. [*That old thing's ready to come crashing down.*]

The john shuddered around me.

I quickly decided whoever it was out there was right. I did need to get moving. I got up from the seat and shuffled out of the privy, my jeans and underwear still around my ankles. Stopping outside the john, I reached down and started to pull my clothes up.

A hand cupped my nearest asscheek.

I jerked away. My mind went blank as I began to turn.

The night was warm, and a full moon was riding the tops of the pine trees when I woke. I felt good, better than I had since dad died. I felt warm and toasty all over, like I did after a night of love-making with my girlfriend -- when I still had one.

I lay naked on a bed of pine needles, my clothes folded beside me. That surprised me, because I wasn't into being naked out in the open like this.

Even that couldn't shock me, however -- I just felt too complete to let anything get to me too much. I felt sated. Sexually sated. And light-headed.

I sat up and felt something pulling at the individual hairs in my treasure trail and the skin of my smooth chest. My hand told me that I was covered in dried flakes. I laughed and pushed myself to my feet as I accepted the stuff was my jizz.

"What a wet dream!" I told myself and wished that I could remember it. I'd had to shoot at least a pint of cum to get this gummed up. My butt was a little sore but I wrote that off as a part of falling asleep on the ground.

I picked up my clothes and started back towards the house. Great-granddad's house. Mine now. I couldn't understand why I was staggering and felt so light-headed. I hadn't even had a beer.

It wasn't much -- a small single-story clapboard with two bedrooms, a sitting room, and a kitchen. Granddad and Dad had kept it up during their lifetimes, using it as a weekend getaway from wives and children. Dad had put in electricity and a full bath maybe thirty years ago. I had inherited it when he died.

I entered through the kitchen but was instantly drawn to the sitting room. I stepped up to the mantle where framed photos of three generations of Taylor men sat. Only one drew me though -- great-granddad's. Something tingled deep in my ass as I studied the tall, blond young man gazing back at me through the years that separated us. My dick immediately stiffened and threatened to go for all seven inches.

Stepping back from the mantel, I broke the spell that had held me. Shaking my head, I turned off the light and headed for bed. Me getting hard for any man was a joke. I'd been porking the ladies since I was thirteen; I wasn't about to start switch hitting now.

It was Sunday evening and I was on my way back to Atlanta and another week with my nose to the grindstone. I spotted the dark-haired guy in overalls standing at the fence separating my property from his before he began to wave me down. His side of the fence was a plowed field. I pulled the Land Rover over and rolled down the window.

"You're the boy who's got the old Taylor place now, ain't you?" the brunette asked, studying me closely.

Boy? Who was he calling boy? He couldn't be more than twenty; he looked maybe sixteen. At twenty-six, no matter which he was, I was older than he was. "Yeah…"

"You're Sammy then?"

I nodded wondering how he knew my name.

He smiled, the freckles on his cheeks spreading wide. "I'm your Cousin Jimmy." He shrugged. "I guess that's close on to third or fourth cousins -- still close enough to be kissing cousins, though."

Kissing? Yeah, right! And I was a just a dumb peapicker too. "Cousins?" I asked carefully.

"Sure. Old man Sam -- he was your great-granddaddy -- he made sure the family owned this whole mountain. He gave every one of his brothers a piece of this here rock back in the twenties, I think it was. His brothers and his own kids."

"That was nice of him," I said checking the sun. I had a three hour drive back to Atlanta.

"Me and daddy and the couple of cousins who still live here year round were wondering, Sammy..." He looked down at his workboots and started digging his toe into the dirt. I waited.

"We was wondering if you'd let us pulp all that timber you got and start farming that hundred acres like most of the others up here do."

"You're saying you guys want to buy it?"

He stared at me like I was insane. "Buy it?" he finally croaked.

"You don't expect me just to give you the place, do you?"

He blinked and it was as if he'd just seen holy writ or something. "Naw, Sammy. The five or six of our families that still farm up here -- we pay 50-50 on anything we make off your property -- just like we do the other cousins who've moved away. You keep the house and come up any time you feel like it. We farm the land after we get rid of the trees and we pay you for that."

"I'll have to think about it," I told him. "Why don't you come by next Saturday -- you and your dad -- and we'll talk..."

I watched him turn absolutely white. Sweat beaded across his forehead.

"Are you all right?" I demanded and wondered where the nearest hospital was.

"Yeah," he whispered, grasping the passenger door so tight that his fingers remained white. "Only, maybe you should come down to the house instead and let's talk there?"

"Why?"

"My daddy ain't going up to the old Taylor place, Sammy. Nobody does if he wants to stay healthy."

"What?" I cried in surprise before I settled back down and stared at him until he started making sense.

"There are things that happen to a man who goes up there -- things that've been happening for more than sixty years now." He shook his head emphatically.

"What kind of things?" I demanded.

He gritted his teeth and looked back up the way I'd come. He smiled and I could tell it was forced. "Just rumors. Stuff to scare the little kids away from exploring where they've got no right to be."

"What kind of things?"

"Just monster stuff. You know the kind of things parents are always telling their kids." He smiled again. "You come down next Saturday evening and momma'll fix you a real home-cooked dinner."

"I don't..." I realized I didn't even know his last name or where he lived.

His smile grew broader and took over his entire face. "We live in the brick house down at the end of this road where it turns onto the paved county road into town. My name's Jimmy. Jimmy Varnadore."

He stepped back from my truck. "We'll see you next Saturday around four o'clock or thereabouts." He waved as he backed up even further and turned. I sat in the SUV and watched him cross the field and slip into the woods.

It had been a grueling week. Exhilarating as the market nudged up to 11,000, but still grueling. I had decided for the millionth time that being a stock broker was not a fun job. At 26, though, I'd proved I was good at what I did. I couldn't imagine not having the kind of money I made.

I was actually happy late Friday evening as I passed through Rabun Gap and turned onto the county road that would take me out to Taylor Mountain. I wanted the couple of days of rest and relaxation the old house promised me.

I passed the brick rambler that was the Varnadore house and turned onto the hard-packed clay road that led up the mountain to my property. Instantly, my conversation with Jimmy came to mind and I wondered why he and his father were so afraid of the old Taylor place. Sixty years? He had said the rumors about the place went back that far.

That would put whatever it was back in great-granddad's day. I wagged my head slightly and chuckled. Dad had been right the few times we'd talked about the place in the mountains, these hillbillies were superstitious. They probably didn't have any black cats around, either.

I hadn't even unloaded the SUV when I felt the urge to go down to the privy. Curiosity, need -- even desire -- they hit me full-force as my feet touched the ground. I resisted and the urge grew stronger. My dick got into the act and got hard inside my jeans.

"Well, why not?" I chuckled to myself and shrugged. Still chuckling at how silly I was being, I started around the house, heading for the woods and the old privy. I was hard by the time I reached the first tree.

"Sammy boy," I told myself as my fingers traced the outline of my dick through my jeans, "you've got to stop thinking with this thing of yours."

I stood in front of the old outhouse, its door fallen off, and wondered what had ever possessed me to step into it last week. The thing was ready to fall down. I had been lucky as hell it hadn't collapsed on me.

I unzipped my jeans and carefully pulled my seven inches through the soft cotton of my briefs. One thing I didn't need was any more scratches on my dick like those I'd found last weekend. I hadn't even been able to jack off the first couple of days I was back in Atlanta.

I pulled the tee-shirt over my head and unbuttoned the waist of my jeans. I was bemused by how hedonistic I'd got the two times I'd been up here as I pushed both jeans and underwear over my butt.

Fingers brushed across my asscheeks.

I froze. And slowly started to look over my shoulder to see who was there.

My mind went blank.

I woke naked and lying on the same bed of pine needles as last week. My clothes were folded neatly and lay beside me. My body was as sated as it ever had been after a night of fucking. My butthole was sore but felt good too.

I was hard as a rock and covered with jizz. And light-headed again.

Clouds scudded across the night sky, hiding the moon. It was dark among the trees. And I could see clearly all the way up to the house.

My thigh itched, right beside my ball sack where the leg joins the torso. I scratched myself and was surprised to see blood on my fingertips. Not much, just enough to know what it was.

I brushed off the surprise as I stood up. "Sam," I said to myself, "you lie down on pine needles to jack off and you're bound to get pricked."

I brought my fingers to my lips and licked at the traces of my blood. "Neat," I mumbled as I tasted the copper. I reached down and wiped the wound with my fingers and brought them back to my lips. "Very nice," I told myself as I sucked the blood off them.

I stayed hard as I walked up to the house. I was still hard and naked as I entered the sitting room and went directly to the mantle. I started to stroke my dick as I picked up the photo of great-granddad and really studied the man's image this time.

Piercing eyes gazed out at me. I figured he'd probably just returned from the First World War when the photo was taken, he looked so young and proud in the picture. He had strong features and shorned blond hair, but was a good looking man. My thigh itched where I'd pricked it on the pine needles. My strokes along my dick became faster.

I set the photo back on the mantle and let my hand carry me towards an orgasm.

Walking back to the bedroom afterwards, I decided that, if I ever did bend over for a guy, it'd have to be someone who looked like great-granddad. Not that I was, of course. I just needed to go hit the circuit again and find me a nice little filly.

Until I did, though, I figured it was okay to jerk off to a picture of a man I'd never known and never could meet; I'd get over it fast enough when I had the real thing spread before me. It'd be just like that first year after puberty hit me between the eyes. I'd sometimes beat my meat thinking about some of my friends -- until I got my first piece of pussy. After that, I hadn't even thought about queer stuff. Until now.

I showered and shaved Saturday afternoon -- and debated dressing in a suit for my dinner with the Varnadores down the mountain. I stood looking out at the copse of pine trees as I toweled off. My ass started itching -- deep up in the bowel. I wondered if I was developing hemorrhoids. I also knew

with certainty that I didn't want to wear anything fancier than clean jeans and a golf shirt.

Jimmy met me at the door, a big grin plastered across his face. "We're mighty glad you decided to join us, Cousin. Come on in. We've got fried chicken, mashed potatoes and gravy, green beans, and biscuits." He rubbed his tummy like a little kid seeing all his favorite food in front of him.

I stepped into the house expecting my instincts to cut in. Greetings as friendly as his usually meant there was a shark in the water waiting for me to wade in deep enough. I only felt his genuine friendliness, though. His father and mother were just as friendly. I decided that, maybe, corporate ethics hadn't found their way to Taylor Mountain. I was coming to like the place anyway, but finding nice people was making it that much easier for me.

The two Varnadore men and I sat in the living room and sipped iced tea while Jimmy's father repeated what Jimmy had told me the week before.

I grew increasingly uneasy as the elder Varnadore laid out his plan but kept a poker face throughout. After all, I played high stakes poker five days a week downtown; it was the only way good stockbrokers made money for their clients.

Only, I didn't understand my sense of unease. Varnadore's idea sounded reasonable to me. It made me money and didn't require an investment from me. Every emotion inside me hated it, even as my rational mind accepted it. An irrational part of me saw it as a threat, a way to destroy me.

"Let me think about it this next week," I told the older man. I smiled disarmingly before he could marshal his arguments and start using them again on me. "I need to check it out -- that's the way my mind works," I told him. "And, right now, I know nothing about farming or cutting trees."

"That sounds fair enough," Jimmy chimed in, and I thought I saw his father glower at him for a moment.

It was late when I returned to my little frame house on the mountain. As soon as I stopped the Land Rover in front of the house, I had the urge to go down to the outhouse and its copse of trees. It was stronger than the night before. Demanding. Impervious.

This isn't me! I realized even as my feet touched the ground, my eyes bulging. I tried to pull my feet back into the Rover, but they weren't leaving the ground. They pulled me off the car seat and I had to grab the door to steady myself.

I started for the pine trees at a trot, throwing off clothes as I went. My hard dick led the way. I was naked by the time I reached the bed of pine needles and threw myself on them. I panted as I waited - and tried to understand what I waited for.

[*You're mine, Sammy boy. Mine, damn it all to hell!*] The words washed through my head. I sat up and looked around fearfully.

Nothing. Nobody. Just me lying out under the trees. Naked. With a

throbbing hard-on. I realized I also had an itch deep in my ass too. What the shit was going on? I started to push myself to my feet.

Something hit me. Like being tackled back in high school football. I was bowled over and fell back onto the pinestraw, the breath knocked out of me. I lay there for a moment, sucking like mad to pull air into my lungs. I felt my legs being lifted and spread. My dick throbbed.

I looked down at the blond guy with the sharp, handsome features who, somehow, had got between my legs. On whose shoulders my legs rested. I felt something wide and hot at my hole and knew what was about to happen.

[*You're mine, boy. Understand that and accept it. Now and forever.*]

The thought simply appeared in my mind, spreading across it to claim possession. My butthole tingled in agreement.

His dick began to slide into me and my sphincter opened wide to admit him. I stared down at the man's hard body as inch after inch of his pole claimed me, as I willingly surrendered to him. I was in shock.

My dick belched a load as a thick mat of pubic hair pressed hard into my balls. I moaned and shuddered and shot my load as he remained buried in me, watching me.

He leaned into me as the last of my jizz oozed out of my piss slit. His face was a smile as it descended towards mine. I reached to his shoulders and pulled him down to me.

As his tongue pushed into my mouth, he began to pull his cock from me, inch after inch of it. I groaned around his tongue at the emptiness developing in me, and I moaned in pure pleasure when he began to push back into me.

We continued to kiss as his hips flexed and humped his dick slowly in and out of my ass. My cock stayed hard between us. My fingers explored his smooth back, caressing down to his asscheeks and up to his neck.

I came again, my jizz spreading across my chest and belly by our bodies rubbing against each other. I rode the waves of pleasure coming out of my ass and knew I had everything I would ever want between my legs.

I moaned and bucked. I broke away from our kiss and then raised my head to find his lips again. I shuddered. I grabbed fistsful of pinestraw. I felt the night air caress each pore of my skin. I was awash in perfect pleasure and never wanted it to end. My dick stayed hard and rode between our bellies. And the guy just keep on drilling my butt.

After I'd come down from my second orgasm, I started to study this guy pumping my hole with his big dick. It wasn't that I wasn't enjoying the continuing fucking. I was. Waves of pleasure still crashed through me. But it was like my mind had washed closer to shore so it could stand up even as it was being buffeted by those waves.

I was able to think again, something my ass and this guy's dick hadn't let me do when my back hit the bed of pinestraw.

I figured, first off, that there was no use denying what was happening to me or how much I liked it. I even wanted it. This wasn't any damned dream.

Somehow, I'd become queer without even knowing it.

Trying to figure how that happened, though, was a no-brainer. I was what I was, and I'd be looking to fill my ass with dick from now on out. I made a mental note to myself that I had to start using "gay" and drop "queer" from my vocabulary.

Second, the guy with his dick in my butt looked familiar. He'd raised up on his knees, lifting my fanny two or three feet off the ground while he continued to plug me, and was gazing down at me intently.

I'd seen him before. I just couldn't remember where.

He grimaced and began to pound my bottom with short fast strokes. A wave of pleasure crashed over me and pulled me back into quivering mindlessness as my body strained hard for another orgasm.

He growled, his voice a hoarse animal cry, and his face turned to the sky. Tendons bulged in his neck as he shoved his dick all the way into me and I felt it pulse over and over again.

My cock erupted, a rope of jizz landing on my chin. The second splatted on my chest. The third pooled in my bellybutton. I picked the one on my chin up with my finger and slipped it into my mouth. It was a little salty -- almost like my blood -- but not bad.

[*That was the best yet, Sammy boy,*] that damned voice inside my head said, pulling me out of my satiation.

I opened my eyes and saw the top of his head. His face was buried between my legs. Nerve endings told me his lips were on my thigh just below the junction of leg and torso. My ears told me he was making slurping sounds. It felt good, whatever he was doing. My dick started to grow again across my crotch.

"What're you doing?" I asked and stretched, enjoying the feel of my muscles pulling under my skin. Liking the feel of his face buried between my balls and my legs. Yeah, I felt good all over, even if my butt did feel a little sore.

He looked up from between my legs, his lips glistening with red blood, and smiled.

It struck me then. "Oh, shit!" I groaned. It was barely midnight. We were in the woods. And I was seeing everything as clearly as if it were noon.

"What have you done to me?" I demanded, sitting up and chastely closing my legs. My dick was hard and I had a maddening itch up my ass, but I wasn't about to get fucked again until I knew what was happening to me.

[*Good! You're staying calm, boy. And with just the littlest control at that.*] He nodded. [*I like that in a Taylor.*]

I stared at him. This man who had shown me that I was queer. This vampire who'd been slurping my blood. This creature talking to my brain without opening his mouth. This whatever he was.

I accepted that I was at a real disadvantage with him. But I knew how to buy and sell stocks better than anybody in Atlanta -- often from very weak

positions. I wasn't about to let this situation I was in stop me from operating from a position of equality with him -- or better.

"Okay," I told him. "First off, you're going to start talking to me using your mouth. I want you out of my brain. That's off-limits unless I invite you in. Understood?"

He studied me for a moment and then slowly nodded.

"We're getting somewhere now," I said, grinning and pushing myself to my feet. I ignored the dizziness. "Second, I've never done anything gay before -- but was shooting load after load just now with you dicking my butt. What did you do to me?"

He snorted. "I didn't do anything to you, boy," he said in a thick twang that hadn't been heard in north Georgia in more than forty years -- since everybody had television and Walter Cronkite taught us how spoken English was supposed to sound. "I eased your resistance a little and relaxed your muscles -- but you did the rest all by yourself."

"This wasn't the first time, was it?" I was remembering the two times before that I'd found myself naked and lying on the same bed of pinestraw.

"I've fucked your fanny off every night you've been here, boy. I just helped you forget the other times so that you wouldn't be too weirded out afterwards."

I nodded. I'd figured as much once I'd finally started putting two and two together. Shooting three loads with a hard dick in my butt was probably too much for anybody to control. I'd done it myself. I was gay, all right.

"What are you?"

"A vampire." He grinned up at me. "What did you think I was, boy?"

"Who are you? I've seen you somewhere. Are you from Atlanta? Did you follow me up here?"

He laughed. "I'm your great-granddaddy, Sammy boy. You were named after me."

I stared up at him and finally remembered the picture on the mantle. "You're him?"

He nodded.

"Is your being a vampire why none of the locals will come onto this property?"

He laughed. "That and the sex. Not many boys in these parts are willing to admit to liking a hot rod in his asshole."

"Why haven't they come up here with wood stakes in hand looking for you? You've been killing off people for -- what? -- sixty years or more?"

His face became a frown and he scowled at me as he sprang to his feet. "Boy, these are my kinfolk around here. I killed a couple of Huns in the Great War -- before I got hit and went to the hospital. I don't kill kin! None of us do."

"How do you feed?"

"A little here and a little there. A lost less than I took from you -- it doesn't take much."

I reached around to my crack and moved a finger down to my hole. Except for a dampness I figured was sweat, I was dry. "Shouldn't I feel your cum in my ass."

"No, you shouldn't." He wagged his head slowly. "I can have an orgasm -- as many as I did when I was a seventeen-year-old tomcatting all over this mountain. Only, I can't shoot a load any more."

Silence enveloped us. I was full of half-formed questions but wasn't going to ask them until I'd thought them out. I already accepted I'd be seeing a lot of my great-granddad.

"Are we through with these questions and answers, Sammy boy?" he asked, pulling me out of my thoughts.

I nodded. "For the time being," I told him.

"Good. Then we can get down to business."

"What business?" I asked, suddenly suspicious.

"Putting a stop to this tomfoolery about cutting down the trees on this property."

"It sounded pretty reasonable to me..."

"I live here, Sammy. And so will you. I don't want my trees gone and I don't want to have to walk through open cornfields."

I shrugged. "Okay. So I just tell the Varnadores no..."

"That isn't enough with those boys. They want something, they'll talk sweet to you until you give it to them. You've got to establish control over them and never let go."

"How am I supposed to do that?"

"Go on up to the house and get a couple of hours of sleep, boy. I'll get young Jimmy up here..."

"Get him up here?" I cried. "That guy's scared of this place."

He laughed. "You'd be surprised at the number of men who sleepwalk on this mountain, boy. He'll be here." He blinked and then frowned. "Do I have permission to enter your house, Sam?"

"Sure you do."

His hand cupped my butt. "This is mine, Sammy -- just as you are. Do you understand that?"

I knew with complete certainty that my ass was going to be fed a lot of dick in the future. I wasn't even surprised that I looked forward to it.

"I don't want to have to control you, Sammy. I want ours to be an equal partnership." He squeezed my butt and I nodded. "Go on and get some sleep, boy. It's going to take a little while for me to get Jimmy up here and spread out on the bed for you."

I felt sleepier than I ever remembered feeling and knew great-granddad was behind that. I didn't like it but knew there was nothing I could do about it yet. I started towards the house. And stopped and turned around. "Just one question..." He shrugged. "Am I becoming like you?"

He chuckled softly. "You're one slurp away from being one of us now. Just the taste of my blood will send you over the edge, Sammy boy."

- 227 -

"Dad and granddad?" I asked, imagining them rising out of the coffins I'd seen them put into.

"They're dead, Sammy." He shrugged. "Back when I'd just become a vampire and your granddaddy was a strapping young man of twenty, he made me promise to leave him alone -- him and his sons. He didn't say anything about his grandson." He grinned. "I always keep my promises."

"He'll wake up and see us, Mr. Taylor," Jimmy Varnadore whispered. I could taste the fear in his voice. I could sense the heat of his blood as it flushed his face. My dick immediately tented the sheets.

[*Why shouldn't he, boy? He's going to own you before the night's out. He's going to fill you so full of his load, you'll be leaking from your ass for a week.*]

"Sweet Jesus!" my cousin groaned. "You promised nobody'd ever find out that I liked it. If daddy ever finds out…!"

[*I told you nobody would bother you about it, Jimmy -- and they ain't. You're not the only boy up her on the mountain I've diddled. And you're not the only one who likes it. Boys up here all have a little sugar in their tanks, including your daddy. Get on the bed, boy.*]

"But Sammy…?"

[*Sammy's going to fuck your brains out tonight, boy. You gonna be so full of him that you'll never again want to be without his dick buried in your butt.*]

I sat up and pushed the sheet off my body when I felt the mattress give under Jimmy. I smiled as the Varnadore boy stared at my erection. "You're as big as he is!" he croaked finally.

[*Get your mouth down on his thing now, Jimmy,*] great-granddad told him. [*Make love to his dick while I open you up for him…*]

Jimmy continued to hesitate.

[*You start licking now, Jimmy. You bob for his apples. I want your butt up in the air calling to me.*] Great-granddad brooked no further dissent.

Jimmy leaned towards me, his face hovering over my pride and joy as he got to his knees and hiked his ass. Then he was lowering his face. I felt his lips opening as they moved over my knob.

I was in his mouth. His tongue spread across the bottom of my cockhead like a wet, warm chute. His lips traced my shaft lower and lower.

Great-granddad climbed onto the bed behind Jimmy and positioned himself. Jimmy's lips had just got to my pubes when his butthole was invaded. He gasped around my dick as old Sam Taylor spread my cousin wide and opened him up.

Jimmy started to bob on my dick then. His left hand came up to cup my nuts while his right went under his belly to grab his own hard-on. Great-granddad started to fuck him real slow with long, deep thrusts. Jimmy Varnadore moaned continuously as he deep-throated my dick.

[*You're opened up good now, boy,*] great-granddad told him and smiled

The three of us lay on the bed together with me in the middle.

"Your daddy asked me to get involved, Jimmy -- when we talked a little earlier -- to get you settled down," great-granddad told him, propping up on an elbow to see over me. "So, here's what I've worked out. You and me, we'll go down to Atlanta with Sammy tomorrow night. We'll get you into college at some school there. The only people you give that butt to are us. That'll be the way things are going be, at least until you finish school and Sammy's ready to join me completely."

"And after that?" Jimmy asked sitting up, his attention on great-granddad.

"We'll have to see. If Sammy still wants you, we'll make you like us sometime afterwards. If not, we'll make you hungry for pussy, like I did your daddy about twenty years ago…"

He raised a finger. "That is, if you and your daddy don't try to dig up my land anymore. That daddy of yours understands that Sammy owns you now, he's gone and dropped his scheme for the time being. I just plan on making sure it stays dropped."

Jimmy looked from one to the other of us, finally settling on me. A smirk grew across his face.

"I'm yours now. I'm all yours -- and Mr. Sam's," he said. "You better get used to it, because I'm not ever letting you shove me off on some girl -- neither of you."

I nodded slowly. Out of the corner of my eye, I saw that great-granddad was beaming. Thank God I'd already accepted that I was gay. Now all I had to do was decide that I wanted to be a vampire so I could be with him forever. I looked back at Jimmy.

With *them* forever, I corrected myself, knowing damned well that Jimmy wasn't about to be left out.

The Willows
Grant Foster

I was physically and mentally exhausted. I couldn't sleep. I'd lost weight. My concentration was totally shot.

Consolidated Mining vs. Winfield had dragged through the courts for months and when it finally came to judgment, I had lost. I was devastated by the verdict because the firm's founder had made it crystal clear at the outset that my future with the law firm depended on a favorable outcome.

He had hinted that I'd be asked to become a junior partner if the case went our way. His mention of the consequences of failure had been less hint than veiled threat. Since the verdict had been handed down -- I'd lost on an obscure technicality that really had little bearing on the merits of the case -- he had maintained a stony silence.

After a few days of the cold-shoulder, I tendered my resignation. I figured a clean break was simpler and healthier than a long, slow slide into limbo. After I had cleaned out my desk, I felt better; but I was still jumpy and strung-out.

I needed a vacation before I started job-hunting. I just didn't have a clue as to where I wanted to go. I knew I wanted total peace and quiet but wasn't sure how to find it.

I almost threw the brochure away without reading it. It arrived in the mail tucked in a stack of bills and Visa card applications and was on its way to the recycling bin when I saw the postmark. Destrehan, Louisiana, didn't exactly ring any bells, but I did recall that one branch of my mother's family was from some little town not far from New Orleans.

I called her, but she was less than helpful, claiming not to remember anything about family matters. She reminded me that Louisiana was hot and bug-ridden. I racked my brain while she chattered on about my sisters, but couldn't make the connection -- if, in fact, there was one.

After I hung up the phone, I looked at the contents of the envelope again. It wasn't exactly a brochure, more like a personal letter with an elegant ink drawing of a beautiful old home above the letterhead. The text read like an invitation to a country home. Of course, given what places like this charged, they could well afford to sit down and crank out something a few cuts above the standard brochure. I was assured that I would experience perfect peace and idle away my days in languid bliss. It sounded exactly like what I needed, so I picked up the phone and made a reservation. The next morning I took a taxi and caught a flight to New Orleans.

I was already beginning to feel less stressed out by the time the plane landed. I ducked into the men's room at the airport to freshen up. I hardly recognized myself. It was the first time in almost six months that I wasn't

wearing a three-piece suit.

The stranger dressed in the scarlet tank-top and shorts who was staring back at me from the mirror as I washed my hands hadn't even shaved. I was pale, and I had lost some of the hard-won definition I'd been working out for years to achieve, but a quick assessment of my reflection assured me that all wasn't lost. I still had decent muscle tone, my belly was flat, and my ass was still doing a fine job of filling the seat of my pants. I flexed and winked at my reflection.

The man who'd been standing next to me suddenly moved three sinks to the south.

I grabbed my bag and walked jauntily out of the bathroom, viewing my resurgent vanity as a good sign. I hadn't even reached my destination and already I was feeling renewed.

The second I stepped out of the airport, keys to the rental car in hand, I started to sweat. The Louisiana heat was a physical presence, but it seemed a benign one. Besides, it would force me to remain lazy and lethargic -- it definitely wasn't a climate that lent itself to thoughts of jogging or heavy exercise. I was looking forward to total relaxation and indolence for a few days. If I got bored, then maybe I'd drive back to New Orleans for a little fun and frolic in the Quarter.

"You have a safe trip now, sir." The young man who checked my papers before I drove out of the rental car lot was easy on the eye. His short-sleeved shirt bared a nice expanse of muscled arm. Maybe it was just my imagination, but I had a feeling he was eyeing me with more than casual interest.

I took the papers from him, smiled, then drove out towards the freeway. One thing was certain, the loss of my job had pumped new life into my libido. I was horny as hell. Of course, I hadn't had sex with anyone except myself for months. It was just one of many things that definitely had to change in my life.

By the time I turned my rented BMW off the narrow two-lane road and drove through the elaborate wooden gates of The Willows, it was almost sunset.

I marveled at the beauty of the scene that unfolded as I drove along. Huge live oaks draped with lacy curtains of Spanish moss lined the graveled drive. Jasmine, growing pale and waxy beneath the trees, scented the air with its heavy perfume. Emerald lawns, perfectly clipped, rolled away on both sides as far as the eye could see.

When The Willows came into view, I stopped the car and stared in amazement. The house was perfect -- an antebellum mansion of unbelievable beauty, rising out of the shadowed landscape like a pristine Greek temple. Tall white columns stood ghostly sentinel at intervals around the structure and French doors opened from all the rooms onto the wide, shaded verandah. I put the car back into gear and continued up the long, tree-lined drive to the front door.

No one rushed out to greet me, but that wasn't too surprising, considering I hadn't been able to tell them exactly when I'd arrive. I walked slowly up the broad, shallow steps, crossed the wide porch and knocked on the big double door. There was no response. I tried the knob. The door was unlocked, so I ventured into the cool, shaded hallway. The only feature that clearly emerged from the gloom was a wide, spiral staircase rising gracefully to the second floor.

"Hello. Anybody here?" I called.

No response. I walked further in, and the door closed behind me with a dull thud.

"May I help you?" The voice was a honeyed baritone.

"Christ!" I dropped my suitcase and spun around, my heart pounding against my ribs. My nerves were still more frayed than I cared to admit.

"Sorry, but you startled me," I said by way of explanation, surveying the man who stood in the shadows by the front door.

Maybe I'd expected to see a southern belle in a hoop skirt come gliding out onto the verandah to greet me upon arrival -- I don't know. All I knew is, the man in front of me was definitely not the welcoming committee I'd been anticipating.

He was tall, slender, compactly muscled -- he wore mud-clotted knee boots and his filthy clothes. His dark hair was curly and unkempt, hanging down almost to his broad shoulders. His eyes flashed a tawny gold beneath the shadow cast by his jutting brows. His sensual lips were reddish-pink in contrast to his pallid skin. His teeth gleamed in the shadowed gloom like pearls. His hands hung limp at his sides, but you could see the corded muscles of his forearms and the thick veins that bound them, wrist to elbow. I had no idea how he'd managed to get right behind me without opening any doors, yet there he stood, a puddle of dirty water pooling around his feet.

"Welcome to The Willows," he said, his voice sweet and lilting in its southern cadences. "You're Marley." He caressed the name, breathing a whole world of meaning into it.

"That's right," I answered, more than a little surprised that he used my middle name. Then it all came back to me. I shared the name 'Marley' with an obscure ancestor who, as I had discovered while snooping in old family records, had been gay. Needless to say, my strait-laced family hadn't been particularly happy about this discovery. There had even been talk of having my name changed legally, but I'd nixed that idea. Mother had pouted, but never brought the subject up again. No wonder she hadn't been very helpful when I called her yesterday.

"I'm Philip Marley Chamberlain. I'm expected then?"

"Oh, yes, everything has been prepared for you. I am Etienne." He gave me a courtly bow which was oddly at variance with his ramshackle appearance, but which quite charmed me, nonetheless.

"It's nice to meet you, Etienne. Look, I'm all tired out by my long drive

and this incredible heat. Do you think you could show me to my room so I can rest up a bit?"

He gestured towards his boots. "You see," he said quietly, shrugging his broad shoulders.

"Oh, sure, I guess I can find my own way."

"The room at the end of the hall, Marley, as always."

"Pardon?" I said as I picked up my suitcase and turned back to Etienne. He was gone. A shiver flashed along my spine as I stared at the corner where he had been standing. He had slipped away as quietly as he had come in, leaving me alone in the wide hall with only a small puddle of water to indicate where he had stood. I must admit that I was a little unnerved as I climbed the broad stairs to the second floor.

I entered my room, closed the door, stripped out of my sticky traveling clothes, and sprawled out across the huge four poster bed. Etienne was definitely a hunk, I thought to myself as I ran my hands up and down over my sweat-slicked torso. He had an unnerving way of appearing and disappearing, but I definitely hoped he'd pop up again soon. Hell, at this point I'd even take him all muddy and wet.

A slight breeze ruffled the gauzy curtains draped across the windows, then swirled lazily across to me, warm and soothing against my bare skin. A ceiling fan turned slowly overhead, droning softly like a big, lazy insect. I needed to shower, but first I closed my eyes -- just for a moment.

The heavy curtains parted slowly, and Etienne stood before me, naked, head held high. I had forgotten somehow how beautiful he was. His skin, pale in the late afternoon light, was smooth and cool as marble. A thin line of dark, silky hairs split him in half, running from the hollow of his throat down into the dense cloud of his pubes. His nipples stood out thick and hard from the squared planes of his broad chest. His muscled back was reflected in the pier mirror mounted between the two pairs of French doors at the foot of the bed -- the wide shoulders tapering to a narrow waist. His legs were long, well-formed, furred with a dense dark growth that stopped abruptly at the point where the globes of his delectable ass began to swell out of the planes of his strong thighs. The cheeks were pale, dimpled, without flaw.

The flames of my lust rose in my belly as he stepped across the bare cypress floor to the bedside. He stopped, hands held out, offering himself to me. I reached up and closed my fingers gently around the shaft of his cock, already rising up from between his strong thighs. I pulled him towards me.

"Marley," he whispered as he climbed into the bed on top of me. He straddled my broad chest, the hair on his legs tickling along my sides as he settled against me. The head of his big cock brushed against my lips. My tongue flickered lizard-like from my mouth, barely grazing the hooded knob. He sighed softly and his prick twitched violently for a few moments before settling heavily against my mouth once again.

I took the silky foreskin gently between my lips, tugging it forward and

away from the swollen, shiny glans hidden inside. I slipped my tongue between the sheath of skin and the sweet fruit it covered, probing and digging in the tight, hot space. I heard his gasped intake of breath and felt his thighs tense against my sides as he thrust forward, forcing his way into my mouth. When I dug my tongue into his gaping piss slit, searching for the first sweet drop of his honey, he squeezed his dick from base to tip, drizzling sticky juice onto my greedy lips. I licked them, then raised my head slightly, urging him to probe my mouth.

He leaned forward, bracing his hands against the ornately carved headboard of the bed, tilting his pelvis forward so he could more easily slide his stiff cock deep into my throat. I grabbed his balls and pulled them back against his asshole, pressing my palm hard against them. He looked down at me, eyes heavy-lidded, watching me suck, watching my rough tongue as it flicked lazily at his swollen cockhead.

I pulled teasingly at the thin line of hair bisecting his perfect body. I rubbed the ball of my thumb against the thick brown points of his tits and his muscles flexed. He bucked, pumping his long dick deep into my throat. I bit down, raking my teeth along the shaft, pressing my lips against the pulsing veins that coursed along his throbbing length.

I could have been content to lie there and suck him till his thick, creamy life gushed down my hungry throat, but Etienne would not have it so. He moved back, knelt between my legs and scissored them apart roughly. He bent his shaggy head and lapped at my sweaty crack. I clenched my fists when he nipped at my asshole, tugging the short hairs around the sweaty, puckered flesh till I groaned with pleasure and my prick snapped up tight against my flat gut.

"It is good, Marley?" he whispered softly, his breath warm on my balls. Etienne rubbed his spit around the spasming ring of my sphincter, then pushed his long forefinger into me.

"It's very good, Etienne," I sighed, pulling his head down to my chest. "I want you."

He guided his long thick prick to my asshole, found his target, and thrust forward. My cry of ecstasy was cut off abruptly as his long tongue snaked into my mouth.

He sealed his lips against mine, then blew his breath into my lungs. A wave of raw passion flowed through me, washing away all conscious thought, making me his minion, taking away my will.

I wrapped my legs around his narrow waist, opening my body to his frenzied thrusting. I was overwhelmed with the sheer animal power of the man -- his pelvis grinding hard against my aching butt, his balls slapping against my tailbone, his hands clamped hard against my shoulders, his fat dickhead pounding my prostate. The intensity of it took my breath, pushing me closer and closer to the point of no return.

He rocked back on his haunches, pulling me up with him, still driving his hard prick in and out of my yielding body. He fixed me with his

glittering eyes, willing my obedience. Unable to speak, I nodded. He smiled at me, his teeth gleaming.

I felt his breath, hot against my neck, a moment of sharp pain, then a bliss transcending anything I'd ever known. My skin began to tingle as our bodies pressed tight together. I felt his heart, pounding against my chest, strong and steady. The pulse became a roaring tide, deafening me, engulfing me.

"Yes, Marley," he moaned, his lips against my ear. My heart beat as his heart, now in synch with that sweet point of union between us, his cock in my body, his strong arms wrapped around me, thrusting, driving, carrying both of us towards the ends of desire.

"Etienne," I whispered and knew he completed me.

He raised his head and smiled at me, his lips scarlet, his face and chest flushed -- rosy, warm.

Scarlet ribbons fluttered down my shoulder across my chest. My head was heavy, my eyelids drooped, my world contracting to the point where his cock pistoned in my guts.

I was finished. Jizm boiled up from deep in my balls. The first jet of my cream flew between us to splatter my chest.

My spasming sphincter brought him to a climax. He stiffened and threw back his head, calling my name as his hot spunk spouted into me, filling me full of his hot, sticky life.

"I'm cumming," he cried. "Hold me, Marley. Until forever, Marley. Oh…"

"Marley. Are you there? Wake up."

I swam slowly back to consciousness, willing my eyes to focus on the dusk-shadowed room. I must have fallen asleep almost as soon as I lay my head on the down-filled pillows.

"I'm here," I called out groggily. "I fell asleep. Just give me a minute or two to wake up."

I lifted my head and pulled myself slowly up against the massive headboard of the bed. When I looked down and saw my cock curved up against my belly, resting in the pungent white puddle, I had to laugh.

It had been a dream then, the steamy imaginings of an exhausted tourist in a strange bed.

I hadn't had a wet dream in ages, but there was the evidence, strung out like liquid ropes against my chest and belly, mingling with the sweat that sheened my body. Evidently, Etienne had gotten under my skin even more than I had realized. It must have been his rough-and-tumble looks as he stood there all muddy and wet from his work. That, coupled with the warm intimacy of his eyes and his deep, resonant voice. That, and something I couldn't understand.

"Your dinner will be ready soon, Marley," he said through the door, interrupting the thought. "I just wanted to make sure you didn't miss the

appointed hour."

"Thanks, Etienne," I called out. "I'll just take a quick shower. Don't worry, I promise not to miss dinner."

I stretched lazily and tucked my hands behind my head, watching the fan's blades circle in the gathering gloom.

I started down the stairs just as the grandfather's clock on the landing chimed eight. There was a light coming from the dining room, but the rest of the house was cloaked in gloom. The long mahogany table was elaborately set for one. I was obviously The Willows' only guest.

Food was set out on a heavy sideboard between two of the French doors that opened at regular intervals around the room. Beyond the verandas, there was only deep, velvet darkness.

There were three bottles of wine ranged beside the single place set for dinner. All were heavily encrusted with cobwebs. Bad marks for housekeeping, I thought wryly as I reached for the nearest of the bottles. I wiped the neck carefully, then poured some into the first glass that came to hand.

It was rich and full, blood-colored, the bouquet so heady and complex that it must have been developing for a very long time. I filled my glass and drank it down in two long swallows. It warmed my throat and tingled in my belly like a subtle fire.

I started to get up to fill my plate, then decided to have yet another glass of the wine. It, too, went down easily; but I felt the effects of the alcohol. The humid night air in combination with the heat generated by the wine made my skin burn beneath my clothes. As I poured a third glass, a blood-red gush of wine sloshed over the rim of the heavy crystal goblet and trailed across the white linen.

When I reached for my napkin to soak up the mess, a jagged streak of lightning flashed white in the distance. In that instant of illumination, when the night turned livid day, I saw him. At least I thought I saw him. It was Etienne, of course -- the man who had invaded my dream earlier in the evening -- although what he was doing naked on the lawn I couldn't quite imagine. The light faded abruptly and then I saw nothing.

My attempt to mop up the wine ended in disaster. I clipped the bottle with my elbow and tipped it over. It eluded me, rolling along the center of the long table, spreading a dark stain like a swollen river on a flood plain. I jumped up, then suddenly realized that I was dizzy. I was struggling to regain my balance when the lightning flashed again. He was there. I was certain that I had seen him this time.

A gust of wind billowed the curtains and extinguished the candles on the table. My cry of alarm was blotted out by the rumble of thunder. When I crossed to the French doors, the curtains sprang to life, wrapping me in their silken folds.

Panicked, I thrust out my arms, trying to push them aside. The wine,

my steamy dream, the sight of Etienne, naked on the lawn, all combined to fill me with a tingling sense of urgency which I could neither define nor ignore.

In pulling free of the draperies, I wrenched the heavy brass rod which held them away from the wall. It crashed noisily against the mahogany sideboard, sending a tray of decanters to a sudden and violent end.

I stumbled out onto the broad veranda, my eyes struggling to adjust to the velvet gloom of the warm Louisiana night. The lightning flashed again, closer now, and again I saw him. He was watching me, hands outstretched, his big prick curving mightily up against his washboard gut. His balls dangled heavily, swaying back and forth between his thighs as he moved towards me.

"Marley," he called, his voice uncertain, supplicating. "Come with me, Marley. It's so lonely here. Please come."

"Etienne?" I replied, unsure of what was happening, only aware of the weirdness and sensuality of it all.

For one fleeting moment, I hesitated. His dark eyes flashed, skewered me, took away any thought of flight. I was so horny I could hardly breathe. I had been ever since I woke up from my nap. My wet dream had only served to make me more ravenous for sex, for the touch of Etienne's hands against my skin.

Stumbling across the grass, I tore at my clothes, kicking off my shoes, almost falling as I fought my way free of my trousers. I tore my shirt open and as I reached him.

I stood before him, trembling and naked.

His touch was like electricity on my skin. He stroked slowly down my neck, over my broad chest, pinching my nipples hard between his fingers, drawing me closer, till our cocks crossed like two swords. His long cock rubbed against my belly, leaving a thin trail of glistening slime in its wake.

Our bodies pressed together -- my flesh hot and fevered, his cool and soothing to the touch.

I clasped his narrow waist as we continued to grind against each other, prick mashed against prick, pubic bushes -- black and golden -- tangled inextricably together.

Finally, he released his grip on my tits, only to lower his head to my chest and continue his ecstatic torture of the tender flesh with his teeth. His hands grasped my butt, forcing the cheeks apart, probing my crack with his long, thick fingers.

I clasped my hands around the strong column of his neck, lifted my legs, wrapped them around his waist.

Lightning flashed again, and the heavens opened, pouring warm rain over us in torrents. It came down so hard the big house behind us was totally obscured from view. It plastered our hair flat against our skulls and cooled my fevered body.

Etienne pressed his lips to mine, his long tongue tickling against the

roof of my mouth. I savored the taste and texture of him. He responded by probing at my asshole, his strong fingers slipping deep into the yielding channel.

"Fuck me, Etienne," I moaned. "I want your cock in me. I want to feel your cum pumping into my body again. Fuck me."

He turned then and carried me across the manicured lawn, into the deeper gloom beneath the moss-hung oaks. I clung to him, his muscle-knotted torso shifting against me as he walked quickly and surely over the uneven ground.

He stopped and knelt, still holding me in his strong embrace. The lightning flashed as I opened my eyes, revealing his chiseled features. His eyes flickered with golden fire, the thick brows arching strongly above them. "I've waited for you, Marley," he whispered thickly. "I've waited so long…"

"Oh, yes," I replied, held in thrall by his incredible sensuality. "I want you, Etienne. Now!"

He pushed me back, not onto the ground, but onto something else, something hard and flat and smooth to the touch. He knelt between my outstretched legs, lifting them till the crook of my knees rested on his broad shoulders. Then he fell forward, impaling me. His cock filled me, stretching my guts to the sweet point of pain. In that instant, we became one body, one flesh, melting together into one complete being.

His balls slapped wetly against my bottom as the rain continued to fall over us. It streamed in rivulets across his shoulders and down his wide chest where it channeled between the swell of his pecs, along the thin line of hair bisecting his torso, then down to his crotch. From there it flowed between my legs and into my pubes, plastering them flat around the base of my swollen, bouncing prick.

Lightning flashed feverishly and thunder rumbled and crashed in a steady crescendo. Etienne reamed my throbbing hole, pounding me to ecstasy. Then he lowered his head and pressed his mouth against the swell of my chest. There was a pricking sensation, then the heat gushed out of me.

My heart began to slow, pumping now in rhythm with his pistoning prick. I felt my limbs grow heavy, my fingers numbing till I could no longer feel the strong arms I struggled to grasp. I watched the top of his sleek head and his broad, rain-slicked shoulders as they began to fade to silence.

"Etienne!" I groaned, my lips barely moving.

He raised his head, his gaze unfocused like a man drunk on too much wine. He saw me, shook himself, pulled me up against him. I watched his finger slash across the heavy curve of his right pec, just above the nipple. A tiny mouth gaped in the perfect skin, spouting warm, dark wine. He pressed my mouth tight against it and I felt the heat begin to flow back into my body like pale fire.

"Suck," he whispered. "Suck me, Marley. I've waited for you. I've waited. Suck, my love. Suck."

I began to tremble as my strength returned, heat coursing through my veins, my cock harder and more sensitive than it had ever been before this moment.

Etienne humped me like a wild man, and my own juices were starting to boil up, ready to explode across my rain-washed torso.

I could hear faint groaning, whimpering sounds deep in his chest as his prickhead began to swell perceptibly against my aching prostate.

Just as I was pushed beyond the precipice and gave myself over to the first intense rushes of orgasm, a burst of lightning brought the whole scene into sharp focus. We were in what had to be the family cemetery.

A marble monument rose behind Etienne, white and eerie in the blinding light. The words engraved in the silvered marble glowed and remained etched on my eyelids, even after the aching intensity of my feelings had rolled my eyes back into my skull.

ERECTED TO THE SACRED MEMORY
OF
ETIENNE HENRI MARTINON
1837-1865
BY HIS BELOVED MARLEY.
I WILL WAIT ALONE FOR YOU, MY LOVE,
UNTIL BEYOND THE END OF TIME

"I'm cumming," I shouted, my whole body spasming with intense pleasure. My cock flexed and a blast of jism jetted out of me, shooting up over my head and splattering on the slab of marble at my head. I no longer knew whether I was in this world or the next -- and I no longer cared. We were together now. That was all that mattered.

Etienne cried out his ecstasy along with me. I gripped his biceps and held on fiercely as his hot life flooded into my body. A final spasm shook me and I sank into the sated void.

"Marley?"

I fought my way back to consciousness.

"Marley!"

"Yes, my love?" I opened my eyes. He was so beautiful.

"I waited, Marley. I waited for you."

"Yes, my love."

"We're together now, Marley."

"Yes, my love."

His skin was translucent alabaster.

"Forever, Marley. Until beyond the end of time."

Blood Bank
Holden Wells

"Mark?"

A hand on my shoulder jarred me. The trash bags under me crunched as weight shifted. I was burning up and I was freezing all at the same time.

"Mark?"

I wanted to wake up, and already I could feel the dull pain in my kidneys that had plagued me the last couple of days returning and I was gasping for breath. Blackness mercifully came over me again and saved me from it.

I didn't hear my name this time; instead, I swam from the depths of deep sleep on my own to find that I was no longer in the alley. I lay on my back -- no, not lay -- reclined, as in a dentist's chair. And I was restrained in a familiar way.

With great effort, I cracked open an eye and peered down my body. A needle in my arm let blood pump into a clear, thin tube that ran ... Somewhere.

I settled my head back on what I knew to be a smooth, dark red vinyl headrest and closed my eyes.

It was okay. I'd been here before.

When I came around next, it was for real, finally, and I was in bed. I sat with the sheet puddled in my lap and traced my jagged memories backward to when I first realized I wasn't going to be able to stay awake anymore and had to get myself to the nearest semi-soft, semi-out-of-the-way place. Or hospital. I guessed I made it as far as a trash pile in someone's alley.

Mono, I thought. Must have been mono. I'd had it before, when I was fourteen. 'Course, when I was fourteen and had it, it didn't hurt to pee. And I'd been able to breath all right. The things you can ignore, though, when you'd rather not face them.

After a yawn and a stretch, I took in the small room -- one I figured was stuck in the far back of Cale's apartment.

My clothes were folded on a chair. Clean. I had to piss. I pulled on my jeans over my morning hard-on and padded to the door to look for a bathroom.

My hand hovered above the knob and I wondered if it was locked.

Which was ridiculous; I knew Cale. Everyone knew Cale. And if I was piecing the fragments of memory together correctly, then Cale had found me in the alley and brought me back to his place.

The door wasn't locked. Cale wasn't a monster for Christ's sake.

I found him in the kitchen, standing over a pot on the stove, dressed in

khakis and a loose white t-shirt.

"You're awake," Cale said, mouth turning up. He held a hand over the steam rising off the pot.

"You fixing something to eat?" I asked, hunger taking precedence over politeness.

"Um, no." He laughed. "Sterilizing needles."

"Ah." I raked my hand through my hair and watched him. It was different seeing him like this, standing in the morning sunlight. I didn't know he could do that. On the street, we only saw him at night. His dark hair slipped forward as he turned back to the pot and I was left with a memory of a smile playing at the corners of his mouth and an almost bashful look in his eye.

His head jerked up. "But you need to."

"Huh?"

"Eat. You must be starved. Fuck." He looked around the room. "I haven't picked up the juice and cookies for tonight, yet. I don't have anything."

The thought of juice and cookies -- stuff he'd feed us after we made our blood donations -- turned my stomach a little, but -- yeah -- I was hungry.

"It's cool," I said. "I can get something…" When I leave. I didn't want to leave. How many of us ever saw this part of Cale's apartment? Or this part of Cale? I'd never heard of it and, trust me, when the weather was crap and business slow, we huddled and speculated about Cale quite a bit.

"Tomorrow," Cale said.

I was about to tell him that he was a little out of touch with humanity if he thought I could wait another twenty-four hours without eating.

He dumped the water out of the pan, the needles clattering against the bottom of the stainless steel sink, and continued with, "Tomorrow you can go out and get something, but today you should take it easy." He dried his hands on his pants. "I'll go get the cookies and juice, and pick something up for you, too."

I wished he'd stop saying cookies and juice. "You don't have to," I said, and that might have been the first time I ever told a grown man he didn't have to go out of his way and do something for me.

"Something from McDonald's?" he asked. "Egg McWhatever-it-is?"

I smiled. "Muffin. Egg McMuffin. Two, with ham."

"Okay." His gaze flitted back to the sink, the needles. I was interrupting his routine. But then he said, "Okay," again and patted his pockets. Keys, wallet: everybody did that, even vampires. I leaned against the doorway.

"Okay, I'm going then." He grinned. Sharp teeth flashed and without thinking I ran my tongue over my own dull ones.

"There are towels in the bathroom. Shampoo. Whatever you need."

I watched him leave.

"I was sick," I said later. Two days later? Maybe. Anyway, I wasn't sick anymore.

"Mmm-hmm." He was reading. Cale's living room reminded me of the stacks in the basement of the library in my hometown. Books upon books upon books. But then, with eternity lying before you, I guess you had time for reading.

I had time for it, too, once, when I was young enough for summer to be considered an eternity. Every other day -- sometimes every day -- I rode my BMX four miles to the library, books bouncing behind me in the bottom of my backpack. With a confidence only an eleven-year-old can possess, I was certain I'd exhaust the little library of books by the end of summer, and I said as much to the librarian. Said it to him twice, at least. And when he told me that I needn't fear because they had a whole stockpile of books in the basement, my face split into a grin.

There were books down there, all right, and that wasn't all, but let's not blame the librarian for the fact that I grew up to make a living off of hustling my ass. I'm sure he was only a little part of it.

"You didn't drink it," I said to Cale now, meaning my blood.

"No. You were sick."

"Why'd you take it, then?"

Cale flattened his hand on his page and lifted his gaze to a spot somewhere in the middle of the carpet. "I guess I just enjoy that part of it, too. It's not always about eating."

I tipped my head back and studied the ceiling. I used to read, but I seem to have forgotten how to let books absorb me.

"You want to help tonight?" Cale asked.

"You serious?" I asked, sitting up.

Cale shrugged. "It's not a big deal."

My ass. I'd never heard even a rumor of anyone assisting Cale.

The bathroom door was cracked. Steam billowed out. I didn't hear water running, though; he must have finished. I stood by the door -- against the door, practically -- and listened. Then I put my knuckles to the wood and pushed. It swung open easier than I expected.

Cale, running a towel over one of his thighs -- the lean, muscled thigh of a healthy twenty-eight-year-old despite his rumored 'true age -- looked up.

"You need the bathroom?" he asked.

He pulled the towel over his crotch, giving it a quick rub, and then straightened as he continued up his abdomen to his chest ... My eyes went back to his thigh though, the inside of which held a neat column of tattoos -- letters, in sets of three. My gaze climbed them like a ladder until I reached his cock, heavy and half-hard below a shock of dark brown hair that rose in an inverted V towards his belly button.

Since he'd taken me in, he hadn't lain a hand on me, hadn't asked for

anything. Was it because he was a vampire? Or was he just straight?

"Mark...?"

"Uh..." I pulled my gaze to his face. "I, uh, have your change." I held out a fist containing a couple crumpled bills and some coins. He'd sent me to buy the cookies and juice for tonight's donors. I obviously wasn't completely over the mono yet; I didn't sneak a single cookie on my way back from the store.

"Oh. You can keep it."

"What the fuck are you doing here?" Kevin asked.

"What's it look like?" I buckled his right wrist to the arm of the vinyl chair with his palm facing down. This wasn't the arm Cale would be drawing blood from.

"We'd been wondering about you. One or two guys speculated you'd found a sugar daddy, but the rest of us figured you were just dead."

"Gee, thanks."

"You looked like hell."

"I had mono."

"Then Count Dracula gave you a transfusion and you were right as rain?"

"No, shithead." I pulled the buckle on his left wrist tight. This arm was palm-up.

"You're not gonna stick me, are you?"

I'd asked Cale the same thing, at once sickened by and curious about the prospect of piercing someone's skin with a needle.

"No, I'm not."

"Thank God for small miracles. Hey, Cale."

"Kevin. How are you tonight?"

He shrugged.

"Business slow?" Cale swabbed Kevin's arm with an alcohol-soaked ball of cotton.

"Yeah. How'd you know?"

"It's been busy here lately," Cale said with a smile. He didn't just take blood from people; he paid them for it. Some guys -- me included -- came as often as he allowed, which was about as often as the Red Cross would have allowed, too. We came because it was easy money, the chair was comfortable, and Cale was a mystery. A handsome, dark mystery. Other guys, though, came only when they were desperate, and some of those guys had been by the past few days.

"It's the weather," Kevin said. It had turned suddenly and unseasonably chilly and wet lately.

"Maybe," Cale said. "There you go. I'll be back in a bit."

Blood pumped into the tube hooked to the inside of Kevin's left elbow, pumping faster as Kevin clutched and released the roll of taped-up bandages Cale had put in his fist.

"So, you fucking him?" Kevin asked me.

I shook my head, entranced by the flow of dark red liquid.

"You know why he ties us down, don't you?"

Again, I shook my head. My gaze left the tube and traveled to the leather cuff around Kevin's wrist. Then to his lap, and the bulge in his jeans.

"Because..." he said.

"Because why?" I slid my hand over my own bulge. Kevin shifted his hips. Rubbing myself, I dropped my knee between his.

"Because the blood, the boys ... They turn him on."

"Do they?" My hand dropped to the front of his jeans. I could have argued with him -- boys didn't appear to do anything for Cale -- but Kevin had me caught up in the possibility of it now.

"Oh yeah," he moaned. "They do," he continued, remembering his end of the conversation.

I stretched myself over him. "So how's tying them down help?"

"Because he can control himself, then. As long as the thing he wants isn't coming on to him, isn't trying to touch him and pull him close, he can control himself."

"You're full of shit," I said in his ear, but I pictured myself walking into that steamy bathroom earlier, and this time I pictured myself backing him against the sink, grinning, wanting him, daring him to take me. I rubbed my cock against Kevin's thigh. "So what happens if he doesn't control himself?"

Kevin pushed his hips up. "He loses it and then ... Then he rips your neck open and by the time he comes to his senses, you're dead."

"Rips you're neck open, huh?" My hand was between our bodies, squeezing his cock. "Like this?" I opened my mouth wide and clamped down on the side of his throat. He arched into my mouth. I ground my crotch on his thigh, then ran my tongue over the ridge of muscle in his neck.

"Yeah," he said, "Yeah, bite me, fucker!"

I did, but not for real. I wasn't a vampire. I didn't want to taste blood. And I didn't think Kevin wanted me to break skin, either, but he was bucking under me, as much as the restraints at his wrists and ankles allowed, and saying, "fucker, bite me." I grabbed the other side of his head to hold him still while I sucked more of his neck into my mouth, slobbering on it then licking the slobber off. He groaned, "Shit. Shit. Shiiit!" He stiffened before he started to shudder.

Panting, I pushed myself up on my arms and look down.

"Oh man," he said, with a little grin, his eyes closed.

His spit-slick neck shone yellow in the light from the ceiling.

"Are you planning to molest all my customers?" Cale asked in the kitchen.

Leaning against the counter, munching on a hot dog I'd just boiled in

the needle pot, I said, "Maybe."

He gave me a smile that showed he knew I wasn't serious.

But still. "What if I did?"

He shrugged. "It's your body."

"What if you wanted it?"

He'd just replenished the cookie tray Kevin had wiped out. I remembered when I used to scarf 'em up, too, when I gave blood here. Cookies and juice and sometimes donuts. But they just didn't sound good any more.

As Cale slowly folded the top of the cookie box closed, he said, carefully, "What?"

"What if you wanted my body?" I asked. "Or do vampires do sex?"

"Why don't you go let him in?"

I was about to ask who when I heard a knock at the front of the apartment. Sucking the fat from the hot dog off my fingers, I passed through the book maze of the living room and into the front parlor, which was the only room his customers ever saw.

"What the fuck are you doing here?" Miguel asked when I opened the door.

"What's the tattoo on your thigh all about?"

Cale was in his usual chair, reading. I'd already ducked my head to check out the cover -- some faded and worn Charles Bukowski paperback. Yesterday it had been Vonnegut. The day before, Michael Crichton.

"Hmm?" Cale said, pretending he hadn't heard me.

I dropped onto the couch and folded my hands behind my head.

"How old are you?" I asked. If you asked three guys on the streets Cale's age, they'd give you answer a hundred years older than the previous guy's answer.

"Mmm ... Eighty-two? Eighty-three? What year is it now?"

I rolled onto my elbow and stared at him. "That's it?"

He dropped his book in his lap. "What? Do I look older than that?"

"No, it's just ... We all thought you were, like you'd been around forever."

Picking up his book again, he said, "Well I haven't. I was born in nineteen twenty-one."

"And the tattoo on your thigh?" I pressed.

Without looking up from his page, he said, "Those who came before me."

"You have a habit of intruding," Cale said when I pushed through the door of his bedroom. His pajama bottoms rode low on his hips. My gaze fastened itself to the line of hair at his belly button, and I imagined I could make out the dark shape of his cock under the thin fabric of his pants. I'd apparently caught him just as he was pulling the covers back to get in bed.

"I know." I didn't leave.

"Well?" he asked after half a minute. He rubbed his chest with the flat of his hand.

"Why'd you bring me here?"

"You were sick, and sleeping in a pile of trash."

"I'm better now."

"Yes."

"So why do you let me stay?"

"You help out."

"You didn't need help before." I pushed the door shut with my back, leaned against it. "You don't actually need help now. Business might have picked up a little this week, but it's far from a mad house out there."

Turning his back to me, Cale picked up a pillow and plumped it between his hands. "So? It's nice to have the help. I do the same thing every night and it gets tedious after a while." He dropped the pillow back on the bed. "Which reminds me, I need you to run an errand tomorrow."

"Okay."

He faced me again, his hands on his hips. "Anything else?"

"Why do you tie them down?"

He grinned. "Maybe it's like Kevin said."

"What?" Knowing full well what, but distracted, realizing that Cale had heard us talking. Had he seen us, too? Watched?

He crossed the room and stood in front of me, put his hand on the door behind my head. "Maybe I just can't control myself and I'd kill you all," he said, his mouth still pulled back in a wicked grin.

"Nah." I pushed him away and realized it was the first time we'd touched since he'd carried me home and tucked me in bed in the back room.

"Cale?"

"What?" He'd headed back towards his bed.

"Do vampires have sex?"

"Go to bed, Mark."

"So come on, tell me. Does he have a coffin back there? Dirt from the motherland? Have the mirrors been removed from the bathroom?"

It was Donny this time, grinning as the blood pumped from his arm. I sat on a wheeled metal stool beside his chair and pushed myself back and forth, back and forth.

"No coffin. No dirt, except what you assholes track in." One of the ways I'd been helping out was in cleaning up. Not my favorite part of the job. Dry-humping the occasional customer was much more rewarding. "And I shaved in the bathroom mirror this morning."

Late, late morning. Cale needed less sleep than I did; he stayed up till all hours taking care of customers, and then woke when the first rays of sunshine spilled through the windows. After my first couple days here, I'd settled into my usual schedule of late to bed, late to rise.

"But can you see him in the mirror?"

"Not if he doesn't stand behind me when I'm shaving."

"Does he?"

"No, you asshole. You're finished." I began disconnecting him.

"Where's he keep the blood?"

"Freezer chest in the kitchen."

"You ever see him drink it?"

I shook my head.

"Come on, there's gotta be something strange you can tell me about him."

"He lets people like you into his house," I offered, but I was thinking about the errand I'd run for him, to an art supply store where they'd handed me a small paper sack. Out in the parking lot, I'd peered inside. It contained a single bottle of blue India ink.

The last of the customers had gone for the night. I was sweeping the parlor -- dirt, cookie crumbs, and clear plastic wrappers shed like skins from the straws on juice boxes. My stomach growled. I wanted a steak; maybe I'd talk Cale into coming out with me.

"You ready?" Cale asked.

"For what?"

My eyes followed the brown paper sack in his hand as he set it on the stainless steel tray beside the blood donation chair.

"For all the stuff you want to know about."

I let out a nervous laugh. My face felt cold as the blood rushed out of it. "Is it just going to be a lecture?" I asked, my eyes going back to the sack.

He took the broom from my hands. "I want you to take your clothes off."

"You're not gonna bite me, are you?" I felt stupid. My fingers tingled so I pumped them into fists a few times.

"Mark, relax."

Right. I'd lived with him two weeks and known him much longer than that. My imagination was running off with me. On the other hand, this was a man who'd stolen blood from a sick person, just because he liked the process of taking blood. Sure, he'd taken care of me afterward, but...

"Get undressed." Cale's eyes were clear; nothing like the assholes who'd tried to get something over on me in the past. I had a choice and could go either way. Stay here or hit the streets. I didn't mind the streets, but...

"Mark?"

I nodded and dragged my shirt over my head. Then pulled off my socks, the bottoms of which were brownish gray from the floor. Cale didn't watch. He opened the sack and pulled out two things he must have stuffed in there after I brought the India ink back: a cardboard card stuck with sewing needles and a spool of thread. As I pushed my jeans off my hips, he

licked an end of thread and held it near the point of the needle. Then, slowly, carefully, he began winding the thread around the thin shaft of metal.

When I pushed my underwear down, my cock bounced up and smacked me in the stomach. The air felt good on my body. I stepped out of my briefs and stood waiting to find out what happened next. Idly, I fondled myself. The harder my dick got, watching him, wondering, the more removed I became from my powers of judgment.

"Come here," Cale said, taking a step back from the chair, his attention focused on the thread he was wrapping. "Sit down."

After a moment's hesitation, I approached the chair, laid my hand on the headrest. My fingers fell on the middle part, the part that had been worn smooth by the backs of countless heads. The heel of my hand rested on the edge where the vinyl was brighter and more porous.

"Go on."

I heard a soft pop. He'd broken the thread with his teeth.

After filling my chest with air like I was about to plunge into a tank of water, I knelt on the chair, and then turned and settled back, reclining in it, bare skin against vinyl. It was still warm, a little, from the last customer of the evening. Chuck. Big Chuck. Twenty-three and still hadn't lost his baby fat, and that's exactly what it looked like on him, too: baby fat. But some guys liked them soft, and the fat had the bonus of making Chuck look much younger, so Chuck didn't do too badly on the streets. I shifted my ass across the same vinyl that his ass -- clad in sweatpants -- had shifted on not twenty minutes ago.

I had the arm rests in my hands, my wrists lying in the open cuffs. I'd been in this chair to give blood so many times, it was instinctual.

"Ready?" Cale asked, his voice competing with the rush of blood in my ears.

"I'd be more ready if you told me what was going on."

As Cale buckled my right wrist in, palm down, he said, "I'm marking you."

"With?"

He pulled the cuff around my left wrist, pushed the tongue through the buckle. "Those who came before you."

My heart beat like a hummingbird's wings against my chest. Cale settled one of my ankles in the straps at the foot of the chair and buckled it down. Then the other. I swallowed. His hand moved up my shin onto my thigh, as he stood up.

"Ready?" he asked again, his palm sliding over my cock, making it leak a warm spot like spilled blood onto my stomach.

"What are we doing here?" I asked, pressing my head against the vinyl.

"Shhh." His knee dropped between my legs. He put his thumb to my lips. "I'm not going to hurt you. Well, not much more than getting a tattoo usually hurts."

"It's just a tattoo?" I asked, my fear beginning to fall into disappointment.

"Yeah, it's just a tattoo."

I watched him pour India ink into a small dish, then lay the needle against the dish's edge, letting the cotton thread wound around it soak up the ink.

"Be right back."

I watched the thread become bright blue. In a minute, he returned with a small plastic tub sloshing soapy water over his hands. He washed my thigh with a washcloth, then with alcohol-soaked cotton.

I'd never had a tattoo, had no idea what to expect. He placed a warm hand at the top of my thigh and picked up the needle.

Our eyes met. I nodded.

He bent and began to pick out the first letter of the first initial of those who had come before. At the first touch of the needle to my skin, my thigh muscle jerked. Even so, a heat scuttled from my balls up to my nipples, making them feel as though they were being scraped by the same needle. I lifted my head to watch him work and instead saw my cock unfurling. He glanced up and a smile flashed across his face before he turned back to his work.

The final letters -- hours later; Cale was meticulous at his work: prick, prick, prick -- were CAM.

"What's your middle name?" I asked.

"Adam."

He cleaned my thigh. I was chilly. Itchy patches of dried precum marked my stomach and my other thigh, but my cock was soft now and resting on my balls.

"I'm marked," I said, watching him smear A&D ointment over my new tattoo. "Now what?"

The breath rushed out of me as he unexpectedly dropped onto my chest, bringing his face within inches of mine. As he pushed my hair back from my forehead, I saw the sharp tip of one of his teeth glisten in his mouth.

"Do you still want to know if vampires have sex?"

The fear that had vanished when he'd told me it was just a tattoo came thudding back. My cock regained interest, too.

"I still want to know why you tie us down."

He licked the ridge of my ear. His body was warm on top of mine, his jean-clad thigh rough against skin made sensitive by thousands of needle pricks.

"And what happens if you bite me. And why you marked me."

"I tie you boys down because it's kinky. I only have boys come up here because I like boys. If I bite you..." He dragged a fang along my throat, making me gasp and tense. "You'll end up with a hole in your neck. And I

marked you…" He pushed up onto his hands and looked down at me with dark eyes made even darker by his dilated pupils. "because you were dying, and now you're the next."

"What?" I tugged at the cuffs, tried to sit up.

"Shhh," Cale said as he pressed his mouth, cool and a little chapped, to mine. I thought I felt his fangs through the padding of his lips. I knew I felt his cock pushing again my pubic bone.

He kissed my chin.

I said, "Why me?"

"I've always liked you," he breathed against my skin. But then, as though worried I'd jump to conclusions, he lifted his head and looked me in the eye. "But I wouldn't have, if you hadn't been sick."

"It was just mono."

He shook his head, then ducked and nestled his cheek against my jaw.

"Let me up."

"Yep." Without getting off me, he unbuckled one wrist, then the other. He started to crawl back to get my ankles, but I stopped him, catching his neck in my hands. He looked up at me.

"What was it?" I asked.

"Septic shock."

"Huh?"

"Blood poisoning. It's brought on by an infection…."

The irony -- saved from blood poisoning by a vampire -- knocked a laugh from my chest. "What kind of infection?"

His eyebrows drew together. "How should I know? I'm not a doctor. Anyway, it should be cleared up now."

"What's gonna happen?" I asked.

He lay his head on my chest. His thumb rubbed my hip. I closed my eyes and swallowed.

"It's slow," he said. "You've probably noticed your eating habits changing. You don't want sweets and sodas."

Water and meat, that's what I craved. "And…?"

He shrugged. "Eventually, you'll want your meat rawer and rawer until you're eating flesh."

Intellectually, the idea repulsed me, but it was the earlier mention of sweets that had actually turned my stomach; the word 'flesh' made my mouth water.

"And then you'll be living off donated blood." He picked up his head, sought my eyes again. "Like me. It's not so bad. And there's plenty."

I curled my fingers in his hair and tipped my chin up, closing my eyes. Maybe it hadn't been long since he'd 'saved' me, but apparently it had been long enough for my body to know, to fucking know that drinking blood was a poor second prize.

"It's not that bad," he said again.

"If you bite my neck, and make a hole, does it heal?" I asked, my eyes

still squeezed shut. The word 'flesh,' the very fucking word was filling me, stiffening me, charging me up.

"Not you, not yet. But on me it does." He'd moved up again, so that we were chest to chest. His fingers pulled my face down to look at him. "Do you want to bite me?"

I ran my tongue along my teeth, my dull, flat teeth.

"They'll fall out," he whispered. "Your new ones are growing in behind them already, but it takes time."

He thrust his hard-on against my thigh and said, "Bite me anyway."

I wrapped my arms around his head and pulled his neck down.

"Bite me," he said as my teeth slipped over his skin, so I closed my eyes and thought of flesh -- saw it, meaty, wet, and ripe, in my brain -- and ripped at his throat with my teeth, gnawed, and ripped, and he gripped me harder until I panicked that I wouldn't be able to breathe, but then blood seeped over my tongue and I forgot breathing, forgot everything but licking and sucking and biting to get more, the whole time feeling him buck against me like he was coming out the hole I'd made in his throat, coming and coming and coming.

Just when I thought it couldn't feel any better, his hand pushed between us and closed around my cock. Then he jerked his neck from my mouth and crawled down my chest. Through heavy-lidded eyes, I watched him run his tongue over the head of my cock. At the same time, I slid my tongue over my own lips, tasting his blood all over again. It went straight to my head, making every nerve in my body jangle. As Cale's tongue pressed against my slit, every one of those buzzing nerves pulled towards it, screaming for more. Cale caught my eye and grinned, exposing razor-sharp fangs that made my breath catch in a fusion of unease and anticipation.

"Uh!" My neck arched back and I clutched the armrests as his hot mouth closed around me. He had those dangerous teeth safely tucked behind his lips, but I knew they were there just the same, and as he torqued my cock in his mouth, my chest tightened. My breaths came in gasps. I heard a crack and one of the armrests came away in my hand. I dropped it to the floor and reached behind my head, grabbed onto the vinyl headrest. Cale's tongue slid from side to side under my shaft and I felt a groan start deep in my balls, gather intensity, and then climb to fill my chest, my throat, my mouth and finally spill out, low and heavy.

Cale's hand grabbed the base of my cock and pulled at it as he increased the intensity of his mouth work. My ankles fought the cuffs that still restrained them as my hips lifted off the chair. The backs of my eyelids turned the color of blood: pumping, throbbing, living blood. The side of Cale's fist slammed against my pelvis one, two, three more times before I opened my mouth and came, pumping everything I had into Cale's throat.

When he sat up -- when I lay spent and panting -- I saw what I'd done earlier, the mess I'd made of muscle and flesh. He brought a hand to his neck, felt it, then looked at his bloodied fingers and grinned.

"Just you fucking wait," he said. "Payback's a bitch."

"How long?" I wanted to feel his teeth in my flesh. An image of him ripping my neck open while he fucked me from behind flashed through my mind. I shuddered at the thought.

"Couple months, maybe. This helped, though. More of my blood." He pressed the palm that had cupped the wound on his neck to my lips and I licked it.

And then it came to me. "Shit! You weren't taking blood from me that night I woke up in this chair..."

"Um ... No. Ready to get up?" He moved to the foot of the chair and pulled at the buckle of my left ankle cuff.

I sat up. "Cale?"

"Mmm?"

"What happened to all these guys who came before?" I touched the CAM at the bottom of my new tattoo.

"We don't live forever, you know."

"No, I didn't."

He grinned. "Well don't go planning my funeral. I've got a few years left in me."

"So who was this?" I asked, rubbing the next letters up from CAM.

"Bill. William Edward Chance."

"You going to tell me about him?"

"Someday."

"And him? FRK?"

"Him, too. And the others, as much as I know about them."

"And you?"

Grinning, he circled an arm around my shoulder and pulled my forehead to his. "And me. I'll tell you all about me, too." He reached out to me. "Come to bed," he said.

I touched his neck, where I'd wrecked it.

"It'll be better tomorrow," he said.

I kissed it, inhaling the tang of blood.

"Come to bed," he said again, ruffling my hair. "I'll show you how insatiable vampires can be."

This time, I followed.

Momma's Boy
Louis Carr

My son should not have been seduced by a monster.

I thought that I'd left all those creatures behind when I married an American naval officer and ended up in San Diego. By the time of my husband's death, I'd become used to Southern California and had no desire to return to the Philippines and what I had known in my youth.

Cliff had grown up as a totally American boy. He didn't deserve to face the monsters of my homeland; he knew nothing of them. Because he looked and behaved completely human -- a good looking, totally Europeanized human - I had seen no reason to complicate his life by letting him know he might have turned out otherwise.

Aside from skin that burned easily in direct sunlight and an allergy to garlic, he resembled any other twenty-one year old American college boy.

Cliff was skipping school, sleeping half the day, and slacking off at his part-time job. That had started a month ago.

Pleading, reasoning, and yelling had gotten me nowhere.

The way he'd practically stopped eating, on top of the change in his sleep schedule, made me wonder if he might have inherited more of my nature than I'd suspected. Since he didn't know anything about my kind, I couldn't very well ask him.

I wondered -- but the logical part of me didn't buy into that. It was far more likely to be some mundane crisis he was going through. Maybe a girl?

I drew the line at using hypnotic influence on my own son. Mundane maternal snooping was something else -- and acceptable. After all, Cliff was my son, living under my roof.

I searched his room. The only thing I found that didn't fit the kid I'd known for twenty-one years was a receipt from a night club called Subic Bay. My nose wrinkled in disgust when I saw the address. It was in a seedy part of Chula Vista near the Mexican border.

If the kid wanted to get in touch with his roots, I wondered, why didn't he start at home instead of visiting some bar that no decent person would enter?

About an hour after dark, I drove by the front of the Subic. It was everything I'd imagined it to be -- a shabby, one-story building with its name on the roof in blue-violet neon letters -- the bottom of the B burned out.

An acid brew of worry and anger started to simmer in my gut.

Slowing the car to a crawl, I surveyed the parking lot. Cliff's green compact caught my eye at once.

I wasn't sure whether to feel relieved or not. It depended on what he

was doing here. For all I knew, the Subic could be a drug hangout.

If it was? Should I tip off the authorities and get the place raided? I didn't give that one much thought.

This was a personal matter and, if some candy man got between me and my child, the cops could pick up the gory fragments later.

I drove around the block and found a parking space under one of the widely scattered street lamps.

Walking back to the club, I stepped into the dim, shadowed main bar. I shrouded myself in a psychic veil, a projection of 'Don't notice me, I'm not really here' as I entered.

The room held more patrons than I'd have expected on a week night. A soap with British accents played at low volume on the TV. Aromas of alcohol and masculine musk teased my nostrils. I noticed that there were no women customers.

I saw Cliff immediately, at a table up front, conspicuous with his shock of blond hair. At that moment, one of the servers set a tray down on the end of the bar and slinked over to him.

Like the rest of the staff, he wore silver toreador pants and white ruffled shirts with red sashes. He had black hair tied back in a ponytail, strikingly pale skin, a boyish figure, and a peculiar violet tinge in his aura.

Cliff stood up and hugged the server, following up with a lingering kiss.

I stared at them in shock.

I wanted to get between them, pull my son out of the place, and demand an explanation. I wanted that, but knew better. I glided closer.

I fought to hold my shield intact and steady my heartbeat at the same time. A click of recognition snapped the scene into focus. The other two waiters and the bartender were also male. Men were holding hands, and a pair in a corner booth were kissing. Cliff's -- friend -- squeezed his rear end as they rubbed against each other.

If I'd been human, I would have blushed.

My son's problem wasn't a girl after all! Cliff was -- oh, shit! -- gay.

My mind immediately started dumping blame on me in torrents. It took several moments to get through the first waves of guilt and get my feet firmly back on something solid.

I told myself that it didn't matter if he was or not -- or whose fault it was - and squared my shoulders and made myself study the two boys.

Cliff's health, mental and physical, came first. I could worry about the other stuff later.

The waiter was a beautiful young man with Eurasian facial features, a poster child for the Pacific melting pot. That strange shade in his aura kept bothering me, though. I felt that he was more than he appeared, but I couldn't pin it down.

Now what? I could hardly storm over to a table in a gay bar and demand to know the boy's intentions. I watched them cooing to each other

over drinks -- a beer for Cliff, something fruity for the Filipino boy.

I figured then that moms were the last to be told their baby boys weren't going to make more baby boys. I could live with that, though. What I couldn't fathom was why Cliff's health and behavior had disintegrated. Lovesickness and sleep deprivation alone couldn't have reduced him to such a wreck.

Had this person turned him on to some exotic drug? Could a chemical dependency account for the odd colors in the boy's aura?

They finished their drinks and headed for the door, arms around each other's waists. I slipped outside, pausing at the edge of the parking lot to watch them. They were a pair of dark silhouettes leaning against Cliff's car in another embrace. After a minute of that, Cliff opened the door to let his companion in, then settled in the driver's seat and started the engine.

I dismissed the idea of following them. I had a general idea of the situation and hardly needed more evidence of my son's gayness. Instead, I went back inside and dropped my illusion of invisibility.

Perching on a bar stool, I ordered a white wine. The bartender, a short, stocky man with salt-and-pepper hair, served it and pushed a fresh basket of popcorn within reach.

"Could I ask you about that waiter who just left?" I said.

"What's a lady like you doing here?" he said in accented English. "You don't look like a fag hag. Better go home where you belong."

I inserted a touch of hypnotic compulsion into my voice. "I need some questions answered about that boy."

"Ramón? What about him?"

Rather than asking straight out whether the waiter had drug connections, I decided to start simply, with another psychic nudge to make the bartender cooperative.

"How long has he worked here?"

"Couple, maybe three months." I heard nervousness in the man's voice.

"Do you know anything about his past? I mean, where he's from -- where he worked before?"

"Lady, he's legal and he never misses his shift. What else do I need to know?" He started to move down the bar.

I increased the mental pressure and switched from English to Tagalog. "Wait," I called to him. "I'm just wondering if he goes out with many different men."

"What are you asking all this for?" he said in the same language. "He steal your husband?" A smirk punctuated the question.

"No, that's my son he just left with."

The bartender's expression turned serious. "Don't worry too much about him. He's not the first, probably not the last. It never lasts long with Ramón."

My chest tightened at the thought of having to comfort Cliff for the fickleness of a male lover.

- 256 -

"I don't want my son hurt. Is Ramón into drugs or anything like that?"

"Not that I ever heard."

I sensed an undercurrent of hostility laced with fear in his comments. "Then, what should I be worried about?" I demanded.

The bartender muttered a word that sounded like -- no, it couldn't be. "What did you say?" I asked, fighting against the worry growing in me.

"Danag," he repeated more distinctly.

I took a deep breath to tame the racing of my heart.

"What do you know about danag?" I demanded.

"Just a fairy tale. Nobody believes that stuff anymore. But if I did..." he glanced around and lowered his voice, "that's what I'd call him."

"Why?" I couldn't keep the sharpness from my tone.

"Bloodsucking monster, that's what he looks like. You must've heard the legends back home. Like vampires in the movies."

I reminded myself that lashing out at this superstitious fool wouldn't help my son.

"Not quite like the movies," I mumbled.

"The story goes that they used to live with the hill folks, the Isneg tribe," the bartender continued, warming to his subject. "The danag worked with them in the taro fields, and the farmers gave blood to feed them. Until the demons got carried away and started draining people to death."

The danag were my people and I'd heard it differently. We hadn't become greedy; the mortals became selfish. They began refusing to donate the small amounts of blood they could easily spare. So my people had no choice but to take it by force. I drew a deep breath to quell my anger.

"If this boy seems not quite human -- well, our people have tales of other kinds of vampires. The aswang and the tiyanak, monstrous ravishers who entice and drain men without mercy..."

I tried not to remind myself that they were always portrayed as female.

Outright fear shadowed his eyes. "I can't talk, I got work to do," he mumbled and hurried towards the end of the bar, where one of the waiters stood with a tray and an order slip.

With a command for him to forget he'd met me, I hurried back to the car, my thoughts churning like a storm-racked sea. The young man with Cliff wasn't one of my kind, but could he be something else that wasn't human?

All the rest of the night, I mulled over what Cliff's lover might be. I recalled the aswang, a birdlike night-flyer disguised as a lovely maiden by day, and the tiyanak, also in woman shape, draining blood with her long, hollow tongue.

They were always female in the legends, but I couldn't see why they didn't have male counterparts. Human storytellers never knew the whole truth, anyway. Near dawn, I fell asleep mulling over the problem and dreamed of Ramón swooping into Cliff's window on black wings, shrieking

like a banshee.

I woke up groggy the next afternoon. After stumbling to the bathroom and splashing my face, I tested Cliff's doorknob. Not surprising, it was locked. But that wouldn't stop me from checking on him. I wouldn't even need to use my inhuman strength to break into his room.

The house's indoor locks were a joke. I shrugged on my robe, collected a miniature screwdriver from the kitchen, and broke in. The job took about five seconds.

I wasn't worried about waking Cliff. Lately, he slept almost as heavily as one of my kind, dozing through alarm clocks, and had to be shaken for two or three minutes to force so much as a groan out of him. I was hunting for signs of bloodsucking.

The heavily curtained bedroom, dim and stale-smelling, felt too warm. He'd closed the floor vent to cut off the flow from the air conditioner. It occurred to me that he'd been overdressing for the weather recently. Another possible symptom of sickness or of becoming like me -- or of anemia.

I leaned over the bed and peeled Cliff's sheet down to the waist. I saw the marks on his bare chest then. Leaning closer, I stared at them in the dim light.

I sucked in my breath and swayed, grabbing the bedpost. These were not the razor-like incisions he would have received from a member of my race. They were tiny punctures, at least ten of them. I swallowed the snarl that threatened to rise in my throat.

No, Cliff wasn't growing into a predator like me. Just the opposite.

What had that bloodthirsty thing done to him?

My thoughts crashed over me, great sprays of foam, and became nothing. I didn't know what to do. I could lurk in wait for Cliff and tell him -- what? That his boyfriend was a legendary monster? From those wounds, I had a good idea of what kind, too. For the moment, though, the best I could do was try to reason with him on a more mundane level.

When he staggered out of his bedroom, he was dressed. I intercepted him with a glass of milk, which he automatically chugged. "Weren't you supposed to have classes today? And your boss from the marina called to find out why you missed work twice in a row."

He thrust the empty glass into my hand. "Save it, Mom. I'm late for an appointment."

"With Ramón?"

"Huh? Who?" The innocent pose didn't look any more convincing than it had when he'd skipped school to go to the video arcade in fifth grade.

"That boy in the tight pants you're seeing," I growled. "Some riffraff you picked up in a bar."

Instantly I wished I could take the last words back. "Cliff, I can accept that you're -- not straight. That's not a problem. There's a lot about Ramón you don't know."

A cold mask settled over his face. "You followed me. What the hell makes you think you can butt into my life that way?"

"You watch your language, young man..." I bit off the end of the sentence. "Cliff, I'm trying to stop you from making a terrible mistake. I only want what's best for you. That boy is ruining your health."

Never before had I felt more tempted to use mind control on him.

"You don't know a damn thing about what's best for me!" he yelled.

Clutching the doorknob, he turned to glare at me. "Don't wait up tonight. I'll be spending the night at his house." Cliff stalked out and slammed the door. A few seconds later, I heard his car roaring down the street.

I didn't bother trying to follow him, since he would cover several miles before I could get my car out of the driveway. Instead, I went to the Subic where I'd get Ramón's address from the manager.

Like most Europeans, the people of my homeland prized garlic as a remedy against 'demons'. The way the plant affected me, I couldn't use it as a weapon. If Ramón turned out to be what I suspected, though; a common household ingredient harmless to me would disable him.

The thought of bursting into a strange house and catching my grown son in a compromising position made me squirm. But I couldn't do nothing while Cliff deteriorated into an anemic zombie, either.

I had some notion of disillusioning him by making Ramón show his true colors. If that didn't work, I had no compunctions about getting rough with the creature. This was my kid the pretty little monster was feeding on.

At the club I pulled right into the parking lot, which was fairly empty. I didn't see Cliff's car; he must have gone straight to his friend's home. I took a stool at the bar and ordered a club soda from the same bartender who'd been serving the previous night. "Is Ramón off tonight?" I asked.

He blinked, apparently struggling with the ghost of a memory of our conversation the night before.

"Yeah, he hasn't been in."

"I need to see him. Could I speak to the manager?"

"Speaking."

"Well -- I really need to talk to Ramón. Could you give me his address?"

"No way, lady. Employee information's confidential." He turned his back to rearrange a row of bottles.

I stretched over the bar to tap his shoulder. He turned, his forehead creased in a frown of annoyance. When my eyes trapped his, his face went blank.

I trailed my fingertips down his arm to his hand. My touch made his heartbeat speed up. Hunger stirred in the pit of my stomach. I ordered it to settle down. "Tell me the address."

He recited it.

"Good," I said. "I'm leaving now. Forget you saw me."

In the car, I consulted my street map again. A few blocks of driving took me out of the commercial district along two-lane, badly-lit streets farther south into a dingy residential neighborhood. I inched past small houses with weedy yards, sagging front stoops, and peeling paint. The address I'd memorized proved to be a one-story cottage not much different from the others, except that it had no lights on. Cliff's car was parked in front of it.

Driving around the block, I parked, then walked back to Ramón's place with my bulky purse hanging from one shoulder. I was prepared for the Tiyanak I was sure the boy was.

Inside the dark living room, the air smelled of incense. Judging from the few lumps of deeper shadow I saw, Ramón didn't go in for much furniture. I stood inside the door and listened to my son groan.

"You want it again?" a silky sweet Filipino voice asked.

"Give it to me. Give me all of it, Ramón!" my son hoarsely commanded him. "Yeah! Oh, yeah…"

I knew what they were doing. I shivered as I accepted with finality that my son would never know a woman as his father had. I debated storming in on the two men and finding Cliff under his lover, being the waiter's woman.

I decided I didn't want to see that. Hearing it was enough. I waited, listening to the sounds of my son's orgasm climb towards a crescendo.

Cliff's moans finally grew softer and I heard Ramón thick accent. "Sleep now, Blondie," he cooed. "Sleep and feel me in you."

In the hall, a faint, wavering light beckoned me towards a bedroom on the left as I began to move. I heard heavy breathing and a pair of heartbeats. The scent of blood cut through the incense fumes. I stopped in the doorway and looked in at my son's lovenest.

By the flame of a single candle on the dresser, I saw Cliff, with his eyes closed, sprawled naked on a double bed next to an open window. Ramón was between his legs, crouching over him.

I had an ample side view of the couple. My son's eyes were closed, his labored breaths slowly returning to normal. With Cliff's legs spread wide, Ramón was sheathed to the hilt in him. The creature's hand moved along Cliff's manhood. Their auras blended in a lurid scarlet fog.

A sinuous tube the thickness of an electric cord stretched from Ramon's gaping mouth to Cliff's bare chest. The monster's tongue pulsed with the liquid flowing through it.

Just as I thought! Tiyanak!

"No!" I cried. "That's my son's blood!" I took a couple of long strides towards the bed. "Get off my son, you…"

Ramón reared up and glared at me with a loud hiss. His tongue retracted an inch or two. His eyes glowed crimson.

"Get away from him," I snarled. Entranced by the monster's spell, Cliff didn't react.

Ramón rolled his tongue back into his mouth and pumped his manhood in and out of Cliff's bottom, watching me watch him.

He whispered: "Not likely. His blood has the most tantalizing flavor. Human, but spiced with something extra."

He slid in and out of Cliff again to emphasize his possession. "And he loves me."

"He's enslaved by you more like it, Tiyanak!"

Distant kin of ours and viciously predatory, his kind made no attempt to live at peace with the day folk.

He pulled out of Cliff, stood up, smirked at me, and wiped a droplet of blood from his lips. "This is most interesting, don't you think? Two beings that don't exist meeting like this over the son of one of them. What do you plan to do about it, danag?"

I smiled -- coldly. We were evenly matched and our spells did not work on the other's race. I reached into my purse and pulled out the box of salt.

"Remember this stuff?" I asked and flung a handful of salt in his face.

It stung his eyes, frosted his dark hair, and showered over his shoulders and chest.

Ramón shrieked. His fingers curled into talons; his face shriveled into a harpy mask. Leathery wings sprouted from his back. Keening in pain, he leaped into the air and flung himself through the window.

Sometimes folk legends tell the truth.

I rushed to the bed and stared down at Cliff. Blood beaded from several fresh punctures. There was no time to moan over his condition, though; we had to get out before the monster recovered and came back.

I shook him until his eyes opened.

"Mom?" he asked sluggishly. He sat up, flushing a dull red as he realized his nudity, and snatched the sheet over his lap.

"Oh, God! Mom, what are you doing here?"

From his tone of voice, he was too mortified to be angry.

"Listen to me, Cliff..."

This situation was a clear exception to my rule against hypnotizing my own child. I gave a hard mental shove, overriding his will.

"Ramón is dangerous to you, and you to him. If you care for this young man, you will never see him again. This is for his own welfare. You understand?"

That wasn't a lie. If Ramón ever got near Cliff again, I'd rip the bastard's head off, an outcome definitely not conducive to his welfare.

"Yeah." Cliff slurred the sound as if he were drunk or drugged.

"You will not return here or go to the club. You will not attempt to call or contact him in any way. And you will forget the details of your -- love play. Is that clear?"

"Right."

His eyes sagged shut; he began to sink back into a stupor.

"Wake up!" My sharp whisper jerked him into momentary alertness.

"Stand up. We're leaving now. You have to walk to the car."

With my strength half-dragging him, he got to his feet, tugged on his clothes, and made it out the door.

"Mom?" he mumbled as we entered the living room. "How'd you get here? Where are we going?"

"Home. Where you're going to get ten or twelve hours of sleep. When you wake up, we're going have a nice, long talk."

He hung his head and looked at me mournfully. "You mad at me?"

"No, Cliff," I sighed. "I was just worried. It's all right that you prefer men, but you have to be careful. When you're rested up, I'll explain why."

I accepted that I'd made a mistake in keeping him ignorant of his ancestry for so long. If he'd known the truth about me, he might have been on guard against Ramón. If that creature tasted a 'not quite human' flavor in his blood, he might have more of my nature than I'd supposed. We had a lot to talk about.

The Body And The Blood
Philip Markham

Five years ago, Anton killed a man. He would be compelled to do it again soon. As it was still a relatively new experience for him, he enjoyed draining his energies to the last so as to get the full effect from his replenishment.

Robin was older and had taken blood far more times than Anton had. He maintained a façade of jaded practicality about the act itself but still flirted with danger by running himself low. He also affected something of a moral attitude to his hunting: he sought willing converts. He recognized his own hypocrisy for, when he allowed himself to lie close to oblivion, no ethical code would persuade him to embrace it. Once, he had eaten in order to live; now he drank in order not to die.

For decades, they had found each other's food; and it was Robin's turn to do this for Anton. He was watching as his golden boy's time approached. Robin noted how, as his need grew, Anton became paler and more tired. That was not to say he looked any the worse for it; on the contrary, his encroaching ill health leant him a romantic ennui, an interesting pallor: a watery kind of beauty.

They embraced -- Robin's sleek body still pulsating with life; Anton contented himself be used. It was strange, he said. He fancied his condition affected his personality as well as his general health. He said – rather grandly – that his very soul had become tired.

Robin, fully aware that his lover had not possessed a soul for almost a century, said this was rubbish. He was enjoying stroking, feeling, licking – he had the virility for both of them and was finding fulfillment in being his partner's source of energy. Tonight, he felt that his passion for Anton was stronger than sexual desire, stronger even than Anton's increasing need.

In his present state Anton's skin, usually so brown, was luminous, more than usually so in the twilight of dawn. He pulled Robin on top of himself.

Robin kissed him. "Let me give you some of my seed," he said. "It'll give you strength until I find a donor for you."

"Do it then," Anton replied and eased himself onto his front. Robin began to massage his shoulders.

"You want it this way?" he asked quietly. "I thought it did more for you if you drank it."

Anton mumbled a protest into the pillow but he wasn't to be allowed to get away with that: Robin insisted on the mumble being better articulated.

"I want you inside my arse," Anton said, smiling. "I want you to fuck me, OK?"

Robin nodded and his fingers pressed hard on Anton's shoulders. He kneaded the flesh at the top of Anton's spine and then, using his knuckles,

he journeyed downwards, vertebra by vertebra, until he reached the dusting of hair in the small of Anton's back. His hand slipped into the cleavage between the buttocks and rested there, taking in the warmth of his lover's body heat, feeling the dampness of sweat.

He watched Anton's impatient bucking for a moment before he parted the cheeks and replaced his hand with his hard penis. It went in easily, causing no more than a throaty groan of satisfaction from Anton.

As Anton's body became solid with his lover's meat, Robin's too, swelled with a phantom cock inside his own arse. He took his enjoyment from fucking at the same time as relishing a fantasy of being fucked himself. He knew well the divine weakness Anton was swimming in, the completeness he was deriving from being filled.

His cock, already buried to the hilt, seemed to go further and further with each thrust. Anton's body and Robin's cock were one -- a wonderful feeling spreading from deep inside the gut and enveloping the penis and an urgent, sensation firing from the penis into the gut, stirring it into a swelling emotion that unified them both. Semen boiled inside Robin's scrotum before it spurted out of his body and into Anton's.

Presently, Anton allowed his lover to pull out and they held each other. The sun had struggled through and lit the winter sky. Anton looked towards the window and his tired face, defined as it was by low, sharp shadows, looked wonderfully handsome.

"Oh, damnation!" he said. "Another fucking day!"

"By the end of it, I'll have found you a nice one," Robin said. "When you're ready to take him, he'll be ready for you."

Jordan Mitchell hadn't wanted to go to a New Year party; he would rather have been at a club with Devlin, his new partner. Indeed, that is exactly where he would have been were it not for one of the secretaries at work. She had kept one of Jordan's fraudulent sick-days from their boss and so had been able to blackmail him into being her escort. She was, she said, sick of her friends using her as the fountain of all gossip; this way, she would at least be sure of being the subject of it for once.

Jordan had been standing in a corner of the neat, naff living room, idly daydreaming about a bomb falling on semi-detached suburbia. His companion was getting drunk and spreading office scandal. There was only one decent man in the entire room: a slim youth whose light brown hair fell attractively across his eyes. Nobody seemed to know who he was. Miss Gossip insisted he was straight but, as she fancied him as well, Jordan suspected her judgment.

He was wondering what his partner was getting up to when the young man looked him up and down in an obvious fashion. "You're about the only thing in this room worth bothering about," he said after he'd come to stand beside Jordan.

Personally, Jordan wasn't enthusiastic about his own appearance; it had always been more of a problem to him than an asset. At school he had been bullied for looking like a girl; at work his colleagues had joked about his soft features and fair hair and had even gone as far as calling him 'Jodie'. Men usually supposed him to be submissive and even a little stupid.

He had finally stopped trying to make himself more rugged when he'd met Devlin who went for active, younger types and whose athletic body and lean good looks were worth the compromise. True, Jordan had taken to wearing a hint of a beard – just enough to shadow his jaw line, but he no longer harbored a secret ambition to resemble a Canadian lumberjack.

"I was thinking the same thing about you," he said. "Please tell me you're on your own. If you're not, I'll slit my wrists."

The stranger took Jordan's hand in his and examined his wrist as if he were weighing up the prospect and imagining the effect such an action would have. When he was quite satisfied, he beckoned for Jordan to follow him upstairs. In the back room, on a bed piled high with coats, they lay down together.

The stranger immediately tore at the waistband of Jordan's trousers as though he were a starving animal.

"Easy boy!" Jordan said. "It isn't going to wither away. Take your time."

The youth's head went down to Jordan's groin; making small, snarling noises, he tore away at the material until his teeth and tongue found Jordan's erection. He had it inside his mouth within a second. Jordan closed his eyes and, raising his hips, he gave in to pleasure.

"Here it is," he gasped at last. "Here's my cum!"

He ejaculated into the eager mouth and then lay back while the stranger wanked himself over Jordan's chest. Jordan liked cum on his skin. His boyfriend called it his primeval instinct: he loved to mark himself with his partner's body fluid. He wanted to smell the cum on himself and leave it there until it seeped through his pores and became part of him.

He watched the semen spurt over himself. Then he rubbed in the quickly-drying fluid and closed his eyes contentedly.

Later, as the chimes of Big Ben kept everyone else at the party engaged in schmaltz, the two men sneaked out.

"I have a friend," the stranger said. "He'd like to meet you."

Jordan turned and looked at him. The boy's eyebrows almost met in the middle and his eyes were large and dark. Handsome was not a word that came into Jordan's mind often but it described this man perfectly. He was fine, masculine, young – he was handsome.

"If your friend is anything like you, he can have me anytime," Jordan said. "What's your number?" He knew that he would never call. He never did.

Yet, Jordan had just made the mistake of agreeing to an assignation with a hungry vampire and vampires, like elephants, never forget.

Time passed and Jordan's love affair with Devlin metamorphosed into a strong friendship that survived the best part of a decade. Jordan had his one-night stands; Devlin, being older and more cautious, did manage the occasional adventure. He accepted what Jordan offered, wished it were more, and devoted himself to mild eccentricity.

Tonight found Devlin in a theme bar that advertised a welcome for Gay Goths and Ghouls, all of which he thought was rather fun. However, his choice of watering hole had less to do with his penchant for the macabre and more to do with the attractive bar staff. Being, as he thought, the only man over forty present, he wouldn't have stayed long had he not fallen into conversation with a blond beauty of rare quality.

The younger man, who didn't mind Devlin's hand on his knee, apparently wished to be regarded as a Goth in that he wore his hair long and dressed in a tasteful Edwardian suit that was probably new and had no doubt cost a fortune.

In this sanctuary of the avant-garde, Devlin behaved conventionally. He was a man on his own, sitting at the same table as another man on his own. He wanted to speak but felt he had to wait for an excuse or an invitation.

Then a bizarre, drunken creature wreathed in cobwebs (and not very much else) ordered his drink in an incongruously shrill voice and the blond boy laughed; Devlin accidentally met his glance and the invisible barrier between them lifted.

"Do you come here often?" – No, neither of them came here often – a short silence – then an exchange of names: "Devlin" – "Anton".

Unlike Spiderman, Anton had a rich voice with clear English vowels. Devlin appreciated this since, as a youth growing up in Ireland, he had taken the trouble to acquire the same for himself. Their conversation gravitated from criticizing the fake ambiance of their present location to discussing the esoteric interests they held in common.

"Gay men and vampires are very similar in lots of ways," Devlin said. "Our desire for eternal youth; our nocturnal habits; the unreasonable fear we instill in so-called normal society; the lonely quest for another of our own kind; knowing each other by guesswork and secret signs. Wouldn't you say that vampirism is a perfect metaphor for our condition?"

"Vampires seek blood only when they absolutely need it." Anton said, half-ignoring the question. "It contains their life force – prana, the Hindus call it. You can get degrees of it by feeling the vibrancy of a crowd; from raw fruit and vegetables, eggs, yogurt, cheese and fresh milk – and from semen of course." He paused for a moment to collect his thoughts.

"It's like running off rechargeable batteries: you can keep topping one up and topping it up but in the end it has run out and you need a new one. That's when the vampire bites." He said 'bites' with some relish, showing his perfect teeth and clicking them together. "Do you think you would recognize one if you met him?" he asked.

Devlin said that he didn't suppose for one minute that a real vampire would demean itself by coming into this bar. Anton wasn't so sure. He nodded over to a handsome youth who was sitting a little way off and who was watching them with a faraway expression on his face as though his head was filled with beautiful music.

"He's lovely, of course," Devlin said. "He has boy-next-door looks and the sense not to spoil them by attempting to be stylish. He certainly looks out of place in here but I regard that as a mark of good taste, not of being one of the undead."

"You think he's attractive?"

Devlin thought the boy was attractive. Though he certainly wouldn't have said so, he found him marginally preferable to his present companion whose symmetrical features and flawless skin were almost too perfect. The boy had floppy brown hair and a long, pale face; his mouth curled slightly upwards and his brows almost met on the bridge of his nose. Devlin thought him quite beautiful.

"You don't know how lucky you are to be young," he told Anton wistfully. "I would give anything to be that age again and know what I know now."

Anton smiled knowingly. 'That beautiful creature over there is older than you are; he's even older than I am."

Devlin assumed he was being gently sent up. "I know," he said. "I shouldn't make such a thing of my age – or anyone else's for that matter."

"I'm serious," Anton went on. "I know him; his name's Robin. He's very old indeed."

Devlin had spent his teens and twenties wishing he were thirty. He had wished them back ever since. Now, at fifty-four, his entire youth seemed unclaimed and unappreciated. He knew that the time would come when he would look back on his present age as relatively young, but that thought horrified him even more.

Anton leaned over to him in a confidential manner. "You have to make sacrifices in order to stay youthful. Believe me." A shadow crossed his clear face. For a second or two, Devlin could almost have been persuaded that he labored under the heavy weight of long experience but the notion vanished as soon as Anton smiled again: he couldn't possibly have been more than in his late twenties. He was being facetious.

The boy they were observing had finished his drink and was searching through his pockets for change. He looked across at Devlin and Anton and smiled.

Anton rose to his feet. "I'm going to invite him to join us," he declared and, without waiting for Devlin's permission, he did exactly that.

A fortnight later, Jordan and Devlin arrived on the steps of a palatial house. They stood in the presence of huge, double doors of good old English oak.

Ever since they'd left London, Jordan had been hoping the accommodation would be outlandish. He pointed to the rusting bell-pull, which was labeled with the one-word command: RING. He joked that it was the type of contraption that should summon a hunchback butler. He put on a cracked, high-pitched voice and said "*Enterrrrrr!*" After Devlin had laughed, Jordan said it was a good job they weren't characters in a horror film because if they were, he wouldn't advise doing any such thing.

Devlin plonked a kiss on Jordan's forehead and rang the bell. Doleful clangs echoed down what they imagined to be miles of long, cobwebbed corridors.

Jordan laughed. "It's Rocky Horror!" he said. "Do you imagine your friend has them doing the *Time Warp* in there?"

"No," Devlin replied. "I expect they're sacrificing virgins."

"We're safe then," Jordan said flicking back imaginary curls. "Or at least *you* are – I'll have to make sure I'm no longer of any interest to them as soon as I possibly can."

He hoped, for Devlin's sake, that this weekend was going to go well. It could be a recipe for disaster, though. Devlin hadn't said much other than he'd met his new friend in a tacky bar, that Robin was beautiful, he was not in the least bit gregarious, and he had been ill for some time.

Jordan turned to take in the view of the gardens. If Robin could afford to rent this place, even for a weekend, he must be worth more than his good looks. It was magnificent! Grass rolled gently down to a neglected ornamental lake; reeds had taken over but a black swan still floated through them, apparently unconcerned.

Jordan was about to say that you didn't see black swans that often when the door was opened.

If this was Robin, Devlin had lied about him. Robin had been described as a "lovely faun": this youth was more like a lion. Whereas Robin apparently dressed conventionally: this young man was half-naked with tight, low-waisted jeans; he also had shoulder-length blond hair and a face and body that weren't usually seen outside advertisements for expensive underwear.

"I'm Anton," he said simply. Then, as a statement, not a question, he added: "You're Jordan."

His accent sounded too perfect not to be faked. Jordan didn't care if it was, though; he was more interested in the sight of hard muscle and toned skin. Anton's torso was a perfect V shape; strong arms and pronounced pectorals; a flat stomach adorned with a trail of blond hair leading down from his belly button.

He was aware that he was being admired and he was probably used to it. He breathed deeply, causing his upper chest to swell and creating a tantalizing whisker of a gap between his body and the band of his trousers. He didn't appear to be wearing any underwear.

"You're to let me know if you need anything."

Jordan guessed that Anton's beauty might be a professional asset and would probably be appearing as an item on the bill.

"We're fine," Devlin was saying. He was hopeless! It wasn't by chance that a near-naked boy had been sent to answer the door. This was Robin's way of telling them they were in for a weekend orgy – they were obviously supposed to enter into the spirit of things and get horny but poor old Devlin just *had* to have everything in black and white.

"Our cases are in the car," Jordan said. Devlin looked at him reproachfully. Devlin made it a rule never to talk down to anyone, especially if he was supposed to.

Jordan marched confidently into the house, pausing only briefly to let his hand linger over Anton's glorious chest. There was hair there – just a little -- and golden so it didn't show unless you looked for it. Anton allowed the gesture but didn't respond. Jordan later swore that he noticed his cock swelling beneath the faded denim but Devlin didn't believe him – or chose not to.

Despite the forbidding edifice, the corridor was light and quite pleasant. Jordan would have quite liked the idea of weekending in Dracula's castle but the airy, well-lit interior was, nevertheless, a pleasant surprise. Anton was ahead of them now and was waiting patiently with their luggage as Jordan took in his surroundings.

"It is very old," he said in answer to Jordan's approving glances. "The owners had the entire place redone when they bought it. They didn't like the dark, you see."

"You're not dark anyway," Jordan said, about to drape his arm around Anton's shoulder. He was meaning to be seductive but Devlin evidently thought he was going a bit too far and poked him in the back for it.

Jordan paid him no heed. Devlin wasn't any great advert for self-control: he'd happily fuck his way out of middle-age if he thought it would help.

The walls were decorated with fine samples of homoerotic art from various periods. Amongst them there was a painting of a boy who looked very like Anton – a lovely, strong, blonde creature sitting by a lake and looking wistfully across the water. In the center of the lake there was a black swan – similar to the one Jordan had noticed outside.

He stopped and looked hard at the picture, comparing its subject to Anton.

"It's you, isn't it?" he said at last. "You sat for this one and it's based on the lake outside …"

Anton looked impassively at the painting as though the thought had never before occurred to him. "Do I look like that?" he said. "Perhaps I do. It's very old. It was painted in the eighteenth century."

He pointed to the corner of the picture and there, sure enough, was the artist's signature and the date, 1749.

Jordan was about to say how extraordinary the likeness was but Anton was already halfway up the stairs, Devlin with him. Jordan glanced again at the picture and persuaded himself that the resemblance was more tenuous than he'd supposed at first. It had either been a trick of the light or Anton was already becoming an obsession. His penis began to stiffen in emphasis.

Devlin came into his room while he was unpacking. "*Who* is that man?" Jordan said. "Has your lovely new boyfriend employed him so I won't feel left out? I do hope so."

Devlin didn't answer. He looked in the mirror and sighed. "I'm older," he said. "I always promised myself that when I reached forty I'd seriously consider the surgeon's art."

Devlin could be maudlin about his age if he was given half the chance. He shrugged at Jordan's lack of response. "Well, what do you think?" he said. "It's quite a place isn't it? Don't you think Anton's done us proud?"

"Anton?" Jordan said. "The naked flunky? Did he find this place? I thought you did."

"It belongs to him," Devlin said, enjoying the surprise-effect his words were having. "It has done for centuries, but don't treat him in any special way. He'd hate that."

"You mean it's been *in his family* for centuries don't you?" Jordan said. Devlin often corrected his grammar and it was always nice to get his own back. "That picture I looked at in the corridor?" he went on. "It must be one of his ancestors. And there was I, thinking we were going to be treated to a sex party and Anton was by way of the hors d'ouvres."

Devlin smiled and put an elegant finger to his lips. The fading light outside was giving way to the fake candles in the chandelier. He looked vaguely sinister, but completely at home. "You'll meet him again soon enough," he said. "Now, I know you also want to meet Robin. He's asked me to send his apologies, however. He's resting and will be with us this evening. It's his illness; I hope you will forgive him."

He opened his cigarette case and offered Jordan one of the neatly rolled joints it contained. Jordan took two of them. Anton had supplied the drugs, Devlin explained; they were quite special.

"I'll have a quick smoke and then I'm going to take a shower," Jordan told him. He peeled off his shirt – Devlin liked to see him like that – and threw himself down on the bed.

He may have drifted off to sleep, but only for a minute or two. He woke, picked up the joint from the ashtray, and took several deep draughts. Then he meandered into the bathroom. Devlin was standing by the shower in his underwear.

The thought flashed across Jordan's mind that this was odd: he thought he'd heard Devlin leave the room. It didn't matter much though; it was a safe bet that he had not stripped in order to wash.

Jordan gave a low whistle of appreciation. Devlin, for all his paranoia about his age, looked extremely good for his fifty-four years. Under the

dapper clothing, he possessed a fit body that could make Jordan's cock hard in an instant. Jordan, in his early thirties, had often been referred to as Devlin's pretty toyboy. He felt this was unfair on the older man; Devlin didn't need a toyboy.

The soft dark hair on his legs and chest was damp with the steam that was gradually filling the room: he looked like an Olympic swimmer fresh from the pool. The two men held each other for a while, simply looking into each other's eyes and smiling gently. It was what Devlin called their gay postcard pose: one man dark, hairy, muscular, and strong; the other fairer, smooth, slim, and boyish.

Eventually, Jordan's hands found their way into Devlin's underwear; they climbed further down to sculpt the contours of his buttocks and then further still, feeling the satisfying roughness of the hair in between.

Devlin's smile broadened as he undid Jordan's zip. He soon had the front of the jeans lay wide open and was running his hand over Jordan's cotton-encased stiff cock.

"Get your mouth on me," Jordon said. "Come on. It's been ages since I had your lips on my cock."

There was a throne-like armchair in the corner of the room. Jordan allowed himself to be propelled backwards until he was sitting in it with his legs wide and his jeans in a scrunched heap on the floor.

The steam had really built up by now: it was turning the bathroom into a sauna. Jordan liked saunas: he had a thing about imagining being mauled by men he couldn't see. He let his mind wander off into fantasy.

His shorts followed his jeans. As they were peeled away from his body, he amused himself by running his fingers through Devlin's hair. The soft feeling of lips around the nub of his penis was utterly delicious.

He pushed his hips forward to give more of himself. Devlin sometimes protested at this and told him to take it easy – not to be in such a rush to get everything over. This time the thrust was allowed, and Jordan's entire shaft went in easily.

Jordan loved it: the warm wetness gripping his cock, rubbing hard against it; the nibbling teeth around the base; the wet hands cupping his balls and pulling gently on his scrotum to make him even more excited. Then, when he had been nearly driven to the point of orgasm, those same hands moved up his chest and began to feel for his nipples.

Apart from his cock, Jordan's nipples were the most sensitive part of his body, and he loved to have them played with. This time was special -- Devlin was being amazingly attentive.

Jordan let his chest be gently pulled upwards. Somewhere on the cusp of pain and pleasure, he luxuriated in the glow of sensation it created. He pushed his cock even harder in and out of the anxious mouth that surrounded it; he threw his head back and arched his upper torso, freezing the position for several, delicious seconds. He knew he had to cum.

It wasn't the usual feeling: it wasn't the growing lack of control as his semen rushed out of his body. Instead, it was a desperate, overriding desire to push his cock harder and harder into that mouth, so hard as to be careless of whether he was hurting Devlin or not. He fucked the man's mouth more brutally than he had ever done before and, despite a warning voice in his head, he simply had to carry on.

He shot straight and full, wave after wave of pleasure making his body tremble from head to foot. He hadn't climaxed like that in ages and he said so.

He reached down to kiss Devlin and to lick the cum from his lover's lips but... He stopped. Staring back up at him was not Devlin, but Anton.

"You enjoyed my service?" Anton licked his lips as though still savoring Jordan's semen and he had a knowing, cat-like smile on his face. He was, as before, only half dressed and was still idly fingering Jordan's nipples.

"How did you get in here? God! Whatever is in those joints is powerful stuff: I thought you were Devlin."

Anton rose. "What you do is yours to decide," he said. "Drugs don't alter that fact. You offered yourself to me before you met me; now I have had you."

He stroked Jordan's face. It was a loving gesture but it seemed curiously detached, as though Anton were weighing him up rather than showing affection. He left the room after that. Once he'd gone, what had happened no longer seemed real. Jordan felt like he was waking from an erotic dream.

Devlin, fully dressed, came back into the room from the corridor. He leaned round the bathroom door, wafting the steam in an exaggerated way.

"If you're not going to have a shower turn the thing off," he said. "Or at least shut the bathroom door."

Robin had drifted off to sleep and was woken by a warm, naked body lying down beside him. It could be Devlin, he thought but hoped it was Anton. Like a bride before the wedding, he did not want to see the groom until the ceremony.

Devlin was ready and willing. He wanted what they had more than any of those who had gone before him. Perhaps it was this fact that made Robin uneasy about taking him. Anton, who never felt any compunction about anything, said conscience was for mortal humans.

It was, thankfully, Anton's hand that closed around Robin's flaccid penis and Anton's lips that touched his. "I've prepared everything," he said. "Devlin's boy has arrived with him. He's young and fresh; perhaps you ought to have him and let him breakfast on Devlin after he's transferred."

"I won't steal him," Robin replied. "Devlin has chosen his first convert and Devlin must have him."

Robin lay on his bed and allowed the room to spin around him. The sensation was very familiar to him. In a few hours he would be able to leave this weakness behind him – until the next time. Soon, he would also leave the delicious cravings behind him – for a while at least.

He let his hand wander down to his cock and tried to get it to stand erect; it wasn't going to. Nevertheless, he stroked himself and experienced the ghost of real pleasure. He was getting weaker by the minute. He was glad he would have his donor tonight.

Devlin had often behaved mysteriously and pressing him to drop the pretense was useless. Whatever he was cooking up now would no doubt be revealed in good time, but Jordan wanted to know what it was. He was expecting an orgy and, in one form or another, that was likely to be what all this weekend was about. It wasn't that Jordan objected to an orgy – as long as it was contained within the boundaries of safer sex of course – it was more that he wanted to know what he was letting himself in for.

They were alone together. Jordan didn't demur when Devlin undressed him; in fact, he loved being admired. Devlin came up behind him and his hands found their way around Jordan's body; his fingers touched Jordan's nipples and circled them gently as they kissed.

He pulled Jordan's naked back close to his own starched shirt. Jordan twisted round and began tugging Devlin's bow tie loose. The two men pushed their tongues hard into each other's mouth. Once the tie had been cast aside, Jordan unbuttoned Devlin's shirt and burrowed inside it. "I dreamed earlier that I was having sex with you," he said after a while. "I could only have been asleep for a minute or two. You were really good – and then you turned into Anton and you were even better."

Devlin pulled away abruptly, "What happened then?" he asked, rather sharply.

"Don't tell me you're jealous of my dreams," Jordan replied. "Anyway, you have your Robin waiting for you. I don't see how you can object if I want to lie on my virginal bed and fantasize about Dream Boy giving me a blow job."

Devlin relaxed just as suddenly as he had tensed. "A blow job," he repeated to himself. "That was all? A blow job?"

Jordan was puzzled by his reaction. "Yes, you know," he said. "Where some bloke puts your cock in his mouth and sucks you until you cum?" The dream had seemed very real at the time and Devlin's reaction was making him think: had he been drugged? If so, it hadn't been necessary; Anton could have any part of his body he wanted and Jordan didn't need so much as a gin and tonic to get in the mood.

Devlin hugged him. "I've been thinking," he said. "It's important to tell people what they mean to you," he replied. "I was always glad we've remained friends."

"What's got into you? Is it Robin?" Jordan asked, suspicion forcing itself into his thoughts. This kind of talk was so unlike Devlin. "Is he *very* ill? It's not the Big A is it?"

Devlin actually seemed amused by the question.

"What's going on?" Jordan went on. He tried to make his voice firm enough to brook no evasion but light enough to save face should his suspicions prove to be entirely unfounded.

"I'll tell you," Devlin said. "But you must promise me you won't tell me I'm insane until I've quite finished."

Robin's eyes were dim and his body ached from head to foot. The rush of life, when it eventually came back to him, would be aggressive. And delicious.

Anton was still trying to persuade his partner to change his mind -- to take Jordan and let him then take Devlin as his first. He maintained that Jordan owed them that much for not having made a gift of himself all those years before.

"I was left having to drink from that drunken lout you brought home," he complained. "He was nothing; he was nobody."

"He supplied your need, " Robin said.

"You should at least look at this boy again before you let Devlin have him all to himself," Anton persisted. Receiving nothing more than a weak shake of the head in reply, he finally gave up. "Devlin is lucky; once he's transferred, his first meal will be a splendid one. I almost wish it were my time to replenish. I wouldn't turn him down."

"I should have taken Devlin before now," Robin said. "I shouldn't drive myself to the edge like this. Look at me. I can't even make my prick hard any more. You shouldn't let me abuse myself. I never allow you to sink so low: I save you from yourself – you're not listening to me, are you?"

Anton kissed Robin's toes, one by one, and grinned as though the complaint was so many words of endearment.

Robin had meant it to be but in his frail state, he began to feel genuine annoyance. He knew why he flirted with such feelings – it was the sweet memory of being human. I am feeling peevish, he admitted to himself. I am sinking into life again. If I don't build again very soon, I will die.

He mused on this for a while: living, dying, feeling: they all seemed entirely abstract concepts to him. He noticed Anton was regarding him in a curious way but he wasn't aware why.

"You're crying", Anton said.

"Am I?"

Robin touched his face and examined the wetness on the end of his finger. "You're right," he said. "I really have left things for far too long."

Though he didn't like to admit it, Devlin had felt rather foolish as he told his story. Recounted to an incredulous friend and sometimes partner, it

sounded, as Jordan lost no time in telling him: "… stupid, ridiculous, and fucking *dangerous*!"

Jordan paced, expanding on his theme: "I know you've gone in for some wacky things in your time but this one really takes the prize! Why for fuck's sake can't you – oh, I don't know – become a Buddhist or a High Priest of Satan – or something? Take up embalming and practice on yourself if you must – but this! Devlin, for God's sake, you can't!"

He sputtered to a halt and stopped pacing but only temporarily. Devlin, who had been waiting politely for such a break, raised his head and cleared his throat.

Jordan wasn't going to allow him to defend himself. "Can't you see how dangerous it is? You don't have to have a certificate from medical school for Christ's sake! What if he's HIV positive? You don't seriously imagine a vampire kink is going to involve safe sex?"

Devlin stopped him. If he hadn't, Jordan would have carried on for another hour and there really was no point. He'd already said everything he had to say; now he was repeating himself.

"I shouldn't have told you," he said meekly.

"Why did you then? Perhaps you knew I'd talk some sense into you? I thought I was bad enough with my cheap pick-ups but this makes me look like a responsible person. You're old enough…"

He ran out of gusto then. It didn't need saying anyway – old enough to know better. The words had a certain irony -- eternal youth was possibly the most ridiculous idea he'd heard in his entire life.

"Devlin, I really love you," he began but Devlin interrupted him and, for the first time in many years, he sounded bitter.

"Love? Where has that got me? For years I've been watching myself slowly disintegrate. This is my chance for something else. I'm going to be an evergreen! If it doesn't work, do you honestly suppose I care if the attempt kills me? The only way you can never grow old is to die young "

"You're fucking insane."

Devlin reached into his pocket and brought out his wallet. Inside were two black and white photographs. He gave them to Jordan. "I expect you'll tell me you know who this person is," he said.

In one the handsome, lithe young person dressed in graduation robes posed rather awkwardly. In the other he was lying on a beach more relaxed – caught off-guard perhaps.

"Only you would be vain enough to carry pictures of yourself in your wallet," said Jordan. It was meant to sound harsh, but it came out as affectionate.

"No, it's not me. Not any more. It's the person I was. He's gone, just as the person I've turned into will go. I am going to die – not thirty or forty years from now: in the next hour, the next minute. We die often and every day; we're replaced by somebody else, somebody who is a little older, a

little duller, a little more tired. We don't notice it happening until we look far behind and ..."

He took the photos back and looked at them regretfully. "We're looking at a stranger," he continued. "Dying begins on the day we're born. I am about to stop that process. I'm going to exist within a never-ending pause in the process of life."

Jordan felt like applauding the performance – he was sure that was what it was.

It took him no longer than five minutes to pack and climb into the car but (and it was something he recognized from other rows they'd had) in that time he had calmed down. He watched the rain gathering on the windscreen and tried to call back his righteous anger. He searched through his pocket for a cigarette.

Inside the packet was the remaining joint he had been given earlier that evening. He knew that if he smoked it, he wouldn't be fit to drive for an hour or so. He put the packet away again and started the engine.

It was no good. He wanted a smoke and – what he called his little demon was very powerful tonight – he was going to have one.

Two drafts of the saccharin smoke and Devlin's vampires seemed no more than a whimsy -- stupid, yes, but no more than that. Jordan's mind busily filtered the vampire story, leaving behind only the bits it was willing to accept. He had, he decided, been taking it all too literally. If elderly ladies in picture hats believed they could drink the blood of Christ every Sunday morning, why should Devlin be rejected in such a perfunctory way?

He didn't relish going back and admitting he'd overreacted. He still felt the principle of his objections should have been respected, but Devlin needed to be looked after. Doing so would not be easy: he would, no doubt, be behaving like a dog on the beach and his minder arriving back would be as welcome as a short leash.

At least, that's what Jordan's brain was trying to tell him, but the world was growing foggier by the second. He left the car and staggered back through the garden. He ducked under trees to escape the rain but splashed through numerous puddles and simply laughed at the drenching. As he neared the house, the downpour began in real earnest.

He collapsed against the wall and realized that he felt happy – really, truly happy. Keeping under the eaves, he sidled along until he reached lighted French windows, the curtains of which had been left slightly apart.

They reminded him of beautiful snakes: the men slithered over each other in a tangled threesome, stomach against stomach, backs arching, straightening – arching again. Wonderful creatures, moving as one: limbs entwined, mouths locked, hands, tongues, cocks – he couldn't tell where one body ended and another started.

Devlin looked directly towards the window at one point. His expression was distant, as though the glass that separated them was the magic mist that stood between two different worlds. Anton, golden and triumphant, was fucking a man Jordan remembered vaguely.

A New Year's Eve party years before: Jordan had gone under duress. The same boy who was now grasping Devlin's cock was the one who had grabbed Jordan all that time ago and pulled him into the bedroom. Jordan had promised to ring him and have a threesome with his boyfriend but had lost the number long before he even thought about calling it. Could that boyfriend have been Anton?

He remember what Anton had told him in the bath earlier. "You offered yourself to me before you met me," he'd said. "Now I have had you."

With Anton still inside him, Robin carefully used Devlin's genitals to guide him to the floor. Devlin's face creased for a moment but the pain was anticipated, not felt. Sliding on top of him, Robin bit into his flesh and locked his mouth there – a baby at the breast. Anton, who had disengaged himself only for the time that took, began to fuck Robin again, building to his climax.

Anton's body stiffened and his face lifted. His lips were a snarl as his hips pushed hard against Robin's arse as Robin drank the blood that trickled from Devlin's neck.

Jordan watched as Devlin's features lost the expression of a lifetime's experience and became a youthful blank. Devlin closed his eyes and surrendered himself to what was to follow. It wasn't a vicious scene; it wasn't terrible. It was warm and loving: and something Jordan only now knew that he wanted.

Robin seemed to glow for a second before he quietly separated himself from the other two. He bit into his wrist and held it to Devlin's mouth. Color returned to Devlin's now youthful countenance, making it vibrant.

Robin stood. He had lost his pallor: having drank his fill he had become sanguine. In the years to come, people would comment on his virility, his robust health. Until, that is, he thirsted again and was compelled to allow Anton to search for another donor. For now, it was over. He stood. Looking like a Hercules in his nakedness, he walked from the room.

Devlin had been still for only a moment. He sat up.

Jordan felt an overwhelming urge to be with him. Unable even to consider stopping himself, he pushed at the French windows. Yes, they were unlocked. Ripping his clothing away as he walked forward he arrived at Devlin's side in a state of drunken disarray.

Devlin gripped Jordan's wrist. His expression changed. Although the years had gone from him, he suddenly looked hungry and ill.

As Jordan lay on the floor before him he was dimly aware of Anton supporting his shoulders. He was raised sufficiently to make him easy prey for Devlin's anxious mouth.

Devlin bit. The two of them writhed together as Anton, like a proud parent, watched Robin's new creation take his first blood.

Bonus Book:
Confessions Of A Vampire

By David Macmillan

Confessions Of A Vampire
David MacMillan

1

Whispering, unchannelled thoughts touched my mind for the first time in nearly seventy years as I stood in my flat.   Disorganized and meaningless, but still bearing my love's signature.

Sergei!

I collapsed into the nearest chair.

Awareness crashed over me. This time I had to protect him. This time, Sergei would again be a vampire and, together, we would seal our bodies off from the worst the mortal world could bring against us.

I accepted that as a given. I had been alone too long -- without Sergei to make my life miserable, yet unbelievably and permanently happy.

But where was he?

His spectral voice now was not faint. It was a loud, random call to me across the spectrums of telepathic thought. He was nearby. But where?

I shuddered. Zürich was a city of several million residents. How was I supposed to find him?

Was he a student? That might well explain the loudness of his soul's whispering to me. But it was just as possible that he was a fifty-year-old butcher two blocks away, two hundred and fifty kilos of man waiting to land on me.

I filtered his whispering from my thoughts. I would search for him now that I knew he was reborn, but I still had things I must do -- things that took precedence. Such as feeding.

The Plattpromenade speared the Sihl River and divided it before it could become the Zürichsee. It was a refuge for the worldly but weary young of Europe.

Young men prostituted themselves along its paths while others shot heroin into their bodies and died as their minds played in the fields of poppy only they could see. Already, in the short time I had lived in the neighborhood, there had been five drug overdoses.

I hunted in wolf form.

As I padded along the cobbled paths of the park, a youth knelt before me, slowly sticking his hand out to me. I sniffed his palm, then licked it. He smiled. His other hand stroked my back. I nuzzled his coat and enjoyed his smell. He was handsome, tall, and lithe. His thoughts told me he was a student at the university, looking to make next week's spending money by hiring out his cock.

His longish hair was light-brown with reddish highlights, his face thin

with high cheeks and forehead, and his skin was light-complexioned, almost translucent under the lamps of the promenade.

My snout went to his crotch and sniffed at his heat. He chuckled and ruffled the fur between my ears. There was no sickly sweet scent of heroin about him, and his thoughts were clear as he looked past my wagging tail for sight of a possible assignation. I nuzzled him and felt his tumescence through the corduroy of his trousers.

Memories of a tongue prying its way beneath his prepuce, lips pushing it back along his shaft, encompassing his sex. A nose against his pubis, hot breath parting the short hairs. Those feelings drew him, drawing him as much as the money did.

He wondered what it would be like to do to others what they did for him. It was a curiosity he resisted vehemently; but it was there, barely submerged beneath his surface thoughts. That and the curiosity of what it'd be like to be mounted as some of the men who'd hired him wanted.

My careful planning for my resurrection had given no thought to my sexual needs. Though not considered, my lust had taken care of itself by finding this lad. It didn't take me more than a moment to decide that I would hire him to keep my libido satisfied until I once again held Sergei in my arms. His memories held this youth's name and where he lived.

I wanted this Emil Paulik. I wanted to worship Eros with him. To relieve his curiosity. But gently. Kindly. Not tonight, but when we could together explore his fantasies leisurely.

He stood; and I sensed a middle-aged man approaching us, a man whose thoughts were already concentrated on the lad's endowment. I wagged a farewell to the youth. I had my own transaction to find. My canine bowel growled in anticipation.

My dinner sat alone on the darkest path in the park that was the river island. He wore a thin shirt and denim trousers. His hair and beard were wild, uncombed and unwashed. His thoughts were incoherent, sliding towards unconsciousness as the autumn night's chill held him and consumed his pain.

He did not stir at my touch on his hand and his skin was already as cold as my own. I nodded to myself as I accepted that he would not live out the night, even if I did not end his lost life for him. I changed back into human shape, standing before him nude.

Lifting him, I carried him into the bushes beyond the path and laid him on a bed of leaves. It was the best setting I could provide him for his encounter with the man on the white horse.

I pulled his trousers to his knees and used my preternatural sight in the darkness to find the needle tracks along the inside of his thigh. I wagged my head at how close they had come to his scrotum. The young man before me was in the last stages of his addiction, all but his largest veins were collapsed. Baring my teeth I plunged them into the artery at the joint.

2

Emil Paulik was leaving a macro-economics class when I found him in the business school building of the university the next afternoon. I wasn't at all sure what it was he was studying, but he looked good as he left the classroom.

"Herr Paulik," I greeted him as he entered the corridor. He stopped and turned back to me, his face showing surprise but no fear or suspicion.

"Yes?" He moved closer to me through the flow of young bodies.

I smiled. "I'd like to speak with you this evening -- if you can make the time available."

He thought of the girl with whom he shared his flat and what kind of excuse he would have to make. I sensed his appreciation of my appearance.

"It concerns an income of several hundred francs a week," I said and fought against the smile that threatened my face as his thoughts raced.

"When?" he asked, all thought of the girl gone.

"At eleven -- in your favorite park?"

His eyes were blank for the merest moment. Then, he nodded, a jerk of his mane of brown, unruly, but healthy, hair. "Until eleven o'clock," he said and smiled -- and waved as he started to resume his journey towards whatever followed his class in macro-economics. He halted and glanced back at me. "Your name?" he called back.

I had a date. Such a strange word. The lad had certainly understood the context of the park and money; he even thought he knew what would happen.

I almost enjoyed the weak afternoon sunlight as I stepped into the open square.

"Herr von Maribor?" Emil Paulik asked from the darkened path on the promenade that evening.

"Would you like a coffee?" I asked. Sergei's mutterings oozed through the corridors of my mind, tantalizingly close now that I was with the student from the university. Close, but still incoherent. I forced them from my mind. I had every intention of satisfying one of my hungers with the man before me and did not need a dead lover reminding me of his resurrected presence.

"No," Emil said.

I felt his apprehension at being seen with another man at this hour, at the assumption others would make of what we were about.

He smiled weakly. "I think we need to discuss the terms of your proposed contract." He rubbed his hands together in the chill of the park.

"I live quite close," I said as I mentally eased his suspicion of me. "It's warm there and we can have wine or a whisky while we work out our arrangements?" Nudging his thoughts, I increased both his curiosity and desire as I made the suggestion something he wanted.

"I think..." He shivered and nodded, glancing away from me. "Let's go."

"I couldn't really talk this afternoon," he said as he sat on the sofa and watched me remove my gloves and coat, still wary even with my vampiric reassurances.

"I understood that," I answered and mentally reassured him again. I smiled as he opened his coat and relaxed.

Oh, yes, I told myself. My sexual hunger would be well-satisfied. My eyes roamed leisurely over his body, imagining its every contour beneath his clothing.

"What do you have in mind?" he asked, mentally alert so that he could control our negotiations.

"I would think five hundred francs a week should help you remain comfortable in the winter ahead." I pulled my wallet from my suit jacket, retrieved five notes from it, and placed them on the end table beside him.

He stared at them, unconsciously licking his lips and calculating. "That's a lot of..."

I felt caution rising in his thoughts. I fielded it as it rose into his consciousness.

"You're not a student?" he asked, looking up at me.

"I'm not," I told him.

"I haven't seen you in the neighborhood before today."

"I've only recently arrived in Zürich," I said.

He nodded. "And what are you buying with this money, Herr von Maribor?"

I moved to the sideboard. "Pleasant interludes, Herr Paulik -- for both of us."

He studied me as I poured him a brandy. I hesitated before pouring myself a drink. Unlike microbes and viruses, alcohol did enter my blood stream -- directly. Much more immediately than it did with mortals. I didn't want to become intoxicated.

"And how do you expect us to play these interludes?"

"Play?"

"Are you into bondage? Or sadism?"

I was shocked; gentlemen didn't do those sort of things in my sexual fantasies.

Emil chuckled. "From the way you just reacted, I assume you're into vanilla sex?"

I shrugged, trying to link the spice to some sexual practice while hiding my ignorance.

"And what would you have me doing during these meetings of ours?"

He had put his curiosity and the fear that accompanied it into words. I could feel the desire to leave in his thoughts, a desire to avoid his own nature. I eased his hesitancy.

"Whatever you feel comfortable doing," I told him, though I knew my words were not exactly true as I spoke them. He would do what I wanted him to and what he feared doing. Yet, I would ensure he was comfortable doing it.

"Five hundred francs..." he mused to himself. "How many interludes a week do you expect that to buy?"

"Once, twice -- as many as you're comfortable with."

My answer satisfied him. He made his decision.

He stood and, raking the notes from the table, slipped them into his own wallet. He smiled at me as he slipped his coat off and tossed it casually on the other end of the sofa. Sitting back down, he picked up his snifter and brought it to his lips, now totally relaxed as he anticipated the sexual adventure ahead.

I touched his thoughts. He liked what he saw and was more than slightly curious at what I had in my basket.

Basket? What a strangely descriptive word.

I quickly heightened his curiosity as I increased the desire growing in him. I felt his tumescence, stymied at the moment within the confines of his clothing.

"May I show you my bed?" I asked.

Emil rose to his feet, a knowing smile pasted across his face, sexual energy permeable between us. His manhood elongated along his leg beneath his trousers now that it could move. "Show me the way," he mumbled, lust already making his voice husky.

"What should I call you?" he asked, the whisper of a smile crossing his lips as he eased his trousers down his legs. "It won't feel right to continue with Herr von Maribor as intimate as we're going to be."

I thought of Sergei. "Call me Karl as my lover does."

"You've got a lover?"

I felt resistance in his thoughts before I heard it in his voice. "He's far away, Emil, and I don't even know when I'll see him next -- and we're here. Together. Now."

An image flitted momentarily across his thoughts. He and I walked along the Plattpromenade together holding hands as lovers. It was the dream in that image that had him at the point of accepting what his nature wanted to do.

I reinforced the image, turning the relationship into one of equal friendship. One of mutual admiration. I gave it warmth and feeling and began to undress.

He relaxed again. Sighing, he began to slide his pants over his feet. The question of his committing himself again relegated to the realm of possibility -- if it felt right when it finally appeared between us.

I stood before him in just my briefs and watched his eyes widen as they followed the tube of my manhood reaching proudly across the front of my

abdomen to jut several centimeters out past my hip.

"You're a big one, Karl," he mumbled.

I smiled at the hesitancy appearing in his thoughts. "Not too big. And it doesn't matter at this moment." My hands went to his smooth, tight chest.

"You're cold," he mumbled, losing himself to my touch.

"I suspect you'll warm me up, Emi." I used the familiar form of his name. I wanted him past conscious recognition of his prostitution. I wanted him relaxed completely, giving vent to himself to explore our interlude.

My fingers followed the mounds of his buttocks. His eyes were glazed with growing lust, his conscious reservations behind us. He reached between us and yanked my underwear down, exposing me.

My fingers ascended along his back as he began to kneel before me, his hands pulling the cotton from my hips onto my thighs and, finally, to my knees where they fell to my ankles.

His fingers tugged gently at my scrotum as the sensation of the warm wetness of his tongue touching the underside of my shaft shot through me.

Oh, yes. He would definitely warm me this night.

His lips found my glans, pushing the foreskin back along my shaft as he descended its length. He was doing far more than I'd prepared him to do.

This was Emil Paulik released from self-restraint and doing what he wanted. I mentally gave him the way to take me without gagging, freeing him to enjoy his exploration of his needs as he gave me pleasure. He was awakening me, arousing the needs I had denied myself for sixty-four years. I relaxed.

Emil began to slow as time passed about us, his body surrendering to the fatigue that was the aftermath of the immediate hunger. His jaw ached, becoming noticeable to him even through his desire. His knees grew tired of pressing against hard wood.

I could not ejaculate. I had not done so since Sergei visited me on my death bed in 1874 and gave me immortality. With Emil, I came close. But, despite his best efforts, I was still dry, my testicles churning uselessly in their purse.

I pulled him to his feet. "Come, Emi," I told him. "Let's make ourselves comfortable."

I laid him on the bed and explored his chest with my tongue, forcing myself not to bare my fangs and use them.

I found his manhood as he bucked against me, a wild stallion knowing it faced taming and wanting it, yet resisting still. I dived down on him, taking him completely, as my hand gripped his testicles, twisting their covering. He moaned and humped instinctively against my face.

I trailed a finger beneath his scrotum as my lips moved up along his shaft to catch his foreskin with my teeth and pull it over his glans. I found his anus and eased a finger in as I again descended his manhood.

He groaned hoarsely, his hips bucking and his thoughts incoherent as he accommodated my invasion.

I worked a second finger into him as I watched his testicles tighten against the shaft of his manhood and stand guard there as he neared orgasm. A third finger joined the other two as I again pulled away and played with his skin.

"Jesus!" he groaned. "Gott!"

I tasted him then, as I felt him shudder beneath me. His sphincter clinched against my fingers and his body went rigid.

I climbed between his legs. He shuddered again as I raised them to my shoulders. Still holding him with my lips, I looked up along his body to find him gazing down at me.

"Do it," he murmured and let his head fall back against the pillows.

I lifted his buttocks to meet me. I let his manhood go and trailed my tongue over his abdomen to his chest, replacing my fingers inside him with myself. Sucking at a nipple, I eased past his sphincter.

My lips sought his as I pushed into him.

His eyes opened and sudden fear spread through him. "Use a condom," he groaned and moved to push me away.

I blinked. A condom?

Of course, I knew what one was. But to use it with another man? Why? I pushed past the fear at the surface of his thoughts, searching for an answer.

He bucked in an attempt to escape me. I touched his fear and helped him relax, helped him shove it away. His struggle ceased beneath me and I felt the heat of his erection jutting up to press against my abdomen as he accepted me inside him, his body grinding itself against my possession of him.

AIDS. A disease with no cure. A disease that destroyed a man's immune system until it tired of its struggles and left the man open to a multitude of opportunistic diseases. Until one killed him. A disease caused by a virus and carried by blood, transmitted by blood to blood. The tiniest wound, the most microscopic tear, was enough to permit the virus into a body to begin its work of destruction.

I allowed myself to consider the situation even as my pubis pressed against the insides of his warm thighs.

I could bleed from a vein or artery. I could be wounded as any mortal could but healed within moments. I could tear back skin and meat and open a vein to share my immortality. But could I carry this virus? Transmit it? For thousands of years, vampires had feasted on human blood. We had feasted on those eaten up with syphilis and cancer -- and were unaffected.

Could this new virus be sufficiently different from all those of the past that a vampire could carry it and transmit it?

I didn't think so. History was on my side.

I wasn't sure, however. And I wasn't going to take a chance. I could not endanger this man with the risk.

But what did I use as a condom? They were not something an

intelligent man with what was to become known as a Socratic tendency had carried when I first learnt of sex or fell in love with Sergei. This AIDS was an unknown threat when Sergei had re-entered my life and I had made love as wildly as a ninety year old vampire as I had as a man of twenty-four.

I did not have one of the things.

"Tomorrow night, will you come to me, Emi?" I whispered against his ear.

"Tomorrow?" His voice was dreamy.

I pulled myself from Emil's warmth. "I'll have condoms then," I mumbled and found his lips with my own.

He sat up and stared at me. "I've got one in my wallet," he said, sheepishly accepting his willingness to surrender himself.

"Do you want to use it?" I asked, forcing him to make his decision without any nudges from me.

He shivered as he slipped off the bed and picked up his trousers. A moment later, he looked from the foiled packet now in his hand to me and back again. He shivered again and tore the packet open. "Be still and let me put it on you."

As he spread the condom open along the shaft of my manhood, he stared into my eyes, looking for the soul some say lies within them. "I don't understand why I'm doing this," he mumbled and climbed back onto the bed with me.

I smiled and then winked at him as he opened his legs to me and lifted them to my shoulders. He pulled slowly on his erection as I entered him, concentrating on it and the feelings emanating from his working it.

"You just have a supply of them here tomorrow," he told me as he ground his buttocks against me experimentally. "You can fuck me, Karl; but you've got to protect me when you do."

3

I entered the park to hunt. It was early evening and still warm enough for mortals not to have donned coats against the coming night's chill. Instead of drug addicts waiting for their piecemeal suicides to become reality, I found the gendarmerie patrolling the paths I had trod only two nights before. They had frightened off both the addicts and the rent boys.

I, too, was frightened off. I moved my hunt to the lake at the eastern edge of Mythenquai below the university, but the chill there was earlier and fiercer than along the promenade. I moved into the city and changed into wolf form.

A man careened into the rubbish bins set at the mouth of an alley off the Sechseläutenplatz. I watched him collapse.

I came upon him and sniffed him carefully.

My eyes widened when I realized there was no heroin in him. He was simply a drunk. I touched his mind again and found a picture of cardboard

boxes lashed together that was his home deep in this alley.

The man was homeless! Like the men in America I had once read about who rode the rails across their country during the depression.

He was like the addicts who congregated in Switzerland from across Europe. Instead of heroin, however, he used alcohol. The descent was the same, only slower.

"Nice doggy," he mumbled as tried to pull himself up. He collapsed back onto the pavement and slipped into his own private world.

Looking at him, I realized that derelicts were as useful as food as were their younger associates in the park. They were also far more plentiful than those lost young of the park.

Alcohol entered my blood and affected me, unlike heroin. But it left me with no unpleasant aftermath as it did these lost men and women of the streets. It also did not leave my mouth tasting sickly sweet.

There were so many, I didn't have to kill. I could fill my hunger daily. The next morning the derelict would be up and about, only marginally weaker than he had been the day before. There would be no sudden increase in their population's deaths to draw official attention. My feeding habits were no longer in danger of exposure.

In human form, I squatted touched the man's shoulder.

"You--!" the drunk growled, his eyes opening to glare at me. "I got no use for you faggots." He made to push himself to his feet. "Go find yourself a woman. Leave me alone!"

I soothed his thoughts and helped him to his feet. He stepped deeper into the alley at my urging. Fear and hatred rode his thoughts even as I made them languid.

I sank my fangs into his dirt-encrusted neck. Not deep, but deep enough. His eyes were glassy and his head lolled on the dirty brick wall of the alley when I left him.

I was happy to be in Zürich in the autumn of 2004. It was proving to be good to me. I could not imagine a reason for leaving it.

Emil was in love.

With me.

I had been the first to take his virginity, the first to whom he gave himself. Now, I held his love in my hand, freely given.

Mortals!

"It's only you I want, Karli," he told me as, straddling my hips, he reached between his legs and took a firm hold on my manhood. He began to lower himself.

"And my five hundred francs a weeks," I mumbled, thinking that I was making a joke.

He stopped his downward movement, my knob pressing against his pucker. I knew then that I shouldn't have mentioned money. What was no more than a jest to me was an insult to him when it came to the agreement

between us.

His face slackened as if I had struck him with my fist. His hand fell from me as he began to raise himself off me.

"Emil..." I reached for his hand.

He shoved me away and both his knees gained the mattress.

"Emil!" I cried as he began to pull himself over the bed. I reached out to him again, having to use my supernatural speed to take his arm before he could reach the edge of the bed.

"Let me go!"

When I didn't, he turned back to me, his eyes dead. "Please, sir."

Scheiße und Blut! I had used much the same joke with a lad in Paris a hundred years ago and he had thought it was funny. Mistresses of whatever gender had certainly changed over the century.

"I didn't mean to hurt you," I told him and continued to hold his arm. I saw the tears glinting in his eyes. "I was attempting to make a joke," I explained. "Obviously, my joke fell flat."

"Under a fully loaded lorry," he mumbled.

"Will you forgive me?"

His eyes still seemed dead, but he studied my face in the near dark of the bedroom. "I need the money, Karl. I have to keep up the rent on my flat..." A tight, fearful smile crossed his lips and disappeared. "Unless you're willing to let me move in here with you."

My heart shuddered.

Move in here? Live with me? See me avoid the sunlight when it again carried heat which was one of the two things that could kill me? Know me for what I was?

With Sergei's specter practically howling about the garret all the time? With me waiting for his third incarnation so we could again be together for ever and ever? Never!

Emil still watched my face, waiting for me. I realized finally and fully that I was in an unpleasantly tight dilemma.

My hand slipped down his arm to grip his hand. I reached out to the other one and took it as well. I kept my eyes away from his smooth chest, forcing them to stay on his watching me. The smell of our earlier sex was still ripe on him. His manhood remained tumescent, the emotional pain I'd visited upon him not yet sufficient shock to have it curling in on itself.

"It's been only a month, Emi..."

"Six weeks and two days," he corrected me, not moving his gaze from me.

"And we agreed we wouldn't do anything precipitous..."

"You said that..." His eyes narrowed. "Where is this lover of yours?"

He pulled away from me and turned to face the wall, leaving me to appreciate his back and nicely rounded buttocks. "He's why you don't want me to live with you," he groaned with sudden realization.

He turned back to face me, his eyes again glistening. "All I am to you is

a piece of arse to hold you over until he returns!"

I stared at him in shock. He had pinpointed exactly my first intentions. But I had grown used to Emil Paulik, had come to enjoy his abandon, and learnt to care for him.

"I think I'd better leave, Herr von Maribor," he mumbled in defeat, his hands reflexively covering himself as he stood.

"Don't do this, Emil," I begged, my voice neutral as I struggled to find an approach that would diffuse our impasse.

"You've already had me three times this week, sir. May I have the rest of it off?" He moved around the bed, picking pieces of his clothing from the floor.

"Emil!"

"When next week should I return, Herr von Maribor?" His voice was unnaturally calm as he stepped into his y-fronts and covered his arsecheeks from me.

"Why are you doing this?" I asked in exasperation.

"Doing what, sir? Surely, I've already given you five hundred francs of pleasure this week. Especially as I'm only your whore until your lover comes to you -- this is Wednesday -- would the same day next week be acceptable...?"

He pulled on his flannel shirt and studiously kept his attention on buttoning its sleeves.

Numb, I watched him leave. Moments later, I heard the door close behind him.

Sergei whispered incessantly, disturbing my sleep and ruining my feedings as the week unfolded.

His memory and his promise had destroyed a beautiful relationship as it budded. I doubted Emil would return on Wednesday.

I had hurt him. I had insulted him. His heart and his honor.

He was a proud young man from a world I did not yet fully understand.

In his mind, he had given himself to me because he loved me. Our late evening and early morning hours had become comfortable ones in which we sated our sexual appetites, but also ones in which he explored his own nature even as he linked it to me.

I realized I had accepted his gift of himself. It was my duty to help him now.

I could mislead him. I could tell him I would accept him as my lover and allow him to sever his ties to the life he had built. I could even mislead myself as I deceived him. I could tell myself that Sergei no longer mattered, that Emil was enough.

He *was* enough.

Only, there was *also* Sergei, alive again and in Zürich, unconsciously gibbering his presence to me.

I would not mislead Emil Paulik. And I would not deceive myself.

Deceit was a vice I either had never learnt or had forgotten.

When I rose late Saturday afternoon, I missed Emil. I missed him more than I had missed him the evening before. I had become used to him by the last week of November, even comfortable with him. Now, as December began, I was close to falling in love with the student from the Universität Zürichs.

I struggled with that as I showered.

If I gave him immortality ... But most vampires committed suicide as their families began to die. Decapitation and heat were the only deaths we could know. All it took was exposure to a cloudless summer day and the long minutes of agony to end vampiric life. Or the brief moments of hell it took to burn away flesh in a crematorium.

Could Emil handle that impulse to destruction that was so much a part of vampire psychology? I doubted it. Even with me at his side. Loneliness had proven to be a monster difficult to tame once immortality was introduced to humanity.

As I walked through the night towards Emil's flat, I knew what I should do. For him and for me. I should blot out his memories of me.

My own pride, however, demanded that he remember me better than he did. I would give him the choice.

I reached out my senses before knocking at the door. To use Emil's newly acquired American word, I scoped it out.

I froze with surprise, my fist nearly striking the door. There were three of them inside! Emil and the woman who lived with him -- and a strangely blank male. Only through Emil's mind was I able to know he was American.

I reached for their thoughts. Emil still hurt at what he saw as my rebuff, but he was past his initial burst of pain. He even laughed at something the American had said and hoped his application was accepted at the bookstall on campus.

They were drinking cheap Chianti and eating the woman's freshly cooked kugels.

The three of them seemed to know each other well. Again, I attempted to touch the American's mind. Nothing. He was a cipher to me. Emil felt the wine he had already drunk and wondered what the other man would be like in bed.

The American's name was Tom MacPherson, an exchange student at the university. I had Emil look at him.

This Tom MacPherson had thick black curly hair, almost unmanageable. Emil could imagine running his fingers through it, feeling its silky smoothness. Tom had a lean face, full lips, aquiline nose, a high forehead, and piercing blue eyes. His skin was pale but dotted with freckles. His shoulders were wide and his chest deep beneath his jumper and Emil remembered he had been a swimmer as an undergraduate at his university

in America. He imagined undressing him with no help from me.

I could imagine the rest as well as he. I looked for the reason for their get-together and found this man shared two classes with Emil.

I touched the woman's thoughts. She was mildly suspicious that Emil would keep dinner going long enough that he could feign being too tired to satisfy her sexually when she finally had him in bed -- as he had already done every day this past week. She liked Tom, but she wished he'd leave. I left her thoughts as she wondered with whom Emil was sleeping, mentally ticking off women she knew from the university, women he knew, women they both knew.

I jotted a note asking that Emil meet me late Monday afternoon at my flat and told him it was most important. I left the note wedged between the door and the jamb.

We would meet as civilized men, perhaps over whiskies. Civilized and relaxed, we would treat our situation as adults. If he asked me to, I would ease his memories enough that he could again enjoy his girlfriend as well as remember me fondly. And I would give him a sum equal to his five hundred francs a week through the remaining school year. Monday I would draw enough money from my account.

Ach! The best laid plans of mice and men . . .

Sunday evening, I sat in my well-lit living room, listening to Mozart's Nachtmusik on the tape deck Emil had convinced me to buy and relishing my serenity now that I had my life once again organized.

I was aflight on memories of my youth, carried along by the musikmeister's fleet music when someone started to pound on the door.

I pulled myself back to reality. The hammering on my door continued. I crossed the room and flung it open, ready to wither even a gendarme with my gaze.

Emil stood there, his fist raised to beat again against the wood. I saw the hurt and anger written across his face. Fear touched his countenance as he recognized me, fear mingled with embarrassment.

"Emil!" I said in surprise. "Do come in."

"Nyet!" a muffled cry rose from behind him on the darkened landing.

"Why did you come to my flat and leave this fucking note?" Emil demanded and blandished a piece of paper, righteously indignant, not hearing his companion's cry.

"I wanted to settle things between us in a civilized manner," I said and heard his companion's groan of pain as he crumpled to the floor.

"Who is this with you?" I asked, stepping out onto the landing going to the stricken man.

"He..." Emil paused, caught between the anger that had brought him and the inexplicable collapse of his friend.

I lifted the unconscious man and carried him into the flat past Emil. I recognized the curly black hair and wide shoulders from Emil's appraisal of

Tom MacPherson the evening before.

Emil watched from the doorway as I lay his friend on the sofa. I touched the unconscious man's swirling thoughts. They weren't blank this time, but there was nothing on the surface of them that explained his collapse or his unconsciousness. I delved deeper as I knelt beside him. And touched the thoughts percolating up from his soul, lacing their way through every other thought.

Sergei!

I sat back on my haunches and stared at Tom MacPherson.

"Is he going to be all right?" Emil asked as he entered.

"Shut the door," I told him but did not take my eyes from my Sergei returned.

"What's wrong with him?" Emil asked again. He approached the back of the sofa, concerned for his friend.

"Why did you bring him?" I demanded.

"I…"

I glanced up at the man I had almost been willing to give myself to and mentally shuddered. How could I ever consider doing that with Sergei so close? How could I hurt so completely any man as I nearly had this Emil Paulik?

"I was afraid of you," he managed, his face reddening with embarrassment.

"Me?"

"I love you and you -- all you wanted was to fuck me." He looked away, avoiding my eyes watching him. "Then you left that note. I was afraid to see you alone. I was afraid you'd get me in bed again…"

I rose. There was nothing wrong with Tom MacPherson but his recognition of me. It had taken Sergei's last incarnation two days of unconsciousness for his spirit to awaken and establish its recognition of me throughout him.

Sergei's spirit had learnt well that time; the American was well on his way to having recognition of me as part of his very being. He bordered on consciousness already.

"Does he know you and I were intimate?" I asked as I lowered myself into my chair, continuing to gaze at the unconscious man, studying this incarnation of Sergei so I could recognize him as well as he would recognize me.

Emil's hesitation pulled my eyes to him. I scowled as I realized Emil had become pale.

"He knows?" I demanded.

"Karl, I was so hurt when I left here that morning," he mumbled as he slumped against the nearest wall. "I went to his flat. I couldn't stand the thought of my girlfriend knowing -- and I had to talk to somebody."

I nodded and forced myself to smile. "Please, Emil, be seated. Would you like a whisky?"

He nodded numbly and moved around the sofa to the chair across from mine as I reached to the sideboard and poured a glass for him.

"I needed to understand how I'd managed to foul everything up so badly," he continued as I handed him the drink.

"He knew you were seeing me before?"

"No. But he knew I earned extra money by hiring myself out on the promenade. I had told him about that one time when he complained about being so poor -- back in the summer, just after he'd arrived at the university."

"And you told him about our arrangement? About our relationship?"

He nodded. "Tom isn't gay -- that's why he wouldn't go down to the promenade. But he understood. He's from some city in America where there is a similar park, and many of his friends earned money the way I was doing. Some of them were gay. That's why I went to him -- he would understand better than anyone I knew."

"Apparently he did understand. He was there at your flat last night."

He stared at me. "How did you know that?"

I sighed. Now that I had Sergei again, Emil and what we had were my past. He deserved an explanation, however. He deserved the truth. I hoped he could accept it.

"I read your mind. Before I wrote the note."

"Read my mind?" He stared at me suspiciously.

"Emil, you've known me less than two months. I hope, however, that you know I would never set out to hurt you, though that's exactly what I did." I shuddered.

"You're going to have a very hard time understanding what I have to tell you. You'll have an even more difficult time accepting it. I'll start with what I am."

"What you are?"

I nodded. "I'm almost 160 years old, Emil." I watched his brows rise. "I'm a vampire," I said before he could object.

He laughed. "You almost had me going there, Karl," he said, his humor momentarily stronger than his hurt.

"I am." I opened my mouth and extended my fangs. "I won't hurt you, I promise. But you must understand this part of me to understand everything else. Will you hear me out and not be afraid of me?"

He nodded dubiously, staring at my extended canines.

My nose grew into a snout as fur covered my body. I could no longer sit on my buttocks. My ears grew long and pointed as my skull sloped back from my eyes.

I hopped down from the chair, padded across the room, and sniffed at his feet as he stared at me, my tail wagging. I licked his shoe with a wolf's long tongue. I barked at him when he instinctively pulled his hands away from his legs. The look of horror on his face satisfied me and I returned to my chair.

I shaped my body into human form again and smiled across at him wryly as I reached for my underpants lying on the chair's cushion. I dressed as rapidly as a vampire is capable with preternatural speed.

"See?"

"Mein Gott!" he groaned and gulped down his whisky. He continued to stare.

"I have never hurt you, Emil -- not physically. I am not about to start now," I told him to reassure him.

"I've seen you in daylight."

"In the autumn and winter -- when the heat of the sun is weak. Even then, I must cover myself. Summers, I must stay away from sunlight all together."

"That's why you wouldn't let me move in with you?"

I nodded.

"Why...?" He paused looking about the room. "Why didn't you simply possess me? Kill me? Or make me like you?"

"I grew into manhood when honor and duty still meant something," I explained. "I contracted with you -- I was honor-bound to stay within the agreement of our contract."

"But I fell in love with you. It was more than our arrangement. Totally different."

"And I was in danger of falling in love with you. After you left, I decided on exposing myself to you and, if you wanted me still, making you like me."

"I'd have done it," he answered slowly. "I -- I'd still do it."

"No." The word was a slap against his face.

"I couldn't," I hurried on, "it wouldn't be fair to you, Emil. Most vampires become suicides because they cannot stand the loneliness and melancholy that is our existence."

"I'd have you..."

"And no one else. Friends grow old, family members die. Daytime activities are no more. You have plans and hopes for your future -- those would all be for naught. Besides, I wouldn't be there to lessen your pains."

"Why the hell not?" he demanded. "If I'm willing to be gay for you? I'd even be a vampire for you! You owe me something in return. That's what love is supposed to be about. Two people helping each other."

"That's true, Emil. But I have a lover."

"Scheiße! I've heard that one before."

"You've heard it, but you didn't understand it before."

"Who is he?"

"He's lying on the sofa right now," I answered.

He turned to look at his friend. "Tom? He isn't gay."

"All humans are bisexual, Emil. We have bodies and minds with which to enjoy sex, to make it a recreation..."

"Science is keying in on the gene that makes us gay."

"A gay gene? It's more likely that any sex gene they find enables man to enjoy his sex instead of enduring it in order to procreate."

His face broadcast his disbelief.

"Emil, I can go to almost any young man in Zürich and offer him several hundred francs and anonymity -- and he will permit himself to be buggered. With but a little preparation and foreplay -- and enough mental suggestion to lessen any fear he has -- he will be aroused by the experience, though he hasn't done it before."

After long moments, he seemed to accept the possibility I suggested. "Okay. So, given we're bisexual to some degree, how does this make Tom your lover?'

"Do you believe I'm a vampire?" I asked as prelude.

He stared at me a moment. "I'd better. I've never seen another human with fangs like yours. And I can't imagine a human changing to a dog and back."

"Then, there is something else a bit less difficult for you to accept -- reincarnation."

"Reincarnation?" He laughed nervously.

"At the first anniversary of Wilhelm I becoming the German Emperor, I met a young Russian nobleman who was a member of the Tsar's embassy to that event. We fell in love."

"In 1872?" He stared at me in disbelief.

"I was twenty-four years old."

"Mein Gott!"

"Sergei was a curious man and one who did not like the thought of growing old. Somehow, he found a vampire who had fled the Paris Commune that followed the German occupation of France and made his way to Odessa. Sergei paid him to give him immortality."

Emil rolled his eyes, trying not to believe me even as he remembered my demonstrations.

"I visited him in 1874 in Odessa and came back to Vienna stricken with some disease. I was at death's door and had only hours left to live when he arrived. He gave me his blood, making me a vampire as he had become."

His eyes lit with understanding. "You're telling me this Sergei is Tom here…?"

I nodded. "He first died in 1905 during the Bloody Sunday riots in Petrograd. He came back to me in 1935 as Würther, the curate at the church on my lands in southeastern Austria. When we fled the SS in 1940, they killed him. Now, he lies there, returned again to be with me."

"How did he die the first time?"

"Some Cossack decapitated him during the riots."

He grimaced. "And the second time?"

"Shot."

"Vampires can die from bullet wounds?" he asked suspiciously.

"I don't think so." I shrugged. "I only know of decapitation and

extreme heat."

"So, how did he die from bullets the second time?"

"He refused to become a vampire."

"But he slept with you?"

I nodded.

"And he loved you that time too?"

I nodded again.

He assimilated what I had told him, gazing all the time at the youth still unconscious on the sofa but beginning to stir. "Why have you told me this?" he asked finally.

"So you can understand why I cannot be your lover."

"What're you going to do to me?"

"Nothing…" I chuckled. "Or, rather, I'm going to give you 14,000 francs tomorrow after I have visited my bank -- as a token of my friendship for you."

I frowned then, remembering I was leaving him exposed as a homosexual and alone now that I had Sergei. "I can make you forget me and what we had. You can return to your girlfriend and live comfortably with her."

"I want to remember you -- and what we've had, Karl," he said and he looked down at his hands. "I want you to remember me too. I want a chance to win you if things don't work out between you and Tom."

"Really?" I stared at him. "And you wish to retain this gay awareness you've acquired?"

He nodded. "I want us to stay in touch wherever you are."

"You won't as you grow older and know I don't."

"I'll still be holding onto the hope you'll give me what you plan on giving Tom."

"Vampire blood or love?"

"Both."

I sighed. "I can only give you immortality -- and I'd rather you wait until time has healed the wounds I've caused you. Then, you can be sure."

Tom groaned and I touched his mind. In amazement, I found him at the brink of consciousness already. I found confusion as well as awareness of what I was and what we had been. I also found resistance to that awareness.

He felt me, and immediately there was only the blankness I had found when he was at Emil's flat. The American youth stirred on my sofa.

"He'll be able to walk in another few minutes," I told Emil. "He's rebelling against his knowledge of our past." I smiled at him. "I'll carry him to the outer door, but you'll need to help him home."

4

I gaped at Emil in shock. The late autumn sun had already sunk into the mountains. Only two days ago, I had had the American lying on my sofa

unconscious from his spirit's recognition of me. Now, he was flying westward above the Atlantic.

"Karl, I'm sorry," Emil told me again, his hand reaching between us to touch my arm, its fingers gripping my biceps.

"Unglaublich," I mumbled as knowledge of Sergei's flight continued to consume my thoughts.

Unbelievable.

Unmöglich. Definitely impossible. Sergei had come to save me in his first life. He hadn't resisted me in his second. But now he fled me. Halfway around the world.

"Take this, Karl," Emil told me and I looked at him, seeing him then. Him and the glass of whisky he held towards me.

"I…"

"Drink it," he said. "It'll help." I knew what it would do to me and help wasn't the word I would use to describe its effects. Numbly, however, I took the drink and swallowed half the glass without tasting its contents.

I felt it almost immediately, however. My legs were weak under me and I felt stupor begin to descend over me. I collapsed into the chair behind me. And I did not take my eyes from Emil's face.

"Tell me what happened -- everything from when you helped him home," I said and set the glass on the table beside me.

Emil sat in the chair across from me. "He kept mumbling in a language I didn't know. It sounded like Russian…"

"He'd have still been Sergei then," I confirmed. "Go on."

"Halfway to his flat, he changed to German -- it seemed like a flow of consciousness -- but nothing was really coherent, Karl."

"He went from Sergei to his second incarnation then…" I touched Emil's thoughts, reliving his memories and hearing Würther speak again. Hearing him again tell me to leave him on that bloody field of edelweiß. The pain as the bullets tore through his side, crushing bone and lung. And his refusal of immortality.

I shuddered. There were times the past definitely was not better than the present.

I smiled bitterly. "He was reliving his second life with me," I told him. "It was a flow of his memories." Emil became blurred as my eyes glistened with tears.

"Karl!" He pushed himself out of his chair to kneel before me. "You're bleeding!"

His words pulled me back from my tears for Sergei, dying in a field of wild flowers as Würther. "Where?"

"Around your eyes." He was kneeling at my side. "Are you okay? Should I call a doctor?"

I pulled a handkerchief from my front pocket and wiped at my face. When I peered at him again, my vision was clear. The handkerchief was bright crimson, the color of arterial blood. I chuckled.

"I'm all right, my friend."

"You're sure?"

I nodded. "You saw tears in my eyes."

"Tears? As red as blood?"

"Vampire tears are blood, Emil. All of our body fluids are blood."

He sat back on his haunches, still watching me closely. "You aren't just saying that? You aren't going to die because your life partner fled you?"

"Sit back in the chair and finish your story, Emi."

"I helped him into his room and made him sit down. I didn't leave until he started acting like himself."

"What did he say after he again became the American?"

He chuckled. "He said he had just gone tripping on the weirdest drug he ever met, a flashback..." He saw my puzzled frown. "There are drugs that make you see things that don't exist or that distorts things that do. LSD is one of them."

"He thought he was on these drugs?"

"I'm not sure of that. Americans have such quaint ways of expressing themselves sometimes. It might have been just his way of explaining what had happened to him."

I nodded.

"He didn't say much more than that. And I left..." Emil smiled wryly. "I had some things I had to think about, and he seemed to be okay."

"You saw him before he left?"

"I went to the airport with him, Karl -- four hours ago. He said he was leaving early..."

"Early?"

"We still have another fortnight of classes -- before the holidays."

"Go on."

"I asked him why. He told me he had learnt a lot of things about himself, things he had to think about and decide if he wanted to accept."

"Did he say anything about me -- or our past together?"

"Not directly. I kept trying to pin him down..." Emil looked down at his hands, unable to meet my gaze.

"He said there were a lot of things he didn't understand. He had to get away from Zürich, away from everybody here, so he could look at them, face up to them."

"Then he didn't reject me?"

"No, Karl, he didn't. He needs breathing space is all."

"Breathing space?" My brows knitted in confusion. "He's mortal -- he breathes naturally. The cells of his body needs the oxygen his lungs pull in from the air..."

Emil chuckled. "It's an expression; it means he needed to put distance between you -- what he's learnt about you and him -- and himself."

My mind was clearing. Fortunately, alcohol's hold on a vampire was short-lived. I rose and began to pace.

I had been a fool not to keep him here and watch over him as I had the curate who had been his second incarnation. Honor had demanded I not force myself on him, however. I hadn't even attempted to contact him in person.

Now he was in America. Or would be before I could do anything about it. With supersonic jets, he was already past London, and probably past Iceland as well. An image of the map of the United States floated through my thoughts.

It was so big!

"Where was he from?" I asked, daring to hope this youth knew that much about the man I already knew I must follow.

He shrugged. "I don't think I know. He was reading at the University of Maryland. Wait! He said he was from Baltimore in the province of Maryland."

I sank onto the sofa, shaking my head at the impossibility of finding Sergei. I could steal into the registrar's office -- if only I could work computers, I could go into his records at the university.

My whirling thoughts stopped then.

I could find everything the university knew about this student enrolled in it. All I had to do was again see the hacker who'd given me my new identity.

"Are you going to try to follow him?" Emil asked.

I nodded. "I can find his address, his home..."

"Do you want me to go with you?"

I stared at him.

"I know -- if we find him and he wants you -- you're his, Karl. But you need me to help him accept you and what you offer him. Otherwise, he may just fly off again and you'll never be able to find him."

"You'd do this?" I asked in surprise.

"I love you, Karl. I also understand that you don't love me. You care for me, though. You like me. You're willing to be my friend. I'll accept that." He smiled wanly, tears glistening in his eyes. "It's the only thing I've got -- and you need my help. You can't move about easily during the day."

"It may take a while to track him down -- can you afford to be away from the university that long?"

He nodded. "This is my last term. I'll simply ask my professors for papers I can write to gain credit for the courses. There'll be libraries there, won't there?"

"I think Baltimore is near the national capital," I said. "Surely, there are good ones in Washington you may use."

He smiled tightly. "May we sleep together too?"

"Is that what you want?"

He nodded.

"Then you shall have all of me that I can give you, Emil. What about your flat?"

"I'll give my girlfriend the money you gave me. It'll pay for the flat and keep her in food for a year at least." He looked away. "I don't have anything else left here."

I chuckled. "I don't envy you that meeting, my friend."

He smiled wanly. "I don't envy you yours when we've tracked Tom down."

We were airborne on a late afternoon flight to Paris where we would change to something called a Concorde which promised to have us across the Atlantic and at Dulles Airport near Washington, DC, in four hours -- leaving me with more than three hours to find my hotel and barricade myself against the coming sun. Given what I had already experienced of this world I had awakened to, I believed the company's propaganda.

Emil leant towards me as we rose over Paris and said: "You're fucking me tomorrow before we do anything else."

I shook my head in amusement. A month ago, Emil Paulik was a young man not about to hike his backside for anybody, a young man hell-bent on someday marrying and fathering children. I had eased his fears and took his virginity partly by guile. I was still amazed at how far he had come since with no help from me.

He had forsaken his girlfriend and, with her, his future plans of fatherhood. He was truly comfortable as what I had once known as an invert. He was equally as mercurial about immortality. The world had truly changed from the one I knew.

5

"I want what you promised last night," Emil said, the moment I woke. "I've been sitting here for two hours waiting for you to awake and give it to me."

He rose and I saw he was naked and erect. He slipped into the bed beside me.

"I don't have a condom," I told him as his face neared mine.

"You're a vampire, Karl. It's a pretty safe bet I don't have to worry." His lips found mine as he moved to lie on top of me, grinding his sex against mine.

His knees rode my sides as he pushed his body far enough up my abdomen for him to free me, his bollocks and manhood trailing across my skin. He descended the length of my body then. His arsecheeks reached my crotch and spread to expose himself; I was fully erect. He guided me into him before he broke our kiss and sat up, impaled.

"God!" he groaned. "I was beginning to wonder if I'd ever feel this thing in me again." He sighed. "It feels so good, Karl." His sex drooled as it rode my stomach.

He let me make love to him for a few more moments. "I want you to

just lie back," he told me then and smiled down at me. "Let me do the work."

He began to ride me, his manhood slapping me each time his cheeks ground into my pubis.

I reached up to pull on his nipples, my fingertips spreading out to caress his chest.

He closed his eyes and moaned as he continued to ride me. And reminded me of the rapture the Renaissance artists captured in their pietas.

"I'm close, Liebchen," he whispered and increased the speed of his movements. His manhood smeared my abdomen continuously with his ooze.

My fingertips caressed from his nipples to his hips and back to his chest again, caressing him as they sensed the growing tension in his body.

It had been a fortnight since he so angrily left me -- a long fortnight. We weren't just engaging in sex, regardless of the arrangement we'd made between us. There was a warmth between us, a sharing that was complete.

We were making love. We loved each other, I as much he. And I wouldn't have had it any other way.

Perspiration beaded his forehead, a thin film shining on his body, as he rode me harder. I touched the surface of his thoughts and felt the feelings fogging his mind.

I gasped with him as fire shot from his bollocks into the far reaches of his body. My every muscle tensed and became rigid with his as he was pushed closer to his orgasm. The knob of his manhood suffused with blood in primordial preparation.

It was as if it was my bollocks riding my sweat-soaked pubes as Emil rocked himself on me in the last moments before he exploded. Before *we* exploded.

He collapsed over me, his face against my neck.

"We need housing," I said as we lay together in the bed, his face against my chest.

"We can stay here," he answered, the movement of his lips against my nipple doing nice things to me, things that would distract me if I wasn't vigilant.

"At four hundred dollars a night? That's nearly six hundred francs."

He sat up, his eyes round as he looked down into my face. "So much money?"

"Tom knows me," I told him. "He knows his past. He warns me away, demanding time alone to understand everything -- to make decisions that may not include me."

"You know this?"

"I hear his spirit's whisperings. Telepathy, you would call it. But these are broadcast."

"We need to find a place then," an all-business side of him said,

erupting from the comfortably satiated youth of moments before. "Do we want a flat or a house?"

"A house," I answered.

"In a gay neighborhood or straight?"

"There's a difference?" I asked in surprise.

"Gay neighborhoods are usually upscale..."

"Why?"

"Because gays spend their money on their homes, Karl," he answered grinning. "We want our sex in comfort and nice surroundings; and we aren't going to have children to waste our money on.

"Very, very upscale areas are mixed -- with educated, moneyed, and understanding straight people predominating. But proletariat neighborhoods usually look rundown and have more crime..."

I laughed. "You're asking me how much money I have."

"I'm merely laying out your choices."

"We'll go upscale," I told him.

He grinned down at me and pushed off me. "We need to find a realtor then."

Emil had been busy while I slept my first day in America. He had ventured into Washington and picked up a thick gay newspaper in which gay-owned and operated businesses advertised, amongst which were at least ten realtors.

While Emil telephoned a realtor to arrange an appointment, I read through *The Washington Blade*, growing steadily more disgusted by the hate it reported.

Two teen-aged sons of some Maryland police chief had come into a known gay cruising area and mugged a gay man. Skinheads congregated at street corners on DuPont Circle to intimidate gay men and women. A Reverend Pat Koughlin preached that homosexuality was a sin and condoned gay-bashing. A Senator called for the United States to send all its homosexuals to a Pacific island so the country could be free of them. Arlington, Virginia, police conducted sting operations against gays. The Christian Center had as its agenda the return of America to family values -- expressly leaving homosexuals out of their concept of family. The Post Office sent unsolicited child pornography to some man in North Dakota and, when he accepted it, arrested him.

This was democracy? This was America?

Wahnsinn! Complete, unadulterated insanity.

What I could not understand was how the country which I had learnt had, nearly alone, defeated Hitler and the Axis could have sunk so deeply into the quagmire of reaction and the fascism that lurked so closely behind it. That was the insanity.

I tossed the newspaper on the bed as Emil replaced the telephone receiver in its stand.

"Did you read this?" I demanded and pointed to the newspaper on the

bed.

"Sure. I had more than five hours before you woke up. I read it. I also read *The Washington Times* and *The Washington Post*."

"Are they gay also?"

He grinned. "They're the mainstream papers." He knelt beside the bed and picked up both newspapers.

"Gott im Himmel!" I groaned as he handed them to me.

"We've got a seven o'clock appointment with an agent in Capitol Hill."

"Where is Capitol Hill?"

"Near the American parliament's buildings. It's supposed to be very upscale. It's not even five o'clock yet..." He grinned. "We've got time to eat."

I picked up *The Washington Times* and started reading half-heartedly, my stomach reminding me harshly that I hadn't fed in two days. I forgot it immediately. With growing horror, I rushed through the rest of the paper in my hands.

"You read that fast?" Emil asked, not sensing my anger.

"Vampires are faster than mortals," I growled. "This trash is a newspaper?" I demanded.

He nodded. "It's the Moonies' paper..."

"Moonies?"

"Some Korean who thinks he's the reincarnation of Christ. His group is everywhere and has lots of money -- they bought *The Times* years ago."

"It's nothing more than a reactionary apologia! It's..." I sought a word that would adequately describe the dribble I had just read, "von Papen's newspaper. They offer nothing, but blame everything on the government."

"Isn't that's pretty standard for an opposition press, Karl?"

"No. If a newspaper must coat its news coverage with politics, it needs to show how its side's positions are different. This rubbish simply blames everything bad on liberals. Even Hitler offered solutions. Only von Papen didn't."

"Who's von Papen?"

I stared at him in surprise. "He invited Hitler into the German government, convincing Hindenberg that the madman could be controlled. The same had happened in Austria when Dollfuß came to power. In Italy with Mussolini. In Hungary and Romania -- each time fascists came to power, reactionaries pave the road to power for them."

"That's pretty ancient history..." He stopped, seeing hurt flare in my eyes.

"Ancient history? I lived through it. I lost Sergei to it once. Your father fought on one side or the other in it..."

"My grandfather," he corrected. "He was French and in the Resistance."

I felt so very old. I tried to believe I was seeing ghosts who were indeed dead and buried. The Nazis were gone. The Communists were gone. Eastern Europe and even Russia were democratic now, emulating their

western cousins. Emulating this country where newspapers, preachers, and senior politicians called for a return to a nineteenth century of fear and hate that existed only in their minds. There were no more von Papens and Marshall Pétains. No more Stalins.

The next four evenings proved hectic. The realtor was avid to sell me a house and have me living in it before Christmas. He was pounding on my hotel door at the earliest possible moment I would permit his appearance. And showing me cold house after cold house -- cold not so much because of the temperature, but because each one felt unlived in. Uncherished and, even, unremembered. I was unimpressed.

I was hungry. Interminable little chats with the imminently cheerful realtor after the night's showings inevitably lasted until two or three o'clock. By the time I had Emil back to the hotel and sexually sated enough that he had gone to bed, dawn was but two or three hours away.

As a bat I flew from our eighth floor window in a city I didn't know as Emil slept. I found derelicts hovering over open grates on the grounds of every large government building. I was giddy from the cheap wine they drank; every morning I went to sleep with the sourest mouth from the crack cocaine they smoked.

By the fourth day of the realtor's exclusive six-month contract, I was ready to buy anything he showed me. I needed the peace my own house would afford me. I needed more wholesome dinners than what I was finding near the Potomac in southwest Washington. I wanted to begin nudging Thomas MacPherson into a decision that included me even as I attempted to decide what I should do with Emil Paulik.

I grew increasingly more fond of Emil each afternoon I woke and found him smiling at me from across the room or felt his warmth beneath or beside me with both our lusts momentarily sated.

The house was large. It stood on its own short block, giving it grounds usually unknown to city dwellers. A black wrought-iron fence imbedded in concrete protected it from the small park in the street before it.

It, too, was cold but still held dim memories of laughter and happiness.

I glanced at Emil and he nodded back at me. "How much?" I asked the realtor.

6

I awakened in my own bed for the first time in more than sixty years, a bed I had bought instead of rented with a hired garret. A new bed with no lumps or sags.

I opened my eyes to find Emil in jumper and jeans smiling at me, warming his backside at the fire across the room.

"Did you sleep well in your own bed?" he asked when he was sure I

was awake.

"The concept of ownership has something to say for itself," I admitted.

He grinned. "I think a firm mattress and springs that don't squeak say much more."

I stretched and pushed the covers from my legs. "I don't remember you complaining before."

He chuckled. "When an experience is new, a man is too involved in experiencing it to be distracted."

"Are you telling me I've become as old and comfortable as a broken-in shoe?"

His eyes widened. "Never!" He crossed the bedroom quickly and knelt before me. "You will never be an old shoe to me, Liebchen." A huskiness was growing in his voice.

His lips touched my thigh and became the caress of a butterfly as they moved upward. "I love you," he mumbled and sent his tongue darting to the exposing glans of my manhood.

I sighed and lay back across the mattress, surrendering myself to his warmth and allowing him to suckle on me.

"So, when do we start looking for Tom?" he asked, sitting up and sliding off the bed.

I stared at him, apprehension suddenly clouding my thoughts.

What if Sergei didn't want either my immortality or my love? I had Emil, of course; but he alone could not come close to providing what Sergei and I had built over a century and longer. I would be starting all over again with Emil.

"His thoughts grow stronger," I told him. "They still continue to warn me away."

I looked down at my hands. "He asks for time. He wants to understand what's happened to him. He wants to make his own decisions without me influencing them."

"You're going to give him this time?"

I nodded slowly. "Until the spring. Three or four months -- what do they matter when we're talking forever?" I was trying to put the best face on it. But I knew it was my fear -- my apprehension -- speaking.

"Do you think you can put up with me until you two get together and decide what happens with you -- and me?"

A frown scampered across his lips but was quickly replaced by a smile.

"I think we should go exploring this capital of America," I told him, smiling reassurance back at him. "And that means a shower for me."

"I need one too," he said, grinning, "Think you could wash my back for me?"

I grinned back at him. "I suspect I could."

As soon as we were under the water jets, Emil smiled and turned away from me, wiggling his bottom at me as he did so. "How about a quickie?"

he asked over his shoulder.

My manhood proudly rose to answer his call.

He sighed as I entered him and pressed his face and hands against the wall of the shower cubicle as he pushed his buttocks onto me in welcome.

When I was buried inside him, he reached behind us and grabbed my buttocks, holding me against him. He began grinding against me then. His eyes were closed, his mouth opened as my shaft rubbing his prostate carried him deep into his feelings.

I reached around his hip and found his manhood bobbing with his movement. I began to stroke him.

He moaned and the moaning of his pleasure became continuous as he worked himself to orgasm.

We strolled along DuPont Circle from the underground station, reading the signs above each converging street, looking for where 'P' Street started up again. I was trying not to remember that I hadn't yet had dinner.

On the southside of the circle, we crossed over Connecticut and approached New Hampshire. I looked along the wide pavement ahead of us to find three youths standing in front of a large apothecary and watching at us as we approached them.

I sensed each man's desire to menace us, but they were under orders to intimidate only. Curious, I extended my vision to see them more clearly.

They each wore jeans, leather jackets, and thick leather, laced-up boots. All three of them had shaved their heads. They wore studs that rode the outer curve of their left ears. It was as if the attire and accouterments were a uniform for them.

I said to Emil in German: "Don't look now, but these three seem to be hooligans planning to have some sport with us." I touched their thoughts again, unwilling to allow Emil to be hurt if their intent changed.

The youth closest to us had caught my comment, his face became a frown as he sought to recognize the language. He smiled when he decided it was German.

"Heil, Hitler!" he cried out, clicking his heels and giving us the formal Nazi salute as we passed them.

Heil, Hitler?

I was in shock. For more than two years I had heard that greeting too many times a day ever to forget it. One answered the telephone and the door with it and said good-bye with it. One greeted people on the street with it. One even greeted waiters and delivery boys with it and sent them on their way with it. I had once suspected a couple ought to begin and end their love-making with it.

I had hated it from the Anschluß until I fled Vienna with the SS a step behind me.

I touched the youth's thoughts. I prayed he was trying to make a joke at our expense, picking up on my use of German.

I felt only a feeling of well-being in him. We were from the Fatherland. We were good people, no matter the area of town we were in or our being two men together. Because he believed every German was a Nazi and racially pure and, thus, good people. I shivered mentally.

How had this happened? Germany had lain in ruins in 1945, its people prostrate before the Allies -- the peacocks dead, captured, or trying to hide themselves from the occupiers. I had read the history of the war since awakening. How could these Americans, who spoke no language but their own dialect of English, be Nazis?

"Why did he say that?" Emil asked, puzzled.

"They call themselves skinheads, but they're Nazis," I growled as we turned into 'P' Street. And felt the three pairs of eyes follow us, respect and something akin to envy in the thoughts behind them. Because they thought we were real Germans, the Meistervolk of Hitlerian insanity.

They were like the young school boys of Vienna when Hitler visited the city after the Anschluß, claiming it forever for the thousand year Reich. I could remember them still in their starched brown shirts and knickers and swastika arm-bands. So proud. So sure. So naïve as to what horror it all held.

How could the grandfathers who destroyed that evil allow their grandsons to revisit it and, like young dogs, dig it up and parade its stinking remains proudly.

Heil, Hitler?

I knew where I would find my dinner tonight. I tried to smile but a numbing fear had descended over me.

7

"What is this Wahnsinn?" I demanded as I read *The Blade*'s first issue of the new year.

"What insanity, Karl?" Emil asked from the dresser as he leant against it to pull on his Reebok trainers.

I glanced over at him and nearly laughed at the lad so proud of a brand name shoe. Reeboks weren't even shoes, they were trainers. For children. But because they were British-made, they commanded a high price and tremendous, even instant, respect amongst young men around the world.

I pulled my thoughts back to Emil's question. "In the Virginia suburbs something called the Christian Center is going through public libraries and taking *The Blade* out of them…"

"Oh, that." He sounded almost bored. "They're just a group of fundies…"

"Fundies?" Emil was picking up much too much American idiom. It was nearing the point that I had to struggle to understand his English any more. And we had made a pact to speak the patois to help me regain my fluency.

"Religious fundamentalists. They say homosexuality is condemned in the Bible -- so, they want anything to do with it removed from public places."

"Emil, these are public libraries! What you're talking about is book burning..," I glanced at the newspaper in my hands. "Or newspaper burning."

"Like the Nazi book burnings all over Germany in 1935?" he asked resignedly, stifling a yawn.

"Yes, damn it!"

"You're seeing things that aren't there, Karl. Over at Georgetown University, I meet the sort of people who will rule this country twenty years from now. They aren't like that."

"I hope," I mumbled. I didn't want to argue with him. I was too fond of him by half. I wanted to be with him, to enjoy looking in the small shops of Georgetown, to enjoy exploring. With him.

Only, he was becoming as blasé as the young Americans I saw -- like the young Berliners I had met in 1930 when last I visited Germany.

"Where are you going tonight?" I asked, changing the subject.

"To the library." He pulled a face. "Where else?"

"You're spending a lot of time at the university now that you've found it."

"I want my degree. That means papers I have to research."

"Are you sure there isn't a particularly attractive young thing who's caught your eye?" I asked, meaning it as a joke.

He looked up sharply. I immediately plastered a grin across my face to ensure he didn't think I was serious.

He shrugged it off, and I dearly wanted to touch his thoughts. Emil Paulik, however, had learnt to feel my touch at the corners of his mind. "I'll probably be after eleven getting back. Are you going out?"

"To feed."

He smiled across at me, only love in his eyes. "You can always have some of me."

I shook my head. "I'll take another part of you, though -- when you get back."

"I want to be a vampire too, Karl!"

"So you can go around being a pain in people's necks?"

"Scheiße!" he growled "You make everything into a joke. All I want is to be with you -- always."

I nodded. "I'll remember that."

"Does that mean you'll do it?"

"Probably. But it's not something you can turn off once you've turned it on. Perhaps after you have time to look at the world without me there to influence you."

"You aren't influencing me!"

I laughed. "I've seen. Go to the library. I become hungry."

He would take the Volkswagen I'd bought us as a holiday present. He would also take me, but not know it. I was suddenly inordinately curious about his evening excursions. After all, he could study and research during the day as I slept; and that knowledge left me mildly suspicious.

Besides, Georgetown University wasn't that far from DuPont Circle, and I was developing a distinct fondness for young Nazi-flavored blood which had not been basted in drugs or alcohol.

"Did you see today's *Post*?"

I looked up quickly at him.

"Some fundy preacher killed an abortion doctor in Florida yesterday."

"They captured him?"

"Of course. He was waiting in front of the body when the police arrived."

I bit as he knew I would. "Why did he do it?"

"He said God told him to do it so that the murders of babies could be stopped."

"Abortion is legal here, isn't it?"

Emil nodded.

"So this preacher committed a murder?"

"He confessed." He picked up the keys. "See you."

I flew along Rock Creek Park towards DuPont Circle from Georgetown. A wet chill hung in the air and snow-laden clouds hovered above the city. My doubts about Emil that had threatened to fester had needed lancing. They were now lanced and he was proved to be but a zealous student, his devotion to me no longer in question.

'P' Street was the largest gay club area of Washington. Three blocks to the east was DuPont Circle and two blocks to the north was the beginning of embassy row that took up most of Massachusetts Avenue.

The skinheads came to watch and intimidate.

In the bars along 'P' Street men from the city and the suburbs met men from the embassies and hoped for a mutually pleasurable evening.

'P' Street had proved to be good hunting grounds for me.

I was fortunate to find a skinhead leaning against the bole of a tree in the small park, smoking a cigarette.

[*Sleep!*] I commanded him as I morphed into human form and watched him slide slowly down the tree trunk to sit on the leaf-covered ground. As I knelt beside him and touched his exposed neck with my snout, I realized that I'd never thought to explore why these young Americans had rejected the democracy of their fathers and grandfathers.

Knowing them to be Nazis had been enough to designate them as my primary food source. I had no knowledge of their intelligence or what had led them into insanity.

Curiosity had always been the bane of my existence.

I touched the sleeping skinhead's thoughts.

Racial purity. White power. The vermin were taking jobs from whites and bringing them down to their level. Kick the inferior foreigners out of America. Queers threatened the white race and took jobs from good family men. The skinheads saw themselves as America's Sturmabteilung, intimidating where possible but handing out beatings where needed.

I had heard that before. Hitler had fostered much the same unthinking hatred in the twenties and thirties. He and his Nazis had died in the flames of the war they brought to the world. I wondered who had resurrected that hatred and transplanted it to America.

I opened the skinhead's coat and shirt, exposing the skin where his clavicle became his neck. Leaning closer, I bit into that spot that would not show when he again joined his friends. And I delved deeper into his thoughts, searching for what this youth knew of the men who gave him his orders.

The image of a paneled room came to his mind, one filled with others like him. Men who would rescue America and save the white race. On the dais at the front of that room, the American flag stood beside the swastika banner. A silver-haired man with a craggy face spoke to the men gathered there as if he were speaking to each one individually. He was the preacher, the skinhead told me deferentially.

He knew nothing more. His knowledge came from two- and three-page tracks that strung together half-thoughts from the Bible with the insanity of *Mein Kampf*.

I finished feeding, told the skinhead to remember nothing, and left. My dinner threatened to tie my stomach in knots.

At home, I sat before the fire and thought.

I thought it not at all illogical to realize the four most powerful countries in the world -- the US, Germany, Russia and Japan -- each had a strong fascist element seeking to destroy democracy from inside. These skinheads then were but the strong arm for something sinister threatening America and, through it, the world.

America was the strongest of the four militarily, though it was no longer pre-eminent in economics or education. It was also the center of the most strident and most developed of the fascist movements. Like the Nazi party command before them, the American fascists had their street thugs on the corners to intimidate the masses but they had something stronger in their fundamental Christianity that would sever citizen from citizen, intelligentsia from Lumpenproletariat, knowledge from fear.

And I was here in America -- at the very center of power and of the conspiracy to seize that power.

If there was a conspiracy, why shouldn't I set out to expose it? And, perhaps, destroy it?

Admittedly, such a question was egotistical. One man -- well, one vampire -- against the Hun, so to speak.

But why not?

I hated fascists. They threatened good people who did no harm. They confiscated the estates and properties of those in disagreement with them. They started wars in which many people, soldiers and civilians, died. And they'd killed Sergei's second incarnation.

My natural inclination was ready to sate my curiosity about the extent and identity of this cancer threatening destruction of America. It included sating my need for blood on those who rode the fear of others to power. I could also add the health of my spiritual bank account, my karma. My inclination would no longer be simply selfish. It would become ennobled, even as both my physical and spiritual needs were met.

The perfect enterprise for a member of a discarded nobility, forced into idleness. The salvation of the mortals who fed him.

It was a bold enterprise that would wed my curiosity, hunger, and spiritual well-being. What I didn't have was the business proposal for the enterprise that would provide me with a skeleton as well as the sinews and meat that would flesh it out. That had been Sergei's milieu, not mine.

All I could remember were the soirees and gala balls. Sergei would prattle so about which captain of industry was whispering sweet rubles to another captain.

The similarities struck me then, a glove across my face challenging me to a dawn meeting. Unglaublich!

Parties on the scale to which Sergei and I were once accustomed seemed a bit outré in the world I now lived in. But soirees? Small gatherings of influential people making deals?

I sat up, grinning widely. I knew soirees. In Paris, in Berlin, in

Petrograd, in Vienna. Oh, yes, I knew them well.

But was the soiree I knew too -- well, refined -- for American tastes? I sank back in my chair.

This was, after all, a country that prided itself on being hardly more than a capitalist version of what Karl Marx had once envisioned -- the land of the free proletariat. A land where anyone could become wealthy if he but had the ambition.

Had attitudes changed so much in sixty years? And did they change from one culture to the next. Fascists -- and their reactionary allies -- pined for the past. A past that never had been except in their own enfeebled minds.

The Nazis had not come from the nobility or the wealthy, educated class. They were Lumpenproletariat, the lowest of the bourgeoisie. I began to smile. There had never been a burgher who wasn't impressed by his betters -- especially, if he thought he was being accepted as an equal among them.

All I had to do now was find the gauleiters and gruppenführers of the new order. They would expose their own closets as well as introduce me to their superiors.

I would stay busy while I waited for Sergei to decide to come to me. And for Emil to finish his damnable papers so that he might graduate university.

I watched the evening news to justify myself further. Stony, hate-filled faces lined the curb before a small building in Philadelphia, the city that once hosted the meetings that gave America it's very freedoms. Some poor woman began to shuffle her way through a double queue of that hate.

"Killer!" a hidden woman screamed and suddenly the rest of the queue took up the cry as men and women began to close in on her. Police pushed through the crowd with their batons.

A pretty face, identified as Joe McCarthy's the executive director of the Christian Center, smiled angelically at me.

"America cannot continue to condone nearly a million murders of innocent children a year," he told me quietly, his eyes holding mine through the medium of television. "We need a government that understands the basic right to life that is so much a part of our country's experience.

"This Congress must continue to undo forty years of humanistic destruction of the American family. It can finish returning this country back to God. The time to do so is now. Jesus demands it."

8

When I awoke the next afternoon, Emil was already naked in preparation for a bout of love-making. His eyes were filled with lust as he slipped under the covers beside me. His warmth against me brought my tumescence to immediate erection even before his lips had found mine.

"I've been needing this since I woke up this morning," he breathed against my ear as he straddled my abdomen and melded his body along the length of mine, his teeth nibbling at my ear lobe, his body moving sultrily against mine.

"You're especially passionate," I managed.

"Your goddamned fascists made it into *The Post* today," he hissed. "You've infected me with your fears. Now, make love to me and help me forget about them."

Our lips met again and his tongue darted between my teeth, into my mouth. I forced my fingers between us to find him as he began to worry my fangs with his tongue.

As his hips moved down along my abdomen towards the erection he knew awaited him, he nipped at my neck and, then, lower, at my left nipple. His drool spread across my chest as his tongue trailed from the first nipple to its mate.

Smiling, he sat up and, reaching behind himself, took my manhood in his hand. Pushing himself up on his knees, he directed it to the entrance of his nether-regions. "Feed on me while you're making love to me," he told me as he adjusted the position of his backside to me.

"You're way up there," I said, sloughing his request away.

He lowered himself onto me. "I won't be after you're all the way inside me," he said, his voice sultry. "Bite me."

"Why?" It was difficult to think logically as centimeter after centimeter of me slipped into his warm, tight canal.

"It's supposed to make sex even better."

He achieved as much union as I was capable of providing and again plastered himself against me. "Bite me, Karl," he mewled. "Feed on me." He began to flex his hips.

I could not think beyond the feel of him. My lips found his neck where he'd exposed it to me. He began to ride me harder. My fangs broke his skin and I began to lap at his blood.

When he'd collapsed to the bed beside me later, our abdomens both coated with his seed, he gasped: "That was incredible!"

His voice was a rasp, his words nearly unintelligible as his chest heaved, pulling air into his lungs and demanding more. His eyes flashed with exultation.

In a hundred and thirty years as a vampire, I had not been as close to total orgasm as I'd came in the moments before. Unproductive testicles had churned within their bag in anticipation of eruption, rising up along my shaft and trying mightily to spew forth the mortality they no longer created.

His gasping breath pulled at me. In our months of sexual couplings, I had never seen Emil so excited that his breathing remained this labored. I studied him more closely, the languid aftermath of sex evaporating as I accepted his ashen pallor for what it was.

I had drank too much. Sex and feeding were so intertwined for me I had difficulty differentiating them even in the most intelligent of moments. I bit him as he first began to ride me. I licked and drank as he worked his way through two orgasms. How long?

More importantly, how much?

I wasn't hungry as I lay beside him. Yet, waking and our sex normally left me craving the hunt -- though I forced the desire from me so that I could be with him. The bruised skin of his slender neck, no more than two centimeters from his clavicle told me what I did not want to know.

There was nothing wrong with Emil's breathing, his lungs instinctively labored to pull more air into them to compensate for the loss of blood that carried it to the cells of his body. I had taken that blood. Far too much.

Had he planned it this way? I wondered, the thought fully realized when it appeared suddenly in my mind.

He gasped, struggling to pull in oxygen to feed his hungry cells, his eyes feverish as if he were a saint seeing a vision.

I touched his thoughts and blushed brightly when I found thought after thought of what he felt for me. Columns of unconnected feelings blossoming into gardens of love.

His pallor was waxen, his breathing remained rapid and labored. I sensed his thoughts becoming more kaleidoscopic, whirling dizzily.

I had known those physical reactions since I first fed on fresh blood -- as I had the feverish pitch of his increasingly jumbled thoughts.

He was dying.

I had finally stolen his innocence and his youth. I had brought him the end of mortal life.

Without thinking, I pushed myself up on my pillows until my chest was even with his face. With the middle finger of my left hand, I pulled back skin and flesh and cartilage, opening a wound between my ribs so close to the sternum it too was partially exposed and I felt the chill of the room's air upon the exposed bone.

I had to give him a new life before his old one was completely gone. Before his jumbled thoughts could slide into the oblivion of mortal death. I had to give him what he had asked for and tie him to me for eternity.

I leant into him, lifting his head and bringing his lips to my breast. With my fingernail I nicked the vein behind the bone and pressed his lips to the hole now open to my heart. To my blood now seeping out onto my chest.

He sucked greedily. Instinctively. As a newborn baby sups at its mother's breast.

I watched for his pallor to change. This was my first effort to create another vampire; I only knew he had to have my blood to survive. I didn't know how much he needed.

An effervescence developed in his skin, the coarseness of his mortal derma smoothing out and becoming even.

I listened in the silence of the room and found his breathing was not as

labored as it had been. I willed my vein closed and pulled away, falling against my pillows. Emil moaned as my blood began to transform him, raising his head slightly and opening strangely clouded eyes. I moved closer to him and helped him lie on me.

My chest healed as I watched his transformation in the last rays of the weak winter sun. My strength returned to me as his breathing slowed and became shallow.

Emil's body changed as I watched, becoming more perfect than it had been. I finally accepted that I loved him as much as I ever had Sergei.

I rose and moved about the darkened room. From beside the fire, I remembered that he was naked and uncovered. Moving back to the bed, my foot kicked the newspaper he'd read as he waited my awakening.

I picked it up and continued on to the bed where I pulled covers up to Emil's chin. Tucking him in. I smiled at the thought and returned to stand before the fire.

I straightened the paper and looked down at its headlines. The picture of a broken high-rise building grabbed my attention and I began to read.

A federal building in Texas had been bombed. Hundreds of people were injured by flying glass and falling concrete, many with crushed or severed limbs. More than a hundred were dead -- most of them small children playing happily in a day-care center. The Federal Bureau of Investigation labeled the attack terrorism. The Bureau of Alcohol, Tobacco, and Firearms muttered darkly of an earlier militia threat against the building.

Militia? There were armies in America other than the national one? Armies that would kill innocent American children in a government building?

I let myself out of our room and went downstairs to the sitting room to turn on the television to catch the latest information on the bombing.

A lorry full of chemical fertilizer was the culprit in the bombing, as it had been in Oklahoma a decade before and New York two years before that. Someone had driven it within ten meters of the front of the building before walking away.

The FBI was already interrogating a suspect arrested shortly after the bombing for a traffic violation. CNN had assembled a truncated biography of the man.

I rose to turn the television off when the anchor finished reporting the bombing. Before I could reach the set, however, he turned to the eighty-fifth burning of a black church in rural Kentucky. I paused to watch yet another atrocity.

There were no injuries or deaths in Kentucky. There were no suspects either. Negro leaders were demanding a federal investigation because all eighty-five churches had served predominately black congregations and the suspicion was that the burnings were racially motivation.

I groaned as the executive director of the Christian Center announced

his organization was promising a paltry reward for information on the church bombings.

I wondered about Joe McCarthy, the executive director of the Christian Center. He claimed to be a conservative. Real conservatives such as Churchill and von Bismarck would turn in their graves! His politics reminded me much more of von Papen's in Weimar Germany.

9

"You were supposed to stop!" Emil cried. "You weren't supposed to do it yet," he continued, his voice a whimper. "I trusted you -- I wanted to know when it happened."

Blood red tears welled in his eyes.

I continued to meet his gaze, saying nothing. There was nothing I could say. The fang marks on his neck were gone. His skin was palely effervescent, smooth as it had never been before. Emil Paulik made a beautiful vampire as he once had a handsome mortal.

He was right. I should have controlled my impulses. I should have pulled back from him even as we rocked together towards his second ejaculation. I should have...

But I hadn't.

His gaze broke from mine and moved to stare up at the ceiling. "It's not your fault," he mumbled. "I kept asking for it. I followed you around like a damned puppy! Wanting you. Wanting to be like you."

Both fists slammed into the mattress on either side of him. "Now, I am."

When Sergei gave me his blood, I had faced imminent death. Emil had been a healthy twenty-two year old mortal. I had been happy to accept life, no matter what sort it was. Emil had had mortal life stretching out before him.

"I'm going to have to get used to it, aren't I?" he asked, his voice that of defeat.

I nodded.

"I'm going to have to kill people now, aren't I?"

"Nothing says you have to drink as deeply as I did. No, you don't have to kill people to feed." I chuckled wryly. "For the longest time before Hitler came, I drank only bovine blood."

"You did?" He looked at me curiously. "I thought you had to have human blood?"

"I did suggest you not read those silly romances," I reminded him. "There's so much you need to learn -- and too much to forget."

"No coffins." He smiled tentatively. "No colds and fevers." He chuckled, but I could sense it was forced. "Not even a bout of nausea when I eat something I shouldn't."

"You'll have that if you eat dead food, Emil -- and worst."

"Dead food?" His face immediately became a question.

"What you've always eaten. You need blood from a living animal to feed..." I sniffed indignantly. "I'm deathly nauseated at just the odor of cooked meat."

"At least, I'm not going to develop arthritis, get old, and have my hair falling out so that I'm bald and ugly."

"There are some advantages," I agreed.

"I can read minds and dance all night every night." He smiled again and this time it wasn't forced. "Yeah. I suppose I can get used to it."

He might be willing to get used to it, but he didn't offer his body for our mutual pleasure. Instead, he rose with newly acquired speed. Even with my own heightened senses, he was mostly blur as he covered himself.

He cavorted around the house, testing his new abilities. I left him alone to explore himself and placed a call to the embassy that set an appointment the next day. The first secretary's fine Viennese-accented German still caressed my ears even after I returned the receiver to its cradle.

"Who was that?" Emil asked. I hadn't heard his approach to the room I had made into an office.

"The Austrian embassy. I have an appointment tomorrow afternoon."

His eyes narrowed as he studied me. "Why?"

"To set up a soiree that introduces me to Washington. To introduce us both, if you'd like," I added. "But you'll soon tire of that sort of night life. There are only so many whispered nothings and assignations a man can accept..."

"Assignations?"

I nodded.

"You aren't going to start sleeping around on me, are you?" His countenance darkened immediately towards anger. "Tom I can accept. I guess I'm even looking forward to him joining us in a way. But he's Sergei; he belongs with you -- with us. I'm not going to share you with anybody else -- especially every little gadfly and rent boy in Washington."

I smiled. This was the Emil I knew -- in love with me, but with a newly acquired possessiveness. "Too often, these soirees can lead to an unused bedroom. But we don't have to accept."

"You had better believe we don't."

"If it's politically useful that the other man -- or woman -- thinks we bedded them, we can leave them with passionate memories of it being so."

He stared at me for a moment and then laughed. "You mean you'd make them remember a shag that didn't happen?"

I nodded.

"Why?"

"It's useful to be nice to a person with even a little power -- it opens doors and makes things happen."

"Just what kind of soiree are you planning, Karl?" he demanded. I watched as he seemed to grow larger and then was standing at my elbow.

"I am an intelligent and curious man, one with an old, established title."

He shrugged. He already knew that, though I hadn't mentioned it.

"I would know why there are skinheads patrolling the gay district of this city, intimidating people," I told him. "I would know why people blow up buildings and burn churches. I would know why this political violence is increasing. I would know the extent of the fascist trappings I see all about us in this city. I would know if we are in danger."

"You're on that kick again?"

I nodded. "Read my thoughts and see what I've seen," I told him.

"How?" he asked as he screwed up his face and seemed to be trying to force his brain out of his skull.

"Relax," I answered and extended myself to the edge of his mind, drawing him back to me, inside my mind.

"Mein Gott!" he groaned a few minutes later.

"You wanted to read thoughts…"

He knew what I was planning.

"I'll help you any way I can. I'll even put up with you fucking some of these fascist pigs if that'll help."

I laughed. "And fuck some yourself?"

He blushed as only a vampire can, effervescent skin blotched with ugly red.

I laughed again. "You must be hungry?" I offered.

"Yeah!" He grinned. "A pizza with lots of cheese…" His eyes clouded and his face became a frown. "I suppose I won't be having that again, will I?"

I shook my head slowly.

Emil most intelligently found research he could do at the university library while I attended the soiree at the embassy in my honor. By nine o'clock I wished I had been as intelligent. It had been eighty or more years since I last attended such a gathering, and my memory of the things had become much rosier than their reality.

I had met the First Secretary of the embassy the week before, the ambassador being unfortunately indisposed. We had agreed my title and position warranted a small gathering in which I could meet men and women of substance in the American capital. He frowned when I specifically requested the members of the party be Republicans and pointed out to me that wouldn't be diplomatic and that Democrats were as willing to meet Austrian Princes as were Republicans.

I prevailed. The First Secretary thought my insistence that the leadership of the Christian Center be included would fare worse in the American media than the inclusion of a far right party in Austria's government had four years ago.

I prevailed. The soiree was set for the first Friday night in February -- tonight. I quickly became viewed by every Austrian in Washington as a reactionary, bigoted arse.

My lips were numb. My face ached from the smiles I'd had to force. The dye on the insides of my shoes was gone, leaving bits of the cow skin as bare as they were when the bovine met its fate. Only my memory kept the names of Congressmen, their wives, and other notables aligned with their faces.

I had stood in the receiving queue until only moments before, meeting

Luke Renfroe, the Speaker of the House of Representatives of the United States, and other Republican party stalwarts who were going to continue revolutionizing America by taking it back to before the Great Depression.

A woman who was the Ambassador to the United Nations twenty years earlier but was now a columnist staggered up to me and peered blearily at me -- she was quickly helped along by an innocuous two-legged male poodle who seemed well-trained at handling his mistress in her moments of distress.

A man with light brown hair and glittering blue eyes stood before me, smiling as he stretched his hand out to take mine. His face was that of an impish and barely pubescent boy. I had seen him recently on the television and placed him now.

"Joe McCarthy," he told me, "executive director of the Christian Center, Prince von Maribor..." His forefinger tickled the palm of my hand as we shook hands.

I touched his thoughts as he again began to move along the line. He was wondering if he dared invite me out later on. I had the distinct impression of the two of us on a bed naked. I gave him a command to ask me before I turned my mind back to the next person to welcome me to America.

I circulated among the embassy's guests and studied Joe McCarthy while keeping half of the reception room between us. I was surprised when I learnt he was past thirty. He looked to be the fun-loving teen-aged boy, well in control of himself in his first outing among adults. The perfect gentleman a hausfrau of the old school would wish of her son. A clean-faced and bright-eyed gruppenführer of the Hitlerjungen.

Joe McCarthy -- a flaming faggot.

I hated what he stood for -- for the evil that should have been burnt from the soul of man by the world war.

[*Invite me,*] I told him from across the room.

I sensed his suspicion of me but felt the heat of his desire as he began to make his way towards me. I watched him politely greet each of his elders, slap equals on the back and laugh. This was one Hitlerjungen Gruppenführer who would go far.

"I'd like a chance to get to know more about you after this little party is over, Prince von Maribor," he offered in a near-whisper as he closed with me in the center of the Embassy's reception room.

I smiled and lifted my brow slightly in question. I wished I had a monocle so I could have done it as well as I had in the days when I was young and mortal.

"Would you like that I join you somewhere?" I asked.

Joe McCarthy chuckled. "You're going to be an interesting man to know, Prince von Maribor. Meet me on the portico of the Embassy at eleven."

"If we're going to know each other as well as I hope," I said, "perhaps

you'll call me Karl."

He grinned. "Prince is a bit formal, isn't it?"

I nodded, again struck by how boyish and innocent-looking this man was.

"Then, you've just got to call me Joe."

"Eleven it is then, Joe."

His thoughts were nearly incoherent with his desire to have sex with me. Unglaublich. But also flattering -- and interesting.

I raised my brow in question as I stepped onto the Embassy's portico and into chilled night. Joe answered my look with a smile which became immediately a scowl as he asked: "You do like fun with your sex, don't you, Karl?"

He had visions of naked Ganymedes dancing in his head. Central to his thoughts, however, was me naked above him as he spread his legs in invitation.

"I've been known to participate from time to time," I assured him.

"We'll get a motel room," he said, taking my arm to lead me out onto the street towards a black Mercedes.

I was curious. How did one preach homosexuality as the fast road to hell while dropping his trousers and demanding to be spiked?

"No-one's going to bother us here," Joe said breathlessly as he sat on the bed and faced me, his hands removing his tie.

He started to unbutton his shirt. "Jesus!" he hissed, "I haven't wanted anybody so much since my cousin was getting me into that barn back in Georgia the first time."

He was to his underpants when he stood to move towards me. "I've got rubbers in my pocket," he whispered just before his lips touched mine.

His tongue was a demon, wrestling with mine for dominion between us, its fevered effort growing quantumly as my fingers slipped beneath the band of his undergarment and began to knead the firm, soft slopes of his cheeks.

"God Almighty!" he whispered as his tongue retreated that he might breathe. "I need it, Karl." His tongue was back then as he directed us towards the bed.

He reached to his trousers, groping with one hand for a condom as the other pulled my trousers open. He found a packet and looked up at me. His fingers trailed up my thigh to find my erect manhood beneath my undergarment.

"Sweet Jesus! Big and thick..." His face became a beatific smile. "Joey's going to have a good time tonight," he mumbled and tore the packet open with his teeth. I had my shirt and tie off when he pulled my trousers and pants down to my knees.

His fingers again gripped me as he began to push latex over my glans. "Uncut!" he croaked. "Lord Jesus, you're really looking out for me tonight."

The condom was unfurled along the length of my shaft in a moment and he lay on the bed. "Come on, let's fuck," he said and spread his legs to look at me through them.

I touched the insides of each of his thighs, descending along them towards his body and knelt on the bed beneath him.

"Fuck me now, baby!" he growled up at me.

My hands neared his groin, prolonging his anticipation.

"Fuck me! We can play later -- please?" His voice was both a demand and a whine in equal measure.

I positioned myself and leant into him, listening to his gasp of pleasure as my latex-covered manhood made its way past his sphincter, hearing the rhythmic thud of his heart pumping his warm, excited blood. I bent closer to him, nuzzling his nipples with my lips as my tongue moved towards his clavicle and the soft, tender flesh of his neck.

I caught myself in time. A dead and bloodless executive director of the Christian Center was not a good idea.

I straightened and, holding his splayed ankles, began to move against his warm, pliant buttocks as he grabbed himself and mindlessly began to pull hard on his manhood.

"Sweet Jesus!" he moaned beneath me. "Come and take me home, Lord!" He ground his cheeks against my pubis. "I'm almost there, Lord!" he cried out moments later, now flailing himself hard. "Jesus, you gotta make me cum!"

I continued in the rhythm I'd given myself and wondered at the religious ecstasy that held this man as I plowed him.

In my experience, devoutly religious Christians had rarely seen copulation as more than a repulsive act they submitted to out of the necessity of producing children. This Joe McCarthy seemed to have his Jesus right here in the bed with us, involved almost intimately in our coupling.

His body tensed against me, his sphincter tightening, and his face reddened in sweet agony. "Oh, sweet Lord, I'm cumming!" he bellowed.

I continued to move against him for the additional moments he took to ejaculate.

He relaxed then, a puzzled look covering his face as he realized I still moved inside him. A grin replaced it. "Keep fucking me, Karl," he said then. "Just bang my ass so I can't sit down for a week. I want to shoot again."

We lay beside each other in the dim light touching us through the window. In more than a hundred and forty years of being sexually active, I had never gone to bed with someone I actively disliked, regardless of his looks. Tonight, I had. Because of curiosity.

I felt sullied. I had yet to learn anything of Joe McCarthy and his organization that helped me to understand their intent.

"I'm surprised," I told him as I traced his lip with a fingertip. "I had the impression your organization considered homosexuality a demonic evil needing immediate exorcism."

He chuckled as his fingers moved languidly across my chest. "That's for the great unwashed -- what you'd call peasants." He snorted. "They're there to be led, Karl. Either we do it or somebody else does it."

He laughed. "I prefer that we do it. We've got the best plan for this country, even the world. The strong, virile white race leading this world into prosperity."

"I thought your president was supposed to do that?"

He grunted. "He doesn't operate on all his cylinders, Karl -- it's the vice president who knows how strong a hand must be -- and he controls that mental retard."

He sat up and looked down at me. "Look how scared people are in this city. Look how little they care for anybody around them. They're lost in their own little worlds -- and don't even know how to connect to the bigger world."

"The president..."

"Look, Karl -- any time something gets done, it's done by a strong man. Pat Koughlin is that man. He'll lead America back to the values that made this country great. He'll lead us into the future with a sure, firm hand."

He reached between his legs and took his shriveled manhood between his thumb and forefinger. "This is how the average American is today -- weak and basically useless." He pulled on himself.

"You fill this thing up with blood and it's hard, strong and powerful. It's going to shoot seed everywhere -- like those Vandals conquering Rome. Like the Christians conquering all of Europe. This country needs something like the blood that goes into my dick to get strong again." He pulled on himself again and looked up at me.

"We cater to the people's fears of a harsh God, their fear of His punishment, and we give them strength just like a porn flick gets my dick hard."

"This is why your people steal *The Blade* from those libraries?"

He chuckled. "That's so little of what we do. But -- yeah -- if you get a society facing one crisis after another -- it makes more and more people afraid. They're like a henhouse that senses a fox outside. In the beginning, it divides them; but it makes each group want strong leadership to tell them what to do. Not maybes, just real solutions..."

"You frighten them with homosexuality?" I asked.

"Sure. That, as well as abortion, gangs, drugs, the axis of evil, terrorists..." He laughed. "That and the horrible state of public education. We sure can't use kikes and niggers any more. We'd be branded racists by the lily-livered press, and nobody would listen to us. Today, they don't dare call us anything worse than conservative."

He reached for me. "We take the Old Testament God and re-define him

in the white race's reality. We ally ourselves with one or another church until we control it. Just like we've done with the Republican party since Reagan..."

He leant over me, his lips finding my shaft.

I gave him images of sucking me off, climbed out of bed, and dressed.

10

I slipped into the car. At six o'clock, in the middle of March, it was unpleasantly warm. Emil was driving.

"I want to stop by the post office before we leave town," he told me.

Trees budded, the earth promised life again after the death of cold winter. It was in moments such as these that I still felt a tinge of regret at what I had lost.

I shrugged and leant back against the seat.

"I finished the last paper last night."

I immediately understood why he was making something of an inconsequential detour.

"The last one?" I asked.

He beamed and nodded.

"You are now a graduate of the university?"

"Not yet. The paper's got to be graded. The university has to credit me with that grade. They have to have a commencement officially to recognize the graduates."

I brushed his objections aside. 'You've graduated, yes?'

"Well..." A smile spread across his face as he pressed the remote control and watched as the wrought-iron gates opened onto the street before us. "I guess you could say that. It's just a matter of waiting until June for the diploma to make it official."

After leaving the post office, he said: "Tell me what you've learnt about your Nazis, Karl. I've been concentrating on these papers these past two and a half months."

"I was starting to wonder if you'd moved into that library at Georgetown."

He grinned. "You know, I was pretty ticked that I had my days suddenly taken from me -- the daylight. But, then, I found out I could just walk into the library and stay there all night."

"Being able to manipulate a lock with your mind does have its advantages at times," I admitted.

"Being able to read without turning on the lights is a big help too."

We turned onto New York Avenue and started towards Maryland. I took a deep breath of the air hitting my face from the wound-down window, tasting the first smells of spring.

"Tell me about your pretty little Nazi, Karl." Emil broke into my thoughts.

"Joe?"

"He's the leader of the Christian Center?"

"It's a strange experience having sex -- making him think we're having sex."

"Is he any good?"

I shrugged. "He was decent that one time -- but no match for you,

Liebchen."

He grinned at me. "We've not been getting it on enough since I died --
want to start correcting that when we get home?"

"Sounds good to me..." I frowned. "Emil, you never died. If you had,
your body would still be dead."

"It's just a term of speech, Karl,' he offered comfortably. "There's not
an easy way to explain how a man ceases being a mortal and becomes a
vampire -- not in any language I know."

"You transform from one life form to another."

"Whatever I did to become the me sitting here -- I want one long romp
in bed with you -- all night long if you're up to it."

I laughed. "I definitely look forward to that," I told him, my fingers
touching his jeaned thigh and stroking it. "I've missed our love-making..."

"Scheiße! We made love four nights ago."

"That was as hurried as it usually is, and you know it."

He blushed, red blotches and streaks breaking out horribly on
effervescent skin. "I wanted to get the last of the notes for that paper."

"How is reaming your Joe McCarthy's arse a strange experience?" he
asked, changing the subject.

"It's..." I paused, trying to understand the strangeness of it and
describe it to myself as well as Emil. "He -- well -- he talks to Jesus when I
fuck him."

"Talks? Come on, Karl! I make all sorts of noise when we're making
love. I probably even say things like..."

"No. It's not like with you. He actually speaks to Jesus."

"Like you're Him?"

"No. Not exactly. He tells me to fuck him harder, things like that. He's
completely aware that it's me plowing him. But, at the same time, he's
talking to Jesus too -- sometimes in the same breath. As if our sex is a
religious experience for him."

He glanced at me as the car entered the Baltimore-Washington
Expressway. "Come on, Karl!" he finally said.

"He says things like: 'Fuck me harder, Karl.' And, in the same breath,
he goes on to say: 'Jesus, help me cum'. It feels strange, Emil -- like that
long-dead rabbi is there in the bed with us. I can't explain it any better than
that."

"That would be a bit weird," he admitted and was grinning when I
glanced over at him. "Other than his being a good lay, what about this pretty
boy?"

"He's the stalking horse of someone named Koughlin..."

Joe McCarthy's memories of the craggy-faced preacher came back to
me then -- for the first time joining with the memories of the first skinhead
who'd fed me on 'P' Street. "Gott im Himmel!"

"What's wrong, Karl?"

The two memories flowed together and I was seeing the skinhead's

unknown Führer with Joe's familiarity of him.

This Koughlin. A preacher. A big name. A man known throughout the country. A man loved by many people. The man with the plan to destroy democracy.

"I know who leads both the skinheads and the Christian Center…"

"Leads? Doesn't this Joe McCarthy give the CC its orders?"

"Not leads -- exactly. Like Hitler didn't lead the SA. Röhm had the SA until 1934 -- then it was absorbed into the SS after the purge that killed him. But Hitler was at the top; he was the ultimate control."

"Who's this American Führer?"

"Remember the skinhead I fed on just before I made you?"

He'd read my thoughts and memories of Weimar Germany. He nodded.

"This preacher named Koughlin," I told him. "He spoke at some function that boy went to. The skinhead looked on this preacher with adoration -- as too many Germans did Hitler back in the thirties. Joe loves him as a god -- at least, as a father-substitute."

"Do you know who this Koughlin is?" Emil asked carefully.

I shook my head and wondered idly how he would know anything about a man so alien to the new Europe that had risen from the ashes of the world war.

"Read my mind, Karl. See what I've heard…" He glanced back at the three-laned motorway. "Just don't mess with what I'm seeing or my ability to react."

I chuckled. "You don't want to find out if vampires can survive a car crash?"

"I definitely do not." He grinned. "Besides, I like this car. You look so good in it."

He had dredged up every memory he had of skinheads, the Christian Center, something called the Aryan Nation, and Koughlin, from Swiss newspapers and his conversations with students at Georgetown University. There were also other memories of newspaper accounts from America about right-wing organizations in the western states killing a radio talk-show host and bombing rural post offices.

For years, Swiss papers had portrayed the accounts of skinheads, murders and bombings as examples of American insanity, but they had been fascinated with Koughlin and the hundred million dollar media empire he had erected.

The craggy-faced preacher the skinhead remembered was the ultimate leader of the Christian Center as well. I wasn't that surprised. I wouldn't be surprised to find he also controlled -- or, at least, influenced -- the fascist organizations bombing government property and killing people. Even with the depression, Hitler had needed to destabilize Germany to become Chancellor and destroy the Weimar Republic.

Koughlin had resurrected that same insanity in America seventy years after Europeans first began surrendering to it and sixty years after Europe

- 328 -

lay in rubble with more than thirty million people dead because of it.

America was already a demoralized country, on the brink of destabilization. Crime was rampant and prisons were overpopulated. The commons -- the under-educated, under-paid, hardest-working members of the bourgeoisie -- were increasingly pining for a strong, moral leader, the freedom of their founding fathers be damned.

Koughlin had definitely situated himself well.

What was I going to do about it? Did I want to do anything about it? What, if anything, could I do about it?

I was still thinking dark, unpleasant, and uncomfortable thoughts when we entered Baltimore.

"I hear we're going to love this place," Emil told me as we locked the car and started towards the intersection on the walk beside the fragrant building.

I peered into the electric-lighted night at this Inner Harbor he had been talking about for a fortnight. "That glassed-in building, right?" I asked.

"That's only part of the whole set-up," he said. "There's supposed to be a brick promenade along the water, a second glass building like that one, a science museum, some three-rigger's supposed to be the oldest ship in the American navy, the national aquarium, restaurants -- lots of things to do."

We had reached Light Street and were gazing at the lighted two-story glassed building as we waited to cross.

"Can you imagine meeting Tom here?" Emil asked, breaking off from the travelogue and rushing along an entirely different thought.

Sergei!

I immediately heard the whispering I had not consciously listened to since Emil joined me in immortality more than two months before. It was no longer inchoate mumblings and warnings that touched my mental ears.

[*I'm ready to meet,*] Tom kept saying over and over again. [*When and where?*]

Emil was studying me closely when I opened my eyes. "What's the matter?" he demanded in a low, urgent voice.

It took a moment to concentrate on him. To bring myself back to standing on a street in Baltimore, Maryland, on a March evening in 2005. "Read my thoughts," I told him.

I immediately felt a slight quivering under the skin and bone of my head as his mind tentatively touched mine, a touch there were no nerves to feel but which I still felt. I watched his eyes narrow as he heard the same message I was hearing.

"Gott im Himmel!" Emil hissed, exhaling air.

"He lives here in Baltimore -- his family does," I said, hesitant now in the face of meeting the mortal man whose soul I had loved for more than a hundred years before he was born.

Emil stared at me, his face stricken. Even without telepathy, I could read his thoughts, the fear of losing me was foremost in them.

"That won't happen," I told him quietly.

"If he won't accept the three of us..."

"It won't happen, Emi -- ever!" I touched his arm. "I won't lose you."

"You've..." He glanced about, his eyes bewildered. "You've got to tell him we -- you -- are here. It's nearly Easter -- this weekend. You said his family's in Baltimore; he's probably at home for the holiday."

"You mean for him to meet us here?"

He nodded. "What do you need to do let him know?" he asked quietly.

"Come on." I pulled him onto the street, formulating the answer in my mind.

"Where are we?" I asked on the harbor side of the street.

"The Light Street Pavilion. Can you answer him from inside the building?"

I nodded. "Why?"

He smiled wanly. "That place looks bigger each step we take towards it. I know I'd want to have a particular location in it to look for you if you were answering me."

It had been almost five months since I had seen Tom and then he had been unconscious. I used my vampiric senses and memory as I watched every dark-haired youth taller than a meter and a half who passed us while we sat in front of a fried potato shop and sipped at what Americans actually dared to call coffee.

"How are we going to handle this?" Emil asked, his voice low in the bright lights.

"What do you mean?"

"Tom knew I slept with you in Zürich -- that's why he was with me that night. He knows I'm gay."

"He doesn't need to know you're a vampire too -- not immediately. But it's going to be obvious we're together..."

"Why?"

"You're eight thousand kilometers from home and, unless you're very rich, students don't normally fly across an ocean and explore a new country."

I shrugged. "You're also with me and he'll know it when he sees you. So what? You're an adult under both American and Swiss law, you can have sex with whom you want and where you want."

"It's not going to make it any easier for you and him."

I held up my hand. "Emil, you and I are not a subject for negotiation. If Tom wishes to join us, then we will accommodate him."

Tears glistened red in his eyes and red blotches burst across his face. "You do love me!" he croaked.

"You have your moments..."

My senses picked up on a tall, slim black-haired youth with a lean face and full lips watching us and I instinctively sought to touch his thoughts.

[*Karli...*] There was the same sense of amusement behind that concise word as when Sergei found me with a young stevedore I had picked up on the Odessa docks while the Grand Duke worked some deal to line his pockets. And his thoughts were shielded. I could read only those he wished me to share.

Emil followed my gaze and started as he recognized Tom MacPherson.

[*Do I meet you mind to mind, Sergei -- or shall you join us?*] I asked.

He approached and smiled at both of us. "Emil, I'm a bit surprised to see you here under the circumstances."

"Do you know who you are?" I asked cutting off a typical Sergei set-up of Emil.

He turned to smile at me. "I hope so."

"I mean are you and Sergei completely reconciled?"

"More than when I was your curate." It was Sergei who answered, but his accent were unabashedly American.

I stared. Not even the curate had managed that complete a union, even in the five years I had known him.

He chuckled and sat between us. "I'm Tom MacPherson in this life, and I'm Tom at this moment, Karl."

"Oh? And are the others forgotten as well?"

"Not for me!" he growled, and I was sure that Sergei alone was speaking at that moment.

He quickly smiled at me and then turned to Emil. "I still don't know whether I need to drop to my knees and thank you for taking me to Karl in Zürich or hate you for it," he told him. "It's taken some getting used to, these different lives always vying for supremacy in me."

"Tom?" Emil said, looking perplexedly at the American.

He chuckled. "One minute, I'm a damned priest trying to be chaste as all hell; the next, I'm some Russian Royal who was more than just a little hedonistic." He glanced over at me. "There are even times when I'm all me -- but they both tell me what I should do each and every damned minute of my life."

"You said you were ready to talk," I said to change the subject.

"Yeah." He glanced at Emil. "But it looks like you didn't wait around this time."

I wasn't sure, but I thought I sensed a slight change in personality. "Emil is someone I love, Tom," I told him. "He loves me as well. If you would join me, you need to join both of us. I think I can safely speak for both of us when I tell you we'll make room for you -- equal space."

"A permanent three-way?" He laughed softly. "Now, that'd be one for the books. Sergei loves it already."

He sat back and glanced from one to the other of us before fixing his gaze on the Filipino food stall before us. "I haven't managed to work it all out yet -- okay?"

I shrugged.

"But this is the way it's going to be until I do. We can be friends, but there isn't going to be any queer shit between us -- me with either of you. And you don't play with my mind to lead me down that path either -- okay?" He looked at me and waited for an answer.

I nodded.

"One other proviso. You stay away from my neck, Karl. I like being young, handsome, and mortal. I'm going to be just as adamant as I was the last time about that."

I saw Emil watching me and reached out to touch his thoughts. [*I can subvert him, Karl. He didn't include me...*]

I shook my head and smiled at him. Both my movement and smile had been at supernatural speed. Emil had obviously caught both. I was surprised the mortal American had too.

He glanced from me to Emil, studying him more closely than before. "So, you're one of the undead now, old buddy?"

Emil jerked, looked to me for an answer and, not receiving one, nodded slowly.

"God! You really are in love with him!" Tom groaned, letting air out of his lungs. "How did it happen, Emil?" he asked and turned back to me.

"Ser -- Tom," I said softly in warning.

"Right in the middle of you fucking his ass, you bit him." He wagged his head. "Jesus! Karl, you never could think clearly when you had your dick in a tight hole."

"Tom!" I hissed as Emil's face blotched nastily.

Tom MacPherson turned to stare and, then, smiled at the young vampire on the other side of him. "So, that's what I used to look like when Karl embarrassed me at least once every time we got together. Jesus!"

"This has got rather personal and I remember you stating personal situations were out between us," I told him quietly.

He shrugged and nodded.

"What is this friendship you offer?"

"I'm still trying to work it out in my head, guys." He smiled sheepishly at me. "I think it'd be fun to hang around you two. I was killed the last time in 1940 and, before that, in 1905. I'm a bit out of the loop..."

"And you're a thoroughly modern man," Emil said.

"True. But one that doesn't know much about the world -- or how you two are hiding being practicing vampires in a world where nobody believes in you any more. Shit! There's a whole lot about this world I don't know. So, what I'm offering is that I learn from you -- but only what I can use in the straight, mortal world."

"All take and no give?" Emil asked quickly and I sat back, permitting him to establish the boundaries of our relationship with this man. He was being far more forward than I could have been, but I wanted our parameters clearly defined as much as he did.

The American hung his head but said: "For the time being at least. Let

me make it plain -- I let Karl start fucking me in the ass like he did my last two times around, I'm going to be gay. I'm nowhere ready to take that step now -- and, maybe, never will be."

He held up a hand. "I know this is only Tom talking and he's only a third of the active personalities and lives inside this body any more. But those other two guys are going to have to do some serious convincing before they get me to bend over for either one of you." He smiled and arched his brow at me, just as Sergei always had.

"Sergei can't wait for me to cement myself to this body by letting one of you two make me. I just don't know how I feel about that, no more than your curate did. I don't have his faith in the church and Jesus, but I'm not ready to start killing people and drinking blood, either."

"But there's a lot you can learn from Karl, so you'll put up with having us around once in a while?" Emil asked, pouncing.

Tom nodded. "Friendship's a two-way street, okay? That means a lot of things that can go down between us with no problem; a lot of things I'd like to think I can contribute to. What I'm saying is there are two things that aren't going to travel that street for a while, if ever -- my ass and my mortal life. If both of you can accept that condition, we can hang out with each other -- you know, do things together." He watched both of us expectantly. Emil watched me.

I took a deep breath, something I had learnt to do at my father's knee when confronted by a weighty subject and had yet to un-learn. "I can accept your terms as defined. Ours is but that Emil is an equal to myself. Any relationship will not be bilateral but must be trilateral."

"That won't be hard -- Emil and I are already friends."

"What type of things does this you enjoy?" I asked, seeking deeper boundaries.

"What do you mean?" he asked suspiciously.

"Do you enjoy the theater?"

"Me?" he groaned and, with difficulty, managed to stop himself from bursting out laughing.

"Sergei and the curate both did."

He seemed to withdraw within himself for a moment, as if he were actually conferring with his past lives. He blushed. "I've never been to a play. But -- well -- I can try most things once, at least," he offered sheepishly.

"The opera? The ballet?"

"You're getting awfully high-brow pretty damn fast, Karl," he growled. "I know, Sergei liked both, and fell in love with *Percival* when you took him to see it in Vienna." He looked from me to Emil. "Maybe. I won't rule it out, okay?"

"What do you like to do?" Emil asked gently.

Tom laughed harshly. "I don't really know. I've been trying to get out of Baltimore ever since I can remember. I got an athletic scholarship to

UMD in College Park because I could swim faster than anybody in this state. And I got that fellowship to Zürich because I spent more time in the books than anybody in the business school. Now, I've got a MBA and can't even find a fucking job. I'm temping over in DC and living at home -- that's what all that effort got me."

"Why?" I asked, truly puzzled.

"The government's not hiring and business has been cutting back all over the country the past four -- going on five -- years now. Since this bastard got into office and pulled the rug out from under the economy."

"But you've got an advanced degree," I answered, still not understanding.

"If I had it from Harvard, I could get on for fifty thousand in New York in a heart beat. But mine comes from Maryland; and that means diddly squat."

I felt his anger at the injustice that his effort and hard work meant nothing. I said without thinking: "You and Emil should get together and develop a business plan."

"And what would that do?" he asked, at the same time curious and trying to push his anger away from the turn our conversation had taken.

"I assume this is still a capitalist world?" I lifted a brow in question at both of them. Emil, who knew me better, nodded.

"A successful investment would mean a good return?"

Tom had caught on to where my thoughts were beginning to lead me and was as fast as Emil to nod his affirmation.

"Why don't we start a business -- together? I have the money but certainly could never be a merchant. But you two...?" I shrugged.

I could feel Tom liking my suggestion, his thoughts were moving rapidly past his initial curiosity. A frown pulled the ends of his mouth down suddenly. "What do I have to do to be a part of this?" he demanded.

"Sergei," I responded in French. "you would ask me such a question? You of all men know me, what I was and still am."

Tom stared at me for another moment before his face and neck began to redden with the sudden rush of blood in his embarrassment. "I'm sorry, Karli," he mumbled in German and I heard Sergei's accented voice speaking the apology.

"Make arrangements with Emil to come over to the house Sunday. You two need to come up with something that benefits all of us," I told him. "In the Capital," I added.

"It has to be evening -- eight o'clock?" Emil said.

"That's pretty late to be alone in downtown DC or Baltimore," Tom answered with hesitation.

"I'll need to feed first," Emil explained and faint blotches rose across his face. "I can drive you back -- or you may stay the night."

"Now wait a minute!" Tom sat back quickly as if struck in the face.

"We have enough bedrooms," I told him.

"Did you mean it?" Emil asked as our car sped up and entered the traffic heading south on the I-95 motorway.

"Mean what?" I asked.

"That you'd put up the money for us to start a business?"

"Why else would I mention it?"

"You could have been setting him up so that, later, he couldn't say no."

I understood and gritted my teeth. "Emil, that calls into question a concept of honor that was bred into me before Sergei made me on my death bed."

My tone was proud. I knew it and I didn't care. I was hurt, even though I knew young Europeans were too much like their American cousins in not knowing what honor really was.

"If you're telling me I just pissed you off, Karl, I'm sorry," he said quickly. "You've been absolutely fair with me -- but you've been single-minded about finding Tom..."

"Apology accepted," I told him. "When we're back at the house, I want you to look through my thoughts of you and him. I don't ever want you doubting my love for you and where you stand again."

After several moments of silence between us, he snorted. "I saw Tom through gay eyes tonight for the first time," he said. "He's a damned good-looking man, Karl."

"Are you trying to tell me you'd rather have him in bed than me?"

"I love you. I like him. And my cock doesn't control me."

11

Congressman Robert Treman cupped my closest arsecheek through the wool of my trousers as I entered the front hall of his Capitol Hill house. I forced myself not to cringe. "We've got some sort of party planned for tonight!" he gushed and aimed his lips at mine. I moved my face enough that they touched my cheek instead.

Joe McCarthy had invited me to an orgy. My first one in America. My first one in more than seventy years.

I was curious if American political perverts conducted their sexual activities as their European cousins once had.

The congressman from southern Maryland was in his mid-forties and beginning to develop a paunch. The dichotomy between his demeanor and his mien was the most memorable thing about him to me. His looks were rough-hewn but fleshing out and softening under the onslaught of middle age. His dress, however, was that of a court dandy, modernized barely from the era of my own youth. A pompous, unctuous peacock.

He was beloved of his fellow Republicans in the Congress, however -- recognized, as some wag had called him, as the most brilliant conservative mind since Vandenberg. I didn't know who Vandenberg was but I knew the

von Papen-styled apologia with which this man couched his description of the new order that he and his cohorts would build.

I raised a brow in question as he righted himself and retrieved his hand from my backside.

Robert Treman laughed. "You Europeans are always so very proper about everything, aren't you?"

"We have our bad moments too," I answered. "What have you planned for this evening?"

He chortled at my admission, right on cue. "Joe called and said he was running behind but for us to go ahead and start without him."

I shrugged. After weeks of meeting Joe McCarthy and helping him to fulfill his fantasies, I saw this congressman's prescription for some sort of party was rapidly beginning to sound like standard fare for at least one well-heeled queen in American fascism's closet.

"But I prevailed on a friend to join us and bring some of his pet whores with him," he whispered.

Instinctively, my brow raised again. I had absolutely no idea what he was talking about.

Treman chuckled and began to lead me into the house. "Jimmy Boyd's brought along four of his best boy agents."

"Who?" My curiosity heightened.

Treman eyed me suspiciously before remembering that Joe McCarthy had vouchsafed me with religious fervor. "He's FBI -- the real thing, not some political appointee."

"A federal policeman is a pimp?" I asked, showing surprise in spite of myself.

He grinned. "You'd be surprised how many foreigners are queer, Karl -- and go hunting young ass or dick when they're in town. Videos of indelicate moments with a chicken have been known to turn even the most unrepentant Commie."

I studied him for the moment it took me to digest his comment and make sense of it. I decided it was best not to mention that Communism took a hit fourteen years earlier that it was still reeling from. There were only the Chinese and North Koreans left -- and the Chinese had left Marx in the mud when they started modernizing.

I told myself that he was saying some agency of the FBI used young American boys to catch unsuspecting foreign homosexuals with their trousers down, so to speak, and turn them into spies or agents for American interests. Was I viewed as such a foreigner?

I forced myself to smile in anticipation and Treman grinned at my response.

"I thought you'd like that," he gushed and clapped me on my shoulders in a uniquely American show of bonhomie. "Shit, man! There's always enough of the cute young things he brings over to go around. Boyd only does one at a time, but he puts on a damned good show. I'm going to take

erection.

The Semitic boy and I watched him cross the room, pulling off his tie as he moved. He had his jacket off by the time he reached his quarry.

"I'm Karl," I offered.

"I'm Johnny," the youth responded.

"Johnny?"

"Well, it's really Hussein -- but there's enough guys in this country who don't like Arabs, I use a nice American sounding name. You're a hell of a lot better than I was expecting when Jimmy told me to come to this party."

"Oh?"

"I've got pretty used to fat old queens who can't keep their hands off a guy's cock." He grinned. "And there ain't no way you're a fat old queen. I ain't seen you on the circuit either..."

"Circuit?"

"You know the bars and hang-outs where they..." He jerked his head to indicate the adults in the room, "hang out and drool for some of what me and these other guys got."

"You work for the FBI?" I asked, glancing over at the man still paddling the boy.

His olive-complexioned skin blanched. "Boyd keeps the vice cops off my butt..." He glanced at the room over his shoulder. "Theirs too. In return, he sometimes sets me up with some foreigner and I tell him what I hear." He grinned. "If he videos the sex, I get paid double -- from him and the john."

"That doesn't bother you?"

"Shit! I like to fuck. And with this equipment..." He gripped his manhood and it sprang immediately into erection. "I don't get many complaints."

I reached along his side to the nearest mound of cheek. He looked down at my arm, the front of my trousers, and back to my face. His features were slack for a moment before he broke into a grin. "Of course, I'm pretty versatile when I want to be."

"That lends itself to a number of possibilities," I told him.

His grin widened and his hands moved to push my jacket open. "I bet," he said softly as his fingers moved it off my shoulders. "I ain't got laid good in a long time."

The jacket fell to the floor behind me. His experienced fingers began to move down the front of my shirt, leaving it unbuttoned in their wake.

"Here?" I asked, acutely aware of the others. After my one extramarital exploration with Joe McCarthy in his world, I had definitely decided I did not like the feeling of being sullied. One on one with Joe, I could help him imagine anything sexual he wanted; I hadn't actually touched him physically since that one time in the motel.

This Johnny, however, seemed ready to have me testing my abilities at

mental slight-of-hand beyond their capability.

"I got nothing to hide," he answered huskily.

Treman was naked and glassy-eyed as he squatted on the floor, pulling the youth with the hose after him.

Boyd stood and positioned the lad he had been spanking in order to mount him. Johnny the Arab was pulling me towards the couch and a blond boy stroking himself.

It began to dawn on me that only two of the boys in this room were concerned with me. The others were sufficiently occupied they needed no control from me. Only Johnny and the blond mattered.

"I'm going to kneel down in front of Timmy here and give him some help," the young Arab breathed. "I want you to give me a real good ride -- okay?"

I nodded.

As he slipped into a mindless rhythm that had his backside meeting each of the thrusts into him that he imagined, I remembered another house in another time.

It had been full summer on the Wansee in 1930. Most of the boys romping naked through the house hadn't yet entered puberty.

The similarities made my projected movements against Johnny's soft, smooth buttocks a continuous reminder of those moments when Röhm and several of his SA aides frolicked with street boys from working-class Berlin the last time I was in the German capital. They and some of the Nazi deputies in the Reichstag were always in search of fun, and the more young boys the better.

They were the same -- those men now dead in the flames of war or suicide and these men of Congress, the FBI, and other governmental departments. They uses the growing power they held to take their fun with whatever they wanted.

Johnny was gasping with a pending orgasm when I felt Joe's fingers touch my shoulder. I jerked as I imagined him seeing reality: a naked, writhing Arab with buttocks grinding against a non-existent invasion.

"Couldn't wait, could you, Karl?" Joe asked, his lips close to my ear.

I shook my head in numbed surprise that his vision had me plowing the lad with no help from me.

"Just save some for me," he said and began to undress.

"That's the first time I've seen that," Tom said as we left the escalator of the underground at DuPont Circle and stepped into the warm April night.

"What's that?" Emil asked.

"The leather boys with all their ear studs." He nodded his head towards them. "They look like they're some sort of kinky -- what do you call them? -- hustlers."

"The skinheads?" I asked as we came abreast three youths leaning against the newspaper vending machines and watching the evening crowd

entering the Circle.

"Those were skinheads?" he asked once we were past them.

"The real McCoy," Emil shot back, a slight smile tugging at his lips at the Americanism. I smiled too, he was becoming so adept at being American. To my ear, his speech had already become indistinguishable from Tom's.

"I don't think we have organized skinheads in Baltimore -- just juvenile delinquents trying to look like Elvis with grease in their hair."

Emil chuckled; I wondered who Elvis was.

"You guys aren't taking me to a gay bar, are you?" Tom asked, changing the subject before I could quiz Emil telepathically why mention of this Elvis was so funny.

"Do you want to go to one?" Emil asked before I could open my mouth.

Tom smiled tightly. "I think I'll pass. Listening to you moaning and groaning your way to whatever you guys have when you get off is more than enough."

"When was this?" I asked.

"Sunday at five goddamn o'clock in the morning." He smiled knowingly, belying the anger in his words.

"Did we wake you?" Emil asked. "You were snoring loud enough to wake the dead when I looked in on you."

Tom turned quickly to face him, his eyes flashing with suspicion. "You didn't?"

"I just tucked you in and kissed your neck..."

Tom's fingers flew to his neck to search for broken skin. "You didn't really, did you?"

"Okay, you two," I interjected, "Tom's at a disadvantage in this tête-à-tête. Shall we talk about something else?"

"We've got a possibility for a lucrative enterprise, Karl," Emil offered, sliding easily from the confrontation. "Tom actually suggested it, though I suspect he was being more than a little factitious."

"What is it?" I asked, taking the bait he offered and hoping that, together, we could draw the American from the fear he had almost fallen into. I wondered at the way they competed so strongly against each other.

"Tell him, Tom."

I sensed the warmth of the mortal's blood spread out over his neck onto his face, a flicker of interest rising in me before I could repress it. Verdammte! I hadn't eaten. I glanced back at the skinheads and smiled.

"There's not much to tell, Karl. I was just sort of fooling around and suggested vampire blood might be the twenty-first century's elixir like penicillin was the twentieth century's. It was more a joke than anything."

Joke or not, I was definitely not interested. Mortal men had discarded vampires as impossibilities; and I, for one, was quite happy to continue being something that didn't exist. [*I haven't fed, Emil,*] I told him. [*Keep him occupied.*]

[*We're almost to the restaurant...*]

[*Look in shop windows -- anything. I'll only be a few minutes.*]

[*You're that hungry?*]

[*I didn't feed last night, and we're going to have him with us until he goes to bed -- no time for a hunt.*]

[*Sorry.*] I felt understanding in his words.

"You guys are talking to each other, aren't you?" Tom asked, looking from one to the other of us.

Emil grinned and led him on along Connecticut Avenue as I held back. "You could do it too -- if you hadn't said you weren't interested in becoming one of us," he told him.

"I didn't say -- Oh, shit!" I heard him gasp as the night enshrouded them both. "Forget I said that. I'm not interested in becoming a vampire and I sure as shit don't need either of you banging my ass for me."

"I thought you'd have second thoughts after hearing how much I was enjoying it," Emil mocked him gently.

"Shit!" Tom glanced to where I was the moment before. "Hey, where's Karl?"

"He'll be back in a moment."

A public toilet stood between 'P' and Massachusetts half a block from the underground entrance. I touched the mind of the nearest skinhead as I moved unseen past them. [*You must relieve yourself now,*] I told him.

He glanced quickly towards the toilet, saw the way to it was well-lit and clear and pointed it out for his companions before stepping towards it -- and me.

I extended my thoughts to the interior of the toilet. A man was washing his hands slowly, hoping something interesting would show up. I told him to leave, making the command strong and immediate.

Hunger was a palpable, growing reality as I rushed into the vacant toilet ahead of the skinhead's arrival, secreted myself in a cubicle, and waited for him.

I scanned the nearby area for other men interested in the facility and turned them away as the youth stepped up to a urinal and unzipped his fly. Continuing to broadcast the warning, I left the stall and approached him. He glanced at me over his shoulder but quickly turned back to face the dirty porcelain in front of him.

I touched his hip and felt him stiffen.

"You want me pissing all over you, faggot, before I stomp your head in?" he growled as he turned his upper body towards me. He looked into my eyes and found himself floating on an endless, unbroken sea.

[*You're through,*] I told him, my mental voice gentle even as it commanded.

His stream of urine ceased, leaving only a drop harbored within the slit of his skinless glans.

I held out my hand and he leant towards me, his eyes still on mine.

[*Shut your eyes and dream pleasant things,*] I told him as I exposed my fangs and they touched his neck.

He gasped when they broke the skin and groaned as they dug deeper. [*Hug me,*] I told him and felt his arms encircle my chest. His manhood grew between us as I lapped at his blood.

The wound I made wasn't deep and the flow of his blood slowed quickly. I was nowhere close to sated; I wanted more.

He ground his erection against me. "Feels good, baby," he mumbled.

I licked his blood and smiled at the direction his pleasant dream had taken. [*A beautiful youth is sucking you,*] I told him. [*Shoot on his face. He wants it.*]

"Yeah!" the skinhead groaned as I pulled away from him and he leant against the barrier between his urinal and the one next to it. His hand gripped his manhood, stroking it as a beatific smile covered his face.

Curiosity touched me with its curse. The skinhead I had just drank from was masturbating to a dream of a boy sucking him off. It was a dream I didn't think his mates would appreciate.

I touched his mind. And found warning emblazoned across his conscious mind. Something's making members of the Spider Fraternity weak near DuPont Circle. Be careful. Stay together. Be strong. Our day is near.

Beneath the warning, his imagined partner was indeed a good looking man. Nothing had happened, but the hint of a promise was there to haunt the skinhead.

A mischievous thought struck me. There were similarities between the skinhead's friend and Joe McCarthy. I told him to loiter around the Christian Center building in Arlington until he could meet Joe. I pulled away from his thoughts then and stepped into the electrically lit night beyond the toilet.

I caught up to Emil and Tom as they were leaving the Uno store mid-way along the block.

"Feel better?" Emil asked. I nodded.

"Where the hell did you go?" Tom demanded, falling into step with the two of us as we began to stroll up the block.

Emil grinned. "You don't want to know."

"Shit! Just because I don't want to get my ass porked or my neck bitten, you guys don't have to treat me like some kid too dumb to know anything," Tom grumbled. "Talk to me!"

"How much do you want to know?" Emil asked quietly.

"Everything."

"Karl was hungry. He left us to feed."

"Christ!" He glanced at me. "Couldn't you wait until we got to the restaurant? A steak's has got to taste better than -- what? -- a hotdog? a pretzel?"

"I can't eat that kind of food," I told him, feeling slightly uneasy at his insistence.

"Why not?"

"I'm a vampire, remember?"

"So, you can't eat with the rest of...?" He stopped and turned to face me. "You...?" He glanced along both directions of the sidewalk and, lowering his voice, continued: "You drank somebody's blood?"

I nodded and he shuddered. "You killed somebody?" he asked even more quietly and the camaraderie that had bound us all evening quickly began to evaporate.

"No," I answered. "The skinhead's still very much alive -- just a little weakened. He'll feel fine tomorrow."

"You sucked blood from one of the guys we just passed?"

"They're a good source of food, Tom," I told him. "They intimidate sane people. They're of no use to anybody -- that makes them fair game to me."

I felt his revulsion, strong and quick, as it swept over him.

"I'm not so sure I'm still hungry," he mumbled.

"Tom," I said gently, "you knew what we were when you decided to be friends."

"I know," he sighed. "But I wasn't really thinking of the bloodsucking." He smiled tightly. "I guess I didn't let myself think about it until just now."

He laughed sharply. "You know, When I was the priest, I wouldn't become like you because of that. Every time I'd get close, I'd remember slurping at some guy's neck..." He smiled at me. "He loved you, Karl -- more than anything, even his church. But he couldn't do that, not ever."

"He died because of it," I answered and my vision became blurred. "He chose..."

"It wasn't such a bad choice. At least, I hope it wasn't. I'm here -- in the flesh."

"You are. And we're both glad you are," Emil told him quickly, a lilt to his voice and I knew he was trying to pull us away from the abyss into which Tom was staring.

The American was silent for long moments and I was only peripherally aware of the curiosity with which passers-by glanced at us. Finally, he shrugged, making his decision and I felt the tension lift from us.

"This is where I ought to run like hell," he said quietly. "It's sort of like finding out your best girl's a hit man for the Mafia, or something."

"You're free to go. Neither of us will bother you..."

"Karl, don't!" Emil growled under his breath.

"No. Friendship with us must be of his own free will," I answered, watching Tom. "And it can't be based on lies or ignorance."

Tom snorted. "No wonder I loved you both times! You're so fucking honorable about everything."

"Would you rather forget what happened here?"

He stared at me. "You can make me forget it, can't you? Just like you and Emil talk to each other with your minds?"

I nodded.

He shuddered again, but, now, it was more a shiver than the body-wrenching movement of earlier. "I had better keep it right where it is -- as a reminder."

He chuckled. "You know, it's real funny. I was feeling like I was out with buddies from school until ... It'd be real easy to just sort of slide into accepting what you offer." He glanced down at the sidewalk. "Sergei's hot for me to do it..." He glanced at Emil and blushed. "He really got fixated on the idea of three-ways."

"Have you ever done it with a man?" Emil asked quietly.

The American's blush deepened. "Yeah. A couple of times back in college. When I was really broke, I'd go to Patterson Park in Baltimore and hustle my cock."

"Did you like it?" I asked as we reached the intersection and looked across Connecticut Avenue to the steak house that was our destination. I was afraid of his answer, even as my heart thudded in anticipation of it.

"Sort of. Shit! Yeah, it was pretty exciting and that made it scary in a way I didn't understand then."

"You do now?"

"Yeah. I've got a soul that's been creaming in its shorts at the thought of hopping into bed with you two for a month. I can see now that it was getting off on what I was doing with those johns who picked me up."

"You don't have to decide to be a vampire to join us in bed, Tom," Emil told him as we crossed the street. "We can have fun together without you making that decision."

"I don't think I'm ready to throw up my hands and start swishing."

I sighed as we reached the east side of the street. "Tom, just because you have sex with a man doesn't make you homosexual."

I quickly outlined my view of man being a sexual animal, one that enjoys its couplings. Now that I knew the sexologists Masters and Johnson had proven my theory in the fifties, I couched my outline in their words as we crossed the street.

"I can almost see myself getting it on with you both-" He hung his head. "Part of me -- Sergei probably -- wants to ... Until I hear myself groaning 'fichset' while one of you humps me -- like you were doing to Emil this morning."

Emil chuckled. "We'll lead you into it slowly, Tomi. Sex needs be fun. The moment you find it's become something else, we'll stop."

"You mean Karl isn't going to be porking me the second my underwear slides below my butt?" he asked with only a trace of humor lacing his words.

"We won't do anything you don't want to do," I told him and opened the door of the restaurant. "Now, let's feed you."

12

Tom and I shared a cognac in the sitting room. I heard the tumblers turning in the outer door and Emil's feet as he stepped into the hall. [*I'm home,*] he projected. [*Give me time to dress and I'll join you.*]

"Emil is back," I told Tom.

"He went to feed, didn't he?" he asked and I feared a return to the tension earlier.

I nodded.

"Was this another skinhead?"

I shook my head. "He has a very negative view of drug-dealers, as negative as mine of skinheads. He was probably over in Anacostia."

"I can almost see offing one of those animals, but what bites your arse about the skinheads? I didn't see them doing anything."

"It's a long story."

"Tell me."

"Tom, I'd need to share it mentally with you. That way, you'd get a direct infusion of my memories without my prejudices coming into play."

He shrugged. "Do it."

"That's very difficult when you're not a vampire."

"Jesus!" he groaned. "That shit again."

Emil stepped into the room, joining us. "Hi, guys..." He made a production of looking around the room and then staring at us. "You mean, you haven't been getting it on while my back was turned?"

]*Emil!*] I projected in warning.

[*Just joking, Liebchen.*]

"We were waiting for you," Tom shot back at him, a grin on his face.

I looked at the American. So did Emil. "Are you telling us something?" I asked.

The moment for repartee was past and he knew it better than I. Tom's face paled. "Okay, item one is I'm horny. It's been the longest time since I got it on with anyone but Mary Five Fingers here," he said, holding up his hand.

"Item two is I've fucked a couple of guys and got blown by a few more. Maybe I wasn't even twenty then, but I remember it being pretty good -- even if I was scared as hell with Sergei singing sweet songs about how good it was.

"Item three is I'm willing to get into something as long as it's understood we don't do anything I freak out about. Item four is you don't play with my head; and item five is you don't assume I want to hop into bed every time I'm around just because I do it tonight."

I continued to study him, working my way through the restrictions. "I didn't hear you mention specific things we couldn't do..."

"Just that you don't play with my head, giving me wants that aren't mine, and that you don't push me into doing something I'm not ready for..."

"And that we don't look upon you as a regular sex partner just because we get it on tonight," Emil added primly.

Tom turned and smiled his thanks to him.

Emil grinned suddenly, signaling the return of his lilting irreverence. "It's almost two in the morning and we've all three fed..." He raised a brow theatrically and his voice immediately became guttural, his 'W's' becoming 'V's'.

"Shall we show you the room where we will deflower you, good-looking American young man?" He licked his lips in campy anticipation.

Tom stared at the Swiss youth then turned to me. "This is a side of him I never saw in Zürich -- what did you do to him when you made him a vampire?"

"He's the first one I made," I answered, "perhaps I gave him too much blood and it went to his head?"

[*Are you sure, Emil?*] I asked. [*We don't have to...*]

[*Don't, Karl. It's what you want -- what has to be. I've known it from the beginning and accepted it.*]

[*I can be alone with him...*]

[*No!*] His face tightened as he met my gaze, red blotches threatening to break out over it.

[*Do it with anyone else and you'd better hide what you do with them -- I'd be mad as hell but I'd probably forgive you. Tom, and the men he was before, though -- they're real to you. They've been a part of you for more than a hundred years. You can no more separate them any part of your life than you can go without feeding...*]

[*I don't have to rub your face in it, though.*]

[*You won't be. I'm the one who has to accept him -- and learn to love him. He possesses you more than I ever can. If I'm to have you, he comes with the packet.*]

[*You're sure?*] I asked and smiled, hoping he felt the love behind it.

He snorted. [*I had better be if I want to be in your life.*]

"You know, I could really learn to hate you guys," Tom opined from between us, forcing himself into our circle.

"Why's that?" Emil asked, his eyes misty pink with tears.

"You talk mind to mind every time you don't want me to hear you. Were you discussing me?"

Emil smiled tightly. "We'll discuss that later -- if you want."

"Shit!" He pushed himself from the chair and stood uncertainly. "You could almost convince me to join the vampire brigade too, with all this interesting shit going right over my head all the time."

I rose. "This is where you back out of this adventure or commit to the duration," I told him, pulling him away from his fantasies of vampires.

He looked from me to Emil and back. "I don't have to do anything I don't want to, right?"

"Come on, American," Emil told him with a grin. "I've never fucked

one of you before."

"Emil!" I snapped as Tom froze.

Emil looked sheepishly at Tom. "I'm sorry. Let's go enjoy ourselves."

At the top of the stairs, Tom slowed as Emil went on into the bedroom and I made to follow. I turned back to him and saw his face was ashen as he stared at the open door to the bedroom I shared with Emil.

"Uncomfortable?" I asked.

"Yeah. A little." He snorted. "A whole lot. I think I just gave birth to an armada of butterflies and they're in my gut."

"Then don't do it. You have the bedroom next to ours, sleep there."

"It wasn't sleep that worried me," he answered but grinned.

"That's got to be your decision entirely, Tom. Go to your bed if the thought of doing something with us makes you uncomfortable."

He laughed. "Sergei would never stop kicking my butt if I backed out now. I think even that prude of a curate would be right in there with him."

"It's not backing out. It's what makes you comfortable. That's your body -- not mine or Emil's, not even Sergei's -- you've got to decide how to derive pleasure from it."

He took the last two steps and stood before me. His lips twitched in a grin. "Are you going to stand out here talking me to death or are we going in there and get it on?"

"I'm going in there and find several hours worth of pleasure before I sleep. Emil has the same intention." I smiled and started for the room. "What you do is your decision."

Emil already lay naked on the bed as he smiled a greeting to me. I shoved off my shoes and crossed the room, pulling off my shirt. I had lowered my trousers over my hips when Tom growled from the door: "Do you two mind some light? I can't see in the dark."

"What's to see?" Emil called out to him chuckling.

"I never looked at a cock up close before -- except mine."

"You just fuck them, take their money, and leave?"

"Emil!" I growled. "Turn on the light," I told Tom.

Tom stopped when he saw me standing at the foot of the bed in just my y-fronts. He turned to face the bed and saw Emil lying there. He blinked his eyes and turned back to me. He crossed the room to stand beside me.

"I don't like you in those," he said in French, his voice Sergei's. His fingers reached out to touch my chest. "Sweet, lovely Karli," he breathed in the curate's voice.

Emil stared at him in disbelief. Tom kissed first one nipple and then the other.

[*He -- they -- want to make love to you, Karl!*]

"Let him make his own decision, Sergei," I told him. "Don't influence him."

Tom's body jerked slightly, and I sensed he was the only presence in his body. His tongue continued to touch and taste my nipples, learning the

contours of my chest, moving over it as his hands opened his shirt and shoved it off.

His body moved to music only he could hear as he stepped out of his loafers and began to unzip his jeans. In moments, he was naked and his tongue had begun a downward spiral as his fingers slipped beneath the elastic of my underpants.

Kneeling, his lips pushed the prepuce of my manhood back along its shaft as he forced himself to swallow most of me. His hands moved along the backs of my thighs to find and, then, knead my buttocks as he began to bob on my sex.

"Let's get on the bed, Tom," I said as I massaged his back.

He stared at me as he rose and took a step backward, his erection complete. "Jesus!" he croaked. "Is it going to be like this every time we...?"

I chuckled. "If I remember correctly both Sergei and Würther were prone to lose themselves to passion."

"But that...!" His eyes blanked for the briefest moment. "You can't cum, can you?" He glanced over his shoulder at Emil. "Neither of you?"

"If you mean ejaculate, no," I told him.

"I've had some damned good orgasms since I woke up undead," Emil continued from the bed.

Tom glanced from one to the other of us. "Should we -- uh -- you know, use rubbers when we get to that point?"

"Parasites can't live in us," I told him. "I don't know about AIDS specifically, but you tested other sexually transmitted diseases with my blood in your second incarnation..." I shut my eyes for a moment forcing the memory of that field of edelweiß from my mind. "They died instantly."

"We've got to try it with the HIV-virus." The erection jutting from his groin began to lose its strength as his mind embraced the new thought. "Can you imagine how big this would be if you and Emil can kill AIDS too?"

Emil had slid across the bed, his eyes riveted to the mortal's manhood and rounded as it became merely tumescent. "His bell end stays uncovered!" he whispered to himself.

"He's circumcised," I told him. "Most Americans are."

Tom blushed under our discussion and Emil's gaze on him. I felt the warmth of his blood spreading through his skin and shivered at the tinge of hunger that went through me.

"It's big and thick like yours, Karl -- and pretty." Emil looked up at Tom's face. "May I touch it?"

"I guess -- Jesus! I feel like I'm under a microscope or something."

Emil's hand was halfway between them. "You don't want me to?" he asked.

"No, do it. Shit! Let me get on the bed and you can suck me off while I'm slurping on yours." He glanced back at me. "You might as well go ahead and pork me so we can get that out of the way too."

"Are you sure?"

He looked away quickly and whispered: "Yeah."

"May I touch your thoughts to make it easier for you?"

"Just to make it easier to take that thing of yours, okay?"

13

With the sun of a late May afternoon on the other side of the house, I sat in the music room and studied the keyboard of the piano that had been delivered that morning. I was again thankful that Tom had become our friend as well as frequent bedmate. Some things, such as piano deliveries, were impossible for vampires without a trustworthy mortal around.

I tried to remember the last time I had played a piano. I was fairly certain it had been the night the Jew from the resistance told us the Gestapo had found us out. The last song I had played as Würther rushed through our living quarters to toss clothes into sacks for both of us had been *Lili Marlene*, a farewell to everything I had ever known. It had to have been; it had been my favorite song since I first heard it in Berlin before the twentieth century began.

Could I even play it now, sixty-five years since last I touched a keyboard? Or would I ruin it? I forced the music from my memory. With its notes and bars now fresh for me, I touched the keys.

Sorrow wrapped itself around each chord as it rose from the piano. Innocence lost, love denied and foredoomed.

I didn't heard the doorbell. I was in the midst of once again strolling under the linden trees of the song, tears in my eyes.

[*Karl, your fascist's at the door,*] Emil projected at me. My fingers collapsed against the keyboard, creating discordance throughout the room. Joe was here? At this house? Why?

I wiped my eyes on a tissue and rose; obedient to my earliest training, I became a host before I had left the room.

Emil was pretending an abysmal lack of knowledge of English as he entertained Joe McCarthy in the parlor. I thought he was even believable and thanked the stars that govern human and vampire destiny that Tom was at Georgetown's medical library in search of strange, quirky things in blood that might begin to explain why Emil and I were exempt from HIV-infection, much less being simply immortal.

"Hello, Joe," I greeted my uninvited guest and, turning to Emil, told him in German he was a believable actor but to disappear. He wanted to watch through my eyes and I agreed to transmit everything that occurred between us to him.

"I'm surprised to see you here," I told the man as Emil left us. I pulled the sliding wooden doors to the music room closed.

"Why're you surprised?" he asked and I noted the real curiosity he felt.

"For one thing, I don't remember telling anyone at Treman's where I lived."

"Oh, that!" He laughed. "Karl, the CC knows everything about you. I had a background started on you before I ever went to that party your embassy threw. I knew you were okay before you ever set foot in Treman's house."

I froze. It took me what seemed to be the longest moments to force a foot off the floor and move it forward. I walked as a mechanical man, a robot. I forced composure over my face before I turned back to Joe McCarthy. "And what did you learn about me?" I asked and hoped I sounded nonchalant.

"You were pretty much of a cipher but we did find that you seem to have a faint connection to some of the preacher's friends in Germany and Austria..."

"I?"

He grinned. "I keep forgetting Europe's about ten years behind us in computer science. We dredged up your grandfather's adoption and his death, your school records -- things like that. We wanted to know whose side you were on."

My blank look alerted him. "This house is about a block from niggertown which scares most people off. But it's -- well, it demands a gentleman; and you have given it what it needed."

"I've had no problems," I told him, ignoring his slur to my neighbors.

His face fleetingly became a leer before it could return to its boyish, naïve purposefulness. "I see why you've not become a regular at Treman's house."

I looked blank again. Try as I might, I had not been able to adjust to the American habit of jumping from subject to subject in conversation. I was still trying to determine the relevance of my physical proximity to Negro homes.

"That German boy who answered the door. He looks like he's got to be close to the best in bed. I can imagine what he'd look like naked in a porn flick."

"Emil?" I asked carefully.

"The sandy-haired boy."

"He's more than a boy..."

The leer returned but, this time, remained. "I bet he is. Is he as good a fuck as me?"

"He's..." I fought against my urge to tell this man it was none of his business, another urge to kill him for what he was and promised to be, and finally accepted the urge to keep things flowing smoothly between us. "He's a good friend," I answered noncommittally.

"Yeah..."

I touched his mind, unwilling to have him thinking things I didn't know as well as to redirect the conversation away from those things into other areas.

He seethed at having found Emil in my house and what he guessed he

was to me. I found his image of me to be tall and well-endowed. I was surprised at the desire to claim me as his own that burnt inside him. I looked into his untroubled eyes and the naiveté that set so well on his boyish face. Nothing of the turmoil of his thoughts showed in that angelic face.

Herr Doktor Freud would have loved to have met Joe McCarthy. Talk about schizophrenic personalities . . .

[*He is nothing to you,*] I told him. [*See him only as a convenience-*]

His anger cooled as he assimilated my command, making it his own without a thought to its appearance in his mind. He smiled. "The reason I stopped by was to invite you to meet Reverend Koughlin."

"When?"

"Tomorrow evening at eight. There's a very special get-together out in St. Mary's county that he's coming up from Tidewater for. I could pick you up if you'd like to come?"

Pat Koughlin. Der Prediger. Der Amerikanischer Führer.

I smiled as invitingly as I could make my face muscles move. "Please," I said. "Yes, I would like to meet him. I've heard so much about him."

I touched his thoughts again and saw the blind love Joe McCarthy felt for the tall, craggy-faced evangelist who was so adept at wrapping himself with the cloak of the Christian God in order to lay concrete plans to destroy America.

Joe grinned. "I'll pick you up at six. You'll be meeting some men who are helping him change America as well."

"Please."

His face went blank, though it colored with the slightest embarrassment. "You understand we don't mix the goings-on at Bob Treman's house with this kind of get-together."

My face was just as blank but held none of his embarrassment. "Of course, Joe."

The Nazi elite hadn't mixed their parties at the cabarets with their orders to send Jews, Slavs, and homosexuals to concentration camps, either. Of course, I understood.

"These men are gentlemen, Karl -- the cream of the crop in America," he explained.

"Gentlemen?" I gazed at him in surprise. "With the amount of vindictiveness coming out of your Congress the past few months? I've begun to suspect your Republican members were each reared in an alleyway."

He stared at me suspiciously for several uncomfortable moments. He sighed finally and said: "You really don't understand, do you?"

I shook my head slowly. "What do I not understand?"

"We have to destroy this president in the American consciousness. The people need to suspect him of everything -- him and his administration. We put him in office and have kept him there; but his usefulness is finished. It's almost time for us to take over."

"Reverend Koughlin can then come to Washington to clean up the mess?" I asked, remembering Mussolini marching his blackshirts to the royal palace in Rome. King Victor Emanuel had had to ask him to enter the government to clean things up, and Italy found it had Il Duce.

"Something like that." He grinned.

"But how will you keep control? A Gestapo?"

"Heavens, no! Technology and local churches."

"The local church?"

"You Europeans have been politically centralized too long. In more and more county and city elections, the only people running are our own. Whisper campaigns -- even full smear campaigns -- keep everybody else out, or destroy them."

He laughed. "Karl, only 20 to 30 percent of voters vote in county and city elections -- even in state elections. Less than 50 percent voted nationally in '96. Our four million members and close allies already control local elections across this country.

"Most of America's polling places are already at churches allied with us. And the Christian Center makes sure every person going to vote knows whom to vote for..."

A dapper Joe McCarthy waited in his Mercedes beyond the gate for me at exactly six o'clock hours the next evening.

An hour after we'd left DC, we pulled into a drive that seemed to have been swallowed by a forest of leafed-out trees. "You're going to like these people, Karl -- they're more your type than Boyd," Joe told me.

I raised a brow in question. He laughed. "They're classy people. Well-educated, old money, good brains -- the kind of leaders who will make the revolution succeed. They're not the foot soldiers like Agent Boyd."

"And they're all homophobic, too -- right?"

He chuckled. "I'd guess most of the younger ones probably swing in private with their own -- but, yes, they do present an unblemished image of sanity and stability to the world."

He pulled in behind another Mercedes. "These people see that America took a wrong turn and got broken. They accept the need for strong leadership -- strong moral leadership -- even if it has to step on some individual rights. The greatest good for the greatest number lies in strictly defining and controlling social behavior, at least, in the short-term -- until we've re-established harmony in the country again."

I nodded complete understanding. Of course I understood. A social deviate of any persuasion wouldn't have courts offering him an attorney and trying to observe his rights once Joe and his friends held power. Unless he was useful, he'd be beaten until he told the police who his colleagues were and then disappear.

As we took the steps up to the door of the manor, I wondered idly how many families in America would learn the fear their European cousins

learnt more than sixty years before if Joe's plans for this country were ever implemented.

A very proper English butler admitted us, ticking Joe's name off a mental list he had memorized, and showed us into a large, tastefully and expensively decorated lounge. Men in expensively tailored suits stood in small cliques of twos and threes, slowly sipping drinks and discussing investments.

"The people on board now are mostly in oil and banking," Joe whispered, watching his betters in awe. "But we're now expanding rapidly through the upper classes. There's been almost a hundred percent growth in those joining us just this past year."

I extended my hearing into the room. I wanted to catch the nuances of these people who would lend themselves to building the new order of a fascist America. Not the thoughts and fears -- but the dynamics of this leadership. These men who viewed themselves as the natural replacements for the class to which I belonged.

Soft, Southern accents and Southwestern twangs predominated. Golf courses were the center around which most of the conversations revolved. I felt no surprise that this gathering of the selected few was entirely white and male.

Bob Treman broke away from his group and came towards us. "Joe, it's good to see you again," he said as he neared us. "Thanks for coming." He smiled pleasantly to me, pretending that he didn't know me.

Joe chuckled. "I'd like you to meet the Prince von Maribor, a sympathizer from Austria. Karl, this is Congressman Treman."

We shook hands and I pretended to bask in the friendly smile of the congressman.

"My Prince, you just make yourself at home," he offered. "Joe here pretty well knows his way around -- stick close to him and see how we do it over here."

I wasn't sure if I had been sloughed off with a mild warning or accepted into the inner circle.

I took a glass of champagne from a passing tray and pretended to sip at it as I followed the leader of the Christian Center from one clump of people to the next during the next forty-five minutes.

Joe and I were near a set of windows facing the drive when conversations stopped on the other side of the room. I glanced over the shoulder of a banker from North Carolina and saw a tall, craggy-faced man with slicked-back, receding wavy hair enter the room. The Reverend Pat Koughlin. The would-be American Führer.

I tuned the conversation around me out as I watched Reverend Koughlin make the rounds of the room.

When he'd reached us, Joe was immediately fawning over the man. I had seen him treat equally with the captains of industry and government. I knew his intelligence to be high -- even if misguided -- and his lust for

power to be higher still; but I had never seen him be a sycophant.

The banker was hardly better.

They were in the presence of their Führer.

Koughlin spoke first with one man and then the other; but I met his eyes searching mine unflinchingly.

"Reverend Koughlin, I'd like you to meet Karl von Maribor," Joe said, leaving off my title.

"You're German?" the preacher asked, his voice warm and friendly, instantly wrapping me within it.

"Austrian -- and Swiss," I answered.

He grinned and offered: "I'm going to be staying here with Bob Treman for a few days, perhaps we can get to know each other better?"

"I'd like that," I answered.

"Good. What time tomorrow is best for you?"

I was surprised at his assumption that I would make time available to him so soon. Still, I had come this far so that I might understand America's descent into a hell Europe had tasted and rejected. "Perhaps around this time?"

"It'll have to be earlier -- say, around two in afternoon, Mr. von Maribor," he said, brushing away my suggestion.

"I couldn't possibly make it before seven, Reverend," I told him.

He stared at me for a long moment. "Whatever," he said finally and turned back to Joe and the banker.

I suspected that I'd been tested and found wanting. I shrugged.

14

I heard Emil and Tom in the sitting room as I let myself into the house. Emil mentally greeted me with an image of the biggest, wettest lips. But, as I neared the opened door of the room, I heard Tom ask: "What's it really like?"

Emil answered: "You mean being a vampire?"

I accepted an offered link to his thoughts and listened as the two of them began to discuss the nature of my being. I stayed in the hall, electing not to join them, thinking that Tom might feel intimidated in my presence but was comfortable with Emil.

"I woke up a whole day after that shag and knew immediately I was different -- and knowing the only thing that it could be was that I had changed into one," he answered. "I don't know if I can put into words what I felt at that moment..." He chuckled.

"You've got to understand I'd wanted to be like Karl ever since I knew what he was. But I was still pissed off when I woke up." He laughed. "It had happened -- the biggest change in my life -- and I hadn't even known it was happening.

"I suppose I expected to be taking my last, gasping breath as some old

- 354 -

troll years from now when it happened." He grinned at the thought. "Then, I'd wake up young and good-looking all over again."

"It's made you better looking somehow," Tom allowed.

"The effervescence?" Tom nodded. "We don't sweat -- we can't. When we change, the pores disappear from our skin; that takes away a certain coarseness I see in every mortal I meet."

"You can change -- into other things?"

Emil nodded. "Just about anything you can conceive of. I've been a wolf, a bat, a mist -- even a panther when I hunted." He laughed again. "Though you've got to be careful about changing shape. It's only your natural body that's affected -- you lose your clothes when you do it."

"Really?"

"Yeah. The first time I did it I had to come back here naked. Walking naked through a city -- even on a winter night when everybody's inside -- is a little embarrassing."

"What did you do?"

"I finally realized that I'd bounded out of the house as a wolf, so I turned myself back into one to make it home."

"You can teleport yourself too, can't you?"

"I've only done if from room to room here in the house."

"You're stronger too?"

"There isn't a man who can touch me if I don't want him to. I can out-run and out-fight any mortal. He can't kill me, but I can kill him. I can see better, read thoughts..." He shrugged.

Tom chuckled and said: "What's sex like as a vampire?"

I felt Emil's face break out in blotches. "It's better. I'm more sensitized as a vampire than I ever was as a mortal. Though I couldn't wait to get over to Karl's flat back there in Zürich, to get it on with him -- I guess I was pretty sensitized then..."

"I know the feeling," Tom allowed under his breath.

"Only, it's a whole lot better now. I can go on and on without flagging..." He grinned. "Like you do."

Emil watched the American blush. "Do you love him?" he asked.

"Yeah," Tom blushed deeper. "Only, I love both of you, Emil."

He snorted. "Before I met you guys that night at the Inner Harbor, I basically saw myself falling in love with just one girl and settling down with her -- marrying her, I guess. When I had finally come to a working arrangement with Sergei and called Karl, I sort of thought -- if it developed that he and I went to bed -- that same kind of thing I'd imagined about me and a girl would happen between him and me.

"But there you were. And it sure as hell was obvious you weren't some pick-up like I'd seen you being back in Zürich. That sort of threw me for a loop." He grinned. "The curate was mortified at the thought of a three-way. It took old Sergei a few moments; but, by the time I left you two, he couldn't wait to try it out."

"And Tom?"

"Shit! I wasn't queer. I didn't want to be queer. I don't know -- a one-on-one with a guy I liked wasn't exactly queer to me. But two guys? No way!"

He chuckled and I saw his neck and face blaze through Emil's eyes. "But I sure did come around soon enough!"

It was late; dawn's approach threatened the night beyond the windows. In the bedroom above me, the American slept the sleep of the satiated. Emil restlessly had gone in search of a drug deal he could disrupt. I sat before the piano, my eyes closed, and allowed my thoughts to float where they would.

Tom. He was so different than I had allowed myself to expect in Zürich as his spirit's incoherent whisperings touched my thoughts night after night. He was definitely his own person; though there were flashes of Sergei's two incarnations when I least expected them.

I wondered if the personality that soul now wore was an improvement over the others I had known. I didn't see it but that meant nothing. Improvements in nature came in small gradations. Just this evening I'd seen Tom fall asleep against Emil's bare chest, the Swiss youth's arms around him.

The curate would have been horrified at the thought of sex with anyone but me or being seen showing affection to any man. He would never have trusted himself enough to cuddle against another until sleep came to him.

And Sergei? He had liked his sex and was indiscriminate about where he found it -- as long as he was the instigator. As long as he had control. Even with me. Even after he'd given himself to me, he wanted to be the one to initiate things. I chuckled to myself. Sergei actually pouted the few times I made an opening move on him.

I suspected sex was certainly not the most accurate gauge by which to determine spectral advancement. But every act of it was as much a combination of the personalities of the people involved as it was the actual mechanical coupling of bodies.

There had been occasional other partners when Sergei and I were exploring our sexual union. But he never submitted to anyone but me; it was an absolute limit he held himself to. His second incarnation had been chaste by comparison, though just as passionate in his love-making. Sex to Würther had been just that -- love-making -- and never anything less. He had sex with me because he loved me; and he gave himself to me totally.

Tom enjoyed our romps with Emil as much as Sergei ever had a menage-a-trois. But he shared himself equally with both of us, something his predecessors would never have done. There seemed a simple joy that rose in him as we touched and fondled our way towards a coupling. And it didn't matter who was doing what with whom.

I smiled at the memory of our shifting union just past us. I had touched his thoughts as he straddled Emil and began to lower himself onto him. Out

of curiosity, nothing more.

In the jumble of images I encountered, I found warmth for both Emil and myself in equal measure. An acceptance of us and a desire to be with us, doing what we were doing. Deeper within his thoughts was the same acceptance but a stronger, more complete desire to simply be with us, singly and together.

In the month since he first fought his way into our bed, Tom MacPherson had come to love us both, in equal measure.

At least one thing had gone right.

I played the overture to *Eroica* as the first streaks of purple spread across the eastern sky. Beethoven had always soothed my soul and was the perfect welcome to the coming dawn.

I was already bored and it was only early evening. The house felt empty. My lovers were gone -- Emil to San Francisco to research some idea he had for a business. Tom had gone to visit his parents in Baltimore for the weekend. It was only Friday.

I was bored -- and lonely.

Unglaublich. Most unbelievable for me.

So, what was I to do to while away the hours and days before I again had the companionship of at least one of them?

I watched the news on the television and learnt twenty feet of an interstate parkway in Arizona had exploded into boulders of tarmac, killing three motorists and injuring a score more. I turned it off. I did not want to hear how unsafe America had become in its heartland or of the country's destabilization.

I entered the music room and forced myself to sit before the piano, exposing the keys that gleamed up at me. Beethoven?

No! Too strong. Even overpowering for how I felt now in my loneliness.

Mussorgsky?

Never! Too dark and foreboding. I would have Slavic demons threatening me the rest of the night and in my dreams through tomorrow.

I smiled as my fingers touched the keys and brought forth the unabashed joy only Mozart gave his every composition. I played *Eines Kleine Nachtmusik* in its entirety, uplifting my spirit and feeling his joy touching me from across the centuries. The music lifted me from the doldrums I had descended into as I had watched my lads leave me with the sun sinking beyond the city of Washington last night.

And put me in the mood to dance the light fantastic.

With whom? Who did I know? Emil and Tom -- but they lived with me and were gone.

Joe McCarthy and Bob Treman -- I knew them as well. Too well. I knew them from their orgies and McCarthy in the additional roles of Koughlin's organizer and apologist -- Martin Bormann, Rudolf Hess, and

Josef Goebbels reincarnated in one body.

They were it. I had single-mindedly immersed myself into the American fascist movement and, doing so, denied myself the opportunity to make friends.

I became pensive when lonely -- and morose, a Russian with his bottle of vodka, crying in it before it was half gone. My Slavic ancestry exposed itself.

Having nothing else to do as I roamed the house. It was Friday night and I did not want to sit at home alone.

I smiled. Joe McCarthy, despite the monster he was, had a pretty face and willing libido. Somehow, he'd learnt to hide the monster behind that pretty, innocuous face. And I did so enjoy feeding his fantasies -- even as I kept my body removed from them.

Joe McCarthy was locking his car as I turned the corner below Treman's house.

"Good God, it's you!" he groaned from behind me.

I turned, recognizing his voice. "I was thinking of you, Joe," I told him.

"I've been thinking about you the past week and a half," he answered. "Since you pissed off the preacher."

"Pissed him off?"

"He's had the word put out that the organization has no interest in you."

My eyes rounded in surprise with no mental effort on my part. "What does that mean?" I asked quietly and wished I'd kept up my attendance at Treman's orgies.

"It means, Prince von Maribor, that no right-thinking Christian better have anything to do with you."

"That sounds ominous, Joe. What's he going to do, put out a fatwa..." I tried to remember the term used in the awful American gangster flicks to which the lads were addicted. "A contract on me?"

The leader of the Christian Center snorted. "We don't do things like that."

I caught the wisp of a thought behind his bland exterior that said they certainly did do such things and that Joe had been involved in the discussion of doing it to me.

I decided I wanted much more information -- and wanted it immediately. [*You want me,*] I told him. [*You need me to plow you.*]

The blandly cute, naïve face contorted with his struggle between duty and desire. His manhood, having no such struggle, tented the front of his trousers.

[*Drive to my house,*] I told him. [*You'll have all of me -- all night, if you can handle it.*]

"Why don't I drive you back to your place, Karl?" he asked huskily, his mind leaping into my bed.

I smiled knowingly. "I think I'd like that," I told him.

He had his shirt unbuttoned before we were inside. I had led him, yes; but I could not make him this willing.

"You don't know how I've missed you this past week and a half," he mumbled as I opened the door. "It's been hell, imagining you with that -- that boy of yours." His fingers pulled my shirt out of my pants and crept under its material to caress my back. "And then the preacher's decision came down. I didn't know what to do I hurt so bad."

He giggled girlishly. "Now, I've got you back, Karl. I'm going to feel good."

"Just for the night," I warned him gently.

"No!" he grunted, misunderstanding me. "I'll find some way to make the preacher reconsider. You'll see..." His fingers were past my hip and worked their way beneath my belt to get inside my trousers. "I want you more than you can know, Karl. You bring out the good in me, better than anybody ever has."

He stayed with me as I stepped inside the house, his fingers groping their way down my abdomen. He gripped my erection as I led him into the sitting room.

He pushed his clothes from his body. "I've just about stayed celibate since our last time. I've kept myself pure for you, you bring me so close to Jesus."

I nuzzled his neck as he pushed his y-fronts over his hips and wiggled out of them. I touched his thoughts as he began to undress me but was unable to find anything but a tidal wave of sexual anticipation.

He struggled with desire-driven fingers to unfurl the condom along my shaft and, sighing when he had it on me, leant back against the sofa and raising his legs in invitation. "Fuck me good, baby," he breathed as I helped him see me pushing into him.

My lips returned to his neck.

"I want to feel Jesus with us tonight."

Even fantasized sex brought out the hunger in me and I had not thought to feed before I started for Treman's house.

He imagined that I entered him. "Oh, sweet Jesus!" he gushed, already reaching for rapture before his fantasy of me could begin to move in him.

I could let myself taste him a little, I told myself. Not too deep. Just enough.

"Sit with me, Jesus!" Joe cried out. "Oh, yes! I'm so close. Thank you, Jesus! I need it to do right. Oh, God!"

I sat beside him and my fangs pressed into the soft base of his neck as his first orgasm sprayed over his abdomen.

Koughlin didn't trust me. He thought I was naïve or frivolous or both. A dilettante. Or, perhaps, a plant.

He feared what I knew. Who in the organization I knew. He doubted Joe because of the man's defense of me. His first instinct was to dispense with me. Joe had responded by defending me even more. Pat Koughlin

responded by doubting him even more.

They had left it that I could live if Koughlin didn't hear any more about me. If I simply faded into the nothingness from which I had come.

"Sweet Jesus!" Joe cried, immersed in his rapture as I lapped at his blood. "Do it again -- it's so good!"

I quit, letting the punctures clot before he was seriously weakened. His fantasy of me continued to plow him with a constant, unchanging tempo. As he talked to the dead rabbi who was de-Judafied and divine to him, I pushed through the frothing sexual thoughts surging across the forefront of his mind. I went deeper than I had ever gone, careless in my search as I knew he'd remember nothing of it.

When he wanted something done but didn't dare bring Koughlin into it, he went to Treman. He suspected the man had his own connection to the preacher, separate from his. That was all right, though -- they both liked dick and that bound them together as tightly as their devotion to their leader.

He had seen the banks of new computers at the center of Koughlin's media empire and was amazed at the thirty people constantly feeding information into them. The preacher had been smiling as he pointed out that everything was there, including a back-up of every CC file in Joe's own office.

Another thought lay beneath the surface of sexual emotions sweeping and crashing over him, his instinct trying to keep it hidden. The Semitic-looking rent boy had told him he had seen me with two men.

I kept the movement of his image of me plowing him even and explored the thought further. Joe had raged at my having two boys while I kept my relationship with him to our meetings at Treman's home on Capitol Hill.

"Oh, Jesus! I'm close. I'm real close," he gasped under me, his fist flailing his manhood. "Watch me shoot, Jesus!"

I held the thought his instinct didn't want to consider, looking at it again and hearing the boy's description of Tom as well as of Emil.

He knew about Tom!

I searched for a connecting thought, one that showed him doing something about the rent boy's report. But, if there was one, it was lost in the whipped waves crashing through him as he achieved his second orgasm.

He smiled beatifically and reached fingers up to touch my face. "I've fallen in love with you, Karl," he mumbled softly as he lowered his legs.

His image of me lay pressed against him, its lips and nose against his neck below his ear, its breathing slowing. His fingers traced random circles across its back.

I sat on the sofa and smiled at him, marveling at the pretty, naïve face that peered at the empty space between his legs.

Pretty face, monstrous soul. That was Joe McCarthy.

He pushed himself into a sitting position so his eyes met mine on an

equal level, his image of me blending with reality. "Who's this new boy from Baltimore you've got?" he asked, his voice neutral as he sought to see into my soul.

I had seen his question coming. His rage had been in his thoughts even as the Arab boy was taking him on the couch only two nights before.

I smiled at him. "Does he matter?" My fingers trailed upward along his thighs.

His tumescence was stretching again towards erection. "He does," he answered but found it difficult to maintain his anger as both his body and thoughts began to want more sex. "If I'm going to run interference with the preacher for you, I want more than just a piece of you at some orgy now and then."

"Tom's just a nice boy I've met," I said.

[*Sleep!*] I instructed him. His eyes closed and, a moment later, I was rewarded with a soft snore as his head sank back into the pillows of the sofa.

I stood and began to pace. Joe knew about Tom, and Tom was a mortal. I had searched Joe's thoughts as deeply as I dared. I'd delved so deep that, without the immediacy of sex, he would have known I was there. But I still had too little. I needed a spy at Treman's orgies.

I wasn't willing to be that spy again. Controlling libidos and having them imagine things not happening was admittedly fun, but the companionship was unpleasant at best.

Before I examined those thoughts further, however, I was going to feed. I was hungrier now than when I encountered Joe McCarthy in front of the Treman house.

15

As a bat, I touched on a bush across from the underground entrance at DuPont Circle and extended my senses for a skinhead presence.

One sat on the concrete ledge above the underground across from me. Another lounged against the 'P' Street wall of the apothecary that faced on the Circle. I would have smiled if a bat's snout allowed me that when I recognized him as the youth who had sated my hunger several times in the months I'd been feeding on skinheads.

I remembered that I had sent him to the Christian Center headquarters. I hadn't found him in Joe's memories, however; and wondered how he had managed to break my command.

Pushing the thought away for later exploration, I searched for the third skinhead I had learnt to expect. He was two blocks away, leaning against the apartment building facing 'P' Street park and watching men enter a leather and levi bar across the street. I took wing immediately. Dinner was served.

Alighting in a bush at the edge of the park, I hopped to the ground and

changed into wolf form. [*Come into the park,*] I projected to the skinhead. [*Come.*]

He looked around suspiciously as if searching for a body to put with the voice in his head. [*Come!*] I told him, putting immediacy into my command. He cast a glance up the street to where his companions loitered unseen two blocks away and pushed away from the building.

[*Take the steps. Enter the park,*] I commanded.

He crossed the street and descended the steps. I made my way silently down the hill through the bushes, following him.

I yapped at him in greeting and trotted across the open grass towards him, my tongue lolling. I felt his suspicion as he watched me for a moment before looking at the steps to the street. [*Don't fear,*] I told him. [*I'm just a dog. A friendly mutt.*]

"Here, pooch," he called softly to me, holding out his open hand in welcome.

I licked it as he knelt and the fingers of his other hand scratched between my ears. He was pimply-faced and pasty-skinned. A teen-ager already going to fat. I sniffed his crotch and nearly reeled at the scent of unwashed sweat and the dried remains of a day-old masturbation.

I touched his thoughts and found anger that he couldn't beat up some of the queers he was seeing. His orders were to watch and intimidate. His mind gave me the image of the youth sitting on the ledge above the underground as his leader.

I hadn't thought to kill him earlier. I also had no reason not to. He was a Nazi, a bully, and unclean. His continued life was meaningless, and I could fill myself completely if he did die.

I opened my jaws as my snout ascended his body from his crotch. He fell backward as I pushed against him, his eyes bulging in surprise. My jaws snapped closed over his jugular before he could scream. He gurgled, weakly trying to push me away as I lapped greedily at his spouting blood until he was afloat on the Styx.

Gorged, I flew back to the Circle and found the blond skinhead who had fed me in the toilet several times over the past several months. I couldn't approach him in bat form and dared not return to the wolf shape of moments earlier -- any more than I could appear before him in human form. As a wolf, I would be connected to the dead man I had just left on 'P' Street; as a man, I would be naked.

The skinhead was bored. He was also horny. For months, he'd been anticipating sex with the man who would remind him of his lost friend, the anticipation blotting out interest in the mousy girls he'd used to relieve himself. He'd stationed himself in front of the Christian Center every afternoon but hadn't seen the man he needed to satisfy what I'd awakened and intensified. Two gay men strolled past him, ignoring him, and he grew tumescent at the unbidden thought of a three-way.

[*You'll have it tonight,*] I told him. [*All of it.*] I strengthened his lust,

- 362 -

expanding it to cloud his every other thought. The skinhead would be nothing more than a clothed sex organ straining to explode when I was through with his thoughts. [*Go to your leader,*] I told him. [*Convince him to join you. Ride the tube to Eastern Market. You'll be more satisfied than you can imagine. Both of you will.*]

He grinned as he started along the pavement towards the underground. He reached for tokens as he loped across 'P' Street before crossing to the circle.

I flew home and dressed. Then I imagined myself at the Eastern Market underground exit to meet the two skinheads when they arrived.

They rode the escalator to the surface, my skinhead's companion still demanding why they were leaving their position on the circle without their companion and before their relief had arrived.

The other skinhead was more attractive than the one I was directing, cleaner cut compared to his rougher-hewn looks. This was going to be more fun than I first imagined -- once I had them back at the house and Joe McCarthy awake, two pretty monsters were going to be ravished before the night was over. Joe was hardly a virgin, and these stormtroopers? They would never be virgin again.

And, to coin an American expression, fuck condoms. These two and Joe were monsters. They were three men who actually deserved to get AIDS.

[*You're horny,*] I told the better-looking skinhead. [*Your friend is taking you to get laid.*] He looked around, his eyes widening as his groin reacted to my instruction. I gave the rougher looking skinhead directions to the house and turned back to work his companion.

The youth fell back a step and watched his companion's buttocks flex as they started up Pennsylvania Avenue to Sixth Street. He was confused, unable to understand why he was looking at the other skinhead's backside and thinking of riding it. Wanting it. More than anything he had ever wanted before.

[*It's all right,*] I told him, soothing his confusion. [*You're going to have great sex. You're going to have as. Tight ass to drain your balls -- better than any pussy ever.*]

He smiled, letting the thought take hold in his mind. His smile widened as the two of them turned onto 'E' Street and moved into the residential neighborhood behind Pennsylvania Avenue. He rubbed his crotch in anticipation.

I opened the electronically-locked gate and left the front door ajar. In the sitting room, I melded into the shadows behind the naked Joe McCarthy. I wanted to laugh. I almost did but resisted the impulse because it was too early for Joe to awaken.

"You sure of this?" I heard the good-looking skinhead ask the rougher one as they passed through the gate.

"Why the fuck you think the gate's open? We're expected."

"So's the door," the good looking one announced moments later. "You think we ought to go in?" The door pushed open and I heard two sets of boots enter the hall.

[*The fun's through the first door to your left,*] I told the rough one, preserving him as the leader on this escapade in his mind. [*Leave your clothes in the hall.*]

I could hear them undressing on the other side of the door even without my unhuman hearing. "You got a cute butt," the good looking one said, giving voice to his thoughts.

"You think so?" his companion asked hesitantly.

"Yeah."

He snorted nervously. "Let's see what's in this room. If it gets wild enough, you might even get a piece of it."

"Yeah?"

"Only, I'm going to have some of yours too. Just remember that if you get any more ideas about my butt."

I grinned broadly. You could instill hate in a boy, but you couldn't take his curiosity from him -- even when you had made a monster of him.

[*You're going to wake up to all the sex you can want,*] I told Joe. [*Hard dick at both ends. It's safe; Jesus sends it. Just for you.*]

Joe McCarthy was tumescent and rubbing sleep from his eyes as the rough-looking skinhead pushed the door to the sitting room open.

"You look ready for some fun," he told Joe as his companion moved in close to peer over his shoulder.

The first skinhead jerked and quickly glanced behind him at his mate who grinned back at him, his manhood pressed against the soft mounds of his buttocks. I made both of them see the groaning pleasure that was to be theirs when they had an erect cock plowing their nether-field.

The blond skinhead grinned. "Later," he said. "We'll let that be your desert."

I sent him to make Joe's intimate acquaintance. The leader of the Christian Center didn't disappoint me. He raised his legs and spread them before the youth was halfway across the room. "Fuck me," he breathed to the skinhead who went to his knees before the sofa and leant into Joe. "Take me to Jesus."

The good-looking one held back, watching as his mate slipped between Joe's legs and push himself into him. His eyes widened and his hand instinctively gripped his manhood, beginning to stroke it in time with his companion's movement in Joe.

[*You want it,*] I told him. [*You want your friend's ass.*] His fingers grasped his own arsecheek as he pumped himself. He moved across the room to stand behind his companion.

He rubbed his erection across his friend's flexing asscheeks, his eyes glassy.

[*Put it in him,*] I told him. [*Just take it slow until he's adjusted to you.*] I

grinned as I showed the first skinhead how to open himself.

I touched the second one's thoughts as he ground his pubis against the insides of his companion's cheeks and found waves of pleasure washing over him. Diving beneath those, I searched for the person who gave him orders.

It was truly interesting what I learnt when I was having fun -- especially about myself. I almost didn't realize the dawn creeping across the Maryland farmlands between the District of Columbia and Baltimore. The skinheads had graduated to Joe straddling them, taking them both at the same time.

Poor Joe. He hadn't even flailed himself into another ejaculation when, at my suggestion, he stood up, disconnecting himself from the lads beneath him. They were automatons as they proceeded to dress. The skinheads immediately forgot the house and how they had happened to come there.

Poor lads. They'd remember their first time together and with Joe. They would never remember me or my house. I left the newly acquired sexual awareness with each of them as well as the willingness to get together with Joe any time. Outside on the street in Joe's car, they would give the head of the Christian Center their names and phone numbers; he would invite them to Bob Treman's house tomorrow night. And I would have access to their minds for everything they saw or heard.

I lay in the reinforced dark of the bedroom Emil and I shared with Tom MacPherson, a satisfied smile covering my face. With Joe's new sex partners, I would know everything that went on at Treman's house and not have to be there.

What bothered me as dawn streaked across the sky above me was that I would never learn how the different heads of Koughlin's Hydra fit on the body -- not from the orgies Joe and his friends had. I would still not know what sinews connected them to it. Regardless of what I eventually decided to do with what I learnt, I needed to know those sinews. Without them, I was but another Cassandra moaning my litany into the wind.

I realized then that Joe McCarthy had handed me the means by which I could make every connection I would need, and I had failed to understand the significance of that knowledge until just now. He had looked upon a roomful of computers and Koughlin had told him that they connected his various efforts and brought them all together. Koughlin's operation had even duplicated everything his menions had on their membership and activities.

I needed another hacker.

I lay back on the bed and closed my eyes, inviting Morpheus to visit me. I was going to have fun at the preacher's expense.

Heil Prediger!

My weekend had been a productive one as Monday's dawn began to

streak the eastern sky. True, I had learnt that my winsome personality had failed to convince Reverend Pat Koughlin of my sympathies for his plans for America. But my failure with him appeared to be my only one. I convinced myself that I had circumvented it nicely.

Joe McCarthy was in love with me -- as much as a psychopath could be said to know love. I had placed two well-endowed, young, and nearly inexhaustible American youths with more stamina than intellect inside Treman's orgies reporting everything they saw and heard back to me. Best of all to my way of thinking, I had arrived at a plan that used both the information I already had and would glean from my spies to discredit the preacher and his American fascists.

I slipped into what writers of purple prose once called the sleep of the just.

I woke to a sense of nearby violence. Beyond the window louvers, I sensed hot sunlight beating down on the house and violence on its grounds.

[*Karl! Help!*] Sergei called to me in fear and pain.

As I pushed back the bed covers, my body was already changing. As a wolf, I bounded from the room and flew down the stairs. A kaleidoscope of images flitted through my mind.

Two skinheads had trapped Tom inside the grounds. They were behind the tall bushes along the drive. One black leather-clad tough held Tom's arms as the other hit him. His jaw was already a mass of pain and he was on the verge of losing consciousness.

I willed the front door open as I neared it and rushed through it almost before there was room to do so. All four of my paws left the verandah at the same time as I propelled myself over the azaleas along its border into the yard beyond.

Heat hit me, burning me through the coat of fur that covered me. Steam rose along the ridge of my snout and streamed past me as I raced across the yard. I anchored myself in Sergei's thoughts.

"Son of a bitch faggot!" a rough voice hissed.

"Hit him again!" another voice egged the first one on. "Kill the fucking queer!"

I broke through the last column of bushes. And sprang. My jaws snapped closed on a leather-clad arm drawn back in preparation of delivering another blow. Teeth tore through leather and sank into human flesh.

My flesh burned. I shook my head, holding the arm in my teeth, ripping its leather and flesh further. I let it go, turning to face the other skinhead still holding Tom. Beside me, the one I had wounded sank to the ground, shock growing across his mind as he stared down at his mangled arm.

"Nice doggy," the youth holding Tom from behind said, fear palpable in his voice. I growled. He reached for a knife at his waist as I took a step towards him.

"Sweet Jesus!" the tough groaned, dropping Tom and stepping back as he tried to pull his knife free. I sprang, my jaws open, aiming for his throat.

His windpipe was crushed as he fell. I pushed away from him and turned back to his companion. Steam rose along my spine and a clump of fur and skin fell from my body. I felt no pain. I thought only of killing the barbarian invading my home.

[*Karl, no!*]

I stopped, staring from the bleeding skinhead to Tom struggling to rise to his feet. "Get inside now!" he commanded me. Sergei commanded me.

His voice brought me to my senses -- and to the pain. "Leave them," he told me, taking a cautious step towards me. "Get out of the sun now."

I didn't want to. I wanted to kill the intruders. But awareness grew as more skin blistered under my fur. I groaned and started towards the house.

I was weak and growing weaker. The verandah looked impossibly far away.

"Move it!" Tom growled from directly behind me.

I slipped through the branches of the bush and left fur behind. I felt the heated concrete of the path sear the pads of my paws. I whined in pain.

"Run, Karl!"

I was too weak to run. I gasped as I left half my tail on a branch of another bush. I saw the steps then. Impossibly lighted by the sun, gleaming white across impossible meters of grass.

Pain. I had never known such pain. I could barely move.

One foot forward. Then another one. I fell. Skin and flesh pulled from my hands, exposing bone.

I was in human form again, unable to hold another form still. Naked. Crawling on my hands and knees towards the verandah. Towards the house. Towards safety. My body would repair itself -- if I could but reach the house.

Skin fell from my back, crackled on the grass and burnt into nothing. Fleshy fat sizzled across my exposed backside.

"Come on!" I heard Tom's voice grunt above me as I felt his hand reach around me and grasp my chest.

I fainted.

His jaw set, Tom pulled me towards the verandah, ignoring the odor of my burning flesh, his mind refusing to see bared muscles as skin stretched and broke across my shoulders.

He was Sergei infusing Tom's mortal body with unnatural strength to carry me, pulling me into the blessedly dark interior of the house and, lifting me into his arms, toting me back to the bedroom and laying me on the bed. He was still Sergei when he called to Emil across the width of America, strong and clear -- and demanding.

Sergei. Not Tom. The immortal soul who had played with me when we frolicked together across an innocent Europe and who kept me sane through more than a hundred years of insanity with his love for me.

I was unconscious. My body burnt beyond the ability of human medicine to save -- had I been mortal. But I was a vampire, an evolutionary advance upon mortal humanity. Immediately after my body was out of direct sunlight, it began to repair itself. Cell by cell, sinew by sinew.

I remained unconscious, kept that way by a body that could re-build itself from even worse damage than this. A phoenix rising from its own ashes.

16

Sergei remained with me the three days and nights that followed.

He was still Sergei when I opened my eyes the first time since I stumbled and collapsed on the grounds under the hot afternoon sun of late May.

His face was drawn and his eyes feverish from lack of sleep, but he smiled at me. "You were close, Karli," he told me in accented American English.

I didn't understand. I remembered nothing after lying down Monday.

He chuckled. "You very nearly died in your attempt to save me, dear one," he explained.

Weaker than I could imagine being, I brought my hand to my face and felt the new soft skin that had grown there. And felt no eyebrows. My fingers moved to my scalp. I felt only stubble but no hair.

He reached out and took my hand, pulling it from my head, his face was a comforting smile. "It burnt off."

"My hair?" I managed to ask, still grappling to understand.

"Exposing one's nude body to direct sun-light was always the favored method of suicide among vampires in the old days, Karl." He shrugged. "At least, until Dr. Guillotine perfected his painless method of decapitation. You came close to dying Monday; another half minute out there and you would no longer be with us."

It took me long moments to work through his explanation and there were wide gaps in my understanding. But I did comprehend the one reality that explained the strangeness I felt in him. "You're Sergei, aren't you?" I asked.

He nodded. "You needed me. Emil wouldn't have known what to do; and Tom was in a state of shock, his jaw broken."

"Broken?"

He chuckled. "I had need to repair it so that I could tend you, dear one."

There was a timid knock at the door. [*Enter!*] Sergei called without turning and Emil cautiously opened the door to look in on us.

"Is he awake?" he asked and Sergei nodded.

Emil studied me and I could see in his eyes how horrible I had to appear. [*Will he live?*] he asked Sergei.

I smiled at his telepathic query. Emil, so young and innocent still, had

no idea his mind's every broadcast could be heard by the one who had made him a vampire.

"He'll make it," Sergei answered verbally.

"I suppose we'll just have to get used to him being bald," Emil saidd, forcing a smile to his lips. "Actually, it's sort of sexy…"

"It'll grow back," I growled with a sudden flare of anger.

"Is everything taken care of in Baltimore?" Sergei asked, changing the subject.

Emil nodded, his face drawn. "I had no idea the noise -- or the mess -- a gun could make."

"What's this?" I demanded.

Sergei sighed. "It's been an active three days since you saved me, Karl. The skinheads who attacked me Monday -- they were sent from Baltimore."

"Baltimore?" I looked blankly from one to the other of them. "I thought they didn't have an organization over there?"

Sergei smiled. "They don't show themselves there. But the Gruppenführer for the east coast had his headquarters there. The old Russian proverb applied: you don't shit where you eat. They controlled the street toughs there but kept them from looking or acting like the skinheads elsewhere in the country. So -- voilá -- no skinheads."

"Sergei picked through the brain of the one you didn't kill and found the man who gave him his orders…"

Sergei had? I stared at Tom MacPherson sitting on the edge of the bed beside me. "You can't read minds! You're…"

"Not a vampire?" he finished and grinned impishly. "I had that distinction two lifetimes ago and, though mortal synapses are gods-awfully slow and unwieldy, I have learnt these past three days how to make them function much as yours."

I stared at him in disbelief.

"I was able to call to you back in the winter, remember?"

I nodded slowly.

"And I called to Emil here -- he teleported in from San Francisco only moments after I had you into bed."

I remembered waking up to his being attacked then. I remembered it all and wished I could have at least forgotten the pain of my body melting away from me. "What happened to the men attacking you?"

"You killed one. At least, he was dead when I got back outside to clean up the mess we'd made."

"The gendarmerie?"

He chortled. "This is the city, Karl. An American city in 2005. People don't call the polizei -- even when they're watching a murder being committed. Besides, I suspect people were at work -- the joggers and strollers who might have made such a call. I simply made the one you left alive carry his friend's body into the basement."

"The basement?" I asked numbly.

"I tied him up and Emil rid us of the body that night."

"They found him floating in the Anacostia River Tuesday morning," Emil snorted. "Actually, the police are now looking for the pack of wolves killing drug pushers and skinheads in Washington."

He grinned widely. "I hear there's a new group formed to protect the wolves because of their public service."

"The live one?"

Sergei snickered. "He's still in the basement but has lost his mind. You're going to need to feed soon and you're in no shape to hunt. Emil or I will kill him and drain him for you."

He didn't shudder as he said the words. He didn't even frown. If nothing else had done so, this statement proved he was Sergei to me. Imminently practical Sergei. He had a sick vampire on his hands; he also had a living piece of drek in the basement with more than enough warm, living blood to feed his sick vampire. Voilá!

I hoped the spiritually developing Tom MacPherson didn't know what Sergei was doing. He'd be what Americans were apt to call one sick puppy.

"What happened in Baltimore?" I asked.

"Actually, it was Towson," Emil said. "A suburb of Baltimore."

"So, what happened?"

"There weren't any wolf attacks in Baltimore, Karl," Emil said, stringing me alone.

"What happened?" I demanded.

"There was a cowboy killing in Towson last night, Karl," Sergei offered.

"Cowboy killing?" I looked from one to the other of them suspiciously.

"It's how drug people remove their competition," Emil offered much too blandly for my tastes.

I struggled up onto my elbows and wondered at how mortally weak I was. "Tell me everything!" I demanded.

Emil shrugged and grinned. "I went in and shot up the place, blowing four people away..."

"What?" My non-existent brows arched in shock.

"Let's start at the beginning," Sergei offered quietly. "This Gruppenführer is -- was -- a preacher at a small fundamentalist church -- small enough that he had too much time on his hands. Emil went in last night and killed him and his senior lieutenants."

"With guns blazing," Emil chuckled. "Want to live through an instant replay?"

"Guns?" I asked stupidly.

"One automatic machine pistol actually -- an Israeli uzi."

I stared at him. "I shall take that instant replay," I grumbled as my thoughts touched his. His face went blank as his mind opened for me.

I stood in a darkened church, pews on either side of me and a dais with a pulpit and two large, heavy chairs before me. To the side of the dais was a

closed door -- and light found its way under the door, beckoning me. I heard voices beyond the door.

I smiled, Emil's lips stretching thin, as I stepped to the door and, holding the uzi in both hands, envisioned it open. My smile broadened, my lips disappearing into mere lines, as I stepped into the room and saw three men standing around a battered desk and the other one sitting at it. I felt no other presence than those of us in the room.

"It's been two days and they haven't reported back, preacher," one man grumbled to the seated man.

"They aren't important, Deacon. It was just a favor the Überführer promised one of the Preacher's inner circle -- and those spiders were expendable. If they failed, they can't be traced back to us."

"One of them was in my Sunday School class last year," the man mumbled. "I recruited him."

The seated man smiled condescendingly. "That was last year. Boys go bad all the time: pick up daddy's gun, and start shooting up the school. They'll never trace him back to us -- not to tie us to him."

My finger tightened on the trigger and I couldn't believe how violently the machine pistol jerked. Or how loud its noise. It seemed to take all my strength simply to hold it steady as I sprayed the desk and the men about it.

My ears continued to ring. There was blood everywhere. And holes. In the desk. In the bodies. In the chair. Even the wall. I stepped across the room as I searched the four mortal minds for life.

The Sunday School teacher still lived and I turned him over to find the exit wounds of the Uzi's bullets. I tore the man's shirt open and lapped at the blood and gore from the wounds, knowing he knew I was feeding on him as he died.

I pulled a wad of currency from my jeans and laid it on the desk. I reached into my back pocket and pulled out five small bags containing white powder.

"Where did you acquire the machine pistol?" I demanded as I withdrew from Emil's memory. "And that much money?"

"I've been feeding on drug dealers, Karl," he answered, a shy smile touching his lips. "It's not difficult to come by good weapons -- or money and drugs."

"Money?" I asked dumbly.

"Several tens of thousands of dollars these past few months -- I left a thousand laying around the church basement and enough cocaine to send police dogs into terminal shock." He stretched languidly, proud of himself. "It will be seen as a drug killing which embarrasses the fundamentalists because of the church involvement -- and there's no connection to us."

"It also disrupts the east coast operations of the American fascisti for the next several months," Sergei said with approval.

"Gott im Himmel!" I groaned and collapsed back against the pillows. "Genüg!"

Yes, enough. I had definitely had enough for one day.

Knowing I had survived and was mending, Sergei relinquished his hold on Tom's mortal body. A night's sleep had given the American his unbridled youth back as well.

It was Emil who fed me the next two days. My hearing had heard the skinhead's screams reverberating through the house as my lover opened a vein and drew blood from him as had barbers of old.

Tom studiously and squeamishly avoided being near the house either time Emil practiced his barbering skills, and I found myself wondering just how much alteration to Tom Sergei had left behind.

He should not have been able to hear the skinhead's screams. But, then, he should never have been able to call Emil back from California either -- not as a mortal. He seemed to breathe a day-long sigh of relief when Emil finally drained the skinhead enough there was nothing for his heart to pump.

The bed smelled of putrefaction where skin and flesh had fallen on it immediately after Tom's rescue of me, when my body was still sloughing off burnt and destroyed pieces of me. The sheets were changed but the odor had permeated the mattress.

Both of them helped me to the shower that Friday. While Tom stood under the water with me, lathering me and scrubbing where I couldn't reach, Emil removed the lovely black satin sheets and the mattress to take them somewhere they wouldn't to be found.

"We need a computer hacker," I told them when they'd dressed me.

"Why?" Tom demanded. "Both Emil and I grew up with computers. They were second majors for us..."

"We need to break into Koughlin's computers," I told them.

"No problemo," Emil retorted.

I stared at him for several minutes. Yes, he *had* become too American. I thanked whatever god might exist that Tom had Sergei to direct him; I didn't think I could survive two Americans in eternity.

"There's the Christian Center nearby in Arlington and Koughlin's headquarters in Virginia Beach on the coast."

"An octopus!" Tom grumbled.

I nodded.

"And you want the tentacles that hold these together from their computers? Names and addresses. Passwords even?" I nodded again.

Emil grinned. "We'll need a computer, monitor, and modem -- another telephone line as well."

Have I specifically mentioned just how ingenious the modern young man can be? My lovers especially.

Their most endearing achievement was how quickly and completely they broke into the computers of the Christian Center and, with that providing direction, stripped Koughlin's computers of everything.

My two lovers brought a cardboard box to the bedroom at dusk the Monday after my sunbath, waking me as they struggled with its weight.

"What the hell do you think you're doing?" I demanded in German and tried to look fierce.

They both grinned at me, completely unintimidated. "You wanted everything your piglets had on themselves, yes?" Tom asked innocently.

My eyes widened. The damned box had to be a meter in height. "All of that?" I groaned.

"This was so easy!" Emil cried in glee. "All their passwords were New Testament words or..." He grinned. "If it was an important file, they took the first letter from each chapter of one of the books in the bible to make a password. Of course, they used the King James' version. Their security program was so simple a child could unravel it."

"Leave it there then," I told them. "Now that we know who is who in their organization, it should be easy enough to destroy Koughlin's threat."

"Are you going to kill them all?" Tom asked, a frown spreading across his face. "There are thousands of people doing things for them -- all across this country."

"I'd rather tie them to what they've done and let the media and police do their jobs," I told him and meant it.

"Our boy found out who heads the skinheads nation-wide, Karl," Tom said, looking over at Emil. "But he's kept it from me this past week."

Emil's face was covered with blotches as he watched Tom sit on the bed beside me.

"Who?" I demanded even as I moved my head with its fuzzy patches of new hair to look directly at Emil.

"He's a congressman, Karl," he allowed, shifting his feet as more blotches appeared on his face.

"Who is it?" I demanded again.

"Treman," he mumbled.

"Treman?" He nodded. "Verdammte!" I hissed.

"He ordered the attack on Tom; but, from what I could get out of that preacher's mind in Baltimore, he's completely in control of what they call the Spider Fraternity -- he reports directly to Koughlin in his headquarters."

It was too believable when I forced myself to consider what I knew. In addition to Joe McCarthy and Bob Treman, there was also the FBI man who procured young boys and men for his agency's spy programs as well as the pleasure of his fascist friends.

There was no reason Treman couldn't like boys as much as his friends and still lead Reverend Pat Koughlin's street toughs across the face of urban America. Röhm had certainly done so for Hitler until he became a liability in 1934.

Tying these men's fascism to the power of American fundamentalism was the chasm my sanity sought to avoid. Religion was the bit of honey that made their medicine go down for the masses while it frightened away the

fourth estate even when it should be investigating and exposing the monsters for what they were.

If religion was the cloak behind which they hid, the virulent homophobia of the religion and its leaders was but another smokescreen behind which to hide many perversions, including child prostitution.

Hitler's men had done the same thing in the twenties and thirties. Sending homosexuals to work camps which became death camps while they prowled the working class districts of Berlin for young boys for their amusement.

Treman as the head of Koughlin's equivalent of the SA wasn't unbelievable. What was unbelievable was that he and the others had not been exposed.

"Why didn't you eradicate that piece of drek as you did the preacher and his gauleiters in Towson?" I asked.

Emil tried to smile. But he was a vampire, and nervous vampires don't hide their emotions well. "He's one of the major members of your fuck club," he offered, consciously peering at me and avoiding Tom's face.

My face did show my embarrassment then, with more blotches than Emil had ever dreamed of having. I forced myself to look at Tom, feeling his eyes on me. "I..."

"Don't start," he told me, his voice strained. "Just tell me one thing: did your involvement with this sex club begin before I got off my high horse and decided to socialize with you two?"

"Before," I answered, happy for a modicum of truth to put behind my words.

He nodded slowly and I felt the effort he was making to keep his anger in check. "I'll accept that," he said finally and glanced at Emil with a tight smile holding his lips. "But I'll never understand how you could allow him to do it."

"Tom!" he groaned, wilting under our lover's scrutiny. "I didn't go with him -- the only two men I've given myself are you and Karl."

"But you knew he was fucking everything that'd pull its pants down for his big-assed dick."

"I was trying to find out about Koughlin and his fascists," I told him, interceding for Emil. "That includes the skinheads who almost beat you to death."

"By fucking them?" His voice rose and he wrenched his control over it tighter. "Those goons hate homosexuals -- you're going to go around screwing every guy who doesn't like us? I don't think that'll make them as queer as we are."

I stared at him for long moments, trying to decide how much of what I'd learnt to tell him and attempting to decide if my one time with Joe was a defense.

Finally, I knew what I must do. I said: "Can you put Sergei alone completely in control of your mind -- like when you were nursing me last

week?"

His eyes were troubled as they met mine. "Why?"

"He can read my mind completely, Tom. I want you to know everything I know -- it'll be so much easier than trying to explain everything from the beginning."

I snorted and glanced over at Emil. "Even Emil didn't believe some of the things I told him. He had to see it happening to believe the insanity growing in this country. You can do that if you read my thoughts and know everything I know by becoming Sergei."

He looked down at his hands. "Or I can become a vampire myself and read them as myself." His anger was gone, replaced now by discomfort and confusion.

"Do you want that?"

He glanced beseechingly at Emil and then back at his hands in his lap. "I don't know, Karl. I'm almost at the point I was when I climbed into your bed with this. Only, If I do, I know I can't get up tomorrow morning and go back to eating thick, juicy hamburgers again like I could with doing queer stuff."

He turned back to face me, his eyes blazing from an inner fire. "If I do decide to become one of the undead, I want to know that there's only the three of us -- in bed and out. That's got to be true for the present and the future. Do you understand that, Karl? There won't be any more fucking street kids or preachers or congressmen. No making more vampires."

"Become Sergei," I said. "Go as deep as you will. My mind is yours."

"Read mine too, Tom," Emil told him quietly and joined us. "I want you to know me as completely as you do Karl..."

"Why?" Tom asked, looking up at him in surprise.

"You have suspicions. How I feel towards Karl -- and, perhaps, you. Why I went along with what Karl was doing with those fascists." His smile broadened. "If you join us, we're going to be together for a very long time. We need to be able to trust each other."

Tom looked puzzled. His brows knitted slowly together as a new awareness settled over him. "Only, I'm not sure how to call Sergei in to take over the controls."

"Sergei?" I said, my voice flat, calling to him vocally even as I directed a mental summons to the dead Russian who was still so much a part of Tom MacPherson.

He chuckled, his eyes twinkled. "You called, Karli?" Sergei asked in German.

I took a breath -- a deep one. I didn't relish Sergei digging through my memories as if he were an archaeologist on the trail of an untouched Egyptian tomb. There were private things -- things we never discussed in our two lives together. But I would not allow Tom to choose death over immortality again.

"He is a strange one, mes amis," Sergei said. "One moment, he is far

more uninhibited than I ever could be; the next, he sounds like Saint Thomas Aquinas trying to determine the largest sitting arrangement of angels on the head of a pin."

Emil laughed, red tears misting his eyes, the tension built between Tom and us finally broken for him.

Youth! It takes so little to make them happy.

"Start with me," Emil told him.

Sergei smiled. It was Tom's face -- his skin and muscles and bones -- but it was the smile I remembered from Odessa. "Süßer Emi," he said, "I only wish it had been me making love to you that evening you became one of us..." He chuckled. "But, then, Karl was always the luckier of the two of us."

A moment later, Emil's face went slack and his eyes glazed; I shivered as I watched the physical reaction to one's thoughts being carefully sorted through and then experienced. I slipped off the bed and hobbled across to the desk where my two lovers had left the box of computer print-outs.

I skimmed through page after page of the Koughlin organizational structure, idly looking for names I recognized as I waited my turn under Sergei's mental microscope. Joe McCarthy was there, the preacher's organizer -- Hess as well as his propagandist Goebbels. Bob Treman was there as well, clearly delineated as the trouble-maker who would hasten the fall of America. Man after man I didn't know followed as did their organizations, tentacles stretching across the face of Lincoln's and Roosevelt's America.

I smiled as I realized Luke Renfroe, the Speaker of the House, wasn't one of those Koughlin trusted to be one of his own. The man had proved to be too smart to commit himself for all the world to see so easily.

"Karl?" Sergei called me. I turned to face him and remembered why he alone possessed Tom MacPherson's body.

"Sheiße!" I groaned.

17

Though three-story, Treman's Capitol Hill house was barely visible over the privacy fence that blocked so much from the neighbors and the curious. I growled softly.

I padded along the sidewalk on my own four feet beside Emil. I was as hungry as the American of lore who ate his horse, and I was going to feed myself. Emil had demanded Treman, taking for himself vengeance for the attack on Tom. I accepted I would take leftovers as my serving at tonight's feast.

Tom was more than slightly miffed that we'd both told him to stay home. Our reasoning was partially that he was squeamish, but mainly because he was mortal.

Mortals left fingerprints and footprints. Mortals could not change their

shapes -- even a mortal under the command of Sergei. And mortals died much too easily.

Neither of us had mentioned Joe. I suspected neither of us wanted to think about him -- not after having Sergei probe our thoughts about him. He had become an unmentionable for us in the week since the attack on Tom and my near immolation.

I changed into a mist and rose slowly over the privacy fence. I sensed Emil do the same beside me. We touched the well-watered lawn in front of the house and, in unison, changed back into our wolf forms.

I had never truly appreciated the freedom life was. As we raced across the lawn under a full moon, I understood how lucky I had been -- and enjoyed the physical exercise of our movement.

The front door opened to my mental command.

[*Where?*] Emil asked, looking blankly around the front hall from the staircase directly before us to the closed doors of the rooms off the corridor in both directions.

[*They usually meet in this front room,*] I answered, moving towards the closed door to my left. I halted before it, extending my senses to the room beyond.

Bob Treman grunted. The sound was low, not carrying even to the door for normal ears. I sensed that his mouth was full. I felt but two other mortals in the room and their senses were sexually directed as were Treman's.

[*This one's yours,*] I told Emil as I commanded the latch of the door to pull back. Emil pushed it open with his snout.

"Jesus shit!" a voice cried at the other end of the room. I looked in that direction and found Johnny the Arab youth who worked for Agent Boyd staring at Emil and myself. His eyes were huge, he was naked, and his manhood was buried to his pubis in the congressman's anus. Treman was bent over. In front of him was the young boy.

[*No-one's going to hurt you,*] I told Johnny as Emil loped towards them, his teeth bared. [*You and the child are safe.*]

Even with my mental reassurance, the lad pulled out of Treman and began to back away slowly.

Boyd's young boy was moving hard and fast against the congressman's face, his breathing ragged. His glazed eyes moved from his friend's strickened face and backward steps to look over his shoulder at us, his body close enough to orgasm that it could not stop.

His eyes bulged, fear spreading over him as a fire in a wind, but his hips continued to flex against Treman. The congressman was too involved in his body to have noticed that his sexual partners now had other things on their minds.

"I'm almost there!" he grunted as Emil neared him and opened his jaws wide.

[*Pull out!*] I commanded the boy. [*Move to the other side of the room. Do it now!*] I added, reinforcing the command.

The boy blinked, stared down at his connection to the congressman for the remaining moment it took Emil to reach them. He pulled away as the wolf's jaws began to close on Bob Treman's throat.

The congressman made no noise. Fighting to pull air through his torn throat, Treman stared at the youth crouching against the wall and then at Emil's fur-covered back.

[*Get dressed,*] I told both young boys as Emil began changing into human form, his face pressed to the dying man's torn throat.

I wanted to smile as they both danced to pull pieces of clothing over themselves, hurrying to follow my commands. Fear oozed from their every pore as they both avoided looking back to where a naked human Emil continued to gorge himself on a dying Bob Treman.

[*Leave,*] I told them. [*You will remember nothing of this. Leave.*]

Johnny crossed to the door and peered into the hall. He glanced back at the boy, then me. "Come on, kid," he called, "I'll get you back to northwest Washington. It's safer there."

Agent Boyd was in an upstairs bedroom. He had a new child lying face-down and naked on a desk as he spanked him.

I had forgotten the FBI agent; he was remarkably unmemorable. He was an agent of the American government tied closely to the closet queens who plotted to bring Koughlin's new order to power. He was a man who was more organized than most, even while he was nearly unreadable. And I had forgotten him.

Joe McCarthy knelt in the center of the room between the two skinheads I'd ordered to spy on him while they serviced him.

None of them heard the door open or saw the two wolves Emil and I were enter the room. I circled the room, seeking a better angle from which to take Joe. Emil stayed at the door to guard it. Of the five mortals in the room, only one was going to die; but we didn't need the other four running out into the night screaming.

I padded across the floor, sniffing at the raw sex that permeated the room.

McCarthy was oblivious to anything but the skinheads at either end of him. Boyd was engrossed in how red he could make the boy's bottom. The child's eyes closed, he sobbed but flexed his hips hard as he humped the desk.

I took several fast steps and leaped as I neared the center of the room, my jaws open in anticipation.

"Sweet Jesus!" Joe cried as he lifted off the rough-hewn skinhead. "Help me cum. Make me strong!"

My upper teeth met soft skin and began to sink beneath it into muscle and sinew as I closed my jaws.

My momentum pulled Joe McCarthy's body from between the two skinheads he'd been servicing. I heard his neck snap.

The boy screamed from the desk behind me.

"What the fucking shit!" the blond skinhead screamed as Joe's arse pulled along the length of his manhood. Emil growled in warning to the others from the door. More screams echoed through the room as I changed back to human form.

[Dress!] Emil commanded the other four mortals.

I gorged myself. His blood was warm and I hated him for what he would make legal and what he felt free to take.

The two skinheads stared at me with eyes wide in fear as I stood up, my face smeared with Joe's blood. [Forget this,] I told them. [You will not remember it. Leave. Now!]

Their eyes glazed, they filed unseeingly past Emil sitting on his haunches, watching them.

I turned to Boyd and smiled when he shuddered. I suspected the man, at that point, wasn't even aware of my nudity, but the young boy he'd been spanking was.

[Leave,] I told the boy. [You were nowhere near this house tonight.]

His eyes glazed as his mind began to delete his memories as I commanded him. [Leave!]

"What about me?" Boyd asked quietly after they were gone. He was the only mortal left alive in the room. I was surprised at his calmness.

"You procure children for this rubbish," I growled.

"That's my job. Anytime there's an investigation involving homosexuals, I've got to produce the boys who get the suspects to open up."

Emil changed into human form and stepped across the room. "Investigation?"

The FBI agent nodded, alert to us even beneath pasty skin and an overdose of adrenaline in his blood. "We investigate any organizations that might be a threat to the United States."

"With children?" I demanded.

"With whatever it takes, Prince von Maribor. It's a simple matter of getting through the weakest link."

"Investigate?" I asked suspiciously.

"Sure. We do it with the Klan, all the hate groups -- the American Indian Movement. Even did it with the commies -- any group that's a potential threat to our country."

I touched his thoughts and knew he was telling the truth. He was intent on worming his way into the higher echelons of the Christian Center and exposing it if there was anything dangerous about them. Everything else paled before that goal.

I stood in the center of the room and stared at him dumbfounded.

"Why did you bring those two children to them?" Emil asked, not yet ready to forgive him.

"The kid downstairs? Shit! His old man balls his ass every morning before school. Weekends, he's even likely to bring in a couple of buddies to

fuck the kid for breakfast..."

"Where's his mother when this happens?" Emil shuddered.

"At work. She's a waitress."

"Even if he's being abused at home, it doesn't mean you should have procured him," I said, some of my pent-up hostility at him returning. "How old is he?"

"Eleven. He and the kid who just left was hanging out in the parking lot at the 'Peake downtown when I found them -- selling their buns for twenty-five a fuck."

"Gott!" I groaned.

"They're already into prostitution when you recruit them?" Emil asked quietly and shuddered when Boyd nodded.

I stood, forcing back the revulsion I had held in check for so long. I accepted that this was simply the way the American government did things. It wasn't that different from what the Europeans had done in the thirties and I imagined were still doing.

"What're you going to do with me?" Boyd asked.

"Do with you?" I asked.

"I know you're -- what? Something supernatural. My best guess is that you're both vampires." He snorted. "The old legends have it you don't leave mortals around who know about you."

I thought for a moment. When we entered the room, I had been content with sending him on his way with his memories of us and the happenings in this house removed from him. But that was before I knew he was involved in a FBI investigation of the Christian Center and Reverend Koughlin's political activities.

"What would you say if you knew I had a complete break-down of their organization -- names, addresses...?"

"I'd sure like to see it." He appeared suddenly hungry.

"I would be unhappy to think those records might disappear into the bowels of your country's bureaucracy."

His laugh startled me. "It might happen too. Old J. Edgar was as right-wing as they came -- even if he did wear tutus at some private parties. Some of his boys are still close to the top; Koughlin could have found one or two who would go along with him."

"You don't have the ability to control the information?" Emil asked.

"Nope." He shook his head. "That's too high up for me -- I'd only get a nosebleed. You two want to know how I'd play this scene?"

"Speak," I told him.

"I've got some pretty graphic videos of the orgies I've been to here, that I've brought the boys to..."

"And?"

"Is Bob Treman still alive downstairs?"

Emil shook his head.

"You let those two kids go, though?"

Emil nodded.

"Okay. Let me get a couple of the tapes from my house -- Treman balling the young kid, him getting balled by Johnny, McCarthy with his skinheads..."

"You knew what they were?" I asked in surprise.

He nodded and grinned. "We'll put the vids on the VCR's in these two rooms and call the police in anonymously. That'd take some of the wind out of Koughlin's sails..."

"What about our information?" I asked. "I don't intend to turn it over to you to be hidden -- I want the American public to know about it so there won't be a cover-up."

"That means the press, Prince. And those boys have been cowed by the right-wing -- ever since it got religion."

"Why?" Emil demanded.

"They've been painted red and liberal ever since Senator McCarthy put on his show back in the fifties," Boyd explained. "They exposed Nixon and his crooks and the haters hated them even more. This new crop of crazies covered themselves with religion. The press figured it was better to print who's sleeping with whom than to really investigate real crimes by rightwing Christians."

"Are there any reporters who still have balls?" Emil asked.

"I know one I think does. She writes for *The Blade*."

"The gay paper here?" I asked.

He nodded.

"Will something she writes get into the mainstream?"

Boyd laughed. "Shit! Reporters are all like vultures -- just circling around and around a dead body -- waiting for the bravest among them to land and taste. This woman breaks the story and *The Post* will be on it like stink on shit the next day!"

"This woman -- does she have the female equivalent of testes?" I asked.

He laughed. "She's something even better. That bitch doesn't need a dose of testosterone, not with the hate she's got on for her brother. She'll do it -- and love every goddamned minute of it."

"Her brother?" Emil asked.

"He's the Speaker of the House, mister. And she does ever more hate his fat ass."

"And you'd set up a meeting between us?" I asked.

He chuckled. "If she'll let me read over her shoulder."

"And how about you and us?" Emil asked quietly.

"Are you asking me if you ought to hypnotize me or kill me?"

"You know what we've done here. You know Karl, and you know what we are. That makes you especially dangerous."

He smiled. "I don't suppose you'd trust me?"

"Perhaps we shall," I told him, returning his smile. Mental control of mortals came in different gradations. The simplest was what we had done to

the boys. The hardest would be what I decided to do with him, pinpointing a single command to protect us.

18

The sun was dropping behind the spires of Georgetown University when I finally left the bed Tuesday evening and a sated Emil for a most necessary shower.

"Liebchen," I called to him as I stepped under the jets of tepid water, "turn the air conditioning down so it's bearable in here."

[*Karl! Emil!*] Sergei screamed to us, his fear crashing through my mind in a flood.

I followed the thought back to Tom. I appeared in the twilight-lit courtyard of the George Washington University Medical School building and changed immediately to wolf shape. I barked a greeting to Emil as I saw him appear.

[*Where is he?*] Emil projected to me.

I extended my senses out over the cobbled courtyard, searching for Tom. I felt him at the same time my eyes saw the top of his head as he rode the escalator from the underground station. There were men in normal street-clothes on either side of him and, as they reached the ground, I saw one of them held a pistol against Tom's back.

[*I see them,*] Emil told me. [*What now?*]

We could rush them; but the pavement in front of the underground had too many people on it. I didn't relish attacking the men holding Tom in front of witnesses. There would be too many questions and Tom was unable to disappear as Emil and I could. He would be left to the police and forced to lead them back to us.

[*They won't kill him out here,*] I answered, praying I was right. [*Let's wait until they get him away from all these people.*]

I reached out and touched the thoughts of Tom's captor nearest me, pushing past the fear and determination I found in the foreground of his thoughts as he scanned the milling night students and street vendors picking up their wares for the night.

He had spent hours watching Tom pour over medical books and he wanted to be through with killing him and return to his wife. He was concentrating on making the building, thinking of a first floor toilet in a room full of exhibits. I felt his revulsion at seeing the pickled brains and cranial slices.

He would make it to the toilet, I decided. But he'd never see his wife again. Not in this life. I sent Emil ahead to secret himself there while I followed them in.

Tom had seen and recognized us. His eyes widened as he watched Emil change into a mist and move towards the main entrance. No one else noticed -- or paid attention to the wolf prowling and sniffing about the

courtyard, moving closer to the three men walking towards the building. I touched several passing minds, curious at the lack of interest and was surprised to find I was viewed as only a stray dog, scavenging for food.

I followed the two men pushing Tom ahead of them to the double doors and saw the campus policeman standing just within the glassed foyer. I became mist as the men pushed Tom inside by oozing beneath the door.

From the moment I saw Tom's situation, I wanted to attack. His attackers were as unhuman as a skinhead or drug dealer -- they had given up their humanity and were legitimate prey.

I wanted to kill them but didn't -- for the same reasons they hadn't yet killed their intended victim. I didn't want witnesses.

Past the lobby entrance and no longer surrounded by people, I changed back to wolf form and padded a meter behind them into the exhibition room and through it towards the toilet.

The men pushed Tom into the enclosure between the two doors and I sprang towards the man who couldn't wait to get home to his wife.

The first man had pushed open the interior door and moved inside when my jaws snapped closed on his companion's throat. My teeth sank into muscle that resisted the impulse to tear away. The resistance lasted but a moment before the front of the man's neck pulled away, but it was enough to brake my headlong collision with the wall of the cubicle.

I landed and pushed myself to my feet, growling as I looked about to find Tom.

Emil had sprang towards the other thug as he stood against the door and stared in disbelief as I tore his companion's life from him. His shock had held him long enough for Emil to reach him.

Tom simply collapsed to the floor of the cubicle when he saw my snout clamping shut on the neck of the man behind him. As I looked about to assess the situation, I saw his eyes were wide as he watched Emil pull his man's throat open and began to lap blood and gore from the wound.

I changed back to human form and began to feed as Emil was doing on the tiled floor of the bathroom behind me.

"Jesus fucking Christ!" Tom hissed, pulling himself up the wall to gain his feet.

"Shut up!" I growled at him without looking at him. "Shut your eyes and keep quiet!" There was far too much blood pooling in the man's wound for me to do anything but ignore Tom. I was as hungry as Emil, and this was food.

With a surge of good sense, he did as he was told.

I dragged my man's body inside and placed it in a cubicle after I had fed. Emil did the same with his man, and the three of us stood facing each other inside the toilet. "You're both naked," were Tom's first words since I ordered him to silence.

"You caught us on the way to the shower," Emil chuckled. "There didn't seem to be any time to decide what to wear."

"You killed them," he accused, his face bleached.

"Damned right we did," I said. "They were about to kill you..."

"But you..."

"Scheiße!" I growled. "There's no difference between a bullet to the brain and a throat torn out of a man -- they're both death. Besides, they were no longer human. They had become rubbish. They were legitimate prey and we were hungry."

Tom sank back onto a lavatory, shaking his head. "I never thought ... Jesus!"

"You never thought you'd be murdered by two fascist thugs either!" I sucked in air. "Sergei, explain this to him while he makes his way home."

"Home?"

"We've got to get away from this." I pointed at the two cubicles that now held dead bodies, then at the small foyer that was splattered with blood and gore. "Emil and I can teleport ourselves there. Nobody's going to see us..." I glanced down at my nudity. "Not like this," I offered, my voice softer and carrying a note of humor.

"You, however, have to take the tube home. I doubt even Sergei can move your corporeal body from one place to another as we can ours."

Both Emil and I felt his revulsion at what he had seen.

"Verdammte!" Emil hissed. "We saved you, Tom. You'd have been dead in another minute if it hadn't been for us."

Tom gazed at the closed cubicles for long moments before he pushed himself off the lavatory. "I guess we better get out of here," he mumbled, turning to look at us.

"Do you want us to meet you at Eastern Market?" I asked.

His eyes seemed to plead with mine for the moment he held them. "Yeah. I guess so. I don't think I want anybody else sticking a gun in my back like those guys did."

Emil and I dematerialized and, again at home, dressed quickly for our walk to the underground to meet Tom.

"Our Yank appeared a bit green at the gills," Emil opined as he slipped into his loafers and made sure his shirt buttons lined up with his belt buckle and flies.

"Who?" I asked absently.

"Tom. The boy's been plying me with questions about the functions of every part of my body this past month -- including my privates."

I looked up from slipping on my own shoes. Emil hadn't sounded at all American and that stood out, emphasizing the difference of this line of thought from anything I had heard the past several months. Normally, he sounded American -- or he had since Tom entered our lives. But this was real English I was hearing now, something taught at Oxford. And more than slightly catty.

"What're you trying to say?" I asked and started for the door of the bedroom.

"I'm saying I think Tommy has been edging closer and closer to the big decision, Karl. He was ready to have you sink your teeth into his neck and suck him dry," he offered as he followed me down the stairs.

Now he was sounding American catty. Graduating class of Anywhere High School of 2005.

"You know you don't become a vampire from being fed upon, Emil," I reprimanded him.

"I'm sorry, Karl," he mumbled as I opened the front door and stepped onto the verandah. "I was being a real bitch there..." He fell silent as he followed me out to the pavement.

"Tom's been closing in on making the decision to join us," he began again as we rounded the corner of Sixth and started towards Pennsylvania, his English well-modulated and belying his national origin. "But I suspect he had an overdose at the medical school earlier this evening."

"How else could we have saved him?" I demanded gruffly as we reached Pennsylvania and turned eastward towards the underground.

"I think our opportune feeding upset him," he suggested.

"Verdammte! We were both hungry. That bloody drek was dying anyway. Why shouldn't we feed?"

"You know it and I know it, but he didn't until he was watching us."

"And you're saying?"

He smiled at me, even as he struggled to match my stride. "I think Tom'll shortly be undergoing an identity crisis and we need to treat him carefully."

"Do you really care, Emil?" I asked and immediately regretted the question. I loved him as much as I did Tom.

He didn't take offense for which I was grateful. "I was there as quickly as you were," he answered gently.

I stopped in mid-stride and turned to look at Emil who stopped at the same moment I did. We stood before the art deco exterior of an American cowboy gay bar.

"I've come to love him every bit as much as you ever did," he offered. "Read my thoughts if you don't believe me."

"I'm sorry, Emi," I told him. "The three of us have been flowing smoothly along, true; but I've been waiting for something to come along and touch that fragile façade, to shatter it."

He grinned. "It's not shattered yet, Liebchen -- unless young Tom is a match for Sergei."

I grinned back tentatively. "I doubt he is -- I know I never was."

"Or me. You should have seen him take charge while you were recovering from your sun-burn. Gott!"

Tom was leaning against the wall of the escalator when we arrived. "I thought you would never arrive," Sergei told us both in German when we neared him. Emil glanced sharply at me but, as quickly, turned his gaze back to him.

"Sergei?" I asked, barely above a whisper.

He chortled. "I thought I might be needed to help this American out, miene Freunden -- in what may prove to be trying times for him..." He grinned. "You see, he has acquired some doubts of how he might feed himself if he succumbs to your charms."

"He can drink bovine blood if he prefers that," I grunted, remembering my own experience between the wars.

"He seems to have momentarily forgotten that point this evening as he watched you two."

We were standing at the elevated side of the escalator and I noticed several young men glancing at us. "I think we should perhaps return home," I offered.

"What?" Sergei yelped. "No added pleasures to our evening, my Prince?"

"Scheiße!" I grunted, starting back the way we had come. "Your lad doesn't care much for added pleasures."

"True, he is a bit of a prude," Sergei said and followed me with Emil bringing up the rear. "I find it strange trying to handle some of his feelings -- he sees things so differently from the way I would."

"How long are you going to stay in charge of him?" Emil asked, matching his steps with ours.

Sergei grinned at me. "As long as it takes me to have one of you to open a vein and allow him to suckle."

"Gott im Himmel!" I grunted as we turned onto Sixth Street and began to pass the open-air restaurant there. "He'd hate all three of us if he didn't make that choice himself," I continued in German.

"He already has," Sergei allowed, continuing in that language.

"What does that mean?" I demanded.

He paused to gather in the idiom he was looking for. "He put the decision in my hands, meine Freunden. It is mine to decide if he goes back to Baltimore or stays with you."

I stopped and stared at him. "Really?"

Sergei halted and turned to smile at me. "Why shouldn't he? He was afraid to handle the decision after this evening. And I am as much him as he is."

"No!" I growled. "Each of you are different, even if you are the same soul."

"Perhaps, Karli," he answered softly. "But his personality, the one separate from mine, put the choice in my hands..."

"I'd like to hear that directly from him before one of us lets you suck," Emil said bluntly, staring at him.

Tom's face managed to look wounded under Sergei's manipulation. "Such little faith you have, Emi," he mumbled.

"We're talking a very permanent condition, Sergei," I said. "I want you with us as much as Emil does -- but we don't want to have this incarnation

hating us for making him undead."

The light-complexioned face framed by the mass of dark curls altered slightly. It wasn't something a mortal would have seen, but both Emil and I watched Sergei become Tom again. "This is a decision I can't make, guys," he said in the flat American cadence I couldn't imagine Sergei's Russian soul ever sliding into.

"Tom..." I reached out to him.

"Don't!" He pulled away. "It's not that I don't love you -- both of you. I do. I'm queer as shit and I accept that. I want the -- the rest of it too. But I don't -- not if I have to do what you guys did this evening. I decided to let Sergei make that decision for me."

"You know which way he'll decide," I told him.

He looked down at the pavement and shrugged. "Yeah..."

"Do you want that?" I asked, pressing.

He veered closer to the street and away from me. "Goddamn it! Yes. I hate what you did. But all the rest of it..."

"Stay with us, Tom," I pleaded softly.

"I thought you loved Sergei," he hissed.

"I did -- ninety years ago. I love you now -- and Emil. Emil and I both love you. We want you with us." I sighed, sickened at what I was about to suggest. "Hear them and accept their council, Tom. You're unique among vampires and mortals to have the experiences of these two previous personalities you can consciously draw upon. But let Emil and I see only Tom MacPherson. You're the man we love in the here and now."

Tears welled in his eyes and slipped unnoticed down his cheeks. It was still Tom who was with us when we turned into the house. We continued to maintain the silence that had held us until we were behind the door to our bedroom.

"Will I have to kill people?" he asked suddenly, holding back as Emil and I advanced deeper into the room.

"To feed?" I asked and turned to gaze at him.

"Yeah..." He nodded.

"Ask Sergei," I told him smiling. "He read my mind for you here recently and I imagine he found how I lived between his two deaths."

His brows bunched together as he retrieved the memory. "Cow's blood?" he said in disbelief.

"For thirty-five years. I'm willing to go back to that again."

He turned to Emil. "And you?"

"I'm just one member of this family," he answered. "I'll go along with whatever program we all agree upon."

Tom sighed. He smiled slowly and glanced from one to the other of us. "I guess I'm acting like some prima donna."

"Tom, why make the decision now?" I asked sitting on the side of the bed. "You've put it off these last three months-"

"I've put it off since you woke Sergei up back in December, Karl.

That's when this thing started." He snorted. "I was fighting to stay out of your bed as well."

He glanced down at the floor. "Now, I've lost this one too." He looked back up at me, his eyes searching for mine. "You wouldn't even let me hide behind Sergei now that it's time to surrender."

"You still don't have to decide tonight," I told him.

"The hell I don't! You've stirred up a hornet's nest with these fundies -- and I was right there alongside you. I was seconds away from getting my head blown off in that john." He shook his head. "And those skinheads the other day weren't exactly playing a friendly game of tag with my jaw, either."

He smiled suddenly at Emil and pushed his shoes off as he pulled his shirt over his head. "I think I'd like getting it like Emil did. Remember? You made sure Sergei read your mind before he did Karl's. That seemed pretty nice." He unbuckled his belt. "Do you think both of you can get in on this bloodletting I'm walking into?"

Emil began to undress. "Looks like we're going to have to change the sheets tonight, Karl," he said.

I stood, a bemused smile plastered across my lips as I admired Tom's naked body and rigid manhood standing just beyond my reach. I began to undress as he moved to the bed and climbed onto it.

By mid-week, television talk show hosts dropped their interest in middle-aged women who slept with their teen-aged daughters' boyfriends and began airing former members of the Aryan Nation, the Klan, and militias throughout the country, trying to delve into their sexual practices.

Christian Center bumper stickers disappeared from automobiles in Maryland and Virginia as fast as their owners could scrape them off.

The circus had begun. American style.

Sated, I lay between my two lovers as the eastern sky lightened outside our window. Tom was becoming a vampire even as Emil and I held his unconscious, changing body to ours. I told myself mine had been a full life these past one hundred and fifty-seven years and accepted it was only just beginning. I had forever stretching out ahead of me with these two men to help me explore it.

Tom was waking as I came back from the shower. "You are a sleepyhead," I told him. Glancing over at Emil, I smiled at him as I remembered the heat of our most recent coupling.

"You two got it on while I was transforming," Tom grumbled sullenly. It was a statement.

"We sure did, Liebchen," Emil answered happily and rubbed his buttocks suggestively. "You missed an especially wanton ride into pleasure."

"Shit!"

"I suppose we could show you what you missed," he leered. "I haven't had American ass in two days."

"Count me out," I told them, my thoughts already turning to the evening ahead.

"That leaves the two of us then -- why don't we try it in the shower?"

"Fuck!" Tom growled even as his manhood became tumescent. "All you ever think about is your damned cock."

"Wait until you get it on now that you're one of us..." Emil chuckled. "It's going to open up an entirely new dimension to sex for you."

"Yeah?" In spite of himself, Tom was curious.

Emil climbed to his knees and leant over the other man to take him into his mouth.

" That does feel better!" Tom gasped, staring at Emil.

"Want that shower now?" Emil asked, leering at him.

I dressed and sat on the bed, listening to their mindless frolic under the water jets in the bathroom. Tom would need to feed soon and I wondered idly at how pronounced his hang-ups about feeding habits would be now he was one of us.

THE CONTRIBUTORS:
(Other Than the Editor)

Barry Alexander: *Night Wings*

Barry, who resides in Iowa, is the author of *IN ALL THE RIGHT PLACES* (Badboy, 1997). He is a frequent contributor to gay magazines and has had stories published in the *Best Gay Erotica* and *Friction* anthology series as well as all five of Dave MacMillan's earlier anthologies.

Mark Apoapsis: *Thresholds*

Mark Apoapsis specializes in erotic science fiction and fantasy stories. He started out writing "slash" fiction. This is his first foray into professional erotic fiction. His hobbies are submitting long, uncut stories (the rougher the better) to hard-to-please editors, and wrestling with artistic integrity.

Jordan Baker: *The Hunting Trip*

Although he dabbles in journalism, Jordan Baker thinks of himself as a professional hitchhiker and house guest. He currently lives in northeast Louisiana with a pair of Siamese cats named Topaz and Sapphire. He too has contributed to all of Dave's earlier anthologies.

Richard Bellingham: *Street Angel*

Richard Bellingham is a geek, writer, artist, programmer, and all-around wannabe creative sort. He currently lives in a small coastal town in Kent, the Garden of England, and enjoys a huge number of eclectic hobbies and pastimes. He is the author and artist of Brad the Vampire, an online comic (http://www.jellicle.demon.co.uk), and works in the IT industry.

Murray Brown: *The Right One*

Murray Brown lives in the South with two cats and a lot of dreams. He's always had a thing for men in black so it was a treat to be able to explore his vampire fantasies. When he is not working, writing, looking for Mr. Okay, or serving his imperial felines, he enjoys refinishing furniture.

Louis Carr: *Breakfast In Bed* and *Momma's Boy*

Louis Carr holds a Ph.D. in English and has written numerous works of fiction and nonfiction about vampires. His first gay erotic work appeared in Idol's anthology *DIVINE MEAT*, published by Idol Books.

Bill Crimmin: *Eternity*

Crimmin was born in London longer ago than he'd like to remember. He's attempted to go through life working as little as possible and having as

much fun as feasible. He took to writing because he could do it lying in bed and to writing erotica, because being in bed when you wrote it often proved fortuitous. He lives alone, being too grumpy and set in his ways to share his space, but is worshipped by a small but dedicated team of acolytes.

Peter Eros: *In Like Flint*

Peter Eros is the pen name of a leading Australian-born journalist whofor forty years has written on everything from showbiz to world affairs forleading publications in Britain, Australia and the USA. In '95, he submitted his first gay love story to John Patrick's Star Books Press.Thus far his stories have appeared in 18 of those volumes.

Grant Foster: *The Willows*

Grant Foster has been writing erotic short stories for several years. His first collection of tales—*LONG SLOW BURN*—was published in 2001 and has received good notices. His biographies of legendary pornstars Casey Donovan--*BOYS IN THE SAND*--and Al Parker--*CLONE*--were released by Alyson. This story is Grant's first foray into the supernatural.

Michael Gouda: *The Gift*

Michael Gouda was born and raised in London, England. After a 'mid-life crisis' he left the world of commerce to enter that of education and is now a teacher at a Comprehensive school in Worcestershire, England, teaching English and Information Technology. His short fiction has appeared in Idol's anthology *DIVINE MEAT* and *EROTIC TRAVEL TALES* by M. Szereto. He is working on an adult novel set in wartime London and lives in a limestone cottage in the Cotswolds with two Border Collies and a cat.

Vic Howell: *Hillbilly Blood*

Vic is a died in the wool Southerner but isn't religious about it; after all, he *will* eat a quiche. His adult life has been spent trying to convince editors and doctors that he really does know what he writes about in his articles that have long appeared in their medical journals. When he's not manipulating science to keep his bank account in the black, he tries his hand at gay erotica and has appeared in several Companion Press anthologies. He lives in Atlanta with a predominantly Persian queen and an impossibly opinionated British ex-pat who can make even Vic that there's hope for George W.

Davy Jones: *Anniversary*

Davy Jones has been writing since 1974 but, up until now, it's all been computer software. He enjoys snow skiing, swimming, and horseback riding. He lives in Seattle with his partner.

James Lincoln: *In Every Vein*

James Lincoln lives on the Gulf of Mexico and has been published in several STARbooks anthologies edited by John Patrick as well as magazines like *Freshmen* and *In Touch For Men*. To keep his addictions sated, he edits videos in real life.

Philip Markham: *The Body And The Blood*

Philip Markham (a.k.a. Gordon Neale) has written five erotic novels for the Idol imprint: *TO SERVE TWO MASTERS* and *SLAVES OF TARNE* (as Gordon Neale), and *CONVICT CHAINS*, *THE LOVE OF OLD EGYPT,* and *THE FAIR COP* (as Philip Markham). He was a contributor to the Idol anthology *DIVINE MEAT*. Philip lives in London.

J. R. Mattingly: *Making It A Threeway*

Versatile, Jim Mattingly writes both fiction and non-fiction -- even a poem or two -- and has had several stories appear in *In Touch*. He writes for *The Letter* in Louisville KY and his first published story appeared in the Companion Press anthology *RENTBOYS*. He is currently working on a novel.

Tom Millios: *Dog In The Manger*

Tom Millios was born and lives in London, England. He has worked as a teacher, computer programmer and data analyst. He is now working full time on his writing.

Daniel Ritter: *The Right Of It*

Daniel Ritter is a freelance journalist and has done reference writing, but he'd much rather write about sex. His fiction has been published widely online but this is his first contribution to an anthology. He lives in the Midwest with two neurotic parrots.

Ruthless: *The Great Nothing*

Ruthless grew up in the downtown core of Montreal where he started crashing gay dances and hanging out with bemused cops on the midnight shift while his voice was still squeaky. He has since transplanted from the steamy streets of Montreal to the Canadian Maritimes, on the shores of the Bay of Fundy where the only nightlife involves owls, fog, pine trees and

most of the year two feet of snow. He works full time and writes in his spare time, but has completed three novels and started half a dozen more.

Simon Sheppard: *Amsterdam*

Simon Sheppard is the author of *HOTTER THAN HELL AND OTHER STORIES*, winner of the Erotic Authors Association award for Best Single-Author Collection of 2001, and the nonfiction epic *KINKORAMA: TRAVELS THROUGH QUEER DESIRE*. He's also the co-editor, with M. Christian, of *ROUGH STUFF: TALES OF GAY MEN, SEX, AND POWER* and its up-coming sequel, *ROUGHED UP*. His stories have appeared in over 80 anthologies, including *Best American Erotica*, *Best Gay Erotica*, *Friction*, and *The Mammoth Book Of Best New Erotica* series, and his next short story collection, *In Deep*, is slated for publication by Alyson Books. Visit him at www.simonsheppard.com.

Jay Starre: *Hunting Season*

The first runner-up in the Mr. British Columbia Leather Contest of 2002, Jay Starre keeps busy pumping out erotic stories for gay men's magazines including *Honcho*, *Torso*, *Men*, and *Indulge*, as well as anthologies including *RENTBOYS* and the *Friction* series from Alyson.

Chad Stevens: *Chosen*

Chad Stevens resides in Redondo Beach, California. His erotic fiction has appeared in *In Touch* and *Hot/Shots!* under the name Charlie Stevens as well as several of Companion Press' anthologies. He has sold a video script and is currently working on a novel. In his spare time Chad owns a small graphic arts and web design studio.

Jon Thomas: *Graveyard Shift*

Jon Thomas lives in Illinois where he studies history, among other things, when he's not working full-time at a large state university. He has written a book on web design and several non-fiction articles, as well as contributing a story to Idol's anthology *DIVINE MEAT*.

Holden Wells: *Blood Bank*

Holden Wells listens to too much heavy metal and writes both horror and erotica from a cabin in the mountains of Tennesse. This, his first published story, gave him a welcome opportunity to fuse his two favorite genres. He is currently working on an adult novel set in a prison.

Mark Wildyr: *Night Friends*

An Okie, Mark Wildyr graduated from Texas Christian University in Fort Worth, Texas, with a degree in Government and History. He worked in banking, finance, and administration. Mark is interested in multicultural

interaction and exploring personal development and sexual discovery. He has contributed to anthologies for Companion Press, Alyson Publications, and STARbooks Press. He lives in Albuquerque, New Mexico, the setting of many of his stories.

Shane Yorston: *Sex, Love, And A Vampire*

Shane resides in the Canadian Maritimes and has been published in science fiction, fantasy, and horror. This is his second appearance in an anthology, his first being in *DIVINE MEAT* published by Idol Books.

On a stroll through Piedmont Park, Atlanta GA

ABOUT THE EDITOR

David MacMillan: *CONFESSIONS OF A VAMPIRE,*
Down For The Count

In spite of the comments of some writers to the contrary, Dave is *not* a vampire and he does *not* drink blood. The above photograph, taken in full sunlight, is ample proof of his mortality. He is, however, a British ex-pat living in the American South and wonders occasionally why, when he has London to return to. Over the years, he's written a number of stroke stories and sold most of them -- he's even managed to write some good erotica. He has edited *DIVINE MEAT* for Idol Books and four anthologies for Companion Press in America. He's always on the look out for good writers for projects he's considering. He lives in Atlanta with Smokey, a young queen of dubious antecedents -- though Persian appears to predominate. He also shares rooms with a Southern reprobate.